Kim Lawrence lives on a farm in Anglesey with her university lecturer husband, assorted pets who arrived as strays and never left, and sometimes one or both of her boomerang sons. When she's not writing she loves to be outdoors gardening, or walking on one of the beaches for which the island is famous—along with being the place where Prince William and Catherine made their first home!

Annie West has devoted her life to an intensive study of charismatic heroes who cause the best kind of trouble for their heroines. As a sideline she researches locations for romance whenever she can, from vibrant cities to desert encampments and fairytale castles. Annie lives in eastern Australia with her hero husband, between sandy beaches and gorgeous wine country. She finds writing the perfect excuse to postpone housework. To contact her or join her newsletter, visit annie-west.com.

A SCANDALOUS 'I DO'

KIM LAWRENCE

ANNIE WEST

MILLS & BOON

First published in Great Britain 2024
by Mills & Boon, an imprint of HarperCollins*Publishers* Ltd,
1 London Bridge Street, London, SE1 9GF

www.harpercollins.co.uk

HarperCollins*Publishers*, Macken House, 39/40 Mayor Street Upper,
Dublin 1, D01 C9W8, Ireland

A Scandalous 'I Do' © 2024 Harlequin Enterprises ULC

His Wedding Day Revenge © 2024 Kim Jones

Unknown Royal Baby © 2024 Annie West

ISBN: 978-0-263-32027-5

10/24

This book contains FSC™ certified paper
and other controlled sources to ensure responsible forest management.

For more information visit www.harpercollins.co.uk/green.

Printed and Bound in the UK using 100% Renewable Electricity
at CPI Group (UK) Ltd, Croydon, CR0 4YY

HIS WEDDING DAY REVENGE

KIM LAWRENCE

MILLS & BOON

PROLOGUE

FEDERICO ALLOWED HIMSELF a small smile of professional satisfaction as he flicked through the unedited frames he and his team had taken so far.

Obviously he didn't normally do weddings, but this was no ordinary event. The wedding of the decade was not that original, but neither was it an exaggeration considering the guest list and the news and social media coverage today had attracted.

Some cynics had suggested the timing had more to do with practicality than romance as many of the international high-profile guests had not had to travel far. Many had been in the UK for the previous night's awards ceremony for young innovators in environmental sustainability sponsored by the groom, who had spent the last couple of months in London to smooth the transition of his latest UK-based high-tech acquisition.

Cynics aside, the event had captured the public imagination—everyone was talking about it.

Except the happy couple.

Draco Andreas was known to be a man of few words and all of them to the point. Though it was said that being on the receiving end of a glare from him was worth several thousand-page volumes of words!

As for the bride, well... Normally people speculated

about the dress, but in this case the speculation was about the bride herself. There were only a couple of grainy out-of-focus snapshots circulating online of the prospective Mrs Andreas, which showed she was a redhead, or had been when they were taken, and she was petite.

The mystery had upped the feverish interest in the woman who had bagged the man whose name had become a global brand in the space of eight years. Conspiracy theories abounded on the Internet from the crazy to the crazier.

Federico was just as curious as everyone else and he didn't have long to wait now, according to the schedule he'd been given. He glanced at his watch: two minutes.

He had no doubt that it would be two minutes. The entire event had been organised with nothing short of military precision. Nothing had been left to chance. Even the weather had defied the forecast, which he was happy about. He might be a genius but there was no harm having the weather on his side.

All he had to do now was make the bride look good. He assumed this would not be difficult as he'd never seen a woman who was less than knockout gorgeous on the arm of Draco Andreas, though up until now none had stayed attached very long!

There were jealous individuals who suggested that wealth was a well-known aphrodisiac but, if half the kiss-and-tell tabloid stories were true, even before Draco had been catapulted from relative anonymity to global fame and fortune he'd not exactly had trouble getting a date!

Given his profile today, it was hard to believe that only eight years ago Draco Andreas had inherited the ancestral name and the looks but no money. Most people had expected him to take the route of many land rich but impoverished old families in Italy and elsewhere and sell up, but Andreas had proved to be a man who didn't take the obvious path, and where there wasn't one he built his own.

And he built big!

The mobile app that had been the first thing produced by his tech start-up had revolutionised personal finances for millions globally. Draco was widely held to have been instrumental in changing the financial scene, fostering new technology, supporting innovation and creating a whole new generation of entrepreneurs.

Much of his seemingly limitless energy had gone into his Tuscan family estate, which now showcased creative, forward-thinking green technology, creating jobs and bringing young people back into the depopulated countryside areas.

He did not seek publicity but it sought him. Federico's thoughts turned enviously to the lucky hiker who had captured the recent and already iconic image of the groom-to-be. Draco on horseback complete with sexy stubble, windblown hair and perfect profile looking moody and broody against a magnificent Tuscan sunset as he herded buffalo that apparently supplied the milk for the estate's famous cheese. Well, it was famous now anyway.

Still, you couldn't have everything, including, sadly, an Italian setting, he told himself philosophically. He adjusted a lens and squinted up through the canopy of chestnut trees that lined the driveway to the impressive ancient cathedral that might not have the radiant Tuscan light, but did have its own magical, if austere, aura. His fall-back plan, should the weather break, would not be needed—the sun was shining from a cerulean-blue sky and there was not a cloud in sight.

One of the suited-and-booted security team responded to a voice in his ear and gave the photographer the nod he had been waiting for and he stepped out of the dappled light into the direct sun. He gave a thumbs-up sign to his own team and waited as the crunch of tyres on gravel grew louder.

This was his first sight of the bride, as there had been no informal early glimpses. As accustomed as he was to having the most famous actresses and celebrities pose for him, Federico drew in a sharp breath as she emerged. The bride's days of anonymity were at an end.

His critical professional eye took pleasure in her delicate features, the wide-spaced green eyes and the fact her skin had the pale crystal clarity of the oyster silk gown she wore.

As she completed her graceful exit and stood there, wand slim, the sun catching her burnished hair, he captured the moment. Seriously enjoying himself, he continued to snap. The bride's delicate nose had just the suggestion of a tilt in profile as the solitary bridesmaid bent to straighten her heavy satin train encrusted along the hem with delicate hand-sewn seed pearls.

'Oh, Janie, you look so beautiful, like a dream.'

Jane blinked like someone waking up. Up to this point the entire day had felt like a dream that she had floated through. Floated in the dress that Draco had chosen when she had been unable to make up her mind from all the designer offerings. He'd chosen the flowers too and they were, she decided, making a conscious effort to loosen her death grip on the stems of the hand-tied orchids, beautiful but, sadly, from her point of view, unscented.

She glanced at her small hand as the blood returned to

her fingers, the glitter of her ring catching the sun. Draco had said when he slid it on her finger that it matched her eyes, which was why she hadn't liked to say she would have preferred something a little less ostentatious than the heavy square-cut emerald surrounded by diamonds.

It just wasn't her, not as a student holding down three part-time jobs to make ends meet and enjoying the thrill of being in love for the first time... Of having her first lover and her last—which was just as well. Draco would have spoilt her for any other man.

Draco thought the ring was her, and she was trying very hard to be the person he thought she was.

It wasn't just today that felt like a dream. She felt as if she'd been sleepwalking for the past two months, from the first moment she'd seen Draco and their fingers had brushed when she'd dropped to her knees to pick up the by then empty coffee cup she had knocked out of his hands. By the time she'd got to her feet she had been deeply and desperately in lust for the first time in her life.

His first words had been, 'You are perfect.'

Without considering her words, she had blurted with feeling, 'You are beautiful.'

She had spent the night in his hotel bedroom—they had not left it for the next two days and nights.

Having him want her, having him love her—being loved by the most beautiful man she had ever imagined existing—was all a dream, and she didn't want to wake up.

'Are you nervous?'

Was she? Carrie's voice sounded as though it were coming from a long way away.

Jane gave her head a tiny shake. She didn't want to think, she just wanted to be there in the moment. Nothing else mattered but the fact Draco loved her and she loved Draco, she told herself, repeating the words in her head like a mantra to drown out the other voice saying things she didn't want to hear.

'No, I'm not nervous,' she denied, lifting a shaking hand to her mouth, the full contours delicately tinted a pink rose. 'I want this more than anything,' she added with a husky touch of defiance that faded as she confided breathily, 'I just didn't recognise myself when I looked in the mirror. Love, that's what counts, isn't it…?'

Carrie didn't say anything, she just squeezed her friend's cold hand. Jane took a deep breath that lifted her narrow shoulders as she gathered her skirts and took the first step up the flight of shallow stone steps, wondering how many brides had trod this route before her and how many had been happy, how many lived to regret it.

Halfway up, she paused and turned back to her friend. 'Truth matters, doesn't it, Carrie?'

The sudden question made her bridesmaid blink and give a tinkling laugh. 'Don't tell me you have a guilty secret, Janie, because I won't believe you…' Jane gave her a stricken look and the tall brunette's smile faded. 'Last-minute nerves,' she soothed. 'Just take a deep breath.'

Jane nodded and the deep breath took her several steps up the aisle, right up to the moment that Draco, tall and exclusive, her beautiful Italian lover, turned and looked at her. She saw his dark heavy-lidded eyes widen and felt the possessive pulse of heat that radiated from him reach across the space between them.

She wanted to walk, to run into his arms more than anything she had ever wanted, but shame rushed in, cooling the heat inside her and killing all her joy dead.

As their eyes locked she lost her tenuous grip on her

denial, along with the flowers, which fell from her fingers, a splash of white on the ancient stone slabs.

Her silence was in itself a lie.

She'd kept the secret to herself for two days.

She'd had two days to tell him, to give him the opportunity to respond, and she hadn't because in her heart she knew what that response would be. Draco wanted a child, an heir for the family acres he spoke of with such passion, and she'd been happy about that because all her life she'd wanted a family, she'd wanted to belong.

After her recent doctor's appointment Jane knew the chances of her giving him that were slim to non-existent.

There would be no baby with Draco's dark hair, she couldn't give him what he wanted and one day he'd know too, and hate her. The ache in her chest became a physical pain that hurt more than the physical pain she'd suffered for so long, a pain that now had a name—endometriosis.

She couldn't do this to him. She loved him too much.

With a small, lost cry, Jane picked up her heavy skirts, tears streaming down her face as she turned and ran.

The silence after the sound of her heels vanished was so deafening it bounced off the ancient rafters. All eyes were on the face of the man standing at the altar, a face that seemed carved from cold stone. The fire was in the flames of icy fury in his eyes.

CHAPTER ONE

THE NARROW COUNTRY lane snaked seemingly endlessly through the English countryside, bordered by unruly hedgerows brightened by hawthorn berries beneath canopies of ancient trees. Another occasion Draco might have enjoyed this corner of rural England he had never visited before.

As he lightly gripped the steering wheel of his sleek black car, the tap of his long, tapering brown fingers was the only outward indicator of the frustration that simmered beneath the surface. The overcast sky loomed, threatening rain that reflected his mood.

He could have done without this! The finger tapping against leather got louder. A visit to the site of a development that had become controversial overnight thanks to an overzealous, impatient site manager out to impress—wow, had that one backfired—was not his idea of a fun trip.

The guy had cut corners that didn't need cutting and outraged vocal locals, who had tapped into several media outlets during a lull in the news cycle and hit a community nerve.

A shiny monster of a tractor lumbered into view, trundling along at a pace that seemed deliberate in its disregard for Draco's timetable. His annoyance deepened—the driver was acting as though he were invisible.

This wasn't how the CEO of Andreas Company should spend his morning. The corners of his sensually sculpted lips lifted in a half-smile. At least he had not yet lost the ability to laugh at himself…but who would tell him when he did?

The sad truth was, these days, nobody in his life would. It hadn't always been that way, but he hadn't always been a billionaire. People didn't tell billionaires what to do.

A hissing sound of triumph left his clenched teeth as on the fourth attempt he manoeuvred around the tractor and put his foot down.

This controversy could have been avoided—therein lay the core of his frustration. Draco's initial irritation with the situation had now turned to resentment. This was precisely why he had a team—a capable team, at least in theory, which should not necessitate his personal intervention on such a low-level project. But this had gone beyond the project itself or the financial outlay; it was reputational damage that he was here to repair.

The narrow lane suddenly opened up, revealing the expansive stretch of woodland that had stirred the hornets' nest; a few scattered houses and a church spire were visible in the distance.

He saw the site manager just as the guy spotted him and wisely slunk away into the trees. 'Lazy, cost-cutting…' Draco muttered before he slowed and took a deep calming breath. All it needed was a charm offensive and he did not doubt his ability to smooth ruffled feathers and win the locals over.

And it wasn't all PR and damage limitation. Draco believed in this project and he had the facts and figures to back up his belief. The two similar upmarket eco holi-day villages in his homeland Italy were up and running, bringing enormous benefits to the local rural communities they were set in.

Recognising early on the scope for financial markets to spur investment in conservation had been partly responsible for his meteoric success. Despite the hype, Draco didn't feel his approach was revolutionary. On the contrary, it was practical and simply about recognising the limits of innovation, engaging with stakeholders and using existing tools.

He scanned the crowd as he drove slowly past, heading to a safe parking spot on the grass ahead, noting the inevitable cameras and microphone-wielding journalists as he searched for someone in the melee who looked to be in charge.

Nobody in the chanting, placard-waving crowd screamed in charge to him, but a guy with a dog collar was holding forth to a news channel; he didn't look too rabid, Draco decided.

He manoeuvred to avoid hitting one of the protesters, who banged his placard on the windscreen, and almost collided with a sign for the Manor Hotel. He caught a glimpse of the building in question through a gap in the trees—a square structure of mellow stone—and wondered about the family who had once lived there.

His own family home in Tuscany could easily have gone the same way, but, despite the predictions that it had been inevitable that Draco would have to let it go, it hadn't and he hadn't.

It never would, not on his watch. He pushed away the thought. Today wasn't about preserving his family heritage—that was safe. It was about preserving the firm's reputation.

Then it happened.

In the periphery of his vision he caught the flash of vivid red amidst the muted greens and browns of the countryside. Draco's foot instinctively pressed the brake pedal, his car slowing to an abrupt halt.

The world seemed to pause, the racket receded, the air for the space of a breath was sucked out of the car, leaving a vacuum.

A jolt surged through Draco as recognition, wave after wave of it, reverberated through his body like an electric shock.

Jane Smith!

He had never searched for her. He had no interest in knowing why she had humiliated him, and what her motivation had been remained a mystery. He had put thoughts of her, along with the engagement ring that had landed by courier on his desk, in a deep vault and thrown away the key, if not literally, certainly mentally for the past four years.

He had made a conscious decision not to allow her the courtesy of unpaid space in his head. He had moved on and he congratulated himself on putting the past behind him.

There had been a few moments of backsliding, but he did not count the once or twice he had caught sight of a redhead and experienced a gut-clench of anger…mixed with a hunger he would not acknowledge.

On those occasions the blaze of colour in the crowd had turned out to be some generic redhead.

Not this time! There was no double take or 'is it, isn't it?' moment.

Her face was turned away from him, but it didn't matter. It was the way she held herself—almost like a dancer, slender and graceful—the way she tossed her head. The memory of her amazing full-throated laugh escaped the mental box he had walled it up in... He could hear the sound in his head, seeding itself like an old melody you couldn't get out of your mind. A melody that evoked memories, the good among them all cancelled out by that one humiliating final scene, the one that held no laughter. For a split second, that memory was so strong, the moment he had consigned to oblivion was so here, now and in the moment, that he could taste the humiliation in his mouth.

His eyes darkened to midnight, his lack of control over the physical response of his body only adding to the humiliation. That his control, something he took for granted, failed dramatically fed the anger building inside him.

It wasn't the only thing building—the forbidden images stored away for so long were spilling out.

The sun touching her hair and dazzling him.

His skin tingled at the memory of her touch, light like her soft silky hair sweeping his chest as she sat astride him, and her mouth, not light but... Jaw clenched, he pushed back hard at the insidious mesh of interconnected images and dragged his focus into the present.

The present where Jane Smith's fiery curls were dancing in the wind in stark contrast to the muted tones of the other protesters.

It was only several moments later that he took in the more mundane details: her hair was shorter, more shoulder blade than waist length, and there was...a baby?

The collision of past and present shook loose a raw

hoarse sound from his throat. A baby? He felt the muscles of his belly tighten in rejection of the image.

Why should she not have a baby? She had moved on, he had moved on… It was simply a twist in the tale that Draco hadn't anticipated.

Anticipated! He mocked himself. As if he had anticipated any of this. Why would he? Jane Smith was the past and Draco was a man who lived in the moment.

He could have rejected the flashback but some masochistic part of him allowed it to play out, the moments frozen in time, snapshots of the past, the day they met. Before that day, he would have mocked the idea that the touching of fingers could be erotic.

As he stared at the slim figure, the jeans and boots vanished and she was standing there in a cloud of silk and satin, looking at him with shimmering green eyes and then… The trance broke as Draco distanced himself ruthlessly from the undertow of emotions—anger, desire. And as he released the foot brake, and the car glided silently forward, tucking into a space, he welcomed the opportunity to prove that Jane Smith meant nothing to him.

Why should he need to prove to himself what he already knew?

Jane stood at the edge of the protest. She was aware that, on her back, Mattie, cocooned in a padded suit, had fallen asleep. His little head complete with bobble hat was pressing against her neck.

He wouldn't be asleep for long. He'd need his next feed and— She stifled a yawn. She could really do with a nap herself. Mattie had been awake most of the night. Sometimes, actually quite often, it seemed to her that he sensed she didn't have a clue what she was doing.

Or maybe he was just angry. She was angry, but Mattie...his loss was incalculable. One minute he'd had two beautiful, loving parents and now, because of a stupid accident, he'd got lumbered with her. She glanced around the clearing. Would anyone miss her if she left now?

It wasn't as if the numbers were so few that her absence would be noticed. The cameras, which she had assiduously avoided, had drawn a bigger crowd than expected.

She had turned up at the office of the editor of the local newspaper demanding to be seen, her determination fuelled by righteous indignation and outrage, clutching the proof she'd waved at him, photos of the bulldozers and diggers, the utter devastation, on her phone.

She didn't know what she had expected—an article, a regional radio mention possibly, but definitely not national news. Would she have marched in there if she'd known the name attached to the project that had chopped down the precious trees while the village slept was Andreas?

Jane liked to think she would have.

Andreas... Pathetic really that the name could still evoke such a visceral reaction. It wasn't as if this little project would have registered on Draco's radar. A few trees and up-in-arms locals were definitely below his pay grade!

I really hope it is, she thought. Drawing his attention was the last thing she wanted. She'd moved on.

The sobbing young woman who ran through a churchyard, sidestepped a security guard who looked as if he was about to rugby-tackle her and climbed over a fence, ripping the skirt of her wedding dress to shreds in the process, before she legged it along a cobbled side street—that person seemed like a stranger to her.

She could not imagine what a bedraggled sight she must have looked. The unexpected rain deluge had drenched her in seconds, and it was a miracle that someone had offered to help. God knew how the rest of that day would have gone if the driver of the big SUV with a loud noisy family inside hadn't slowed to ask her if she needed help. Carrie, who unbeknownst to Jane had followed her out of the church, had arrived, breathless and dripping wet, while a tearful Jane was still trying to get her words out to the kind strangers.

The family had given the pair a lift to Carrie's flat, where Jane had poured out her story, or rather dripped it out, while they'd sat draped in towels drinking wine out of mugs.

'And you didn't tell Draco about this?' Carrie had asked.

Jane had shaken her head and did so now to disperse the memory. Why was she thinking about Draco so much lately? she asked herself crossly. Maybe it was becoming a mother to a motherless baby. The discovery that she wasn't able to become a mother had been the reason she had run away in the first place.

She'd thought about writing to explain, but what was the point? He would never forgive her for humiliating him. No, his only reaction would have been relief before the next long-legged glamorous beauty drifted into his life, and not for long. His love life had a built-in revolving door... Not that I'm judging, she told herself with a sniff.

If he'd had a lucky escape, so had she. Watching from a safe distance over the last four years, she had found it pretty obvious that, even if her inability to give him an heir had not been an unsurmountable obstacle, the marriage would not have worked. When she'd been in thrall to him, so desperately in love with the idea of being in love, the future had just been some rose-tinted, lovely place.

When she'd looked back she had been shocked to realise that virtually all their conversations, such as they had been, had involved her trying to say what he wanted to hear. It had never even crossed her mind that he might be unfaithful, and if it had she would have told herself that if he ever got bored with her it would be her fault.

The entire situation had been a disaster waiting to happen. She thought about it these days as skipping the middle bit and getting straight to the end, less pain and disillusion all around in the long run.

'Miss Smith.'

Jane blinked like a shocked baby owl as a reporter from a well-known nature programme appeared, backed by a cameraman.

Oh, God, she thought, pasting on a smile.

'You must be pleased about the turnout today.'

She took a deep breath. 'Pleased but not surprised that people care, that people are shocked and disturbed about this blatant act of environmental vandalism. Ten years ago a survey showed this area was home to four bat roosts, owls lived here and woodpeckers, and innumerable other wildlife have lost their homes. This is a protected habitat, there were tree preservation orders in place, the law was broken and for what? A quick buck!'

The reporter turned to camera. 'That was Jane Smith, who alerted the authorities to this incident.'

Jane gave a deep sigh of relief when the reporter still talking to camera smiled at her, mouthing thanks before he set a new course for the vicar.

'Oh, my, Henry is really enjoying his five minutes of fame,' his wife observed as she joined Jane.

'He's welcome to mine…that was terrifying… God, did I make a total fool of myself? How did he know my name?'

'You're famous—you kick-started this… As for making a fool of yourself, you were actually rather brilliant. Oh, are you still on for book club or have you got another media gig…?'

Jane laughed and sought a firmer grip on her banner.

'Oh, I haven't read—'

'Oh, don't worry, neither has anyone else. Bring a bottle… No,' she mused, then glanced at Mattie, lowering her voice. 'Sorry, you'll be the responsible adult in the room, and don't worry, I'm not cooking,' she added, laughing to herself as she walked off.

Jane had never belonged to a community before. It was nice and at the same time desperately sad that the reason she did was because of a terrible tragedy.

Carrie should be here. Jane didn't want to be living a life that should be her friend's, even though it was a very nice life.

She still couldn't think about Carrie without the almost permanent lump in her throat swelling painfully. Carrie had come into Jane's life during her last year in the care system.

It had been the attraction of opposites. Carrie outspoken, and Jane, who had over the years in care perfected the art of fading into the background, but they had instantly bonded.

Then later, while she had been at art college, Carrie had found her lovely Robert and they'd married and had their baby, though not in that order. The weekend break had been their belated honeymoon and Jane had been trusted with their precious eight-week-old new baby while they were away.

'I wouldn't leave him with anyone but you,' Carrie had told her. 'Just three nights.'

Three nights had turned out to be for ever when the train the new parents had been travelling up to Scotland on had been derailed. Five months ago the tragedy had made the headlines every day, now it got the occasional footnote or personal interest story.

For Jane and Mattie it was never going to be a footnote. It had changed their lives for ever. Jane, who had never thought she would be a parent, was, or very nearly was. The official adoption was in the final stages, and she, a townie, was living in the tiny rural cottage that Robert and Carrie had inherited from his great-aunt.

Jane had been determined to adapt to rural living for Mattie's sake but, in the end, it hadn't been as difficult as she had anticipated. She had felt an immediate connection with the countryside, and had immersed herself in all it could offer, joining a rambling club, learning about foraging the hedgerows and woodland for ingredients for the weekly cookery classes given by a local chef in their village hall. She had been roped into picking litter from the village green with the local schoolchildren and spent an evening joining a guided bat-watch walk.

For the first time she understood the urge people felt to protect the countryside for future generations, for Mattie's generation. This was Mattie's home, his heritage, and the wanton destruction had made her react on a visceral, very personal level.

The sadness that hit her at intervals like a great black crushing wave settled on her shoulders and her placard lowered. Jane edged away. She needed a break and no one would miss her.

Then it happened!

During the interview she had been distantly aware in the periphery of her vision that a big sleek car was drawing attention, but not hers. She had never been into shiny cars. So her glance was incurious as it swivelled that way, no longer incurious when she identified the figure behind the wheel. Everything froze inside her, her breath hitched.

Dark eyes met and held her own… She was fighting for breath.

Her heart rate climbed.

She could hear the blood drum in her ears, so loud it drowned out the little cry of shock that left her parted lips.

It was him—Draco Andreas!

The memories flooded back, not a smooth flow, but a series of staccato images, from a time when she was infatuated by the idea of being in love. She had been blissfully oblivious to his fame and wealth or, for that matter, even the fact, initially, that London was not his home, but that he was there temporarily, for two months.

Back then, he was just Draco—the man who made her laugh, the one who seemed to genuinely care about her, not the CEO of Andreas Company, the man who was now renowned for changing his lovers the same way a normal person changed their socks.

Even his feet had been perfect!

Now that was a weird thing to remember, but it was a lot better than dwelling on perfect other bits!

The baby on her back woke, cried out, perhaps alerted by her tension, and began to fidget. She tightened her grip on the placard, sensed rather than heard the ripple of conversation trickle through the crowd as the tall, exclusive figure got out of the car.

Total mind-freezing panic bubbled up. This wasn't the moment for a confrontation.

That moment didn't exist!

With a quick furtive glance around, Jane seized the opportunity and was relieved when her legs obeyed the order and slipped away into the shadows of the trees.

As she distanced herself from the protest, the sounds faded into an indistinct hum. The familiar terrain of the untouched woodland welcomed her, the solace and peace it normally provided eluding her. It was a shock. She was fine. She just needed a moment—or maybe a year—to gather her thoughts, to reconcile that past with this present without gibbering.

Hands pressed against a moss-covered tree absorbing the texture, Jane closed her eyes. The gentle rustle of leaves and the distant murmur of the crowd might have created a soothing symphony, only it didn't.

Her thoughts were total and utter chaos. All she could think of was Draco's face—the golden toned skin drawn tight across sculpted razor-sharp cheekbones, a broad forehead and a strong firm jaw. The devil, it was said, was in the detail, but Draco had always made her think of a fallen angel, dark and devastating. The details of his symmetrical features were fascinating, mesmerising.

Her stomach muscles lurched as she dwelt on his deep-set midnight-dark eyes set beneath the thick bands of his brows and framed by dark, lush lashes. His carved cheekbones with their knife-sharp angles, dominant blade of a nose, contrasted in a dramatic, stomach-melting way with his mouth, sensual and full.

Authority clashing with sensuality and all utterly, totally male.

She clenched her soft jaw, refusing to be swept away by nostalgia, lust or longing, a weird combination of all three, and she was in no condition to analyse.

She just had to keep telling herself, for sanity's sake, that her life was different now, it centred around little Matthew and the responsibilities that came with guardianship. A gentler life with friendship and kindness, book clubs and village-hall yoga, which had its issues because she was the only person under sixty there—she couldn't include Maud, who had the flexibility of a ten-year-old.

With a determined breath, Jane steeled herself. Draco Andreas might be a part of her past, but she wouldn't let him disrupt the life she had built for herself and the child who depended on her. As she slipped further into the sanctuary of the trees, her thoughts circled around a decision—how to navigate the inevitable confrontation with the man who had once been the centre of her universe. He had surely either forgotten her existence or hated her.

Was it even inevitable?

Would she prefer he hated her than had forgotten her?

How would she play it?

Well, fancy seeing you here.

Oh, gosh, long time no see…

CHAPTER TWO

THERE WAS AN almost audible static hum of anticipation as the tall, dynamic Draco Andreas appeared, impeccably clad in a grey tailored suit and open-necked white shirt.

Jane was sitting in the back row behind a tall man with an even taller hat. She couldn't see the loose-limbed figure but she knew that he'd look perfect. She also knew that the eyes that would be scanning the crowd were more navy-black than brown-black, and his stare managed to give the person that came under their laser beam the impression that nothing was hidden from the owner.

The man in front whipped off his hat and she slunk down in her seat a little more. There were a couple of angry shouts and mutters that faded in the face of the effortless authority projected by the tall, lithe figure who, after walking up the short flight of wooden stairs to the small, raised stage, paused to shake the hand of the vicar before turning to his hostile but now silent audience.

He paused, seemingly perfectly at ease, his dark eyes scanning the faces turned to him, and despite being hidden Jane found herself instinctively shrinking back some more and lowering her lashes.

Not hiding? said the exasperated voice in her head. What else would you call it?

Pride had brought her here, the determination, after a

lot of soul-searching, that she could not allow her blast from the past to derail her life.

Draco would leave her life as he had entered it, casually, and she must react in the same way. She wouldn't allow herself to run away or hide—both, to her shame, her initial instincts—but that didn't mean she had to advertise her presence.

For a board-wielding protestor, she really did have a genuine dislike of confrontation.

Would he even remember her?

She'd changed a lot in four years. When she looked in the mirror these days… When did she look in the mirror?

Juggling her job as a receptionist in the doctor's surgery and childcare didn't leave a lot of time for worrying about frown lines, and running around after a baby meant she had lost ten pounds she could probably not afford to. She knew that her face had lost some of its youthful roundness, and her last hair trim had been a nail-scissor bathroom-sink job…

Also her wardrobe was a long way from the designer clothes that Draco had bought for her. Bought and chosen… She was ashamed now of how malleable she'd been, how desperate she'd been to please him, how she'd allowed him to dress her up like a mannequin doll. She ran a hand over her hair, which he'd been fascinated by. He had gone so far as to extract a promise from her never to cut it; he always wanted to be able to wrap himself in it.

And she had agreed without a second thought.

There was nothing symbolic, she told herself, about the fact that she had lopped eight inches off her waist-length locks two weeks after the non-event wedding. It was just more convenient this way.

Unable to resist the temptation any longer, she bent

her head to look around the man in front and saw Draco was still standing there, seemingly relaxed as he used his charismatic smile to obvious effect. She was not in the fainting zone of that smile, but she still felt the aftershocks of it.

Not recognise her? she mocked herself, retreating once more behind the grey hair, her heart thumping as she recalled that moment earlier when their glances had connected.

Draco had seen her and he had definitely recognised her.

She had read retribution in his face. Draco was not a forgiving man. Remembering his expression, she shivered, her overactive imagination conjuring up an ancient god about to do a lot of smiting!

Even if that smiting was in a twenty-first-century legal as opposed to lightning-bolt way, when you were Draco Andreas that could cause some damage!

Draco had recognised her, all right.

'Ladies and gentlemen,' Draco began, his lightly accented warm velvet voice awakening dormant interconnected nerve endings under Jane's skin in a tingly, painful way. 'Firstly I owe you an apology for the unauthorised tree-felling.' He paused to allow the big murmur to die down before continuing. 'I will not excuse what happened. There is no excuse. I understand your anger. I, too,' he declared sombrely, 'am angry.'

Someone beside her clapped and as Draco's eyes went to the spot and he smiled, everyone there thought he was smiling at them, but Jane was willing to bet that she was the only one whose stomach muscles were dipping and who had an embarrassing ache between her legs.

It was all she could do to stop herself yelling out, It

wasn't me. I would never cheer you… Kiss, touch, taste—that was another matter!

She cleared her throat and reminded herself that all that wild, wanton behaviour was in the past.

The next part of his speech was lost on Jane. It took all her resources to resist the tug of the closed door and the freedom outside, freedom from the insidious sense-killing sound of his voice, and some increasingly disturbing thoughts about his mouth, which was beautiful and sensuous. He had a tongue that knew its way around… Stop that, Jane!

The entire section of his speech that passed over her head must have been good because this time the applause was more widespread. There were even a couple of grudging grunts of approval from a few of the most vocal critics, who had yesterday been calling for dire punishment to be visited on anyone that worked for his firm.

Draco had won them over. Always inevitable, she thought as she glanced around her at the rapt faces turned to the charismatic figure who now held them in the palm of his hand.

The way he had once held her breast in his hand, and in her head she heard his voice telling her it was the perfect size… She gave several sharp shakes of her head, took a deep breath and loosened her top where it chafed her painfully engorged nipples. Under the circumstances it seemed pretty pointless to pretend that the years had lessened her susceptibility to his male aura.

But fancying Draco Andreas hardly makes me unique!

Her lips twisted in a cynical, self-mocking little grimace as she glanced at the villagers. There had to be more than a few heads filled with fantasies involving the tall Italian billionaire, which was fine so long as they stayed fantasies. It was the common-sense-killing reality of falling for Draco that was dangerous.

Of course he had won over his audience; it was what he did. It seemed amazing now that when they had met, she hadn't known who he was. That fact had seemed to amuse Draco, and even when she had known the details she had still not taken on board the mind-boggling extent of his power, wealth and fame.

It was a measure of her infatuation and self-delusion that she had thought even for one insane moment she would have fitted into his life.

That she could make herself the sleek, elegant creature who drifted along at his side saying all the right things to all the right people.

The only way it could have worked was if she'd never opened her mouth, which would probably have suited Draco. He had literally never spoken about his tech company or his role in the world of finance. Their conversations had revolved around the Tuscan estate, his face lighting with genuine enthusiasm as he'd described the place that was to be her home…the perfect place, he'd said, for bringing up children.

It was what she had wanted to hear, she thought sadly. He had been offering her what she had always longed for.

Refusing to acknowledge the pain that came with the thought, she told herself that she had her family now and it would be all the family she ever needed.

As for a man to complete her little family, she didn't think so. Mattie took up all her time and energy. As for sex, since Draco her libido had gone into hibernation and she wasn't about to wake it up, unless one day she was able to separate emotions from sex, and that she couldn't imagine.

She closed down the inner dialogue and tuned back in time to hear Draco say, 'I acknowledge that mistakes were made in the execution of our project.'

She risked another look and saw him spread his flattened palms wide in a *mea culpa* gesture. 'I take full responsibility, and I assure you that immediate steps will be taken, are being taken, to rectify the damage done to the woodland. A comprehensive tree-replanting scheme will tomorrow be initiated, ensuring the preservation of this beautiful ecosystem for generations to come.' Draco outlined his plans for environmental restitution before seamlessly shifting from the eco-project to community welfare, revealing a grander vision that seemed to resonate with the villagers.

You had to give it to the man, Jane thought, trying to view his words objectively—and failing miserably—but his delivery was sincere, if a little too slick. The cranky addition made her feel a bit happier.

'I understand the importance of community,' Draco said, his gaze sweeping across the faces before him. 'And in recognition of your patience and understanding, Andreas Company will fund the restoration of the local church roof—a symbol of our commitment to the wellbeing of this village.'

Nice touch, Jane admitted silently as a ripple of appreciation flowed through the hall. Draco Andreas, the master of persuasion, was weaving a narrative that endeared him to the hearts of the villagers.

He hadn't needed to use his powers of persuasion to get her into his bed, she recalled, her cheeks heating at the memory of that first time, the look of shock on his aroused, flushed face when he had realised he was her first. She pushed the memory away and tuned back in time to hear Draco say, 'As a further gesture of good-will, I am extending an invitation to a member of this community...' Draco announced, his eyes subtly searching the crowd.

Jane pulled back, shifted uneasily in her seat and felt as if they had landed on her. Paranoia, she told herself, looking at the grey hair of the man sitting in front of her and channelling inner calm.

And failing miserably.

'We are hosting an alternative energy eco-training course at my estate. I believe local representatives should be involved in shaping the future of green technology, and, after what has happened to your community and how you responded so robustly, I feel that your insights are invaluable.'

Jane felt the collective gaze of the villagers following as his stare turned towards her, and her chin lifted. This was not an accident.

As the villagers applauded, Jane pushed back her seat and got to her feet, throwing out a few smiling greetings as she made her way to the door with a couple of murmurs of 'Mattie'. Actually, her boss, the local GP who was also a neighbour, had said no need to hurry back when she had offered to babysit.

Jane made it as far as the gate before a voice calling her name made her turn reluctantly back.

'Vicar?' she said, politely waiting for the overweight and very well-meaning cleric to catch her up.

'Jane, dear, I'm glad I caught you. I did want to speak to you before but I was not expecting Mr Andreas to mention it tonight. I hope you don't mind, but when he told me about the course I thought of you. And when we discussed it at our meeting, so sorry you couldn't be there, but it was unanimous. Everyone agreed you'd be the perfect candidate—'

Jane cut him off with a laugh. 'Perfect? I can think of four locals who are a lot more qualified than me...actually more, because I'm not qualified at all.'

'But your enthusiasm and—'

'I am amateur hour and we both know it.'

The vicar looked momentarily flustered, but rallied. 'You started the ball rolling with our protests. You should be the one—'

Jane bit her lip. This was starting to feel like a conspiracy. 'Obviously I am very flattered you thought of me, but—' She bit back a sharp 'I'm not a charity case' and continued with a smile. 'It's out of the question, I'm afraid—'

'You are thinking about Mattie, but I understand there are crèche facilities at the conference, and a bit of Italian sun, a break, is just what you need, my dear.'

His comment confirmed her suspicion...poor single parent Jane could never afford a break in Italy. They meant well but the idea of charity made her hackles rise. 'I burn in the sun,' she said in a flat little voice.

The older man laughed as if she'd made a joke.

'Seriously. There are many more people better qualified than me for this...treat and the surgery is short-staffed.'

'Ah, yes, we discussed this with Dr Grace and she said you are owed holiday so that's no problem. She's already lined up a temp.'

Jane took a deep breath. She could see her avenues of escape closing. 'You seem to have thought of everything.'

'So you agree? I think it would be very helpful in setting up the exchange day with the inner-city school you suggested at the last parish council meeting.'

She sighed and thought, Me and my big mouth. On the other hand, take Draco out of the equation and it was tempting… But Draco was not the sort of man who vanished in a puff of smoke. His presence was not something you could ignore.

It was a mad idea, but she admitted there were temptations: the course would be interesting…and so would seeing Draco's home, his life… Yes, she was curious—who wouldn't be?

She still hesitated, but she was tempted.

Finally she gave a reluctant nod. It wasn't as if Draco would be a visible presence there. While it was great PR for him, she was confident it was the sort of thing that would be delegated.

'There would be conditions, obviously, with Mattie. I'd need more details.'

'Of course, of course, quite wise of you. I'll pass on your request to Mr Andreas.'

'Oh, I'm sure Mr Andreas has more important things to concern him. One of his many assistants will have what I need.'

'Thanks, but I won't,' Grace said when Jane offered her a coffee. 'And you know I love to babysit. I really miss the time when my two were small and didn't answer back—speaking of which, I need to check my lot have done their homework. As you know, they run rings around their dad,' she said with a roll of her eyes. 'You know, Jane, I am so glad you have agreed to Tuscany. You need a break.'

'It's not a holiday.'

'True, but I'm sure that you will find some time for a bit of sun and sea, maybe some down time with a good-looking Italian?' she teased before sweeping out, her ringing phone attached to her ear.

Jane shut the door, leaned back against the wall, closed her eyes and breathed out a gusty sigh. The only sound was the clock on the wall above the open fireplace. She'd have actually welcomed some angry baby cries at that moment if only to distract her from the thoughts swirling in her head.

She had levered herself off the wall when there was a knock on the door. Grace always left something behind.

Pasting on a smile, she pulled it open. 'What have you left this time?' she began.

Her smile wilted and her mouth opened as she raised her eyes a long way to the face of the man standing in her doorway, his dark head brushing the supporting beam of the open oak porch.

'Draco...! Mr Andreas,' she hastily corrected.

If his male aura had made her uncomfortable in the village hall, here she felt pummelled to tight-throated, heart-thudding, mind-emptying confusion by being this close to his unique brand of raw masculinity.

'Oh, make it Draco,' he drawled. The lift of one corner of his sensual mouth became a full mocking grin complete with flash of white teeth as he stared down at her from under his heavy-lidded dark eyes, the lashes so long they touched the razor-sharp contour of his cheekbones. 'I'm on first-name terms with almost all the women I've slept with, *cara*.'

His lazy mockery stung and jolted her free of her confusion—sometimes being angry was very mind-clear-

ing, also it distracted you from thoughts of his mouth.
'And you remember all their names. I'm impressed,' she
snapped back waspishly.

Draco took a mental step back. She was no longer trying
to make herself invisible, a tactic that had always amused
him—the adult equivalent of a child believing she had
vanished if she closed her eyes—and now she was right
up there in his face.

Did she actually believe that a flame-haired woman
who looked like she did, with eyes like that...a body...
He cut off the line of thought before it made an extremely
uncomfortable situation even more painful.

He felt a surge of self-contempt, remembering how, in
the days after she had humiliated him, he had lain awake
at night and in between drinking, aching for her. Now he
looked at her and admired the tilt of her nose, the wide-
spaced, dramatically green eyes, the kissable lips, the
stubborn tilt of her chin... A faint frown interrupted his
self-congratulatory list. The stubborn chin—had it always been that way?

You can congratulate yourself as much as you like,
Draco, but you're still hard as a rock, mocked the voice
in his head.

An image of the bundled-up child on her back flashed
into his head and the taunting inner voice helpfully
pointed out, You won't be getting any, but someone else
is.

This was a departure and not at all the way he had anticipated things going. The Jane he had known always
had a warm sense of humour and a gorgeous laugh but
sarcasm—that was a major divergence.

He studied her, admitting to his spark of curiosity but

not his hunger as he took in the details of the soft contours of her heart-shaped face. Her big wide eyes, darkly fringed, looked back up at him, wariness shining in the shimmering depths, her mouth was still temptingly generous, but the angle of her rounded chin suggested a stubbornness he did not recognise.

As if anxious to dispel any impression that she'd been counting his lovers, Jane added haughtily, with a frown that knitted her feathery dark brows, 'Were you looking for me?'

He straightened up to his full, impressive, lithe and muscular six feet three and looked down at her, the flinty flecks like ice in his eyes and the mildness of his contempt making it all the more coruscating. 'Was I meant to look for you?'

Had she anticipated he would, and had she expected that reaction? Had she engineered this situation? The suspicion lingered, but she would have been disappointed. He had not chased after his fleeing bride. To do so would have made him his father—a man who had been so obsessed with a woman that it had broken him.

Obsessed to the point of insanity. In his father's case, his obsession had been the second wife he had left Draco's late mother for.

Antonio Andreas had indulged his second wife's every whim and all her whims involved money. And when the money to feed her appetite for luxury and excess had run out, and there were no more artworks for his father to sell, she'd predictably left him for someone able to give her what she wanted, leaving behind her young son, his half-brother, who would have cramped her style.

Without her around things could have got better—Draco had hoped they would—but they hadn't. His father, unwilling to accept the reality, had stalked his ex-wife online, and also in person on a number of excruciatingly embarrassing public occasions, begging her to come back to him.

He never seemed to lose his appetite to be humiliated, and, despite everything she had done, would never hear a bad word against her. When Draco, unable to hold back any longer, had spoken out, his teenage self had experienced not just the rough side of his father's tongue but his clenched fist.

Undoubtedly growing to despise his father had influenced his reaction to being dumped at the altar. The objective part of him recognised this. It had been a point of principle not to look for his runaway bride, not to allow himself to even ask why or where, let alone search for her.

And yet here she was. If he'd believed in fate he would have said it was meant to be, but Draco believed that a man made his own fate, not that he wouldn't take advantage of opportunities when they came his way.

Was this an opportunity? he asked himself.

If so, for what?

The revenge his anger craved?

Answers he wouldn't even admit to himself he needed? That he wanted to demand?

A guilty flush ran up under Jane's skin. She didn't pretend not to understand his reference and the double meaning—it wasn't the here and now he was referencing.

'No, I didn't expect that,' she said quietly, adding huskily, 'Why are you here?'

With his mouth lifted into a lazy, self-mocking half-smile, he asked himself the same question now.

To confront her, accuse her of engineering this situation?

Curiosity?

To see first-hand where she had chosen to live in preference to life with him and, he thought, staring past her, with whom…?

'Aren't you going to invite me in?' he asked her, even though it was obvious she wasn't. Maybe she was wondering how she would explain him to the boyfriend or husband? The father of her child, whose existence he still couldn't quite take on board.

'I—' Before she could think of an alternative to the blunt negative that she wanted to blurt, Draco, who was obviously not similarly inhibited by good manners, walked past her. It was a small space and Draco was not a small man.

Instinct made her close her eyes and try to make herself as small as possible, which was, she immediately realised, a pretty pointless exercise and not one that concealed the shameful fact the brush of his hard-muscled arm against her shoulder had sent deep ripples of desire through her entire body. The warm male scent of his body was lingering and making it hard for her to think clearly.

Loving Draco had always been insanity—wanting Draco, she corrected swiftly. The correction made it easier to breathe.

She might now know that marriage to Draco would have been a mistake and could never have lasted, but she was still scarily receptive to him physically.

Fact. Deal with it, Jane, she told herself, showing zero sympathy for this weakness.

How utterly and totally insane was it that she felt almost as bereft at that moment as she had that day she'd run away from the wedding?

Allowing herself a few calming hitches of breath, she turned and followed him into her small cosy sitting room, seeing the space through his eyes.

It didn't feel very cosy. Cosy and Draco? No, definitely not!

She nervously twisted her hands, her skittering gaze drifting around the room, anywhere, quite frankly, than at him. She saw the home that Carrie and Robert had lovingly built together, imagining how it might look through his eyes. Draco wouldn't see the items that had sentimental value, the repurposed thirties sideboard and the recovered rocker, he'd see cramped and slightly shabby.

The idea that he might be sneering made her skin prickle defensively. In the space of time it took her to pick up a toy that had fallen out of the toy box behind the sofa and replace it carefully her chin had gone up and she was able to face him with at least the illusion of confidence.

She had once been so sensitive to his moods that even the thought that she had said the wrong thing, worn the wrong outfit or used the wrong bloody fork would have felt like a failure, not good enough.

Well, this house was more than good enough and she would eat her food with her fingers and to hell with his distaste!

The moment the thought popped into her head she knew it was the wrong one because it brought with it the memory of an occasion when he had used his fingers to feed her a decadent creamy confection, she had sucked cream off his long brown fingers and— She stopped the destructive and criminally self-indulgent memory as she straightened up, one hand on her hip, her free forearm holding her hair back from her face as she delivered a

look that said, Want to make something of the repurposed furniture? Because I will defend it with my life.
She would defend every trivial detail of the home that
had been made with love.

As their glances connected and held she had the satisfaction of seeing a startled expression slide across his
lean features, followed by a slow speculative stare.

'I like what you have done to the place.'

Her eyes narrowed—he hadn't sounded sarcastic or
sneery—but she only lowered her chin a fraction.

Draco could have done with lowering his head. It was
almost grazing the low beams that Carrie had painted a
warm shade of white to make the ceiling seem higher.
Her friend had laughed at the time, saying it was just as
well her husband was short.

The memory brought a lump to Jane's throat and
misted her eyes, and she blinked hard, not wanting to
make an awkward situation worse by crying. It still happened at the most inopportune moments, the grief just
bubbling up. She kept the moisture at bay through sheer
force of will, determined not to look away.

White or not, the beams were not high, and Draco
dominated any space, but the room's proportions made
his presence even more overwhelming. It wasn't just a
physical thing, not simply his size and sheer physicality,
it was the restless energy he exuded.

He was not a relaxing person to be around.

Draco watched as she shook back her hair, which fell
immediately into a fiery nimbus of bronze curls around
her face and shoulders as she planted her hands on her
narrow denim-covered hips and lifted her chin.

Jane took a steadying breath, hiding her grief behind a

facade of defiant belligerence as she waited, determined she wouldn't be the one to break the silence.

She had to wait an uncomfortable length of time.

'You have changed,' he said finally, his eyes on her stubborn chin and the militant light in her incredible eyes. Never during their relationship had she been confrontational—in fact there had been times when her little shrug of acceptance, her placidity, had irritated him. The only time she'd shown fierceness had been in bed, which he hadn't objected to at all! There she had been fire to his dreams with her relentless fascination with his body and her utter lack of inhibitions.

She had never challenged him, she had never used tricks to manipulate him, unworldly to an almost unbelievable degree. Everything about her was the diametric opposite of his grasping, avaricious, conniving stepmother. She had never asked him for anything. In fact she had seemed uncomfortable with the gifts he had given her, politely grateful, but he had sensed her unease when he had filled a wardrobe with designer clothes.

Which made what she had done all the more incomprehensible!

Out of nowhere a memory surfaced, shaken loose perhaps by the perfume she was wearing now, the same perfume she had been wearing when she had pulled herself to her knees on the bed that was tumbled by their recent lovemaking and, pressing her small perfect breasts to his back, wound her slim arms around him and whispered that she loved him. Waiting, he knew, for him to return the sentiment.

Draco had not lied. He did not believe in love, love was the thing that had destroyed his father, but he thought he was gentle. The idea of hurting her had hit him on a level he had never recognised in himself previously or since.

He could remember with shocking clarity looking at the individual freckles on her smooth pale shoulder and breathing in the scent of her hair as he smoothed it off her graceful neck before burying his face in the silky softness.

'We are good together, cara. I can't get enough of you.'

She had smiled when he'd flipped her onto her back and begun to make love to her again, slow and languid this time. There had been sadness in her eyes, but he had pretended not to see it, ignoring the tickle of guilt, which now seemed ironic considering how things had ended.

Hearing the criticism in his voice, she assumed that he was referring to her recent weight loss and shrugged. Jane didn't find her jutting hip bones attractive or the sculpted prominence of her collarbones, so it was not really a surprise that he didn't either, but then her life no longer involved being the person that Draco wanted her to be.

Not now.

There was a freedom in that, she told herself. It made her feel strong…made her like herself, and she was a mother now. She was very conscious that a mother owed it to their child to like themselves, not to pass on their insecurities, teach by example… She had read all the parenting bibles, usually before she fell into a sleep of utter exhaustion.

If only she had had such self-insight four years ago. She had refused to recognise the flaws in their relationship, how unequal, how unhealthy it had been, until she was distant from it, and even then not until the pain of what had felt like a grieving process had passed.

'Actually I'm a perfectly healthy weight,' she countered, her lips tight.

He blinked. 'I didn't mean that,' he snapped back, sounding impatient at her interpretation. 'I meant…you… just seem…different…?'

'Well, it would be more surprising if I wasn't. It has been four years. You seem exactly the same,' she added, not making it sound like a compliment.

'I don't have a family.'

She nodded, thinking of the procession of girlfriends he did have as she watched him dig one hand into the pocket of his tailored trousers and look around, his gaze landing and lingering on the toys.

CHAPTER THREE

DRACO GAVE NOTHING away in his expression as he turned back to her and asked casually, 'Is the baby's father in the picture…?'

How long has he been in your life?

Is he the reason you walked out on me?

He couldn't voice those addendums without acknowledging how much he wanted to know and that was something he could not, would not do.

It came so out of the blue that Jane had no time to control her reaction. Her hand went to her quivering lips as she shook her head, seemingly unable for several moments to speak without breaking down.

Her discomfort, her stress was palpable. He'd be lying if he said he was displeased to sense some trouble in paradise.

Was the man married?

Had he cheated?

Or had he just not wanted the responsibility of fatherhood? Draco wondered, indulging in some speculation as he conjured up a man who was a total loser.

'Is it a joint-parenting situation?' How did that work? He never really had understood, but he supposed if people were willing to compromise for the sake of their offspring… Personally he'd never been big on compromise.

Jane shook her head, not appearing to register the faint mockery in his voice. 'Mattie's father was brought up in the village,' she said quietly. 'He moved away then…he was a stonemason, a craftsman, an artisan. His little company was about to…' Her voice trailed away.

Draco felt his jaw tighten in response to her reverential tone then belatedly picked up on the tense.

'Was?' he queried.

'He died,' she said, her voice as dark as the bleakest dark winter night.

Her hand was covering her mouth again, the mouth that he had loved, the mouth that had driven him crazy as she'd explored every inch of his body. No sex had ever been like what he had experienced with Jane.

It was that sex and the mortal blow she had delivered to his pride, not loss, that had made the months after she ran away the toughest he had ever known.

He had got through it, and part of the joy of being rich was that he answered to no one. So if you holed up in a cabin in Alaska for two months, no one asked you why. Not even the guests at the wedding and definitely not the photographer with the images of the fleeing bride, photos that were now in Draco's possession.

It had seemed a fair exchange to Draco, and when faced with the choice he had offered the photographer had agreed.

'Publish and you will make money but I will ruin you.' Draco had not elaborated before he'd given the favoured option. 'Hand over all the copies, and I mean all, no insurance for your memoirs, and your career will go stratospheric.'

There had been rumours circulating, obviously, but no visual evidence and nobody willing to go on the record.

He was known to be litigious, which came in handy. He doubted anyone had believed his 'mutual change of heart' press release, but no one had actually challenged it.

'I'm sorry,' he roughed out.

Her hand dropped, and her shimmering forest-green stare was disconcertingly direct, almost accusing, which, considering he was the injured party, was ironic.

'Are you?' His face was blank, which she had noticed when they were together was his way of dealing with emotional situations. She had always imagined that behind his mask were real feelings he could not articulate, but now she knew he hadn't said he loved her for the simple reason he didn't.

Draco said nothing.

What could he say? Moments before he'd welcomed the idea of her being unhappy. He felt a slug of guilt and thought, Be careful what you wish for Draco.

The pain in her eyes was… Unable to maintain eye contact, he turned his head sharply. Her vulnerability, her fragility shook loose feelings that were painful in their intensity, but he refused to name them.

'Were you married?'

She ran a hand across her face and gave an odd little laugh. 'No.'

'So being a single parent must be…'

'A learning curve,' she admitted, cutting in quickly. It wasn't a lie, it just wasn't the complete truth.

The silence stretched as he seemed to search for words, which had to be a first for Draco, as he glanced once more towards the toys.

'Do you have family close...?'

'I was brought up in care, Draco.'

The reminder brought the faintest of flushes to the slashing angle of his high cheekbones. 'I know that.'

'It just slipped your mind.' Because it hadn't been important enough for him to remember, she thought bitterly.

'I meant a support group... Your friend Carrie, was it?'

'It's a good community here,' Jane said quickly, not meeting his eyes in case he saw the tears shimmering there and biting down hard on her lip when she heard the quiver in her voice. 'The village is a good place to bring up a child. In a big town, a city, it must be harder. The villagers have been great. I think they suggested me for this course because they think I need a break, that, and the fact I brought the news crew here.' She took a deep breath. 'I can see how it might seem personal but it wasn't, though I think you're owed an—'

'An explanation?' he suggested helpfully.

Her eyelashes flickered against her cheek as her brain froze. She ought to have a practised response, but she didn't. 'No, I meant—' She paused, thinking, What did I mean? 'I meant you can blame me for your bad press but that doesn't mean I regret it, because I don't!'

'No, I don't blame you for the bad press. I blame the incompetent site manager who decided to cut corners. He is the reason I have had to make a detour to the back of beyond, but he won't be troubling you any longer,' he told her and watched her eyes widen. 'Don't look at me like that. I haven't put out a hit on him,' he said, sounding amused.

'I didn't think—' She broke off, a guilty unease settling over her. 'You sacked him?'

Jane had been vocal in her denunciation of the man. She had called him all the names under the sun when she had confronted him in the quagmire that had once been beautiful and tranquil, but despite that she took no pleasure from the idea of his ruin. What did she know? He might have children, a mortgage… She felt a stab of guilt at her part in the imaginary downfall building in her head.

Draco shook his head in seeming disbelief, watching the expressions drift across her face. 'I can't believe you feel sorry for the guy.'

'Not sorry, precisely,' she countered, lifting a hand to remove an annoying recalcitrant curl from her face.

Draco's eyes followed the action, focusing in on the fine-boned delicacy of her wrist, a delicacy that hid the supple strength of her body, lovely toned legs that could wrap tight around him, arms that could—

He tried to halt the memories but it was too late. Heat he had zero control over was spreading through his body, flaring inside him as memories surged.

He remembered hearing the harsh rasp of her breath as he kissed his way down her spine, the little groans as her face dug into the pillow as he slid his hand between her legs, the fierce focus on her face when he entered her and—

One moment she was breathing, the next the air around them had become thick and heavy, making each breath an effort as their eyes locked, green on obsidian. Jane shivered as an illicit thrill of excitement spread though her body. Her entire world had narrowed to his dark stare. She felt as though the protective layers were being peeled away from her skin, leaving her exposed, but she couldn't break the contact.

'Draco…?'

* * *

It wasn't the slurred-sounding, bewildered warning in her
voice that dragged him clear of the erotic spiral of memories. It was a sudden extraordinary, impossible thought
as he recalled the excuses his incompetent employee had
reeled out when he was trying to pass the buck. The
woman he'd spoken of who had violently attacked him.

Jane realised she had been holding her breath. There was
a gentle whoosh as she let it out and smoothed her hair
back from her face. The dangerous thrum in the air had
receded, leaving an awkwardness—at least on her part.

She rubbed her arms where the fine hairs were still
standing on end as if she had just walked through an electrical storm, and silently called herself a fool. She'd been a
foolish, starry-eyed virgin who had fancied herself in love
the first time around. The second time… She caught herself up short, her eyes widening in horror at the dangerous
direction of her thoughts—there would be no second time!

Five minutes in his company and she was already
thinking in terms of inevitable, but nothing was inevitable except the fact there was no going back.

The sexual hum in the air had gone but Draco's stare
remained unnervingly intense.

'What?' she snapped out, wondering if that breathless
moment had been a figment of her imagination, the result
of her hormones coming out of hibernation.

She dashed a hand across her small nose. 'Have I got
something on my nose or something?'

Her comment drew his eyes to the light sprinkling of
freckles across the bridge of her tip-tilted nose. 'Freckles,'
he said, seeming lost in thought. 'Were you—?' he said
abruptly before shaking his head and laughing. 'No…?'

'Was I what?' She stopped, gripped by a chill of horror. If he knew how close she had come to making a pass at him. Pass. It sounded so innocent when what she'd felt had not been innocent.

'Franco…the guy whose career you were so worried about.'

Her lips twisted in annoyance. 'Could you sound more patronising if you tried?' Maybe he was trying. 'And,' she finished crossly, 'I was not worried. I am not about to lose any sleep over him!'

'It might make you feel better,' he continued, ignoring her intervention completely, 'if I tell you he tried to blame everyone else but himself.'

This had been a red line for Draco. The first quality required for good leadership was the recognition that the buck really did stop with you.

'Actually, one specific person who apparently was a foul-mouthed ranting witch who he suspected was not all there.' He tapped his own forehead to illustrate his meaning. 'She also physically threatened him…?' He paused. 'You…?'

'Not violence,' she protested. 'I was angry,' she admitted defiantly.

'It really was you. That is…?' He dragged a hand across his dark hair, making contact with a ceiling beam, and dropped it. Even after the confirmation it seemed barely credible to Draco, who couldn't equate the description with the meek, compliant woman he had once been engaged to.

'What a…'

He blinked as a word he had never thought to hear on her lips slipped out and she seemed oblivious to the fact.

'I ask you seriously—who wouldn't be angry? The heavy machinery had come in the night when we were all asleep. By the time I arrived the other men were drinking tea. It was a done deal. And he, that man, he had the cheek to tell me I was trespassing, which I wasn't. It was a public right of way. As for physically threatening him, I was holding the stick, I didn't use it.'

'You need a weapon for self-defence? I had no idea this was such a rough area.'

Her eyes narrowed in dislike. 'Bruce likes sticks. Bruce is a dog,' she clarified quickly. 'And he belongs to my neighbour. He'd slipped his leash and I was chasing him as I'm faster, and Grace took the pushchair for me. If that man is telling lies about me...'

'Relax, he won't be and he's been given a sabbatical... a long sabbatical.'

Draco blamed himself for the situation, hence his personal intervention. He despised the idea of neo babies being given a leg up the ladder, but he had personally signed off on this appointment, not because on paper the guy had the qualifications, which he did, but because Franco's father had promised apprenticeships to a dozen kids in his laboratory.

'Why didn't you think I was capable of it?' Jane demanded, finding relief from the maze of conflicting churning emotions in indignation. 'I'm capable of a lot more than you ever thought.'

'Yes, that was brought home to me the day you did your runaway bride stunt! If we'd been filming that would have gone viral because you come across really well on camera.'

'What do you mean?'

'Your interview earlier made the evening news bulletin.'

'Oh, God!' she said, horrified. 'You watched the coverage?'

'It was brought to my attention.'

'I thought billionaires didn't bother with the little stuff. They floated around on private jets and went to film premieres.' She stopped, thinking of his companions at the last glittering event he'd been pictured at.

'You wishing you'd stayed around to enjoy the lifestyle?' he mocked.

This first direct reference made her stiffen. 'I think we both know I'd have been a terrible wife for a billionaire. You still haven't said,' she added, 'what brings you here.'

'The eco-management course.'

'Oh, if it's oversubscribed, no problem at all.'

'It is not oversubscribed,' he retorted, framing the words with invisible quotation marks. 'I am led to believe you have…' He paused, his dark eyes glittering as they captured and held hers. 'Conditions?' He folded his hands across his chest, looking amused. 'I am here to hear them.'

Jane blinked in confusion. 'What?' Comprehension dawned. 'Oh, I didn't mean—!' Her shocked expression morphed into a frown. 'The vicar didn't say that, or mean that, and you,' she accused, 'knew it! I needed clarification of the childcare facilities. I'm not leaving Mattie with a stranger for hours on end. He needs continuity after…'

He arched a brow. 'After?' His eyes narrowed. 'Are there health issues?'

She shook her head. 'No, nothing like that. He is very young.'

'I have no experience of babies, but I hear they are very adaptable, but to ease your mind there will be several workshop situations that you can bring him along to,' he said glibly, hoping this was true and realising if it wasn't it ought to be. And not just because he had decided that having Jane within grabbing distance might be… Not that he would grab, he mentally corrected.

Why not? asked the voice in his head.

There was no denying there would be a sort of poetic justice in a role reversal. This time he would be the one to walk away…without an explanation.

No matter how many mental gymnastics he performed it was hard not to hear the word revenge. He was no saint, but he liked to think that taking advantage of a mother who had lost her partner was beneath him.

But it would be interesting to observe her reaction to what she had passed up on.

He wanted to see her regret…he wanted to know why.

He closed down that line of thought, not needing to admit what else he wanted and had wanted from the moment he had recognised her.

It was a weakness.

She was a weakness.

'I will send the prospectus and timetable of events. No one is expected to attend them all, so there is time to spend with your son…there is flexibility.'

She felt a scratch of guilt. When she had seen him she'd assumed he had come here to…well, not be nice and certainly not show consideration. Clearly he had moved on, as, she reminded herself, had she, though not necessarily in the direction Draco thought.

Why hadn't she told him the truth about Mattie's parentage? she asked herself guiltily. His assumption would lead him to think she had moved on, which of course she had, but allowing the assumption to stand meant she didn't have to prove anything.

The guilt remained and she felt uneasy about the subterfuge. She hadn't planned this route; it had just opened up. She had actually assumed he already knew when he'd asked.

'Actually M...' The breath died in her throat when she looked up, the expression on his lean patrician features making her start to babble nervously

'Well, that is very...it sounds good,' she finished, her relief intense when he took the hint and began to move towards the door. 'Oh, w—'

Her warning was cut off as his head hit the low beam where Carrie had inserted the downlighters, the thump made by the collision of his skull with wood sending her stomach into a lurching dive.

Stunned, but not as stunned as he was, she watched with horror as he sank to his knees, his head on his chest. The slow trickle of blood brought her to her senses.

People said she was good in an emergency situation, but actually she just reacted.

She took a step towards him and fell to her knees beside him. 'Oh, my God, I should have warned you... I am...' Fewer words, Jane, said the practical voice in her head, and more action.

'I'm fine,' he muttered irritably.

'Don't be stupid. You are not fine.'

He looked at her through his fingers, which were already red. Luckily she wasn't squeamish. She was guessing it had been a long time since anyone had called him stupid.

'Sit down,' she coaxed, relieved when he managed to plonk himself down on the sagging sofa. She took hold of the hand he had clamped to his forehead. His healthy golden glow had an unhealthy pallid tinge and there were beads of sweat along his upper lip. 'Please don't go all macho and ridiculous… Let me see…'

She thought he was going to push her away, but he allowed her to thread her fingers into his thick dark hair, gently separating the strands to access the source of the trickle of blood that was dripping down his face.

'Here… No, that's the old scar…' she realised, exposing a long white ridge of scar tissue she had traced with her fingertips in the past. She had imagined him earning it doing something action-man and dangerous on the ski slopes.

And didn't that say everything there was to say about their relationship? She had never asked and he had never volunteered the information.

'Here it is…quite deep. You might need stitches.'

'I won't need stitches.'

She glanced at his face. His colour was a lot better. 'If you say so…but unless you want to look like some gory advert for a horror film, you'll let me help. It's self-interest,' she added. 'I don't want to be known as the woman who attacked a billionaire.'

His dark eyes swivelled her way. 'Just the woman who left him standing at the altar.'

Jane froze.

She had half anticipated that the label would follow her for the rest of her life, but it hadn't. Miraculously there had been no photos on social media, maybe because phones had been banned at the wedding, something she had thought a bit over the top at the time.

Her eyes slid from his and the challenge in them—this was not the time or the place for explanations and she doubted there ever would be a right time. If he knew her reasons, he'd be relieved, which she could cope with, but his pity… No, she really couldn't take that.

'I will get something to…' She made a vague gesture and got to her feet.

When she returned carrying a bowl of water and the contents of her first-aid box, Draco was still sitting on her sofa, looking more normal apart from the blood.

'Send me any bills for the furniture.'

She rolled her eyes. 'There is no blood on the furniture.' Plenty on his shirt and a few blobs on the polished wooden floor. 'Lucky I'm not squeamish,' she observed prosaically as she laid the bowl on the restored carpenter's chest that served as a coffee table. 'This might hurt,' she added, trying to sound chattily indifferent when she really wasn't while dipping a cotton swab into the water where antiseptic swirled.

Objectivity was really hard to fake when she was this close to his hard, lean male body, when a thousand memories, tactile and visual, were flitting through her head, and her stomach was performing somersaults as a hunger she only allowed to surface in her dreams dug in, painfully real.

'It's not actually as deep as I thought,' she admitted, her frowning regard on the clean wound where the copious flow of blood had reduced to a steady seep. 'You might not need stitches,' she conceded, taking a deep breath. If nothing else, the act of asking would prove she had moved on. 'But this other scar, that must have been…'

'A skull fracture, which, as I'm sure you're thinking, explains a lot.'

Jane wasn't laughing. He could feel the empathy coming off her in waves.

CHAPTER FOUR

'HOW DID THAT HAPPEN?' This time she didn't need a deep breath; the question came naturally.

'I fell while I was...' He had told the story so many times. Including to the medical staff when he had arrived in the emergency room, but somehow the words wouldn't come now. 'My father punched me. I fell and hit my head on a...'

He stopped. It was the expression on her face that brought home to him what he was doing... Which was what, Draco?

He was not a sharer.

He did not require sympathy or, worse still, pity, so why the hell had he just told Jane a fact that he had never told anyone?

'It was a long time ago and I was an extremely irritating kid.'

Jane sucked in a breath through flared nostrils. She knew that Draco's father was dead, that his only close relative was a half-brother, a lovely skinny beanpole of a boy who she had met briefly the day before the wedding, but in that moment she hated that father with a teeth-clenching passion.

Her small hands clenched into fists of outrage until

the words bubbling up inside her could not be contained and they escaped in a rush.

'He beat you?' she cried, disbelief and outrage throbbing in her voice.

Draco had regretted sharing the moment he'd opened his mouth, but he hadn't been anticipating her dramatic reaction.

'I had a late growth spurt, so not after that occasion.' He'd been safe from his father's increasingly dangerous mood swings. His father had not been the sort of man who would hit out at someone who could hit back. But he had been the sort of man who would hit someone smaller, so Draco had delayed starting university to make sure that the same didn't happen to his little brother. 'He drank himself into an early grave.' And Draco never had made it to university. He didn't feel the loss.

'Good!' she exploded, then caught his expression and refused to back down. 'I'm sorry how that sounds but, well, I hate bullies!' she hissed. Appropriate or not, her emotions could not be contained.

Draco contemplated her fierce expression, the sparking defiance in her green eyes, the hectic flush on her smooth cheeks, and found it hard to believe that he had once considered her a gentle, mild creature outside the bedroom.

The bride he had imagined would create no dramas. Except, of course, her exit from his life had hardly been without drama, he reminded himself drily.

Catching her full lower lip between her teeth, she lowered her gaze and looked at him through the mesh of her dark lashes. 'I'm sorry if you don't like that, but there it is.'

'I wasn't too keen on him either,' Draco responded lightly after a long contemplative moment.

Jane didn't respond. She was struggling with all her strength to escape the hypnotic tug of his dark stare until she reached the point where the necessity to do so didn't seem so urgent, despite the warning bells ringing in her head.

'I always assumed that you had a happy childhood,' she mused, sounding confused as she settled back on her heels beside the sofa. They had been engaged to be married and they had never come close to sharing as much as they had now, when they were nothing to one another.

She shook her head against that deeply bleak thought and, pushing her hair back from her face, tangled her slim fingers in the glossy skein.

She didn't mean to bring up the elephant in the room; it just happened as she blurted, 'Why did you ask me to marry you, Draco?'

Draco's response was equally uncensored. 'I wanted to keep you in my bed for ever.' How long before she had been in another man's bed, the man who had given her a child? The question left him with an odd hollow feeling.

A solitary tear began to trickle down her smooth cheek as he watched, releasing an emotion that he refused to give a name to. He inhaled as it broke loose in his chest, creating a suffocating feeling.

Was she crying for her dead lover, the father of her child?

He leapt to his feet explosively, frustration etched into his lean features.

Jane chose the same moment to get to her feet, and, clumsy in her haste, she almost knocked the first-aid box over. At least it distracted her from the shameful fact that her sensitive pelvic muscles had gone into quivering spasm.

Their impetuous actions had brought them face to face.

Her breath hitched as he caught her face between his big hands and bent his dark head. She saw a glimpse of the hunger in his eyes and refused to allow her heavy lids to close. She would not surrender her control.

The alternative to losing control was taking charge, so she did. Bringing herself up on her tiptoes, she placed her hands around his face, feeling the rasp of light stubble, and she took control, fitting her lips to his.

For a split second he did nothing as he inhaled her scent and then he was kissing her back with a blind, relentless, consuming hunger. Little husky sounds of desperation escaped her throat and were lost in his mouth as the combative contact grew rougher and less disciplined, all heat and hunger.

Then it was over and they were looking at each other—glazed shock duplicated… She saw the moment the shutters came down in his black eyes and decided it was a good thing.

The last thing she wanted was some sort of post-mortem, not that the frustration thrumming through her body needed much analysis.

Draco had always been able to turn her into a person she hardly recognised. It had once felt like freedom; now it felt like loss.

'Well, that was stupid.'

She never allowed herself to wonder what would have happened if her doctor's appointment had fallen after they had married, because she knew. His life since then had proved he was a man who played the field and got bored quickly.

She was aching for something that had never existed, which made her angry, mostly at herself. He had never said he loved her, just that he wanted her, and by now that lust would have turned to boredom. Idiot, she chided herself, focusing on the reality, which was that he had lost no time replacing her in his bed and she was no longer the woman who was seduced by a man telling her he needed her, he wanted her… Even if that man did have a voice that ought, if there was any justice, to be illegal.

'Pleasurably stupid.' He looked down. She barely came up to his shoulder, so fierce, so hot, she did more with a kiss than he had ever imagined possible. 'That's why I proposed, *cara*.'

In other words, just sex.

It was really hard at that moment to remember that she needed more than sex. Actually she didn't even need sex; she needed a quiet, neatly ordered life.

Draco and neat and ordered were a contradiction in terms.

'Oxymoron,' she said out loud, then fielded his quizzical look with a shrug. 'I'd be flattered if it weren't for the fact that your version of for ever, according to what I have read, is about a month,' she said, taking refuge from the ache inside her in the not very pretty truth.

If she hadn't been such a besotted innocent she would have realised at the time that a highly sexed man like Draco, a man who had women throwing themselves at him, would never have been satisfied with one woman.

'The wedding…it wasn't planned. I never intended…' she began before her voice trailed away. 'Just think about all the money you saved on a divorce,' she completed with a laugh that had a fake, hollow sound even to her own ears.

'You signed a pretty tight prenup.'

'Oh, God, so I did. I'd forgotten about that!' It had not been important. She hadn't even read it.

'You think I would have cheated on you?'

Unbelievably he sounded angry. 'Call it a wild guess,' she shot back.

Her anger faded into something far more complex as she watched his eyes drift from her face to her heaving breasts, or actually maybe not so complex, in fact totally basic. She had not kissed another man, let alone had him touch her, since her aborted wedding day.

After the first few months of her existing in a limbo state between misery and more misery, a medical emergency had broken the cycle of despair.

Her endometriosis had flared up, and the acute attack, with pain on another level from the chronic discomfort she had grown accustomed to, had hospitalised her.

As luck would have it, the hospital had been making a push to lower its gynaecological waiting lists and paying private clinics to slash the queues.

Jane had found herself part of this scheme and transferred to a clinic where her keyhole laparoscopy had been performed the very next day. Just in time, the surgeon had said. High on painkillers at the time, she hadn't asked, Just in time for what? And later she hadn't wanted to know.

The procedure to remove the plaques that had been causing her so much pain had been a success, though she had been warned that this was not a cure and in the future a hysterectomy might be the only solution left to her.

Jane had decided not to think too far ahead. This was a reprieve and she had no intention of not taking advantage of it. Cure or not, without the chronic pain her life was changed and for the better. She felt as if she'd been given a second chance—if not to have her own children, then she could work with them.

Her job at the care home had been on a zero-hour contract but that had not been an issue and there were never zero hours in the understaffed sector. The flexibility had meant she could fit in her hours around her pre-nursing college course, the first step on her way to fulfil her new ambition to be a children's nurse.

She'd had a purpose again.

But so much for plans—they were as fleeting as happy endings. Her life had changed again when there had been the knock on the door and the terrible news. She knew she would never be the mother that Carrie would have been, but she was damned sure she was going to try.

She was a mother now and there was no room in her life for the chaos that came with Draco, even had that particular door been open.

'I think you should go. Shall I call someone for you?' she asked, glancing at his head.

'I'm fine.'

Mattie chose that moment to wake and his angry shout drifted down the stairs.

'Your son?'

'Matthew… Mattie…'

'How old?'

'He's seven months. He was eight weeks when…'

He watched the look of loss spread across her face and it hit him. The eight weeks she spoke of, or couldn't, was when the baby's father had died.

'If you'll excuse me… I should go.'

He gave a quick tip of his dark head and without another word was gone. Jane leaned back against the door, her hand pressed to her lips. I kissed him!

The shame was mingled with an illicit thrill of excitement. Her body was still tingling from his touch, and just thinking about the hard imprint of his aroused body sent a pulse of heat through her pelvis.

She breathed slow and deep, trying to gather her scattered senses, then Mattie yelled and, reminded of her priorities, she felt a sharp stab of guilt and flew up the stairs.

Jane almost forgot the printout of her itinerary for the next three weeks and turned back to the cottage to grab it off the table, pushing it into her carry-on bag.

She knew the departure and arrival times, but the details had not included the airline she was travelling on. When she had emailed a request the person she was corresponding with had told her she would be met at the airport with tickets and further details.

She had decided that, rather than book a transfer, it would be more economical to hire a car, which would be waiting for her when she arrived at the rather obscure Italian airport. Her satnav had given her a route that appeared to avoid any major built-up areas and suggested it would take her two hours to get there.

'You've got everything this time?' Grace teased as she got in the car. Mattie was already ensconced in the back seat next to Grace's teenage daughter, who was great with him.

'Definitely sorry about that, but you wouldn't believe what a nightmare it is packing for a baby.'

Grace laughed and nodded to the rear-seat passenger. 'Oh, I would, and it doesn't get any better, I promise you. This one always wants to take her entire wardrobe,' she joked, ignoring the indignant 'Mum' from the back seat.

'Nervous?' Grace asked as they drove along.

Realising she was chewing her fingernails, a horrible habit she had kicked ages ago, Jane gave a self-conscious grimace and hastily withdrew them, glancing at her neat, clear-polished nails before putting them firmly in her lap.

'I've never been to Italy before.' It seemed strange to think that she had once been planning on spending the rest of her life there. She hadn't even considered how difficult that would be or suggested that she accompany Draco on one of his overnight trips home. Her level of acceptance now seemed bizarre to her. 'And I've never been here.' Jane looked around curiously. It felt different from any airport she had been to. There was no parking issue, for starters, and they pulled right into a space outside a small terminal building. 'I've never heard of it before.'

'I've never been here either, but a friend did their flying course from here and obviously I've never been in a private jet.'

'Private jet!'

Grace looked amused by her horrified expression. 'Didn't you realise? Want to get your pilot's licence or need a stop-off point from your end-of-the-garden helicopter pad, this is your go-to airport. It avoids the congestion over London.'

'But I'm not booked on a private jet.' Her initial confidence wavered as she saw a suited figure approaching the car, flanked by two women who looked corporately slick.

Grace unfastened her seat belt.

'Looks like you have bagged the company jet, lucky you!' her friend said, nodding to the logo on the side of the jet on the runway.

Jane followed the direction of her friend's stare while in the back the youngster bounced excitedly and pleaded, 'Send us loads of photos for me to post.'

'Oh, God, no!'

From the back seat the teen piped up, 'How is this bad?' before a glare from her mum reduced her to silence.

Sensing her friend's horror, Grace said cheerily, 'I think you'll find you are. It'll be a fantastic opportunity to meet some of the others on the course ahead of time, scope out the talent,' she suggested with a mock leer.

'Mum…?' This time the reproach came with a giggle.

Jane rolled her eyes, but asked herself if it would be so bad to discover someone nice and normal, not to mention safe, to have some fun with. An image inserted itself in her head of someone who was neither nice nor normal, and as for safe!

'I have no time for men. I have Mattie.' Jane almost choked at the way her prim response sounded, but it was true, and a lot better than admitting Draco was a hard, no, impossible act to follow. Because he made you so happy, mocked the ironic voice in her head.

'Being a mum is not like taking the veil, Jane.'

'Oh, God, gross, Mum!' the teen in the back seat responded, covering her hands with her ears.

'I know things didn't work out for you last time.'

Jane sighed. She really regretted that extra glass of wine at book club, but at least her confidences had stopped at, 'I was engaged once—it didn't work out.'

It was a bit disorienting to have the reception party not only help unload her luggage but coo over Mattie and stay with her as she moved smoothly through Customs.

Wow, she thought as they settled in their seats in the empty cabin, this was travelling, but not as she knew it! She glanced through the window, wondering when the other passengers were going to board. Was she early?

It wasn't until they were in the air that the penny dropped: there were no other passengers!

She was confused. Had other people cancelled, or was this Draco showing her what she had missed by not marrying him?

There was no doubt it was a comfortable way to travel, especially with a baby, who lapped up all the attention from the cabin crew who pronounced him beautiful, but, and she knew it was probably irrational, she felt resentful.

She felt as though she were a puppet who no one had bothered to consult, so no change there. Don't ask, just lavish luxury and she will stay in her box!

But Jane was no longer happy in her box! And she couldn't wait for an opportunity to prove it.

The transfer at the other end was equally smooth. There was no juggling baggage, no issues at all until she was shown the waiting limo.

This was an opportunity with neon sign directions.

The entourage that had followed her exchanged glances and looked nonplussed and alarmed when she shook her head and told them, channelling polite but firm, 'I've got a hire car. I'm driving myself.'

This was a cue for a lot of ultra-alarmed looks and some waving of hands, which, when she stuck to her guns, eventually became helpless Latin shrugs tinged by worry.

It struck Jane as a big fuss about nothing.

'Right, Mattie, let's do this!' she said with false jollity when she got behind the wheel of what the online details had described as a compact hatchback.

Compact was generous and the way the person handing over the car had sternly told her that any damage would incur severe penalties seemed a bit over the top, considering the number of dents and dings in the paintwork.

She also found and disposed of several crisp packets and a crushed soft drink can under her seat, which maybe explained the incredibly low price of the hire. Still, so long as it got her there and it wasn't far. She took comfort from the logistics.

Though not far in miles, the road was scary—there, she'd admitted it—and had to have doubled the distance.

There were several times during the journey when she regretted her decision to refuse the taxi service offered, especially when she had to pull over on a really lonely road to change Mattie's nappy and feed him, glancing over her shoulder at every shadow and sound. When Mattie had subsided, replete, her supply of food exhausted, Jane found herself hoping that the stock of baby food offered by the organisers was more realistic than the description of the hire car.

If not, she was in serious trouble!

The satnav, while accurate and indispensable, had chosen the shortest route, but maybe, she began to realise, not the easiest one.

Of course, the views were incredible, or they seemed that way on the rare occasions she took her eyes off the road for a split second. Those occasions were few and far between because she really didn't fancy driving off the edge of a mountain or ending up in a ditch.

Talk about white-knuckle ride!

When Jane saw the first sign bearing the name of her destination she gave a sigh of relief and felt some of the tension edge out of her rigid, aching shoulders. By the time she reached the massive wrought-iron gates that took her off the public highway she had passed three more signs and the tension was back.

At least when she'd been focused on not driving off a cliff she hadn't been thinking about what would happen when she did arrive, and now she was.

She drove towards the huge, elaborate gates wondering what you did to get inside—ring a bell?

There were no bells that she could see and it all seemed rather grand. Was there a trade entrance?

'Oh!' She actually leapt in her seat then laughed at herself as the gates silently opened. Of course, there were cameras, she thought, trying not to imagine the anonymous eyes watching her as she drove through and began the last leg of her journey.

If this was a driveway, it was not what she thought of as one. She had driven a good half-mile along a mercifully bump-free road through dense forest when the sunken lights alongside the verge burst into life, illuminating the road ahead and revealing an area of manicured parkland with the blue shadowed mountain to one side and the sparkle of sea to the other.

'Oh, wow!' she breathed and she cranked down the window a crack to inhale the salt and pine scent of the air.

It became less a breath and more a gasp when the palazzo came into view. Obviously she had looked it up but the generic photos online did not come close to the full open-mouth impact of this first glimpse, even though she hadn't been expecting a small cottage. But this… The sheer scale of the building standing before her made a statement—presumably something along the lines of 'We are rich and powerful! Do not mess with us!'

If so, it communicated the message well!

Set against the backdrop of dark sea and the first streaks of crimson from the setting sun, it made that statement even more dramatic.

She took in the symmetrical rows of deep identical windows on three levels, the huge baroque porticoed entrance and the impressive sweep of steps that shone white in the fading light.

Would she get a chance to see inside?

This was where Draco had said they would bring up their children. The recollection seemed even more surreal now she was seeing the place, though only as a visitor.

She hesitated, taking her foot off the accelerator as she approached a fork in the road. One quite obviously led up to the house; the other she presumed led to the buildings she could just about make out behind the distant bank of trees and shrubbery.

She had turned the wheel to head away from the palazzo when the figure stepped out of nowhere…one minute there was no one there, the next he was there.

CHAPTER FIVE

JANE SLAMMED HER foot on the brake and closed her eyes, anticipating a thud.

When she opened them, Draco was standing there making her think of some sort of glowering gladiator, a bare inch between him and the bumper of her car. Typical of the man, she thought, still shaking with reaction that he had not even bothered to jump out of the way. Startled, she glanced at Mattie in his car seat, blowing bubbles, oblivious to the near miss.

Her heart contracted with love for him.

Draco strode around the side of the car, his face like thunder, wrenched the door open, and stood there, waiting.

She had seen Draco annoyed before, irritable, and even in a bad temper, but she had never seen him really, really mad. It was an awesome sight in the way a hurricane was awesome, but you still didn't want to be in its path.

She could think of two ways to deal with this—well, three if you counted turning the car around and getting the hell out of there.

Jane didn't count it.

So that left being placatory and apologetic, even if she didn't know what she had to apologise for, or going on the offensive.

She hummed softly to herself, embracing the spirit of rebellion bubbling up inside her as she exited the car and stood there blinking up at him while easing the crick in her back.

Her stomach flipped. She accepted it as inevitable. Only Draco could look as gorgeous with his hair standing up in spikes where he had dragged his fingers through it. He looked very large, very angry and quite desperately beautiful, wearing a black shirt and trousers. His expression made grim look light-hearted.

'I wasn't expecting a reception committee,' she tossed out audaciously and saw his eyes narrow. Weirdly, she got a bit of a kick out of winding him up. 'You look...' her lashes lowered momentarily '...not happy? Sorry— am I late?' she wondered perkily.

'Late?' Her entire attitude was provocative, from the little smile on her pink full lips to the toss of her head.

His temper hit the red zone as he made one last attempt to contain it and then let rip.

Jane stood there and heard him out, waiting in the post-explosion silence before she responded, not in an effort to be provocative, just to get her breath. Nothing on her face showed the heart-thudding effect his diatribe had had on her—he really was awesome.

'You finished?' She watched his nostrils flare as he exhaled and opened his mouth. 'Before you say anything else, it might be a good idea to switch to English. I have not the faintest clue what you just said to me... sorry, *yelled at* me.'

They had planned for her to take an immersive course in Italian after they had married. Draco had begun the lessons in the bedroom, introducing a vocabulary she doubted any language tutor would have offered.

The shameful pulsing throb between her legs made her voice sharp as she continued.

'If you greet everyone this way I can't imagine anyone coming back for a return visit. Your bullying might be acceptable for people who work for you, but I don't!'

'Bullying?' he echoed in insulted disbelief.

She could imagine that women didn't talk to him that way, or, for that matter, anyone, but tough, she decided, enjoying the feeling of rebellion.

'I am not a bully!'

'You yell at people who can't yell back. Well, that is no longer me!'

'I do not yell at anyone, and I never yelled at you!' he countered, clearly outraged at the accusation.

'You didn't have to. I agreed with everything you said!' she pointed out bitterly.

'Because I make good sense, because I always had your best interests at heart.'

'You believe that? Then you're even more arrogant than I thought.'

A look of self-conscious unease drifted across his face before his jaw tightened. 'My temper got the better of me.' The concession appeared to be dragged out of him against his will. 'But that is hardly surprising!'

He had spent the last hour plagued by images of smashed cars at the bottom of cliffs, broken bodies, the lick of flames. No wonder he had lost it, but at least she hadn't understood what he had said.

'If you thought I was going to run you over, I thought I was going to run you over, which was much worse.'

'You think this is about you driving like a lunatic?' He dismissed the idea with an expressive Latin gesture.

'I do not drive like a lunatic. I happen to be a very good driver! If I wasn't a very good driver I would have hit you. Also, I was driving at a snail's pace. But I get,' she conceded, 'that it must have been scary for you.'

He looked at her in utter astonishment. 'You really think I yelled at you because of that!'

She shrugged. 'I haven't been here long enough to make you mad about anything else.'

'You disregarded my instructions for your transfer.'

Instructions. Now that really grated. 'Oh, my God, you really are a control freak. Your office sends out a memo and if it's not followed to the letter you freak out!'

The provocative sound of her mocking laughter set his teeth on edge. 'I presume you were trying to prove a point, though what point I can't begin to imagine.'

'I was not!' She just resisted the impulse to stamp her foot because that would not help the mature and adult high ground she was determined to inhabit.

'So you flouted my wishes, the arrangement I put in place for your and the baby's comfort—'

'You put it in place... Seriously, Draco, you expect me to believe that you even knew what arrangements had been put in place?'

He ignored the sarcastic intervention. To respond would have involved addressing the fact he had been personally involved in all the details of the arrangements for today.

'It is three and a half hours since I received the information that you and the baby were not in the limo sent for your safe transfer,' he said, emphasising the safe. 'I was informed that you were driving yourself in a cut-price hire car!'

'That's just like you, to judge everything on its value.'

'I'm judging it on its brakes, which does not seem un-reasonable. Your actions seem at best childish. I have no experience of what travelling with an infant involves but I am pretty sure that it is not relaxing. Your behaviour would have been mildly irritating had this happened in England on roads you are familiar with, but this is very much not England. The more secure route here would have taken you three hours, the shortcut offered by your satnav two and a half.'

Her guilty expression said it all.

'Have you any idea how many accidents have occurred on that road, how many foolish tourists have come to harm?'

She flinched but maintained a defiant attitude as he hammered the point home.

'All right, it was not a good road.'

The concession didn't cut any ice with Draco, who had spent the last two hours thinking of those blind corners and hairpin bends, his imagination going into overdrive.

He had been first at the scene of a crash the previous month when luckily no one had been seriously injured, and the guy at the wheel of the horsebox should have known better.

Draco knew every twist and turn, every blind corner like the back of his hand; he had cut his teeth and honed his driving skills in this terrain, but even he only used the shortcut in daylight hours, and then in a four-wheel drive.

'You could have been caught out there in the dark.' A fact that had lain heavy with him as he'd waited, feeling totally impotent, and as he'd watched the sun begin to sink, his anxiety had turned to cold fury.

He never second-guessed his decisions but he had re-gretted his decision not to drive out and intercept her.

She could have taken the sensible longer road and there were several points on both routes where the driver had an option—the chances of him missing her were high. For all he knew she could have recently passed her driving test. He didn't have a clue as he had never asked her.

What had he asked her?

You were never that interested in her life story, were you, Draco?

He pushed the tickle of guilt away. He had remembered that she was brought up in care, and he could recall thinking it meant that there would be no embarrassing relatives coming out of the woodwork.

His anger didn't dissipate but it was now diluted by a guilty awareness he was reluctant to acknowledge.

'I arranged for you to be brought here. Why did you not come as arranged?'

Her chin went up. 'Arranged?' She shook her head, making her curls bounce then settle into soft golden coils. 'I did not ask you to make arrangements for me, and I was not included in those decisions. I am very sorry that you have been inconvenienced,' she said with an insincere smile. 'But I had made my own arrangements.'

She watched as a look that on anyone else she would have called bewilderment slid across his lean features. His stabbing gesture was all frustration, before he dragged a hand across his already ruffled dark hair.

'You rented this...' Lips curled in contempt, he launched a vicious kick at the car wheel. 'I do not think much of your arrangements.'

'Do you mind? I have to pay for any damage.'

'I'd pay to get it towed away and crushed. You thought a child would be safe in this!'

The fact that Jane had thought the same thing numerous times during the journey made her respond to his comment even more indignantly.

'How dare you?' she snapped, her eyes flashing green fire. 'My parenting skills are not your business, and at least I don't assume throwing money at a problem is all it takes to solve it!' she huffed contemptuously. 'You can stick your limousines up—' Her eyes widened as she came to a breath-hitching pause. 'I just want to say...'

What do you want to say, Jane?

'I am not your problem and,' she added defiantly, 'I really don't think I'd take advice from someone whose idea of parenting is holding your girlfriend's lap dog while she pouts for the camera.'

His expression moved from fury to blank astonishment before melting into a grin that made it hard to stay angry, actually hard to stay on her feet.

'The thing bit me,' he recalled. 'I had to have a tetanus shot.'

As the tension dissolved Jane covered her mouth with her hand to smother an almost-laugh. She was only partially successful. 'Good!' she growled back.

'I am discovering that size is not a measure of combativeness,' he observed as he studied her face and wondered how it was possible he had never seen or even guessed at this fire in her personality. 'I was concerned.'

'Why?'

The question was so wilfully stupid that he had to wonder if she was going out of her way to provoke him, but he would rise above it, he decided. 'The road I am assuming that you took is not for... Before you explode once more, even locals take the longer route.'

'It wasn't a nice journey,' she admitted, allowing her-

self to be slightly mollified. 'But if there was a car organised this end you should have discussed it, or,' she
corrected very quickly, because she didn't want him to
think she had expected personal treatment, though this
did seem pretty personal, 'have someone discuss it with
me.' All her communications thus far had come via the
office of Draco Andreas. And once the image from a six-
ties spoof of someone gorgeous with endless legs and red
lips sitting on his knee taking dictation had got into her
head, it had been impossible to banish.

It was there now as she said coldly, 'I require options,
not ultimatums. I am quite capable of organising my own
life and making my own decisions.'

'So I am seeing,' he observed, studying the obstinate
set of her round chin.

'Look, obviously—' she sniffed contemptuously '—
you think I couldn't find my way out of a paper bag. But
I'm really not that helpless.'

Draco, his expression indecipherable, looked at the
small finger being waved at him.

'All right, I am sorry if I put you out, but…' It suddenly occurred to her he had made special arrangements
for her… And more troubling, if that was the case, why?
Maybe he just thought she was hopeless and—

Pressing her hands together and closing her eyes
briefly, she called a halt to the flow of disjointed question marks in her head and took a deep breath. 'It's been
a long day and I understand there is an induction session
early tomorrow, so if there is someone to show me to our
room, Mattie—'

On cue the baby began to wail.

Draco watched as she ran around to the passenger
door of the car. Something in her expression as she bent

over the baby seat and spoke soothingly to the sobbing child before she picked him up in her arms made things tighten painfully in his chest.

The cries lessened to a dull roar as she walked back around the car towards him. 'Just point me in the right direction.'

'There has been a change in the schedule. Because not everyone was able to make it on time it was decided that tomorrow will be a free day.'

Jane tried to hide her relief behind a smile but she knew she failed. 'Oh, that's…good to know. Is it far to the—?'

She glanced towards the spread of buildings, their roofs at different levels hidden by the trees, able to make out lights in the gathering gloom.

'Not far, but you are not in the annexe, though if you decide to attend the meet-and-greet supper there later to-night someone will be on hand to escort you.'

A meet-and-greet supper! Perfect to top off the journey from hell and a near-miss collision. Opting out sounded very good to her at that moment. 'Not… I must have mis-understood. So where are we staying?'

'The centre does not have adequate childcare facili-ties. We have allocated you rooms in the main house.'

Jane listened to the slick explanation in silence, her wide eyes swivelling to the palazzo. The sun had al-most sunk and in the semi-darkness it was now lit by spotlights.

'Is there room?' she asked and laughed, even though she didn't really feel like laughing. It was strange to know that once she had been destined to be mistress of the place. She would have arrived here as a bride, not a visitor… She took a deep breath. The point was it hadn't happened.

'Right, okay, where should I…?' Her glance moved from the baby who was nuzzling her neck to the car. Mattie would kick up a hell of a fuss now if she tried to put him back in his car seat.

'I could drive…' Draco looked at the car, imagined the discomfort of fitting his legs into the front seat and decided. 'We will walk,' he announced, showing what she considered an uncharacteristically sensitive appreciation of her dilemma. Or maybe he just fancied a stroll.

'Someone will bring the…car,' he announced, with the confidence of someone who knew there were always people to do his bidding. 'And your luggage. I will show you the way.'

Half down the incline, Draco paused. 'He looks heavy.'

'He's a big boy,' Jane agreed. 'Oh, my goodness, the gardens…' She stared in wonder at the vision stretched out before her. Strategically placed spotlights revealed a series of terraces descending down the steep incline overlooking the sea to one side and the green plain on the other. The terraces appeared to be connected by gates and stairways, and the water from an ornate fountain spilled down the interconnecting levels, ending in a pool in the main terrace outside the palazzo.

'It is quite nice,' Draco agreed, then, with a grin, added, 'English understatement. It rubbed off in school.'

He had never said, but Jane had always had the impression that Draco's English school experience had not been a good one. He had always said that he would not send their children away to school.

The children they never could have had.

'Was his father tall?' Draco kept his voice carefully

neutral. A dead man would be a difficult rival for someone who wanted to take his place.

Luckily Draco did not, but he wanted to know, he thought he deserved to know, if this man was the reason that she had walked away from the altar. Had they already met? Had she realised that she needed to be with this man…that nothing else mattered?

'No, but…' Jane stopped. Carrie had been tall and athletically broad-shouldered, her sparkling eyes and way of looking at the world projecting confidence and hiding her vulnerability. An image of her friend the day she had told Jane she was pregnant drifted into Jane's head, the snatch of conversation playing.

'I don't know how a real family works,' Carrie had confided in a panicked whisper.

Jane, who had been given up for adoption at birth, was equally ignorant of the dynamics. She had never found her for ever home. She'd been on the brink of adoption twice. The first time the mother in the family had become pregnant and they had decided they didn't want Jane. The second time she had felt for a short time as if she was part of a family, but before the adoption had been signed off the husband had been diagnosed with a chronic muscle-wasting disease. There had been tears on both sides when Jane had been sent back to the children's home, but she knew she had been loved and that was something no one could take away from her.

'A real family works on love and you and Rob have enough to spare, don't you think?'

Sometimes you said the wrong thing and others the right thing and this had definitely been one of the latter. She remembered her friend's expression clearing.

'We do, don't we? And he or she will have you for an aunty so that's lucky too.'

Jane's arms tightened around the baby as she hid her face in his soft wispy curls of baby-soft hair for a moment.

'I didn't mean to upset you.' The gruff self-recrimination in his voice made her pause mid-step.

Jane raised her eyes to his face as she took the opportunity to hitch the baby into a slightly more secure position on her shoulder and wished she had not packed away the baby sling, which would have left her hands free.

'You didn't.'

Her swimming eyes said otherwise.

Draco's glance shifted from her face to the baby she held, but the unfamiliar and unwelcome feelings sliding through him did not ease. 'I should take him.'

The abrupt announcement drew a startled round-eyed stare from Jane. 'You?'

She looked almost as shocked to hear him make the offer as he had been himself. The idea of holding something so small and breakable filled him with more horror than a market crash!

He nodded and shrugged. 'Why not?'

How hard could it be?

'But—'

Her reluctance served to harden his resolve. 'There are a lot of steps and it is dark; you can't see your own feet carrying the baby.'

He watched her little grimace of acknowledgment as she pulled the baby in closer, her chin resting on his head.

'I should have driven you down…' But this was one of

the best views of the palazzo and he had wanted to see her reaction. He winced at the insight.

He had wanted to see her regret when she saw what she had walked away from. In the end, though, she had walked away from him, and his ego wouldn't allow him to admit that this inescapable fact still hurt.

'Well, thank you, but the gardens are lovely. I can't wait to see them in daylight.' The light had almost faded completely now, though the path was well lit, and she got a sense of the garden. 'It smells gorgeous. Thank you...' she husked again as Draco bent forward, arms outreached to take the baby from her. She held her breath but still felt her senses thrum when the warm scent of his skin tickled her nose.

'Yep, perfect,' she praised.

Jane lowered her gaze, for some reason she didn't delve too deeply into, the sight of him standing there with Mattie in his arms. The contrast of big man and tiny baby, made her throat tighten with emotion.

'My mother replanted this area many years ago.' Her startled gaze lifted in time to catch the softening around his mouth, the warmth in his eyes, which a moment later vanished as the iron hardness reappeared as if a switch had been flicked and he provided unemotional additional information. 'I tried to reinstate the planting exactly as it was as a memorial to her.'

'That's a nice thing to do.' It suddenly struck her how strange this was, to be standing here talking this way.

When they had been together Draco had never discussed his family much, and when he had it was mostly information about his younger half-brother's achievements. His late father he'd never spoken of at all, she didn't have any idea when he had died, and the only time he had mentioned his mother it had been bare, bleak, bone-dry facts.

His parents had divorced and she'd died a year later.

When Jane had offered sympathy he had closed the conversation down, leaving her in no doubt that the subject was a no-go area—there had been a lot of those.

Jane had wanted to probe but never asked questions back then, had told herself that he would confide in her when he needed to. Now, of course, she knew he never would have.

Their relationship, certainly from his side, had never been about talking or sharing; it had been about sex. Maybe they were talking because they were no longer a couple. They were no longer having mind-numbing, incredible sex... Even then, when she had been so invested in being with him, she had sometimes wondered what, beyond the sex, was keeping them together.

She shook away the thoughts in her head, annoyed with herself for reading anything significant into a casual comment, for making it something more than it was.

Ah, well, the 'keep out' signs no longer applied to her. She wasn't the fiancée trying to say the right thing. Now she could say the normal thing. If he didn't like it, it no longer mattered, she told herself, wanting to distance herself as far as she could from the woman she had been.

'Did you go with her, your mother, when your parents split up?' She half expected him to tell her it was none of her business but, rather to her surprise, after a pause he responded.

'He wouldn't let her take me. And once Jamie was born, I couldn't have left him anyway.'

Jane felt a stab of frustration when he stopped talking. She remembered that feeling of being kept on the outside all too well. His expression was hidden from her by his long, luxuriant lashes, but she'd already seen the regret in the dark depths, presumably that he had told her even this much.

She felt a wave of self-disgust, hardly able to believe that she had meekly accepted his lack of communication as the norm when they were meant to be in a relationship.

'I remember Jamie,' she said, thinking of the stick-thin shy thirteen-year-old she had been introduced to the night before the wedding.

'You made a big impression on him,' Draco said drily, remembering his brother's accusing eyes when he had demanded to know what Draco had done to make her run away.

'How old were you when your parents divorced?'

'Fifteen.'

'So that would have made Jamie…?'

'He was born a month after they married. Watch your step. There's a…' With the hand that wasn't supporting the baby, he caught her elbow as she stepped off into space, or at least six unexpected inches, and landed with a jolt.

'Thanks…sorry, I wasn't looking where I was going.'

No, she'd been looking at him. There was no doubt he was well worth looking at, no point denying the glaringly obvious, and the stubble that was now darkening his cheeks and jawline added an extra earthy… Do not think earthy, Jane, she told herself firmly. She could not allow this to drift towards the obsession she had once felt. No, he was just a good-looking man—okay, a gorgeous man—she had once had a relationship with.

If only he'd let go of her elbow!

How many erogenous zones could there possibly be in an elbow, for God's sake?

'He must be getting heavy. Shall I take him back?' Extending her arms enabled her to escape the skin-peeling contact of his hand and shake off his grip on her elbow without it looking too obvious.

Draco slung her an amused sardonic look. 'Thanks for the offer but I think I'll manage.' The baby was not his issue. His inability to stop staring at her lips was.

CHAPTER SIX

THE BABY OBLIGINGLY let out a howl of anger and, red-faced, started kicking and squirming, which focused Draco's attention on the angry bundle.

'What did I do…?'

Her lips twitched as she watched Draco, none of his habitual 'master of all he surveyed' cool written on his face. Instead there was something that on anyone else you might have called panic.

'Nothing, he's hungry. Let me take him back.'

This time he didn't argue, just muttered something in Italian as the baby was passed between them with no drama, if you discounted the shivers that slithered down her neck where Draco's warm breath brushed her sensitised skin.

Jane began jiggling the baby in her arms. 'Nearly there,' she hushed softly as they reached the lower terrace of the gardens that fed onto the wide stone area in front of the palazzo itself.

The baby responded to her voice and the decibels reduced. 'You are nursing?'

He didn't appear uncomfortable asking the question, but Jane could feel the heat climb up her neck until her face was burning with colour, not because she was embarrassed, but because she felt guilty.

Here was yet another chance to fill him in on the facts. It wasn't as if it were a guilty secret or, for that matter, a secret at all.

Of course, she had a secret, but there was no reason to share it with him. 'No, I'm not feeding him myself.'

'I understand it is not always so easy.'

He understood? The suggestion that he had researched breastfeeding issues might have made her laugh had she not been holding a fretful baby.

'Ah, here is Livia.'

If he sounded relieved, Jane felt a million times more so.

'Livia will show you to your apartments.' He turned to the other woman, who was wearing a dark trouser suit and what Jane rather uncharitably interpreted as an intense eager-to-please expression. She ought to know—she had worn it herself once upon a time.

'This way, please, Miss Smith. I hope your journey was not tiring?'

With a charming smile the woman stepped aside to allow Jane to precede her though the massive ornately carved double doors.

It was like walking into another world. She stood and her head dropped back, taking in the ceiling that appeared to float miles above her head. Works of art adorned the gilded and stuccoed areas of the walls, the remaining walls covered, not in plaster, but with massive mirrors painted with laurel leaves.

Classic sculptures, busts of women with Roman profiles and alabaster faces, stood on the plinths that ran down each side of the massive entrance leading up to a dramatic carved staircase. Marble again like the floor, it swept up to the first-floor gallery where it split, drawing the eye up to the glass dome high above.

Amidst all the classicism was the furniture, large and dramatic pieces, all vibrant colour and ultra-modern clean lines. Two massive sofas beneath the classic plinths were emerald green and the towering steel-framed bookcase a striking red.

Jane stared, not taking in a fraction of the detail.

The other woman, who smiled and stood silent, seemed to understand her awe.

'They made many discoveries during the restoration, but I am sure you do not want a guided tour just now. You are this way.'

She led Jane down a corridor lined with ancient statuary and works of art to a door that opened to reveal a lift, which was not at all ancient. It took them to another floor in smooth seconds, which Jane was glad of. She never had been keen on enclosed spaces.

This corridor was lined with windows that must make it very light in the daytime, but at the moment it was lit by low-voltage lights in the sconces that lined the opposite wall.

'You are here.' She opened the door and waited as Jane stepped inside, not to a bedroom, but to a large living area. The furniture was modern but not statement pieces, just high-quality craftsman-made matching the walls that were painted in a pale plaster colour.

'Oh, do not be concerned,' she said, seeing the direction of Jane's gaze. 'The balcony is childproof.' She nodded to the row of doors. 'Not that that is an issue at his age,' she added with a smile. 'There is a small kitchen.' She pushed open a door and Jane had the impression of white and glossy. 'The other doors are the bedroom and nursery, which interconnect, and the bathroom is shared. I hope this is suitable? There is also one off the playroom, should you wish to use it, but possibly he is not that age yet.'

Jane watched as she opened a door to reveal a bright yellow-painted room that looked like any child's idea of paradise. There was a series of cartoon characters painted on one wall, shelves containing neat stacks of boxes and books on another. The low table with chairs in the middle of the room was empty, but she could picture it littered with toys from the boxes distributed around the room. She imagined a child sitting on the wooden rocking horse.

A child with Draco's dark hair and eyes.

She turned away, a lump in her throat, and began to jiggle Mattie up and down in her arms.

'You're right. I don't think this one will be making use of those facilities...' She heard the door close and was glad.

'Shall I get someone to unpack for you?' The other woman nodded to the luggage stacked in the corner, which Jane had not previously noticed.

Draco's airy confidence that her car would be dealt with seemed justified as her luggage had arrived before she had. She picked up the folded buggy and, with a practised flick of her wrist, unfolded it one-handed before placing Mattie in.

'No, that's fine,' she said, clipping the safety harness. 'I'll unpack myself.' There was not much to unpack. Mattie's things took up most of her luggage allowance. 'This is absolutely...well...' she swept a hand in an expressive gesture around the room '...perfect, but I think,' she began hesitantly, 'that there might be some mistake?' she suggested, feeling the need to double-check. 'I am here for the conference. I'm not a house guest. I am meant to be in the—' She began to feel in her pockets for the course details.

'Mr Andreas did not consider the accommodation there suitable for an infant.' The woman glanced fondly at Mattie, who was stuffing one chubby fist in his mouth, a very serious expression on his face. 'My nephew is his age. He is a very pretty baby too. Oh, the fridge is filled with the formula you requested and some basics for yourself.'

Jane had considered that a nice thoughtful touch when she had filled in the online form. It had saved her a lot of luggage space.

'Thank you,' she said, absolutely overwhelmed by the kindness being shown. 'I feel I'm getting preferential treatment,' she admitted guiltily.

'Not at all. I understand the evening meetings might go on late and it was decided that these apartments will be more suitable, much quieter, less disruption.'

Jane acknowledged a sense of relief. People said nice things about babies, but when it came to a good night's sleep they were less tolerant, and who could blame them? She had pictured sitting down to breakfast with a lot of unfriendly stares directed her way from heavy-eyed sleep-deprived people.

Here Mattie was not likely to bother anyone but her and she had adapted quite well to disturbed sleep patterns. As for the evening meetings, she doubted she would make many.

'It's…' She paused, torn. On the one hand she felt guilty because this did not align with her egalitarian principles, but on the other she was so happy that everything was geared to her and Mattie to a degree she could never have dreamt of. 'Sorry, I'm repeating myself, but this really is perfect.'

Perfect, but an enigma, a perfect nursery, what did she know? This was not her world. Maybe that was how billionaires did it, put in a nursery in case a guest had a baby. Maybe it really was as simple as asking a chef to offer a vegan option.

Or maybe it was something even simpler—this suite of rooms was historically a nursery and no one had thought to change the function when the place was restored, they'd just updated the decor and the facilities? Was it possible that Draco and his brother had occupied the rooms?

An image of a youthful Draco flashed before her eyes, along with the possibly false idea she had that his childhood had not been that happy and it was more than a broken-family scenario. She was overthinking this—just thinking about Draco was overthinking!

When she had agreed to this, she had told herself that, beyond some rousing introductory speech, she would not have to see Draco.

Did you really think that or were you hoping…? She would not even allow the question to form.

The scenario she had imagined involved her seated at the back of a room clapping politely along with the others.

The older woman beamed and, seeming to understand Jane's unposed question, but not that she was fighting the pain of loss with every fibre of her being, added in a confidential undertone, 'I was not here at the time, but I believe this was the old nursery and intended to be so again when…' A self-conscious look spread across Livia's smooth face as she paused, straightened the snowy collar of her white shirt and added, with the forced professional air of someone who realised she had said too much, 'The staff still speak of it. It was a sad time here.'

Jane froze…sad time. Could the woman be referring to the aftermath of her runaway bride act? She felt a slither of unease. Obviously she knew she had made the right decision, but she had been so busy dealing with her own emotions in the aftermath that she hadn't thought about the possibility of a knock-on effect for people she had never met.

She knew that Draco had been angry…but she also knew that his heart had not been affected. How could it have been? She had never had his heart. His ego was another matter.

'I am sure there will be babies here one day.' The comment was delivered with an accompanying confidential smile. 'And in the meantime it has come in useful for you.'

There will be babies!

Just not mine.

'It's really lovely. I'm grateful. I'll have an explore, before I bathe Mattie.' She smiled, hoping the other woman recognised the not so subtle code for 'I want to be alone'.

She really did! The entire day had been exhausting and then the cherry on top, just when she ought to have been recovering after the drive from hell, she had walked straight into Draco, or driven into, and a little too literally for her liking.

He didn't seem to have registered that she could have killed him… Even thinking about that moment made her stomach quiver violently.

Draco was the most alive person she had ever encountered…loved… That she no longer was in love with him did not alter the fact that the idea of him not being in the world was a possibility she simply couldn't accept.

'Should you wish anything...'

I wish to stop thinking about Draco.

In which case coming here was not such a great idea.

'I'm fine,' she said brightly.

To Jane's relief the woman appeared to be moving towards the door and she politely mirrored the action. 'Thank you so much.'

Alone at last, she thought, looking around the room. Focusing her thoughts on the practical and away from the dangerous, she decided to leave the bags and prioritise settling Mattie down. He took his feed well. He became animated in the bath, kicking and splashing, but as she dried him and put him in his sleep suit she could see his eyes were growing heavy. She rocked him on her shoulder, crooning softly until she felt his little body relax into sleep.

She tucked him up carefully in his cot and tiptoed out of the room, leaving the door ajar.

Despite her attempts to dismiss the woman's comments, the words continued to ricochet around in Jane's head as she stood in the nursery that was furnished for the children she and Draco would never have.

Though he would have children—the housekeeper had implied as much. Had the comment been code for Draco having plans to marry? Pressing a protective hand to her stomach, Jane felt her eyes fill with tears... She dashed them away angrily.

She returned to the nursery to check on Mattie, her heart swelling with protective love as she stared down at his flushed sleeping face. Making her way back to the small but well-equipped kitchen, she cleared away the things she had used to make the feed and pushed back the chair she had pulled over to feed him. Through the open window the light breeze blew in the scent of lavender mingled with the salty tang of pine.

She should not be feeling nostalgia or regret. She should feel relieved that things had never reached the point where she had to tell Draco she couldn't have children.

That was one nightmare scenario she had avoided, and so had he. The sentence drifted into her head.

I am sure there will be babies here one day.

She closed the window with a snap and, though the entire place was wired for sound, went back to check on Mattie, who was still fast asleep, snoring softly.

Smiling, she blew him a kiss and banged her head on the butterfly mobile above the cot.

Unpacking her own things did not take long as Mattie's clothes had taken up most of the case. Of course now she knew she could have brought several cases.

She looked at the few lonely items hanging in the cavernous wardrobe. She stood there wondering what happened now.

She knew that to appear suitably keen good manners meant she ought to go to the informal supper, but he had suggested it was optional, and there was no way she would drag Mattie out. Delaying the moment when she was revealed as a phoney appealed at that moment.

Although she was starving.

She was wondering if there was anything in the fridge besides formula to stave off the hunger pangs when a tap on the door drowned out the sound of her growling stomach.

The girl on the other side introduced herself. 'I am Val, the nursery nurse. Well, not really. I help my brother with the bees.'

'Right,' said Jane, amused by the girl's intensity, confused by the mention of bees, and impressed by her excellent English. 'But when guests need a babysitter I help out. I have plenty of experience. I have five smaller brothers. I am here to sit with the little one should you wish me to, though if you prefer not to go for supper it will be delivered here.'

'I…' Jane hesitated and stepped aside for the girl to enter. 'Please come in. Mattie is asleep and normally he sleeps for several hours after his evening feed.'

'Oh, that is so lucky!' Val exclaimed chattily. 'My youngest brother still wakes twice in the night!'

'Look, it's very considerate of you to offer.' Jane paused, realising that it was unlikely the girl had volunteered—this was her job. 'I'm not dressed.' Jane, feeling creased and grubby after the journey, gestured down at her jeans and shirt, thinking that even if she was 'dressed' it would not be very impressive.

'No problem. Even if you don't want to go down to supper I could stay while you shower?'

'I'd probably hear Mattie, but actually that would be great,' Jane admitted, smiling her gratitude. It would be a treat to have a shower without listening out for Mattie.

'Supper is being served at seven-thirty?'

Val saw Jane's face and grinned. 'I don't think it will be a late night—there are a lot of old men with beards.' She looked self-conscious. 'Sorry, that was rude. I quite like beards.'

Jane laughed and the girl looked reassured. 'No problem if you want to take it here.'

The shower, with its array of bewildering controls, was twice the size of the entire bathroom in her cottage…actually, her bedroom. As Jane revolved in the pummel of the warm spray she could feel the knots in her neck and shoulders begin to loosen and she allowed herself the indulgence of enjoying the luxury. She couldn't remember the last time she'd lingered in the shower and there had not been any long, luxurious soaks in a long time.

When she finally forced herself to leave, she felt, if not a new woman, certainly a less tense one. Encased in one of the mountain of fluffy robes, she returned to the bedroom after first glancing in on Mattie, who was fast asleep.

Maybe she would skip supper and just have a glass of milk. Half an hour earlier she'd been starving but now her appetite had gone. She was often so busy that she rarely sat down to a meal, instead eating a sandwich or something on the go. Some days she went to bed and realised she'd forgotten to eat; it was an effort to drag herself out of bed to make a sandwich or have a glass of milk but she made herself—mostly.

If she hadn't the clothes hanging in the wardrobe would look even more ill-fitting than they already did, she thought, putting her travel-creased clothes in a linen hamper and trying not to catch sight of herself in the full-length mirror.

The packet of online information on the course had said there were laundry facilities, which was a relief and a must when you were travelling with a baby, so Jane wasn't really worried about the negligible wardrobe, which took up a couple of hangers and one drawer.

She hastily selected some fresh underclothes, a denim cotton skirt, which, like many of her clothes, felt too loose at the waist, and a sleeveless blouse, pale blue with splurges of orange, that tied at her midriff. She fastened it with a knot but it still gaped sightly, showing a sliver of her midriff. The shirt looked like silk but wasn't, hence the bargain price.

Dragging a quick comb through her hair, she shoved her feet into a pair of sandals and hurried back to the sitting room, where the young girl was looking at her phone. When Jane entered she put it back into her pocket.

'I have decided not to go to the supper,' she said immediately.

'Of course, I will have some supper sent up to you.'

'Actually just a sandwich... Have you eaten? Am I keeping you from your supper?'

'Oh, I've already eaten. There are always sandwiches, salads and so forth laid out for staff on duty during the evening.' She pulled an apple from her pocket like a magician.

'That sounds perfect. Give me directions and I'll go and help myself if you don't mind sitting with Mattie?'

'I don't mind, but you're a guest.' The girl looked doubtful.

'Really, I could do with stretching my legs and getting my bearings before tomorrow. Just direct me to the kitchen.'

'Well, there is a back way that is much quicker—the elevator at the end of the corridor, not the one you came up in. Turn right out the door and just walk to the end. You can't miss. It will take you directly there.'

'I won't be long, and if Mattie wakes...' She pulled out her phone and gave the young woman her number.

'Can't miss it' were, in Jane's opinion, classic famous last words, but actually she didn't miss it and a short while later found herself, not in the main kitchen, but in what appeared to be an anteroom where food was laid along a long table. There was plenty of food left but the room was empty.

There was much more available than sandwiches and salads under their plastic coverings, including a few warm dishes in a heated trolley, which Jane avoided. By now she had totally passed the point of being hungry but recognised she needed food.

With some smoked-salmon sandwiches on a plate, she had intended to go straight back to the nursery, but as she walked past a stable-style door, its top section open to allow the gentle breeze to enter the room, she paused, filled with a sudden longing to breathe in some of that sweet-smelling air.

Carefully unlatching the bottom, she closed it after her and stepped outside into what appeared to be a court-yard. Several storeys rose above it. None of the windows were lit; they just seemed like black empty eyes look-ing down at her.

There was nothing sinister about the central area, which, as far as she could tell, was a neatly tended kitchen garden, which explained the fragrance that had brought her outside. At the far end there was a tall stone arch, and moonlight filtered through.

Standing curiously in the opening, she was transfixed by the view of the moonlit gardens, the gentle trickle of flowing water from the series of fountains blending with the not so distant hush of waves retreating on a shoreline she could not see.

Without intending to, she found herself wandering along one of the paved pathways bordered by lavender that brushed her legs, filling the evening air with perfume as she glanced back to check that the arch was still in sight. She didn't want to lose her point of reference and get lost.

She laughed under her breath, a bitter sound. She'd already lost her way the moment Draco had stepped back into her life. Something about him seemed to disable her ability to think straight, to make rational decisions.

'I'm beginning to think this was a bad idea, coming here. Beginning?' she mocked, looking around the magical setting and huffing a small ironic laugh. Who was she kidding? She had always known it was a bad idea.

But I came anyway.

She had told herself it was a logical choice, that she had been left with no option, but the reality was she could have said no at any point. She could have wriggled out of it, but she hadn't.

'Why?' she asked herself, before closing her eyes as if she could block the answer to her question.

Draco was like a drug. She had gone cold turkey to get him out of her system and it had hurt. She really couldn't let him back in.

Telling herself fiercely that she wouldn't, she didn't register the toe of her sandal had caught in an uneven ridge in the paving until she had left it behind.

With a muttered curse of frustration, she turned back to retrieve it just as the moon slipped behind a cloud.

The sudden darkness was so profound that it was as if someone had switched a light off. She stood stock-still and waited for her eyes to adjust to the light or, rather, lack of it.

CHAPTER SEVEN

THEY DIDN'T NEED to adjust. The moon reappeared, revealing the enchanting gardens and the fact she was no longer alone.

Her heart took a plunging dive before climbing into her throat, a helpless primitive shiver of awareness slithering down her spine, and she shivered, too shocked to even attempt to retreat. As if her secret thoughts had summoned him, Draco, the real flesh and blood one as opposed to the one in her head, was standing there a few feet away holding a wine bottle in one hand and her sandal in the other.

'Is this where I see if the slipper fits?'

She took a step towards him and snatched it out of his fingers... For a second he didn't release his grip. What was infinitely more disturbing was that for a second Jane didn't want him to.

Balancing on one leg, she slid her foot back into the sandal, not taking her eyes off him the way you didn't take your eyes off a dangerous jungle cat about to lunge.

You should be so lucky, mocked the voice in her head.

Though the analogy was not so far out. There was something quite...combustible about him, she decided, her eyes going from the bottle in his hand to his face again as she marvelled at the perfect symmetry of his features that were all dark shadow and light relief, like a starkly beautiful pencil sketch, his shadowed jaw adding to the edgy vibe.

'What are you doing here?' she began in a cranky voice that made his dark brows lift sardonically. 'That is, it's your home, of course you're here,' she said quickly, glad the shadows hid her embarrassed blush. 'I just assumed you would be at the meet-and-greet supper.'

'Me being the host?'

She nodded and he followed the direction of her gaze to the uncorked bottle in his hand. 'The trick of good management is delegation, and I thought you'd be there.'

'Looks like we were both wrong,' she said, struggling to stop her gaze travelling over his long, lean length, and trying not to see the reckless gleam in his deep-set eyes that was probably connected to the bottle of wine he held.

She didn't remember him ever drinking much.

'Don't worry, I'm not drunk, at least not yet.'

The words sounded almost like a threat. Their glances connected and the combustible quality of his dark gleaming stare made her stomach tighten and flutter.

His glance took in her damp hair, which was drying into a nimbus of fiery curls, before his eyes narrowed in again on her face. 'Were you avoiding me?'

Her attempt at laughing off the suggestion sounded pretty feeble even to her own ears. 'I could ask you the same question,' she tossed back. Only she wouldn't because that would have been absurd.

'I should have gone tonight,' he admitted.

She glanced at the bottle in his hand and arched a brow. 'Celebrating?'

'That remains to be seen.'

She refused to be ruffled or think about the hidden

meaning in his words… Actually, was it so hidden? She suddenly felt queasy at the image of a warm body ready and waiting for him in bed.

'Spare me the details.'

He laughed. 'I have always thought the joy was in the detail.'

Jane, who had spent the last four years trying very hard not to remember the joy or the detail of Draco's lovemaking, cleared her throat. 'You still haven't said why you didn't go tonight.'

'I don't remember you being so… Actually, tonight is mostly experts, great people but they can be a bit… intense. There will be a more diverse group arriving tomorrow, more relaxed.'

A nasty thought was forming in her head. Was this all about revenge? Was she here so that he could see her humiliated, exposing her ignorance when she found herself among experts? A moment later she felt guilty for the thought. She had done enough online research to know that Draco's green credentials were not some marketing ploy, that he appeared to have a genuine passion and if he had wanted to see her make a fool of herself he would have been there to watch.

'I'm not an expert,' she pointed out spikily, determined not to fall back into old patterns of behaviour. Her compliant silences were long gone.

'No, you're not.' Except in the field of driving him slightly crazy. What was it about her? He watched through dark hooded eyes as her hand went to the base of her throat and he remembered kissing the blue-veined pulse point.

His desire for her had never made any logical sense. It

had always been consuming, and he had always vowed not to be consumed by a woman.

'Did you want me to make a fool of myself tonight?'

The charge dragged him from his contemplation of the sliver of midriff where the pale skin glowed with an opalescent sheen against the vivid brightness of her shirt.

'Why would I want that?' he asked slowly.

'Maybe a bit of payback…?'

'A boring evening and finding yourself out of your depth hardly compares with being left standing at the altar.'

The guilty heat flew to her cheeks and her antagonism melted into remorse—not that she regretted her decision; she knew it had been the right one, but she wished that she had made it earlier.

'I'm sorry.'

'Sorry?' He considered the word. 'Oh, that makes it all right, then,' he drawled. 'Did you save the article with my face attached on coercive control?'

'What?' Her eyes flew wide with horror. 'But that's not true! And your press release.' Not that it had been his—mysterious sources had managed to subtly distance Draco from the entire event. The story was then buried by a convenient good news story—who doesn't love a royal baby?

'When did the truth get in the way of a good story or, in that particular instance, innuendo?' he said, sounding to her ears astonishingly casual about the whole thing. 'The mutual agreement story was not universally accepted. I suppose I should consider myself lucky no one asked you to contribute to the debate.'

'No one found me and I would never have called you a bully!' she exclaimed indignantly.

'You did earlier.'

She conceded the point with an uncomfortable shrug. 'Well, that was different. I nearly ran you over. I was… you were…'

He arched a brow.

'Impossible!' she burst out. 'I know you are rather overbearing and you treat women with the sort of respect you show your suits, but you are not a bully, no way, and—'

His slow whistle cut across her. 'I really know where to go for a character reference should I need one!'

'Nobody ever found me, but if they had I would not have contributed to a character assassination!' she exclaimed indignantly. 'And you were not at fault, I was, and I never meant to hurt you, Draco, truly I didn't, but it was the right thing, you know that, outside the bedroom,' she said, immediately wishing she hadn't voiced the thought, or at least the bedroom part, because his eyes darkened instantly and the tension in the air made the fine hairs on her nape lift.

'We didn't have a thing in common.'

'Outside the bedroom,' he inserted provocatively.

'That doesn't last. We would have split up by now.'

'I lack your ability to see into the future, especially a future that never happened.'

She sighed out her frustration. This was going around in circles. 'Look I don't see any point in post-mortems. You are angry, I behaved badly, and you deserved an apology, more than just a note.'

'A note!' He shook his dark head. 'There was no note.'

Jane began to rub her bare finger. 'I put it in with the ring—you got the ring?' The idea that the valuable item had gone astray filled her with horror, as did the idea he might think she had kept it, or sold it.

He nodded. 'I read the delivery note. I was aware of the parcel but I did not open it.'

'Oh, right… Well, I wrote a note to say that I was sorry.'

'It was a long time ago. There is no need for an orgy of remorse. We have both moved on.'

She lowered her eyes and nodded. 'I know.'

'And you found another life too? How long did you know the father…?'

'Robert. Not that long.'

His expression hardened at her deliberate vagueness. 'So he was not waiting in the wings to comfort you when our marriage didn't happen?'

For a split second she took the question at face value, remembering how she had felt after she had run away from their wedding.

Then his underlying meaning hit her.

'There was no one else involved in my decision to—'

'Dump me at the altar.'

She winced but then brought her chin up. 'How could you think that?'

He gave a negligent shrug. 'Just a passing thought.' One that had been torturing him since the moment he had learnt of the child's existence. 'Does he walk yet? The child?'

'Mattie.'

'Yes, Mattie.'

'No, he's too young, but according to the books that's when life really changes.'

'Will your cottage be suitable then?'

Her chin went up. 'The cottage is perfect!' she declared

with a dangerous sparkle in her eyes. 'I wouldn't want to live anywhere else even if I could afford it.'

'You struggle?'

'We do fine. The house belonged to Robert's great-aunt.' And it was now Mattie's inheritance.

The small amount she could save might not be enough to enable her to buy a place of her own, but she'd be happy with a rental when Mattie turned eighteen, maybe staying near the village.

'So there is no mortgage or rent.' There were plenty of other bills though. 'I should be getting back to Mattie. Val seems lovely and very competent, but I only came down for a few minutes to grab a bite...'

His eyes went to her hand, which retained the squashed remains of a sandwich. 'Literally, it would seem,' he murmured, before adding in a tone of clipped annoyance, 'Why were you not offered the option of a meal in your room?'

Because he had delivered the question in a 'heads will roll' sort of way, she added quickly, 'I was, everyone here has been super kind, but I wasn't that hungry and I wanted to get my bearings.'

'You should eat.'

His accusing tone made her blink, then frown at the underlying impatience. 'I have eaten.' She gave a small smile of triumph and swallowed the squashed bit of sandwich to illustrate her point.

'A sandwich,' he said with lip-curling contempt. 'It is no wonder you are so...' Draco paused, his eyelids half lowering as his glance skimmed her body. He was prepared for the primal reaction of his body, but not the surge of protectiveness. She looked so small, so delicate, so vulnerable.

Jane raised a brow and allowed the awkward silence to stretch. It was a bit late for him to worry about being polite. That ship had sailed the moment he'd opened his mouth to call her skinny, bony or whatever other unflattering adjectives were going through his mind.

'Not the woman you proposed to in another life?' He was probably thinking he'd had a lucky escape. 'And you're right, actually—I am not that woman. And you have no idea what a relief it is not to have to play that role!'

'So you were playing a role when we made love, playing a role when you couldn't keep your greedy little hands off me, *cara*,' he drawled. 'You are a very good actress.

'I meant meek and submissive—'

'Except in bed—' He had never had such a fierce lover in his life, or one so sensitive to his needs, and not afraid to tell him what hers were.

She lifted her hands above her head and turned her back on him. 'Will you stop talking about—?'

'Talking about what? Sex? You have changed. I seem to recall it was your favourite subject.'

Her eyes narrowed and her chin-tilted pugnacity made him think of a small, cute dog that thought it was large and dangerous—not that she yapped, even when angry. He'd always liked her voice, the softness underlaid with a sexy hint of huskiness that grew more pronounced when she was aroused.

'I lied. I wanted to bag a billionaire!'

A heavy silence followed her words. 'Clearly not enough.'

Jane shed her antagonism like a second skin. She knew how it must have hurt a proud man like Draco to be left at the altar. 'I hadn't met Rob…anyone,' she said, still genuinely bewildered by that accusation. 'Why would you say that?'

'You have a child, you have lost weight, you look like a shadow, you are grieving...' he ground out. 'This much is obvious. It is obvious to your community, which is clearly protective of you. Are you trying to tell me this man had nothing to do with why you dumped me so publicly?' He bit down hard on further emotional incoherent revelations escaping his clamped lips.

Bit late, Draco, mocked the ironic voice in his head.

You can't have it both ways, he thought. Tell yourself you had a lucky escape and you have moved on—he had so many meaningless notches in his bedpost to prove it—and then come across as some sort of victim, unable to move on.

Jane was so astonished by his uncharacteristic outburst that it took her several moments to follow through the processes that had brought him to this conclusion.

Here it was again, another opportunity, red lights flashing, to set the record straight, to correct the facts, to admit she was not a mother.

That she had never loved anyone but him.

She knew that she was a coward, she despised herself for taking shelter in a misconception, but where was the harm? she asked her guilty conscience.

She'd hurt him and he'd survived. At least this way she got to keep her secret, hug it to herself and know she had done the right thing. She deserved some privacy. This was her own private tragedy.

She laughed, and she didn't know why, and saw his face darken.

He looked as if he wanted to throttle her and actually she couldn't blame him. Then she thought about the

stream of beautiful women who he had had sex with…
Good Lord, she had been on the brink of feeling sorry
for him. How insane was that?

'I should have done it privately,' she admitted. 'And
for that I apologise.'

'But you don't regret it.'

Calmness settled over her as she saw babies with dark
hair and beautiful dark eyes. 'Not for one second. We had
great sex, Draco, but to spend a lifetime together…you
know what a bad fit I was.'

The irony was he had, and it hadn't mattered. His desire for her, the elemental fire she lit in his blood, had
bypassed logic.

'I… I have to get back to Mattie,' she said, desperate
to escape before she cried. She turned and ran back towards the lights.

CHAPTER EIGHT

'SORRY I WAS so long.'

The young woman uncurled her legs and stood up from the sofa she had been ensconced in. 'You weren't, and Mattie has not made a sound. He is fast asleep. You have eaten? You didn't get lost?'

Jane struggled to smile back. 'Your directions were excellent.' It was her instincts that were not at all excellent. Her instincts were all wrong. 'I think I will just make myself a tea and go to bed,' she said, feigning a realistic yawn.

An hour and two teas later her yawn was real, but her mind was still painfully active.

This had been a massive mistake. The only question was should she cut her losses now or see it out to the grim end?

She changed into a nightdress and looked at the bed but didn't climb in. The idea of lying there tossing and turning was not a tempting proposition. Instead she did another tour of the nursery suite, looking inside the playroom for the first time.

It really was magical, she decided as she opened one of the cupboards at the end to reveal floor-to-ceiling shelves stacked with games and toys. Wandering over to the twin cupboard beside it, she noticed this one had a key. She turned it and these doors folded back to reveal, not shelves of toys, but a bathroom twice the size of the one she'd used earlier with twin sinks, a massive copper bath and a shower cubicle still emitting a cloud of steam into the atmosphere.

She wasn't looking at the impressive fitments but at the man who was standing stark naked and wet in the middle of the room.

Draco, his face hawkish, the skin drawn tight against the perfect bones, returned her stare with one that glittered with bold challenge. A small, dangerous smile played around his sensual lips, his dark olive skin gleaming gold, the moisture clinging to the dusting of body hair, his long eyelashes.

Her eyes dropped. She couldn't help herself—he was so beautiful, like a statue brought to warm, vibrant life. There was not an ounce of excess flesh on his lean frame to hide the perfect definition of each muscle.

Her heart thudding, her helpless glance slid down his chest, his corrugated ribbed belly and lower. Her breath caught and snagged in her chest as she struggled to breathe. Draco had always represented the epitome of raw masculine power and he was aroused.

Very aroused.

She tried to kick-start her brain and managed a stuttered, 'S-sorry.' She took a step back, only it wasn't. The signals had got crossed in her head and she took a step forward, drawn towards all that magnetic potency.

'I'm sorry, I had no idea that the door…'

He dropped the towel in his hand and turned to fully face her, totally at ease with his naked state. 'It was locked on your side. You opened it, *tesoro*.'

'I didn't know…this is…' She stopped and thought, Why aren't I closing it?

'Because you don't want to?'

She swallowed. 'I said that out loud? 'This is…'

'Come here, Jane.'

She shook her head. 'I won't… I can't. This is a massive mistake.'

He swore. 'We are very good at making massive mistakes together, I think,' he returned sardonically. 'We both know we would have ended up here.'

She shook her head in helpless denial and ran her tongue across her dry lips. If he touched her she'd be lost to all sense and all sanity.

So instead she touched him.

She laid a hand against his chest, feeling his damp warm skin under her splayed fingers and holding his eyes.

She watched his eyes blacken, saw the muscle beside his clenched jaw tighten and felt the pulse of excitement between her thighs. Desire was a thudding presence in her head.

He bent down, his breath on her face as he slid a slow kiss across her lips, a butterfly kiss that left her wanting more. Draco always left her wanting more.

She took his hand and guided it to her breast, then some tiny flicker of sanity pierced the sensual thrall she was on the brink of surrendering to and she shook her head.

'Mattie?'

'Leave the door open and—' He reached out to a shelf and located a control pad. Pressing a button, he raised his hands. 'It activates the intercom in here too.'

'You can listen to me?'

'I love listening to you when you make those little

mewling noises in your throat, that little...' He swallowed and reached out, whipping the nightdress off in one smooth action. It fell on the damp floor in a crumpled heap.

She felt relief and then, when his stare slid lower, a moment of panic. She was too thin, she was—

'Beautiful!'

The throaty declaration made her confidence surge and her own gaze lift.

As they met flesh to flesh, kissing wildly, sparks struck and flamed. Jane plastered herself against him, her small breasts flattened against his chest as she lifted herself on her toes. And when his hands came to span her waist and her toes left the floor she wound her legs around his waist as he carried her into the next room.

A bedroom—the only detail she noted was the big bed.

He laid her in it and knelt beside her as he lowered her head, admitting with a wicked grin, 'I didn't think I'd make it this far.'

'I love touching you,' she husked as her greedy hands explored the hard contours of his chest, his back. She pressed her lips to his chest, only stopping when he tangled his fingers in her hair and pushed her head down onto the bed.

She whispered his name as he kissed her, his hands moving over her body leaving trails of fire and screaming nerve endings. Her fingers slid into his dark hair, holding his face at her breasts as she writhed beneath the caress of his tongue and mouth.

He lifted his head. 'You look like an angel, the wanton wild variety.'

She moaned and bit down on her lips as he slid his

hand between her legs, his finger slipping into the hot moisture of her body.

He only stopped when her finger slid across the velvet hardness of his tip, her hand closing as she tightened her grip around his shaft. Wriggling beneath him, she reversed their positions and moved down his body, tracking a line on his damp skin with her tongue.

A wild animal groan was torn from the vault of his chest as he dragged her up his body until their faces were level, his hands cupping her bottom.

The raw need etched in his face was beyond exciting.

'You taste of me,' he slurred against her mouth as they kissed. 'I need...'

She saw what he was about to do and said quickly, 'No, it's okay, I'm not... I have it covered.'

A strange expression flickered across his face but a moment later it was gone and he nodded. 'I'm safe too. Tested. And when I am inside you there is no one else.'

She could have wept. There had only ever been him. Did he really think she could think of anyone else? 'I need you inside me,' she whispered, sliding her tongue along his lips and then inside his mouth.

As his control broke he tipped her onto her back.

'I have to have you now.'

She silently nodded and strained up towards him as he slid a knee between her thighs, nudging the aching moisture between her legs. She pushed against him to ease the ache, the need.

Then as he slid into her in one thrust she yelled his name, her fingernails digging into his back for purchase.

'You're like silk,' he groaned against her neck and the pulse inside her built and built until they were both on fire.

Then she hit the peak and shuddered, feeling the heat spill deep into her.

'What are you doing?' A heavy arm was flung across her. 'What time…?'

She pressed a finger to his lips and wriggled sinuously from under his arm.

'I have to go.'

He sat up, looking gorgeously rumpled but suddenly very awake.

'It's the rule.'

'Whose rule?'

She ignored the appeal of his white devilish grin, along with the lazy, slumbrous invitation in his eyes as he lay there, his hands tucked behind his head, in a pose that said, I'm yours…come and get me.

She wanted to but this needed saying.

'Mine. Look, if this is going to happen again it will be on my terms.'

His eyes narrowed speculatively as he raised himself on one elbow to look at her. 'Is this because you feel guilty, disloyal that we had sex?'

It would have hurt less if he'd said made love.

There had never been any pretence of love, yet there had been tender moments. A touch, a look that had had the power to bring tears to her eyes, a reaction countered by the longing to hear him voice the feelings that she now knew had been nothing but a product of her own wishful thinking.

She would not make that mistake again. She would accept the reality and enjoy it while it lasted.

She lifted her chin. 'I am not the woman I was… I won't…'

'Say what you imagined I want to hear… Yes, I get

that,' he said sardonically. 'And it is why… I like that idea. I like the idea of sex as equals, no emotional barriers. You are grieving, but we still have needs… Sex is a natural human urge, and I think a lot—I think a lot of being inside you,' he admitted throatily, allowing himself to admit that his desire for her was utterly insatiable.

That had not changed, but his sense of self-preservation made him refuse to acknowledge that her vulnerability hurt him—he always had considered empathy something to avoid.

Nothing that had happened had made him change his mind, except that ship had sailed. He couldn't even pretend an indifference to her feelings.

The silence pulsated.

'Is this why you connived, and if you deny it I won't believe you, you connived, pulled strings and, well, the stuff you do in your sleep, Draco, to have me here in your bed?'

'I did not have to drag you here, *cara*.'

'No, but—' She took a deep breath, planting both fists against her chest as she pushed out, 'There are rules. Don't look like that. This is not a joke to me,' she flared.

'All right, what are your rules?'

Her lips tightened at the suggestion he was humouring her. 'Well, for starters, this stays private.'

'I was not about to invite an audience.'

Jane slung him a look, annoyed that he didn't seem to be taking this seriously. 'You know what I mean, no public displays of…'

'Affection?' he inserted when she stumbled searching for the right word.

She refused to let his sarcastic interruption put her off. 'This is sex, not commitment.' She almost felt stupid pointing this out, but the rule was for her own benefit as much as his. The best way to avoid heartache was by killing dead any irrational expectations before they took root. 'And most importantly you need to understand that, for me, Mattie always comes first.'

The silence that had grown heavier as she spoke stretched.

Draco was not questioning her words, but his own reaction to them, which ought to have been living the dream…? Sex with no expectations of it becoming something else, no romantic gestures or pretending to feel what he didn't.

He was not normally on the receiving end of rules, which might account for the irrational surge of dissatisfaction underlying his response.

'It sounds workable,' he finally responded coolly.

There was nothing cool about the smouldering expression in his eyes as he dragged her down to lie on top of him.

Every cell in her body wanted to relax into him, meld her curves to his hard frame, but one cell of sanity enabled her to draw back. She just prayed he would never know how hard it was for her to roll away. He made no attempt to prevent her.

'I need to get back to Mattie.'

'I will be away tomorrow,' he heard himself say in some sort of reflexive response to the rejection.

Fine.

With her hand halfway to Mattie's mouth with a spoonful of baby gunge Jane was telling him was super-delicious, her own mouth fell open.

She might even be drooling.

'I thought you were away today?'

Her accusatory tone was aligned with the fact that Draco was not away. He was here, radiating an electrical charge of energy that sent her nervous system into shameful overload.

'You decided to eat in the nursery,' he said, not addressing her comment or his presence. He surveyed the table. 'Except you are not eating.'

'I have had coffee and some fruit.' She blinked as someone in uniform appeared with a trolley bearing waffles and scrambled eggs. At least those were the items she could identify.

'I didn't order these.'

'No, I did. You sit and eat. I will feed the baby.'

'You…?'

He arched a brow. 'You think me incapable of managing this task?' he challenged, wondering if she might be right.

Jane, who would have actually paid to see him manage this task, put the spoon down and, lips twitching, stepped away. 'Feel free.'

'When you sit down and eat.' He pulled out one of the chairs beside the open window and gestured.

After a gentle push she took the seat and, actually, the smell wafting up from the bowl of fluffy scrambled eggs was not unpleasant.

She had eaten a plateful and two slices of toast dripping with butter when she broke down, laughing, as the expression of fierce determination on Draco's face vanished when a lump of mashed baby food landed in his eye.

He pulled out a spare chair and straddled it, wiping his face with a napkin. 'I think he has finished.'

'All it took to bring a sex god down to earth was an eight-month-old baby. Who knew?' she mocked, grinning.

'A sex god…you think?' he mused, sliding her a self-satisfied look that made her oversensitive stomach flip as he poured himself some coffee. 'There are limits to my willingness to become an object of mockery. I have fed him. You can remove the food that did not land in his mouth.'

'You gave him the spoon.'

'Good for developing his dexterity and self-reliance,' he came back glibly.

'Seriously, Draco, I thought you were—'

'My plans changed,' he cut in, not quite meeting her eyes. 'So I decided to check on you. Does that break any of your rules?' He found himself really beginning to resent those rules.

'I don't think… No, probably not.'

'I normally begin my day with a swim. Would you care to join me?'

'Mattie—'

'It is my understanding that it is never too soon to introduce a baby to water, and if you are worried about exposing his delicate skin to the sun we have an indoor complex as well as the outdoor pools.'

'Of course you do,' she came back drily. 'Oh, why not? That would be nice, but he might not like it,' she warned.

Draco had managed fifteen minutes of laps, pushing his body to the physical limits, before Jane appeared, and his body reacted independently of his brain to the sight of her standing there in a plain black relatively modest swimsuit, revealing that he had not reached his physical limits at all.

Actually it turned out that, after a first startled, wide-eyed look, Mattie did like the water. So did Jane but who wouldn't?

The indoor pool was Roman themed, decorated from floor to ceiling with mosaic tiles of varying shades of blue all set against a background of gold, which gave a shimmering, breathtaking effect. The murals on the walls were classically inspired.

'You want to swim? I could take him?'

'You want to take Mattie?'

Want, Draco privately conceded, would have been overstating it.

'Any instructions? Keep his head out of the water, is that right?' he teased.

Jane handed him over with an eye roll, trying not to lust too obviously over Draco's streamlined muscular frame and failing dramatically as she handed the baby over to his care, without, despite her reluctance, a qualm.

She always felt safe, at least physically, with Draco and she totally trusted him with Mattie.

She had managed a few lazy lengths of the middle pool—there were three—when she flipped onto her back, floating as she watched Draco, in the shallowest pool, swirl Mattie around before splashing him gently, resulting in the baby's loud gurgling chuckle echoing off the ceiling.

An expression of sadness slid across her face and her heart tightened as she thought of the things that would never be.

One day Draco would make an incredible father.

Despite her belief in his fathering qualities, Draco was not involved in the soothing of the fretful baby post swim or the changing, feeding and settling.

Jane joined him again, very conscious of the heavy

achy feeling low in her pelvis, aware as she lowered herself into the warmer shallower pool that his eyes were watching her every move.

'I need to make some calls.'

She nodded and told herself the bubble of disappointment was irrational. She had made the rules after all.

'Enjoy your day,' he said, levering himself from the pool.

Jane averted her eyes from the tall dripping figure as he slicked back his dark hair. 'We will,' she promised.

'You have plans?'

'I'm playing it by ear.'

It was mid-afternoon when the prickle on the back of her neck alerted her to the fact she was no longer alone.

'He's asleep?'

Without turning, Jane put a finger to her lips and tiptoed out of the room, aware that Draco had followed her. She felt his hand on her shoulder and found herself leaning back against him.

'Is this,' he began, the throaty rasp of his voice against her ear sending electric shudders through her body, 'when I am allowed *my* moment?'

With a deep sigh, her green eyes glowing with slumbrous invitation, she turned in the circle of his arms, straining up to brush her lips against his. 'You are allowed anything and everything,' she husked, her lips moving across his mouth before she slid her tongue between his lips, pushing away the thought that there was a time limit on this bliss. These moments were too few, too precious—she wouldn't allow anything to spoil them.

Her fellow attendees seemed an eclectic bunch and during the introductory talk several came over to say hello to Mattie. At the coffee break Jane sat at an empty table and positioned Mattie's buggy at her side, catching the toy he threw before it hit the floor. She gave it back to him and turned back to her coffee and the screen of her phone, scrolling through the bewildering list of classes on offer, glancing up when a young couple approached.

'Mind if we join you?'

Jane smiled.

'I'm Luciana, this is Joe.' Before Jane could respond she added, 'And we know this is Mattie, he really is a star, and you are...'

'Jane.'

'You made your choices on classes yet?' Luciana asked, casting a knowledgeable eye at the screen of Jane's phone.

'So far I haven't even figured out what most of them are... I really think I might be out of my depth,' she admitted ruefully. 'What does NZSD stand for?'

It was the young man who responded. 'Net zero and sustainability development.' He saw Jane's surprised expression and grinned. 'I know I look Latin but I'm Liverpool through and through. When in doubt I use the "close your eyes and stick a pin in" methodology. Or, better still, get engaged to a local like I did and let her decide for me.'

'Are you calling me bossy?' Luciana retorted, extending her hand to show the sparkling ring on her finger.

Jane made the appropriate admiring noises.

'So you are staying in the palazzo?'

Jane nodded and wondered if that was her role for the next three weeks.

The woman staying in the palazzo.

'I think the idea is Mattie doesn't keep people awake at night.'

* * *

Into the second week of the course, on what had been scheduled as a free day Jane sat down to breakfast. When, for the first time, Draco did not appear to share breakfast with her and Mattie, she realised that without intending to they had settled into a kind of routine.

Recognising that his no-show left her feeling a sense of something approaching loss, Jane realised that her rules were not a guaranteed method of protecting her heart from damage.

'Rules aren't much use if you don't follow them, are they, Mattie?' she told her uncritical audience as she popped him in his stroller, struggling to retain her cheery attitude when she realised that very soon there would be no breakfasts and no anything else with Draco.

She took Mattie for an early morning swim alone, determined that she would enjoy the day, which she had not planned to spend with Draco anyway. She had signed up for the trip to the local town.

It would be more relaxing without Draco around, she told herself. Their shared sexual awareness could make even the most mundane action breathtakingly intimate and made it hard to remember the rules were there for a reason, let alone what they were.

CHAPTER NINE

DRACO APPEARED LATER that day just as she was settling Mattie for his afternoon nap, or trying to.

'Did you enjoy your morning?'

'Very much. It was good to get away.' And the local town, with its historic cobbled streets and harbour, was really beautiful.

'Good to get away from me?'

Soon every day would be away from Draco. She felt her stomach tighten and pushed away the thought, painting on a smile as she surreptitiously studied his face, observing that the same indefinable thing she had heard in his voice echoed in his lean features.

Had he got out of the wrong side of the bed?

It had not been hers.

When Mattie had kicked off she had wheeled his crib to beside her bed. Draco had been lying there, the sheet low over his hips to reveal the light dusting of dark hair on his flat, muscle-ridged belly and broad bronzed chest, one hand behind his head, looking gloriously tousled and, with the stubble on his jaw, even more mind-numbingly sexy than normal as he'd watched her.

He hadn't said a thing.

He hadn't needed to. Having caught a glimpse of herself in the mirror, Jane could imagine what he'd been thinking! Her hair a wild mess of curls, dark shadows under her eyes and her hip bones visible through the thin robe she had quickly pulled on.

She had tried to sound as if she didn't care when she had suggested in a scratchy, impatient voice that if he wanted any sleep he should make the trip through the interconnecting door to his own bedroom suite. Would he make the same trip when his own children were here, or would the nanny be in the nursery while Draco made love to his perfect wife?

Later, when Mattie had settled and she had rolled over to sleep, missing the warm body beside her, she had regretted her generosity.

She ignored the lingering sick feeling in the pit of her stomach and managed to respond to his question with a teasing smile and a negligent shrug. 'Oh, absolutely, you weren't there to cramp my style.'

'You did the usual tourist stuff. You ate?' he added.

'Well, I am pretty much a tourist,' she pointed out. 'And of course I ate. I know you think I'm too skinny, but I do not have to be force-fed.'

'You are not too skinny! You are—' Tough and vulnerable, and the combination shook loose some uncomfortable emotions in him that he was not prepared to own. 'I like watching you eat. When you remember, you eat like you make love—with total commitment.'

The frown melted from her face. 'Yes, well, I love the local cuisine and it's quite nice not to have to cook. I'm a terrible cook,' she confided with a rueful grin. 'Actually Luciana showed me a few places only the locals would know about.' She glanced at the dress, hanging up behind the door, she had found in the incredible vintage shop down a side alley. It had been an Aladdin's cave, a treasure trove of vintage and rare, owned by an equally fascinating woman.

In her mind's eye Jane could see the dress as it would be shortly. Her fingers itched to get to work on it.

'You didn't have to go on the minibus. I would have taken you and Mattie if you'd asked,' Draco observed, continuing to sound disgruntled.

'Mattie was fine. He's a very sociable baby.' Though not, admittedly, today. He was not his usual cheery self. 'And you weren't there,' she said, keeping her tone neutral, then adding brightly before he responded, 'It was actually nice to be part of the group and not the woman who is staying at the palazzo.'

'Has that been an issue?'

She shrugged. 'People are initially wary of the person being given preferential treatment, but Mattie is always a vote winner.' And everyone could see that it made sense they had been given more baby-friendly rooms.

Of course, if they had realised that she was sleeping with Draco she could imagine that situation would change very quickly! Which was a very good reason, one among many, to stick to the rules and keep the sleeping arrangement under the radar. It was important to her for people to know she was here on her own merits, which she liked to think she was, or at least deserved to be.

There were some fascinating characters, and she was learning a lot, some of which would be transferable when she got back home.

Some days…home seemed a very long way away, in another life, but she had to keep her feet on the ground and remember the life she was living now was not real. A week and a half and she would be back home.

'Everyone is very excited about the party tonight.'

He raised a sceptical brow as he looked at her with narrowed eyes. 'Everyone?'

She shrugged. The truth was, when Draco had said that there was to be a cocktail party to celebrate the first of what he intended would be a yearly course and conference and he was inviting some people, she had been concerned that someone there might have been at the wedding and might recognise her. She didn't want to be outed as the runaway bride!

'I'm not really a party person, but yes, I'm sure it will be…interesting. Will there be many of your friends there?' To her dismay she did not pull off the casual part of her question.

'Just spit it out, *cara*.'

'I was worrying that…' The words came in a rush. 'Will there be people there who were at the…wedding?'

'You think they will recognise you? You were hardly there long enough for that.'

The acid sarcasm brought a flush to her pale cheeks. She touched her red hair, which today she had loosely gathered in a knot from which bronzed curls spilled out and framed her face.

'People see the hair.'

'Indeed they do,' he agreed as he thought of the texture, how it looked spread out on the pillow catching the sun and burning burnished gold when she lay sleeping in the morning.

'There is no need to be concerned. It is a different set of guests, diverse, but all people whose attendance will raise the profile of the event and hopefully more to follow. Also I am announcing the launch of a prize for an eco-initiative for young people. These guests are contacts that will be useful. It is not black tie tonight, but I can have a selection of outfits—'

Exasperated, she cut across him. 'We have already had this discussion, Draco, and I'm not wearing jeans and a nice top, if that is what you're worried about.' Actually Luciana, the willowy Italian girl, had offered her a dress that, though mini on its owner, would have been mid-calf on Jane, but with the waist cinched in would have done nicely. She had found a suitable belt but then found the rather nicer alternative.

'I think you look delightful in jeans.' He quite enjoyed peeling them down her slim legs. The top was to his mind nice or otherwise optional.

'I have my outfit sorted. I found something in town this morning.'

He looked dubious. 'There are not many shops in—'

She gave a small smile and sighed at his persistence. 'You mean designer shops and no, there aren't, but there are a few really good small independent stores and I discovered an absolutely incredible vintage shop. The flamboyant elderly lady who owned it had many tales to tell of her time working in the film industry.'

At one point she had brought out an album of signed photos of old film stars, pleased to find an audience that was genuinely fascinated.

Jane had come away with the blue silk thirties dress in really great condition, which was now hanging behind her door, and the promise that the next time she came there would be cakes.

Jane had assured her that cakes would be much appreciated, feeling sad when she'd realised that she wouldn't be here for a return visit.

The dress needed a few tweaks but nothing that was

beyond her capabilities. Would that her life could be sorted so painlessly—a snip here, a stitch there.

'I don't think she does it for the money. I think she just loves beautiful things.'

'You bought a second-hand dress?' He sounded so comically shocked at the idea that she smiled as she gestured to the dress.

'I did.'

'You are wearing that?'

'How lucky I don't need your approval to feel good about myself,' she tossed back. 'It was a bargain. I felt quite guilty.'

Seeing the antagonistic challenge in the eyes turned to him, Draco swallowed the protest on his lips. Obviously she would look gorgeous in anything, but she deserved to wear beautiful clothes and not someone's hand-me-downs.

'So what time would you like to walk across?'

She raised a feathery brow. 'To the party? Oh, I'll make my own way across.'

She saw his jaw clamp but he didn't say a word as he pushed his hands into his pockets and turned to the window. She sighed. Draco's back was very expressive.

She finished folding the last of the baby sleep suits, extracted a grumbling Mattie from his stroller and, performing a soothing jiggle to quieten the baby, walked across to where Draco stood, a tower of glowering disapproval.

'I don't know why you are being so cranky.'

He spun around to face her. 'Cranky?' he echoed, sounding so incredulous at the suggestion that she almost laughed, but stopped herself, realising that might be unnecessarily provocative.

She glanced down at the baby in her arms, whose eyes had drifted closed, but, to be on the safe side, didn't stop rocking him. 'Well, it is sometimes difficult to work out who the baby in the room is.'

His expression of utter outraged astonishment drew a short laugh from her throat...before she held her breath, waiting for him to explode. She released it again when he laughed, reluctantly, but Jane decided she'd take it.

'Well, it is daft, isn't it?' she observed with a smile. 'It's not as if it's a date. We have established that we don't do dates.'

She watched with a sinking feeling in the pit of her stomach as his expression changed, the humour wiped out to be replaced by a dark scowl.

'So you wish to leave your options open. If you go alone you can leave with who you wish.'

His interpretation immediately fired Jane up. She was spending all her time and energy trying to maintain the boundaries and keep to the rules and Draco seemed not even to recognise they were there! If they came down she would have to see that all those self-imposed lines were not just invisible, they were utterly useless. She didn't want her delusions to be revealed, because then she would have to admit she was not in control of this situation. She was not in control of anything. Her emotions didn't recognise any lines, invisible or otherwise, and at some point this was going to hurt.

All over again!

'That's a crazy, not to mention insulting, suggestion!' she retorted, her voice shaking as she clung to her control by her fingernails. 'Be careful, Draco, or I might walk away with the idea you are jealous,' she threw out in frustration, not expecting her words to find a mark.

The words stopped Draco cold.

An image flashed into his head, his father consumed with jealousy demanding that his wife, her bags packed, tell him who the man was she was leaving him for. And she had laughed contemptuously at him, falling to his knees begging her to stay, degrading himself, literally crawling after her.

He stood there trying to shift his brain into gear, the pressure in his chest heavy.

'I am sorry to disappoint you but I do not do jealousy,' he said finally.

She saw his closed expression and asked herself what else she had expected. 'I am aware.'

He looked at her through narrowed eyes. 'Do you still feel guilty for having sex with me so soon after your partner's death? Is that what this is about?'

'I have no idea what the "this" you are talking about is,' she replied, guilt putting an acidic note in her voice. 'And I resent being looked at like I'm a bug under a microscope…a…psychological experiment.' And a liar. She felt several kinds of terrible for taking refuge in a lie that just seemed to grow and grow the longer she hadn't addressed it.

Now it was too late.

'Which is why you can't meet my eyes?'

She met his eyes then, her green eyes sparking fire, and directed a defiant look at him. 'This is not something I want to discuss with you. People do not— I don't feel guilty, Draco. I feel—' She paused and thought, I feel scared stiff, because the illusion that I can have sex and not fall in love with you is making me feel ill, especially as I never fell out.

For a split second she wondered what he'd do if she

voiced the words out loud. He might really think he wanted to know what her motivations were, mainly because he couldn't believe that any woman would say no to him. But he would regret it if I did, she thought grimly.

'So you will have sex with me, but you won't walk a few hundred metres and enter a cocktail party beside me.'

'I suppose that about covers it,' she said, noting her deliberately cheery delivery was making him look even more bad-tempered, in a way that beautiful people and sleek jungle cats looked bad-tempered. 'And will you lower your voice? Mattie is just settling. He has been a bit cranky today.'

Draco watched her look down at the baby in her arms, concern pleating her brow, and something shifted in his chest. It was happening a lot.

She was, he had to admit, a perfect mother.

Some masochistic impulse made him throw salt in the open wound as his inner voice said, A mother, but not of your babies.

Fine by him. He didn't want babies.

When had he decided that he would leave the passing of their dubious genes to his little brother?

Could that change of heart have anything to do with the only woman he had ever imagined being the mother of his children leaving him standing at the altar?

Ignoring the taunting voice in his head, he ground out a frustrated, 'This is absurd.'

'What is absurd?'

'You are being absurd. Are you trying to make some sort of point?'

The moment he flung the words it hit Draco that he could just as easily ask himself the same question.

Why was he getting so hung up on this? It wasn't as

if he *wanted* a relationship. Or was it that *she* very obviously didn't that was getting to him?

Was he arguing with her or his own responses?

Turning her head to deliver an exasperated glare, Jane caught an indecipherable expression on Draco's face, but by the time she had laid the drowsy baby in his buggy it had gone.

Draco watched as she dropped into a chair before hooking one small foot onto the metal rest intended for a bag and on auto pilot began to push it back and forth with a metronome regularity meant to soothe the baby to sleep.

She looked exhausted.

Emotions he kept a tight hold of threatened to break loose in his chest as he studied her face, the shadows under her green eyes, the pallor that made the sprinkling of freckles stand out across her nose and cheeks.

She had looked exhausted last night when she had brought the baby back to bed and kicked him out, so much so that he had heard himself offer to take the baby for a drive. He had heard it said—where, he couldn't remember—that this was helpful for some crying babies.

She had looked at him really oddly and said thanks, but no, thanks, she...they were fine, as if she was drawing a firm line around an inner circle he would never be allowed inside.

Not that he wanted to be, obviously.

'Yes.'

He shook his head.

'Yes, I am trying to make a point. I am going to this cocktail party on my own, not as some sort of arm-candy accessory. Nobody will ever treat me seriously if they think I am your latest girlfriend.'

She made it sound as if it were the worst fate in the world! Controlling his slug of anger and the impulse to respond with a childish retort along the lines of she should be so lucky, which would have made him sound like the total loser she appeared to think he was, he rose to his feet, the abrupt action making the baby stir in his sleep, which earned him a reproachful look from under her lashes.

It was bizarre, almost as if he had walked into an alternative reality. He spent his days sidestepping the women who threw themselves at him, never hearing no if he chose to assuage his physical needs, and here was Jane keeping him at arm's length.

Arm's length was generally where he wanted to be, so the situation should have pleased him.

He dragged both hands through his hair and stalked across to the window before turning back.

'So am I allowed to remember your name?' he wondered with withering scorn. 'Or should I perhaps bring someone else?'

The thought of Draco draped over another woman made her feel physically sick. Her chin went up. 'You can do what the hell you like,' she said with an unconcerned shrug.

As he stalked down the corridor he stopped short when he suddenly realised she was treating him like a sex object…so why the hell was he getting so irate about it?

Considering the way they left off, Jane wasn't sure what sort of reception she would get from Draco at the cocktail party. She was not looking forward to making a solo entrance and was glad she bumped into Joe and Luciana in the cloakroom as she handed in her silk wrap.

'Oh, wow, you look gorgeous!' Luciana exclaimed. 'I just love that dress. I can't believe it's the same one you bought in that vintage shop.'

Jane nodded a little self-consciously. 'Thank you, it needed a few tweaks.' She had stripped the dress down to its basics, removing the fussy frills around the neckline and the gaudy sash to reveal the simplicity of the blue silk underneath, the bodice that hugged and the bias-cut skirt that flared and swished around her calves.

'The shoes are new though,' she said, extending a slim ankle for inspection. 'I haven't got a clue why I packed them,' she admitted, looking at the pointy-toed spiky heels that had been a bargain buy in a sale…impractical but beautiful. 'I felt tall until I saw you, Luciana.'

The willowy young Italian smiled. 'I thought Joe might take me out somewhere. That's why I put this in.' The Italian girl laughed and gave a twirl, the beaded hem of her mini rattling as she did so.

Her English boyfriend, a good foot shorter and wearing a tweed waistcoat over his best jeans, responded with a loud, *'Bella!'* in a Liverpudlian accent and dragged her in for a kiss.

Watching their youthful and carefree antics made Jane feel a hundred years old. They were so spontaneous, so unencumbered with complications—so in love!

'It's gorgeous. If I had your legs,' Jane said, admiring the girl's slim, endless legs with envy, 'I'd wear it every day. You make me feel like a dwarf.'

The laugh, a rather grating artificial sound, made them all turn.

'You aren't tall, are you?' The remark came from a stranger who was peeling off a fur wrap.

Her heels made Jane's look like flats and her silver

dress, which appeared glued to her body, displayed every
curve of her lush, voluptuous figure.

'Hello,' Jane said a little awkwardly, because the normally warm and welcoming Luciana had not responded
at all beyond taking her boyfriend's arm in a tight warning grip.

The blonde with the hard eyes was looking Jane up and
down. Her expression suggested she had awarded Jane
a grudging five and a half, and Jane might have been
amused except there was *something* about this woman.

Reproaching herself for judging by appearances, Jane
forced a smile.

'So are you all part of this *green* thing?' the blonde
asked with another artificial-sounding laugh.

Jane nodded.

'So you are staying in one of those awful rooms?' She
made the en suite facilities sound like hovels and Jane,
who had visited Luciana in hers, knew they were anything but.

Luciana, who was normally friendly to everyone,
stood, her lips tight, but, making an obvious effort to
be polite in the face of the other woman's rudeness, intervened.

'Joe and I are, but Jane is staying up in the palazzo, as
a guest. She has her son with her.'

The woman's patronising smile faded and one of her
pencilled brows rose as her spiteful, speculative stare
turned towards Jane. Her interest was of the malicious
variety, something in those heavily made-up eyes making Jane feel uneasy.

'In the palazzo, how very nice,' she trilled back, making it sound not nice at all. 'I am not allowed up there
any longer.' She placed one heavily ringed hand on her

heart and, adopting the persona of a heroine in a Victorian melodrama, revealed in a throbbing voice, 'But it was once my home.'

Jane heard Luciana mutter something in her native tongue under her breath. It did not sound complimentary.

Home…?

Even though the woman's facial muscles were no longer capable of moving, Jane sensed her frown as she turned her attention back to her.

'Have we met before?'

'I don't think so.'

'Oh, I think so, and I never forget a face…' The woman tapped the side of her head. 'It will come to me.'

It sounded like a threat.

'Do you know her?' Jane asked as the blonde made her sinuous way ahead of them, where a door swung open and she vanished, along with the sounds of chatter and laughter that had spilled out.

'*Sì*, I will explain later,' Luciana said in a confidential aside behind her hand as a pair of servers in smart black trousers and white shirts passed by carrying trays containing arrays of edible works of art, minuscule but pretty. 'Take no notice of her. She is an utter bitch and I have no idea why she is here tonight except if it is to cause trouble.'

Mystified by this uncharacteristic venom, Jane wondered who the woman was and what her connection was to the palazzo. She'd lived there?

Could she be an ex of Draco's…? It was as hard to imagine Draco being seduced by a predatory older woman as it was to imagine him moving one of his overnight girlfriends in.

Jane dismissed the possibility almost immediately.

The woman's face might be lifeless, but her eyes were not young. She fell into step with the young couple as they stepped through the open door.

Jane blinked. The overnight transformation was dramatic! The double doors that interconnected the four meeting rooms had been opened and the space was impressive.

Music provided by a string quartet was playing at one end of the room and serving staff circulated with silver trays among the beautifully dressed guests. There were a few jeans and jumpers from the usual suspects, but even they looked less crumpled than usual as they mingled with the sprinkling of movie stars, politicians and aristocracy.

Jane found herself wondering where she fitted in, and then realised she probably didn't as she grabbed a glass as it was offered. A couple of sips made her feel a little less panicky.

'Jane...?'

Jane tried to place the tall, slim, good-looking young man in a blue velvet tux and then it hit her.

'Jamie?'

Draco's half-brother, no longer a skinny beanpole of a kid, grinned and hugged her. 'My God, what are you doing here?'

'I keep asking myself the same thing,' Jane admitted.

'So are you and Draco back together?'

Jane felt her heart clench. 'No, nothing like that. We are...not a couple.'

Never would be a couple, the depressing thought flashed into her head.

Never really had been a couple. When she had said yes to his proposal, she had not known him... Had she loved him? She had certainly been infatuated by him, but her feelings then, strong though they had been, were a shadow of what she felt now. What she felt now was deeper, stronger, and when she saw him with Mattie she knew what an incredible father he would be one day.

Had his feelings changed too?

She pushed away the question, aware that once she allowed herself to indulge in wishful thinking it would be all the harder to face the reality of the situation when it came time to say goodbye. She had to live in the moment and accept that the moment meant something very different to her than it did to Draco.

Her shaking hand slopped a bit of her wine, and just when she needed it, she thought, draining what was left in the glass.

'You all right?' Jamie asked, taking the glass from her fingers and putting it down on a side table.

'Fine. So Draco didn't mention I was here?'

'We've hardly had a chance to speak. You were the last person I expected to see after—'

CHAPTER TEN

JAMIE'S EYES WIDENED and he winced. 'Sorry, I didn't mean it to sound like that.'

'It's all right. I know what you mean.'

'You haven't changed at all,' he marvelled.

'You have,' Jane said, taking a step back to look at him.

'I'm flattered you didn't recognise me,' he joked. 'And—'

'Jamie, my darling boy!'

Jane could almost feel the energy being sucked out of the young man. She could see the gawky boy he had once been as he froze, turning slowly towards the voice.

The connections were being made in her head as she watched the blonde from earlier kiss the air a foot or so either side of Jamie's face.

This was his mother, Draco's stepmother. Jane's heart went out to him.

'Oh, my darling, you still have the glasses, I see.' She shook her blonde head. 'They make you look so geeky. Tell him,' she said, appealing to Jane. 'Contact lenses or, better still, laser surgery and…' She brushed an invisible crumb off her son's immaculate lapel, her lips twisting into a grimace of distaste. 'You always were a messy lit- tle—' The eyes swivelled slyly towards Jane. 'Aren't you going to introduce me to your friend? I'm Jamie's mother. I know, before you say it, I look too young.'

Jane, who hadn't been about to say anything of the sort, took a deep breath. 'How lovely to meet you—again,' she said calmly, not even bothering to disguise her insincerity. 'So sorry, but Jamie promised me this dance.'

Jamie blinked at her as she inclined her head to the empty space in the centre of the floor, her eyes flashing a message.

'Nobody is dancing,' the woman pointed out petulantly.

Jane took Jamie's hand and laid it on her waist, and after the slightest pause he placed his other in the small of her back.

'They are now!' she cried as they twirled away.

'Thank you,' Jamie said quietly as he held her eyes, gratitude shining in his.

Jane could see the beads of sweat along his upper lip and her heart went out to him as she reflected how terrible it was that a mother-son relationship could be so toxic.

'Oh, hell, thank God you can dance!' she said a few moments later and was pleased to feel some of the young man's rigid tension relax as they moved to the music.

'A lot better than you,' Jamie retorted. 'You have trod on my feet three times.' He laughed and leaned in, his expression serious as he emphasised, 'Really, thank you for that.'

'Any time,' she said, meaning it. 'I suppose I've broken some rule by dancing,' she said, half gloomy, half laughing.

'What's the worst that can happen?' Jamie said.

Jane lowered her eyes and thought, It already has.

She'd been hiding behind the illusion that she was in

charge, she set the rules and boundaries, which meant she was safe, but, for all the smoke and mirrors, it was self-delusion. She wasn't.

She was in love with Draco and the heartbreak coming her way was inevitable, but in the meantime, she told herself fiercely, she was going to enjoy every precious moment of it.

'Wow!' The dizzying circle of alternating despair and determination in her head was broken as she allowed herself to be manoeuvred around another couple to avoid a head-on collision.

The floor was now quite crowded. Several couples of varying abilities had joined them, and the quartet had reacted by switching seamlessly to a slow, dreamy waltz number.

'Wow, you are so good at this,' Jane said truthfully.

'When I didn't make the soccer team, Draco advised me to find something I was good at. Turned out that women like dancers more than they like jocks, or it might just be me,' he said smugly.

Jane laughed. 'Oh, you sound so like Draco.'

'I'm not sure I'd take that as a compliment, Jamie. Do you mind if I cut in?'

Grinning, Jamie released Jane and as Draco bent to say something in his ear he nodded, flashed a grin at Jane and mouthed thank you before threading his way through the dancers.

'May I have this dance, *cara*?'

She nodded, feeling suddenly incredibly shy. 'I should warn you, I'm not a very good dancer.'

'I think that is for me to say.'

He did not pull her into his arms immediately. Instead he took her elbows and held her a little away from him, his head dipping as his glittered dark stare swept down her body.

Jane felt the quiver start deep inside until her entire body was engulfed by a hot tide of sexual awareness... It seemed crazy to her at that moment that she had ever convinced herself she could enjoy him and then walk away.

'You look very beautiful.'

It was not the words, it was his voice, his eyes, it was everything about him that stalled her brain. She knew they were surrounded by people and she ought to be acting normally—she had forgotten what normal was!

'I'm not a very good dancer,' she said as his hand came to the small of her back. She could feel the warmth of his splayed fingers through the silky fabric.

'You said that.'

'Did I?' she said vaguely. He took her hands, which lay loosely at her sides, her fists clenched white, and placed them on his shoulders and put his one hand on her back between her shoulder blades, the other to her waist.

'Follow me.'

A bubble of laughter emerged as a strangled choking sound through her clenched teeth as she realised she would probably follow him over a cliff.

No, you wouldn't, said the stern voice in her head. Because a) he wouldn't ask, b) you are a mother, so your first responsibility is to Mattie, and c) you wouldn't be standing on the edge of a cliff because you are scared of heights.

This sense-inducing line of logic at least gave back the ability to breathe, but only shallowly, as he began to move, no, they began to move as one unit. Draco didn't have Jamie's fancy steps, or if he did he wasn't using them, it was just silky smooth harmony and hypnotic sway, the closeness intense but, in a contradictory way, seductively soothing.

Jane's nostrils flared as she breathed in the warm male scent of him, revelling in the coiled strength of his hard body. Enclosed by his arms, she felt cut off from everything but him—he was everything.

His breath was on her hair and then her neck. 'I saw what you did.'

'I felt like dancing and your brother is a very good dancer.'

'Better than me...?'

'Much better.'

His chest lifted in a laugh. 'Really, *cara*, it was good of you to rescue him. She...his mother, Christina.' On his lips the name sounded like a curse. 'She is a vindictive bitch, utterly selfish, but, more than that, vicious, and let's just say that when they were handing out maternal instincts she was not at the back of the queue. She missed it totally.

'She traumatised him when he was a kid. Her voice could make him shake. It wasn't physical abuse, it was—' He heaved a deep sigh. 'The best thing she ever did for Jamie was desert him.'

'Why did you invite her?'

'Invite?' he exploded, looking outraged, then, in response to her widened eyes, lowered his tone as he explained. 'It seems like she came as a plus one and ditched her escort the moment the helicopter landed. I don't know why she's here but I'm assuming it's not concern for our mental well-being! Look, let's not talk about her just now...' he said, drawing her into his body.

Jane had no issue with this suggestion.

She lifted her head and placed a hand on his chest. 'Draco, the music has stopped.'

He stood still and Jane caught a dazed look drift across his face as he saw the people leaving the floor and others moving in to take their places as the music struck up a jazzy number. Well, as jazzy as a string quartet went.

Jane watched his previously distracted expression clear as he scanned the room with a practised eye. 'There are people I have to talk to.'

Was she imagining the underlying hint of frustration in his lean face? 'We will talk later,' he said, pulling back, but leaving his hand on the base of her spine as they left. The gesture felt possessive, and she found herself wondering if other people saw it that way.

'Maybe we should be careful. People might make the connection, put two and two together and—' She gestured with her head. A few loose curls had already escaped the Grecian coil at her neck that had taken ages for someone whose idea of a hairdo was a comb and shake. 'I think people are looking.'

He stopped as they reached the edge of the area that had become an impromptu dance floor and tugged her around to face him. 'Of course they are looking, you look… That is your second-hand dress?'

She felt his warm gaze move over her body. 'Vintage,' she corrected, her green eyes laughing up at him. 'It is also much greener to shop locally, as you should know,' she reproached, tongue in cheek.

'So true, and here is someone you might like to educate on that subject… Tabitha Greenwood, Jane Smith… Tabitha is a—'

'I know who Miss Greenwood is!' Jane protested, flushing as she smiled at the fashion designer with the international reputation, who was instantly recognisable even if she had changed her hair colour from jet black to platinum blonde. 'Hello,' she said to the woman studying her with open curiosity through a pair of massive pink designer glasses.

'Jane was just lecturing me on waste in fashion. She's a big fan of charity-shop bargains.'

'Actually, I am.' She slung a look up at Draco. 'He is putting words in my mouth and I am quite capable of speaking for myself.'

'Well, that is telling you!' cried the other woman, looking amused by the interchange.

'Actually my dress—'

'Vintage,' the designer cut in, casting an expert eye over the blue silk gown. 'It is gorgeous and, I suspect, updated a little?' She quirked a quizzical eye at Jane, who nodded.

'I can't really do frills.' She grinned and made an expressive sweeping gesture towards her foot. 'I'm too short.'

The other woman, who was a sturdily constructed five nine, smiled back. 'But perfectly formed, as they say, don't you think so, Draco?'

Draco gave her a sardonic smile and said nothing.

'See you later, enjoy…' He paused and swung back. 'Have you eaten anything more substantial than a canapé?'

Jane, who hadn't had a canapé yet and was very aware of the speculative gleam in the birdlike gaze of the designer, shook her head in irritation. 'Don't fuss.' To prove a point she grabbed a handful of canapés from a tray and put them one by one into her mouth. The last one was rather delicious. 'Happy now?' she challenged.

Never as happy as when I am looking at you.

The extraordinary recognition just popped fully formed into his head.

As there was no answering grin, her own smile faded. His expression was about as revealing as bulletproof steel shutters. It made her realise that she had not seen that closed-off look in a while, and she really hadn't missed it!

Watching the tall figure stride away, the two women exchanged glances.

'What was that about?' the older woman wondered.

'Not got a clue,' Jane said with a tight, strained smile.

'I'm here for research purposes and, of course, the champagne,' Tabitha added, grabbing a fresh glass from a passing waiter. 'These days you have to go green or go out of business. What about you?'

'I have a place on the course here.'

'Yes, but you already know Draco.'

'What makes you say that?'

The older woman threw back her head and laughed. 'It's pretty obvious, my dear. I hear you're staying in the palazzo? And yes,' she added in response to Jane's expression, 'I am a nosy old biddy, but I'm only saying what other people are thinking after that dance.'

Jane looked at her in dismay. 'I'm staying at the palazzo because I have my baby with me and Draco kindly put us up there because it's quieter.'

'A baby...?'

Jane could see the wheels turning and thought, Beam me up!

'Mattie, the baby's parents,' she said quietly, 'they died. I'm his guardian.' There was some relief in fessing up even if it was to the wrong person.

The mockery in the other woman's eyes faded, to be

replaced by compassion that brought tears to Jane's eyes. 'Oh, my dear, how tragic.' She squeezed Jane's shoulder. 'I've never been a mum, it just didn't happen, but, you know, I think you will be a really good one. Come on, I have a friend who I know would love to meet you. She is very into vintage as well.'

As Draco did the handshakes and smiles he was aware of Jane in the middle of a diverse gaggle of people who seemed to be having more fun than anyone else in the room.

He felt a swell of admiration, a possessive pride that he knew he didn't deserve as he watched Jane shine, her natural warmth drawing people to her.

A phenomenon he understood totally.

It seemed bizarre that he'd been concerned she would not feel comfortable today. His concern had been misplaced. Four years ago it wouldn't have been. If he'd shown a shred of empathy back then, if he had actually picked up on the signs of stress…and had a conversation about it…the wedding might have gone ahead.

He felt a surge of self-disgust because he *had* picked up on the signs, but he had ignored them, filing them under inconvenience, because beautiful, desirable Jane would always be there, smiling at his elbow and fire in his bed.

It was more difficult to slip away than Jane had imagined but she finally managed.

'You running away from the ball?'

She was good at running, he reminded himself, nursing the old hurt, channelling old anger and resentment as a barrier when he felt himself getting closer to her, when he found himself thinking *family* when he played with Mattie.

Lately the embers of old hurt were harder to kick into life. Logic suggested that it was probably a good thing she would be leaving soon, but he found it hard to summon much enthusiasm because logic was a casualty of the passion that burnt between them, a passion that had not as yet burnt itself out.

Jane's breath caught at the sound of his deep voice. She ignored her thudding heart as she turned, channelling calm that was not even skin deep.

Being around Draco made her feel more alive somehow. His presence heightened her perceptions. A moment before she hadn't noticed the romantic twinkle of the thousands of white fairy lights that wound around the trees that lined the path back to the palazzo, or the scent of rosemary and pine in the soft sea breeze or the moon that put blue highlights in Draco's dark hair and accentuated the perfect angles and planes of his face.

His dark jacket hung open, the white of his shirt was dazzling, and underneath was the silky brown skin and the light dusting of body hair, the directional line that vanished as it met… She inhaled and thought, Pull yourself together woman—focus!

Not on that, she thought as her eyes sank just a little lower.

Cheeks hot, she dragged her eyes to his face. 'Well, I was not running.'

So no excuse for the breathless delivery.

She lifted her heavy silk hem, exposing her calves, and angled a wry grin at her feet, a really safe place to stare at. 'Not in these, and this was officially designated a party, not a ball, also no relation at all, as far as I know, of Cinders.'

'That is a very thorough analysis. I will always come to you for fact-checking. I will rephrase—walking away from the party.'

She tried to smile but it just wouldn't come. 'I want to head back to check on Mattie. Yes, I know Val can cope,' she added quickly, anticipating his response, 'but he's not been himself today.'

'Mother's instinct?' He watched her flinch and took a step closer, a concerned frown tugging his brows.

She shook her head. 'No, just observation,' she said, ignoring the slug of guilt and changing the subject. 'Tonight was a success for you. You must be pleased.'

Was he?

Draco hadn't even thought about it, and the success of this project should have been his main focus—tonight was part of that. Yet the entire evening he had felt as though he was playing a part, saying the right things, and occasionally the wrong thing, while all the time his eyes had been searching for a flaming redhead.

He had brought Jane here with some vague idea of making her hurt the way she had hurt him. At some point the plan had lost impetus and derailed itself…and ironically the only person hurting, it seemed to Draco, was him.

The pain had centred on his frustrated primal urge to possess her. Being lovers ought to have solved that issue, leaving him to walk away when the hunger had burnt itself out. The hunger was still raging and now it came with excess… He refused to call it emotional baggage, but what else could you call it when he looked at her, so small, so vulnerable, so bloody-minded and stubborn he kept feeling the alien urge to protect her.

It wasn't meant to be like this.

Sex should not be like this. It should be uncomplicated. It was one of the most uncomplicated things in life, a need that he prided himself on being able to control. It never got in the way of the more important things.

'It was a success for you,' he countered finally.

'I had fun,' she said, a wistful note in her low voice. *Not with me!*

'It will be something nice to remember when I go back home,' she said with an upbeat smile. She'd die before she'd let him know how much it hurt to say that. 'And I have made some friends I will keep in touch with, and young Val is showing me her brother's apiary tomorrow. I have had a crash course in beekeeping and its importance, not just to the rural economy, but basically the future of the world.' She painted on a smile.

'Yes, he is very entrepreneurial. He's got orders from a major London store,' Draco, who wasn't at that moment interested in bees, told her. 'You could come back?'

The suggestion seemed to surprise him as much as it had her.

'To see your friends, Luciana and her boyfriend—'

'Joe? Won't he be going home next week too?'

'He and Luciana have taken out a lease on one of the studios in the creative hub.'

This was news to Jane. 'Jamie seemed shocked to see me here.'

'I didn't think he was going to get away. He was playing a chess tournament, but it got cancelled.'

The tiredness that had been kept at bay by adrenaline was hitting home as Jane took the few steps across to a carved wood bench, situated to make the most of the incredible view out to sea, which was utterly spectacular. At night the ocean was just another shade of darkness in the distance and the light and magic came dappled from the fairy lights threaded through the branches.

'He's still in college though?' she said, trying to work out the age of the teenager.

'His last year at school. He's thinking of turning professional when he leaves.'

'*Professional?*'

'Chess. He is really very good.'

Jane searched his face curiously. 'Do you mind? Don't you have plans—?'

'I would prefer he went to university,' Draco admitted. 'But that's probably because I missed out. I want Jamie to have freedom, the opportunity to do what he wants and change his mind if that's what he needs.'

'Why did you miss out?'

'My father was not the most caring of parents.'

Jane thought about the scar on Draco's skull and realised that he had stayed around to make sure that Jamie didn't suffer the same way. 'His mother—?' She stopped and shook her head. 'Sorry, I don't mean to pry.'

'Christina used him like an accessory,' Draco responded, his voice as flinty and unforgiving as iron filings. 'And while he was a pretty cute baby she had him wheeled out by nanny for the photo ops and charity events, but Jamie had issues with his eyes. He needed corrective surgery and wore thick glasses…' His lips thinned with distaste. 'Not so cute, apparently,' he finished with contempt. 'She moved on from him and this place and our father had zero interest in him.'

Jane remembered how the comment about his glasses had paralysed Jamie, and her heart broke for him. 'Poor

Jamie.' Or maybe lucky Jamie, because he'd had Draco around to protect him.

'Our father was a man in thrall, so weak so…she was like a drug for him. He had no pride, no sense of duty to this place.' He gestured towards the spotlit palazzo. 'He sold everything he could, sold off land, put families who had lived here for generations off the land, and I couldn't do a thing.'

Jane saw the echo of the remembered pain and frustration in his grim, almost haunted expression and her heart squeezed for the boy and young man he had once been.

'But now you can and you have,' she said gently.

Their eyes met and she watched the steel barriers sliding into place, until his face was an unreadable blank.

Frustration built up inside her. Just as he'd seemed to be opening up he had shut her out again.

'I should go back in, and get it over with,' Draco said, glancing back towards the lights of the building behind them. 'Christina isn't here for no reason.' It would be money. On the rare occasion she appeared it always had been, and if it wasn't for the fact she would stalk Jamie he would have sent her away empty-handed.

'And you are still protecting Jamie.'

'You like it here?'

Thrown by the abrupt change of subject and the tension in the atmosphere, she nodded. 'Obviously—what is not to like?' she said, her heart drumming.

'Does it actually need to end?'

Jane's thoughts raced as she closed her eyes against the chaos in her head… She took a deep breath and met his too intent dark eyes.

'What are you saying, Draco?' Not what you think,

said the voice in her heart, except she didn't know what she thought. You couldn't kill hope.

Perhaps he saw something in her face because he said straight away, 'Obviously I am not proposing.'

The idea that he suspected her dreams was utterly humiliating.

'Obviously,' she said, enunciating each syllable with elaborate care while inside she felt like a total idiot.

'I think we both know, you before me possibly, that we would never have worked as a couple, but if we put our history aside there is no doubt that we have…something…?'

'Sex,' she intervened bluntly.

'Our personal relationship aside, your enthusiasm for this community, they would welcome you.'

'I know you look at me as the cure for some temporary testosterone imbalance!' she flung out wildly as she surged to her feet. 'But I don't see that as my life's work. I already have a life, and I don't want a temporary bit part in yours. My future doesn't involve you, Draco. Do you really think I would uproot Mattie, move to a different country where I have no friends…?' she exclaimed, breathless with indignation. 'My God, you have to be the most selfish, arrogant man in the universe!'

He ground his teeth. 'Why can't we discuss this situation like two sensible adults?'

'Because there is no situation and only one of us is a sensible adult. Thanks for the offer, Draco, but I'm already spoken for. My life is in England.'

The words thrown out conjured the image of Jane throwing open her cottage door, her bedroom door, to some faceless male figure. 'I'm here.'

'Your arrogance sometimes, Draco, is… You think

you're the big selling point?' If that was what he thought it was hardly surprising, given that her feelings must have been obvious. 'I really need to go. I need to get back to Mattie.'

'You use him as an excuse. I'm not going to tell you what you want to hear to keep you here.'

The charge brought a hectic angry flush to her smooth cheeks. Presumably he thought she wanted to hear him say he loved her, and he was right, she realised, despising herself for holding onto a dream. 'I don't use anyone, Draco. I leave that to you! And you have no idea what I want to hear.'

She turned as the tears spilled, before he could see them overflow, before he could tell her that she had wanted to be used.

She had begged to be used.

Draco watched her stalk up the path, spine rigid, chin high. Even in the midst of his anger, justifiable anger, at her attitude, her delicious bottom under the silk, the sway of her hips were a major distraction.

As he watched she stumbled and fell off her spiky heels and the instinct to go to her assistance made him surge forward, only to ask himself what the hell he was doing when she regained her balance and a string of curses drifted his way on the soft still night.

Without turning back, she bent down, pulled off her shoes and, with them dangling from the fingers of one hand, continued to walk up the incline.

The party was still in full swing and he had several people, donors and supporters, that he had to talk to.

He needed a few moments to compose himself before he could do his duty. Where was your devotion to duty a few minutes ago, Draco? he asked himself. He held himself to strict self-imposed rules, rules that meant he would never see his own father when he looked in the mirror.

Do you want rules or the woman you...? His clenched fist turned white as he fought the word before it formed in his head, words he didn't want to say, emotions he didn't want to feel.

He didn't need Jane. He didn't need any woman.

But he wanted her, how he wanted her.

'Going to follow her?'

CHAPTER ELEVEN

IT WAS THE voice that always elicited a visceral reaction of distaste that brought home the fact he had walked, not towards the building, but away from it and towards the palazzo.

'What are you doing here, Christina?' Despite the surgery, or maybe because of it, the years had not been kind to her, or maybe that was the sheer malevolence that he saw behind the perfect features, more perfect now than when she had married his father.

The blonde's over-pumped lips pouted. 'You forgot my invite.'

'The only invitation you'll get from me is to go to hell,' Draco informed her in a deceptively mild voice.

'Oh, well, if you're going to be like that…but I'll make allowances, Draco. Someone said no to you, so you are bound to be feeling a bit—'

'You were eavesdropping!'

'Before you ask, I heard enough.' The spiteful tinkle of laughter bounced off him. 'Poor Draco knocked back. You know, you reminded me of your father for a moment there.'

She watched the colour drain out of his face and smiled a complacent cat-like smile that left her eyes hard as stone.

'Grovelling comes easy to the Andreas men.'

Denial was his first response.

Fury was his second and then—after he searched his memory for proof she was wrong—relief.

'Thank you,' he said softly.

He was not his father. He was his own kind of fool.

An expression of incomprehension flashed across the blonde's face.

'What for?' she said warily.

'For making me realise that I am nothing like my father.' His father had been many things, including deluded, but he had not been a coward, he thought in self-disgust. Whereas he had been a blind coward who had exiled himself from so many possibilities because he didn't have the guts to admit what he wanted.

To admit what he felt.

Jane hadn't walked away because he wasn't telling her what she wanted to hear, because he took pride in telling it the way it was…not sugar-coating it.

He had asked her to leave behind everything she knew and offered her nothing in return.

She had walked away because he was too much of a coward to say what she wanted to hear. He was too much of a coward to admit what he felt for her.

That he loved her.

He glanced at the spiteful face of the woman opposite, impatience, not anger, in his face now… He wanted this charade to be over. He saw his stepmother's expression falter a little, but she rallied and was back a moment later, her malicious smirk in place.

'She has quite a mouth on her, that girl. I wouldn't have thought she had it in her, but then you never can tell, can you? From those sweet and innocent butter-wouldn't-melt appearances.'

He did not move, and he did not raise his voice when he said softly, 'You will not speak of Jane. Is that understood?'

The older woman, shaken despite herself by the dark implacability in his eyes, took an involuntary step back.

Draco folded his arms across his chest. 'What do you want?'

'Oh, I'll get around to that, darling, but first tell your little playmate that I have remembered where I saw her... I never forget a face.'

'Leave Jane out of this. You will not go near her. I do not want to hear anything you have to say.'

'Oh, you will want to hear this. She has a baby, I hear—'

'Christina...' he said, a warning in his voice, a nerve clenching and unclenching in his lean cheek.

'Did I ever tell you about...? Well, probably not. But what was it—four years ago? I forget, but I had a little accident. I think Spiros was quite pleased to know he was still man enough, but thank God we were both on the same page.

'I went to a clinic in London. Mind you, if I'd known they had started taking NHS patients,' she said with a little moue of distaste, 'I would have gone elsewhere, but, still, it was sorted.'

The dismissiveness of how she said 'it' made him feel sick, especially when he thought about how for many women this was a decision that they did not make lightly, that they wept over. 'You had an abortion.'

'That's what I just said,' she replied with a bored sigh. 'I am a young woman, Draco.'

'Why would you think this would interest me?'

'Ah, yes, well, as I was being wheeled to the theatre I passed someone else on their way out…red hair, white face.'

His lean face froze, the skin pulled tight across his sharp cheekbones as her meaning hit home. 'Liar!'

'Ask her yourself if you don't believe me.'

'I won't, I don't need to,' he said, even though they both knew he would.

And when he did?

Having delivered her malice-laden bomb, his darling stepmother vanished, leaving just the stink of her choking perfume behind, where to and with whom he frankly didn't give a damn!

Draco didn't give her the satisfaction of knowing that her poisonous darts had found fertile ground. He pulled it together and went back into the party or—as his inner voice said—did a Draco Andreas.

Next thing he knew he'd be referring to himself in the third person.

It was a good two hours later when he finally left and made his way through the grounds to the palazzo.

Four years…four years…he tried not to connect the dots but by the time he entered the hallway they were a solid directional line.

He remembered the small scars on her smooth belly and the way she had dismissed them, not quite meeting his eyes when he mentioned them. Could they be connected to…?

An image of her holding the baby floated into his head. She was the perfect mother to another man's child.

Had she aborted his child?

He prided himself on not being judgmental when it came to the choices women made about their own bodies, but this was not impersonal, this was as personal as it got—his child. Grief of something lost to him tightened like a fist in his belly. His hands clenched at his sides. This was not something he could consider with cool neutrality.

He had to know.

She owed him some sort of explanation.

Would she be waiting for him to climb into bed beside her? He pushed away the image that floated into his head of her warm and soft, sweet-smelling body as she smiled a sleepy smile and reached for him.

As he entered the nursery corridor he slowed slightly, a frown puckering his brow. His housekeeper, wearing a dressing gown, and a member of her team were standing there deep in conversation.

'Livia… What is happening?'

Their expressions and the tears on the normally cool and collected face of the housekeeper made his stomach muscles clench in anticipation. It didn't take a genius to see that he was not about to hear good news.

It wasn't good news and, though he had to prompt the woman, he eventually got the story.

Mattie was ill, a doctor had been called but they didn't know when he would be here, because some form filler on the other end of the line was asking so many questions before they would confirm his attendance.

Draco walked in, and took in the scene at a glance.

The baby was crying in his crib, young Val standing beside it, tears streaming down her face, while Jane, still wearing the blue silk dress, had the phone in her hand. White-faced, she looked haunted and was visibly shaking, but there was a firm determination in her voice as she spoke.

The anger that had kept up the walls of emotional isolation he had been sheltering behind dissolved. Everything inside him ached for her. He felt her fear and desperation.

'No, not that I am aware of. No, I am not the baby's biol—'

'Give it to me.'

'Draco!' she cried, relief in her voice as he took the phone from her limp grasp.

She took a step away, her arms wrapped protectively around herself, aware on one level that his presence could not make everything right but, oh, it was such a comfort just not to be alone.

He was speaking Italian but, unlike her, she could tell that he was in control of the conversation.

He was not begging, he was demanding, and it seemed to make all the difference. He paused occasionally, covering the receiver as he relayed a question to her in English before giving her response in Italian.

Finally he put the receiver down.

'Marco…' he began, pausing when she shook her head. 'He is the head of the paediatric intensive care unit. He will come with the air ambulance, which is already in the air, and in the meantime we are to cool Mattie down, open windows, strip off his sleep suit.'

'Thank you…oh, thank you! That is…just thank you, Draco,' she said, looking at him with shining eyes.

Draco nodded and walked across to the cot.

Trying to be as cool and calm as he appeared, Jane went to the crib. Mattie had stopped crying and the silence was somehow worse than that awful keening sound had been.

It was like undressing a rag doll and he was so hot.

'He is still very hot and so, so floppy.' Her voice broke as she turned away and laid her head against the warm solidity of Draco's chest, which was right there when she needed it.

She allowed herself the indulgence of staying that way for a few moments before she pulled herself together and stepped back.

'Val has gone to get a fan.'

At that moment the young woman arrived without a fan, but with welcome news. 'The helicopter is here. Oh, I am so, so sorry...'

'No, this is not your fault,' Jane said firmly as she clasped the younger woman's hand.

Draco watched her take the time even in the midst of her own fear to reassure the younger woman. A small snuffly cry made him glance down to the baby lying there, his sweaty face as pale as milk, and he felt things shift inside him. 'He looks—'

The door opened and a young man about Draco's age appeared.

Jane watched as they shook hands but did not waste time on pleasantries.

'Mrs—'

'Miss Smith, Jane,' she said.

'Well, let's have a look at this young man, shall we? While you tell me what happened.'

The examination was gentle but thorough.

'I suspect this was a febrile convulsion. We can confirm that when we have him at the hospital. For the present his temperature is high, and I will give him something for that before the transfer and also put a line in to give him some fluids.'

'Thank you,' Jane said, half scared to voice the question that was uppermost in her mind. 'Will he be all right?'

'I know it looks scary but little ones are very much more resilient than people think. I suspect there is an underlying infection.'

'You will run all the tests necessary.'

'*Sì*, Draco,' he said, turning to Jane. 'Try not to worry. He is in the best of hands.' His calm confidence worked its magic.

'Ah, here is Nurse now.'

A young man appeared, carrying a medical bag under each arm.

'We will get him ready for the transfer. You will be coming with us, I assume.'

Jane nodded as the two men bent over the cot, blocking her view of Mattie.

'Thank you,' she said in a quiet, sincere aside to Draco. 'You made that happen... I am so grateful. I will keep you in touch...'

'I am coming with you.'

'I should say, no, it's fine, but I'm not going to,' Jane admitted, feeling tears prick her eyes. 'I was so horrible to you.' She quivered, blinking away the salty tears of emotion trembling on the tips of her eyelashes.

'That is not important now.'

Her throat full and icy fear still gripping her belly, she nodded. 'I promised I would take care of him.'

Promised who? The dead father, he assumed. 'And you have, you are, you are an incredible mother.'

Her head bent, she sniffed, missing the look of pain that slid across his taut, lean features.

The helicopter journey was relatively short, the staff

were really comforting, which Jane appreciated, and Draco's presence meant she didn't have to worry about following the conversations when they slid into Italian. The transfer into the hospital was performed with no issues and the medic's obvious competence was reassuring.

She had moved out of the way while the medical team gathered around Mattie, but she didn't take the seat offered. She couldn't sit still.

'He is in the very best hands,' Draco said, watching her.

She nodded. 'I know, it's just...'

The medical team moved away from the cot leaving one nurse at the bedside. The senior doctor walked across to them, smiling.

'Well, it is just as I thought, there is a viral infection, simple upper respiratory. He had a febrile convulsion, frightening, but not indicative of anything else. Now that his temperature is down and he is having his fluids replaced he will be back to normal very quickly. We will keep him in overnight for observation and, all being well, which I am sure it will be, he can go home tomorrow.'

Jane closed her eyes and gave a deep shuddering sigh before opening them and clasping the medic's hand in both of hers. 'Oh, thank you, thank you so much.' Before she released his hand with a self-conscious, 'Sorry.'

'Delivering good news is one of the best parts of my job.'

She watched Draco walk with him towards the door, her smile fading as she thought about the bad news he had to deliver too often, but not today and not to them.

'They will put a bed up in here if you wish to stay, though I have an apartment here where I will be staying.'

'No...no, I'll stay here, thank you.' She looked at him,

noticing for the first time the lines of strain etched around his mouth. 'I am so sorry. I'm sure this is the last thing you wanted after—'

'Now is not the time.'

She set her lips in a straight line to stop the stupid quiver. He was allowed to sound brusque at the very least.

'You have my private number?'

'I don't have my phone.' She realised that she didn't actually have anything.

He seemed to read her mind. 'I'll organise some things for you and have them sent over.'

'It's half one in the morning, Draco.'

He looked at her with the hauteur and arrogance that often infuriated her and other times made her smile. At the moment it just made her feel safe.

'How is that relevant?'

'Silly me,' she said with a wobbly smile.

A small bag of essentials—toiletries, nightclothes and a change of underclothes—arrived an hour after he'd left, also a phone with a note attached saying, 'I've put my number in it' in Draco's bold, sloping hand.

Jane didn't anticipate getting any sleep, but, although the nurses were in and out all night to check on Mattie, she did manage two long stretches of rest, and after a wash and fresh clothes she felt almost human.

She was on her second cup of coffee when the doctor and Draco appeared.

Her eyes skated across Draco, noting the tension emanating from him, and the dark shadows under his incredible eyes, but then not everyone liked hospitals. Well, nobody liked hospitals, but for some people, often the sort of people who never had a day's illness in their lives, the medical environment, the reminder of human frailty, was tough to take.

'Good morning,' she said to the doctor, who returned the greeting before he walked across to the cot and consulted his tablet.

'Well, all the results are clear, no underlying issues. He is good to go.'

Jane bit her lip. 'He seems a bit cranky this morning?'

'He's got a cold so that's to be expected. You know the drill if his temperature goes up?'

She nodded. 'Are there any things he can't do?'

'Well, flying should be avoided for a little while. The upper respiratory infection would put a lot of painful pressure on his little eardrums, and it is hard to tell a baby how to release the pressure.' He turned to Draco. 'How are you thinking of getting back to the palazzo?'

'Would he be better staying in town for a day or so?'

'That would be the ideal solution for this young man.'

'Couldn't I drive?'

'It would be preferable to flying,' the doctor agreed. 'But the drive is… What, Draco?'

'Not an option,' Draco said flatly.

Jane clamped her lips over a retort that would no doubt have sounded churlish and ungrateful. She'd been happy for him to step in and smooth the way in an emergency situation, but now that had passed she really didn't want him to think he could carry on.

At some point she would have to make that clear.

'I could book into a hotel?'

Draco slid her an impatient look. 'Do not be ridiculous. You will be quite comfortable in the apartment. You will drop in and see the patient, Marco.'

'I will.'

Jane was pretty sure that doctors in his position did not do house calls, but she wasn't going to object.

'I don't want to be a nuisance.'

'Then stop talking rubbish,' Draco advised tersely.

She had the impression that had the doctor not been there he would have said more.

It was the doctor's presence that similarly stopped her protesting beyond an 'I'm not the sick one' when someone brought a wheelchair for her to sit in while she carried Mattie.

The surgeon wheeled the chair himself, which drew a few startled looks as they made their way to the main foyer of the ultra-modern building.

'Am I allowed to walk now?'

Draco, after a pause, moved to take Mattie from her arms.

Being held by Draco, the baby looked so tiny and the big-man-small-baby image, especially when the man was Draco, made Jane's throat tighten with emotion. But then, after the last twenty-four hours all her emotions were incredibly close to the surface, and her control, even given the traumatic events, seemed extremely fragile. Scratch the surface and she might start crying or laughing or shouting—most of the time she didn't know which direction her emotions would take her!

Free of the baby, she was able to get to her feet and shake hands with the doctor, who responded with a smile and added, 'Oh, I got the notes through from your family doctor and there was nothing significant in the medical history to be of any concern now or in the future.'

Jane nodded, relieved.

She had felt a moment of panic the previous night when asked if there was any medical history in the family he should be aware of. She had been forced to explain that she was not Mattie's biological mother. She had passed on Grace's name, pretty sure that, as their family doctor, the GP, who was also Mattie's godmother, would know the medical history.

'I should know about these things. It just didn't occur to me...' she admitted with a flash of lip-biting self-reproach.

The handsome medic shook his head and placed a comforting hand on her arm. 'Parenting is a balancing act. The most important thing is to enjoy the experience—they grow up very quickly. You're doing a great job,' he added warmly before he left them.

Jane flushed with pleasure at the compliment.

Standing too far away to hear what was being said, Draco could see the warmth of the exchange and the pretty flush that brightened her heart-shaped face.

Jane secured Mattie in the car seat fixed in the not-child-friendly back of the low-slung powerful car that she suspected had never seen such a piece of equipment before. Now, if you were talking a fur stole or an item of feminine underwear...?'

Torturing herself with the visions that came with those items, she belted herself in beside him, her smile widening as he gave a gummy grin.

'Sit up front. There's no room back there.'

'There is for me,' she said stubbornly. Her knees pressing into the driver's seat was infinitely preferable to sitting beside Draco.

'What was that about?' Draco asked, looking at her in the rear-view mirror.

She looked bewildered.

'Marco is married with children.'

Jane blinked. 'You think I was flirting with Mattie's doctor!' The ludicrousness of the suggestion drew a gurgle of laughter from her, and beside her the baby joined in.

In no position to see the flash of shock in his eyes, all Jane heard was the silence from the front that was interrupted by the sound of a car horn.

Draco growled out something that sounded not polite in his native tongue and pulled out of the parking space. The memory of his claim that he was never jealous came back to mock him as he drove out onto the highway.

The hospital appeared to be situated on the outskirts of the city but every now and then Jane caught a glimpse of the spires and golden buildings of Florence.

It was beautiful but, strangely, she felt a sudden longing for home and all things familiar, and with the longing came an image, not of her cottage, but the palazzo, backlit by the warm afternoon sun.

The instinct shocked her. It could not be a good thing to become so attached to a place over such a relatively short period of time. Or maybe not the place, but the people—the person who lived there.

Well, you'd better become unattached very quickly, she told herself sternly as she stared at the back of Draco's neck, where even though he kept his dark hair short, it was beginning to curl.

She was quite glad there was zero conversation during the journey to Draco's apartment. Jane had been trying to name the different landmarks she glimpsed and wishing she had a guide book when tall wrought-iron gates ahead of them opened and he drove into a courtyard. The sound of traffic was muffled by the trees and the rows of fountains and lush greenery bordering the cobbled area.

'This is beautiful!' she said, craning her neck to see the wrought-iron balconies on the top floor of the three-storey building.

'Just the one apartment. We have offices on the ground floor, so no commute when I am here.'

'Offices?' she exclaimed, thinking, Not as we know it. 'Where are the cars?'

'It's a public holiday here this weekend and the main entrance to the office is around the other side of the building. There are not so many staff. It's just a small hub specialising in…' He paused and spared her the techno speak before adding simply, 'Mostly it is IT-based here, and my office. The pool and gym in the basement are open to the staff, but feel free.'

'I really don't think I'll have the time.' Or the inclination. She took a deep breath. 'I doubt I will be here long enough. As soon as Mattie is able, we will—' Then, because he might think that she was including him in the 'we', she added quickly, 'Me and Mattie?' Hearing the question mark in her voice, she flushed and, seeing his perceptive appraisal, wished the words unsaid.

It wasn't that she would ever give his proposal of staying serious consideration, which was just as well because, from his expression, he wasn't going to make the offer again.

Probably thinking he'd had a lucky escape. Last night must have brought home that she and Mattie were a package deal and, as great as he was with Mattie, the baby was not his responsibility.

One day he'd have his own children.

'Me and Mattie. I think we might go directly home

from here. I'll have already missed some of the course and it seems pointless—'

His strong jaw quivered as his dark glance slid from the baby to her. 'We will discuss things later.' The situation had necessitated a delay in confronting Jane, but there had been no lessening of his need to demand answers. He had spent a sleepless night with his stepmother's spiteful words pounding inside his skull like a jackhammer.

The careful placement of his words, the undercurrent in his voice, brought her head around to face him. She blinked, confused by the explosive tension pouring off him in waves, and turned back to the task in hand.

'Let me do that,' he interrupted, watching her struggle with the anchoring straps on the unfamiliar baby chair. Mattie, who had dozed off, carried on sleeping.

Jane eased herself out, taking care not to hit her head in the car built for looks and speed rather than its family-friendly qualities.

Draco did not hit his head and the car seat came away in two deft clicks and snaps.

Walking into the building's spacious entrance hall, he ignored a wide marble staircase and led her straight to a lift that whooshed upwards.

Inside the apartment was the same mix of ancient and modern, eclectic contemporary pieces set against old stone and wooden panelling.

'I thought you'd like Mattie to sleep with you tonight.'

Jane wanted to ask if he would be sharing her room, but she didn't. The tension she had sensed earlier was even stronger in him now.

Draco couldn't wait any longer. 'I know.'

She blinked, met his hard dark eyes that glimmered

like obsidian pools and it hit. He had overheard her conversation with Marco when she had told the doctor that she couldn't have children.

'Oh, I know I should have told you but I knew how you'd react.'

He just couldn't believe what he was hearing. 'So you knew how I'd react.'

'I suppose that some men might not mind, but I knew how badly you wanted a family, Draco, and at the wedding I knew I just couldn't do that to you.'

As a shaft of anger pierced him like a blade the faint white line around his sensually sculpted lips grew more defined. The idea that she had been carrying his child and known it, concealed it from him… It was almost as if he were standing outside his outrage. To embrace it would mean a loss of control, acknowledging a pain that he might never move beyond.

CHAPTER TWELVE

'YOU KNEW YOU were pregnant at the wedding.' It sounded so calm, so civilised, so careful. It was only careful to preserve the illusion that what he was feeling could be considered logically.

She felt utter confusion when he raked her with a cold stare.

'P-pregnant?' she stuttered out. 'What are you talking about...?' She suddenly realised to her horror that they were talking at cross purposes. 'No, that's not right...' She lifted her hands in silent appeal but saw her words had no effect on him. 'That wasn't how it was, Draco, just calm down and listen to me. I can explain.' Explain that she had wanted to guard her secret. She'd fooled herself that it had been to protect him but wasn't his anger justified? She had been protecting herself, like a wounded animal seeking a quiet corner to lick her wounds.

'It is a bit too late to lie now. My stepmother was at the same abortion clinic as you. She remembers you well. So don't try and deny it!'

Never forget a face.

The woman's comment came back to Jane.

Like cracking a safe, the clicks in her head continued until the truth of what he was thinking, of what he thought of her, was revealed.

The irony of what he imagined the truth to be was not lost on her as her horrified despair became fury at the flick of a switch.

'I'm not going to try and deny it,' she told him, all cold disdain and hot flashing eyes.

'So you admit it?' he condemned, past the point of taking prisoners. For the past twenty-four hours he had imagined she would deny it and they would laugh together, because how could the woman he knew was willing to sacrifice everything for her child be capable of that? But no, that wasn't happening. This was the reality that he had to accept.

'You know something? I think you want to think the worst of me.'

'Do not try and deflect.'

'Yes, I was at that clinic. I was an emergency admission.'

His anger faltered for a split second, but then he remembered her saying that she had known at the wedding and she had hidden the truth from him.

'You had a miscarriage?' Alone, hurting, afraid. He took a deep breath. 'Talk to me. I will listen.'

It was the fact he thought he was being the big man that really got to her. 'Oh, wow, that is so good of you,' she drawled, her voice dripping with sarcasm.

'I just want to know why,' he blasted out, finding her anger and aggression bizarre. 'Do you not think I am owed that much? It was my child.'

'No, Draco, it wasn't your child. There was no child,' she told him bleakly. 'I did not have a miscarriage. I couldn't have a miscarriage because I can't have a child.'

'You are talking…?'

'I saw a doctor two days before our wedding. He told

me that I had severe endometriosis. Look it up,' she added in response to his blank look. 'It was,' she admitted with a slightly hysterical laugh, 'a relief. I had a name for the debilitating pain and the symptoms. The relief didn't last,' she added, turning her haunted green eyes to his face. 'Then he delivered the double triple-whammy—that I would never likely be able to have children.'

'But you have Mattie.'

Her glimmering smile now held sadness. 'I do, I have Mattie,' she said, her chin lifting. 'But only because his parents died. You remember Carrie? Mattie is her son.'

'Why on earth didn't you say so right at the beginning? You let me think…'

'Everyone in the village knows. I suppose I just assumed that you'd find out and it was quite nice to pretend…no!' she self-corrected with a fierce little shake of her head. 'Mattie is my son.'

He had wanted answers and he was getting them but not the ones he had anticipated. 'What were you doing in that clinic, then?' he growled, finding it disorientating to have things no longer slotting into place in his head.

'I was there because my endometriosis had caused internal issues, bleeding.' She couldn't bring herself to say life-threatening but the situation had been. 'And I needed emergency intervention.'

'Surgery…? The scars…?'

She nodded. 'From the laparoscopy.' She cleared her throat and struggled to organise her thoughts when all she wanted to do was wail. 'I was spared a major incision.'

She spoke so quietly, without any emphasis, but her words cut into him as brutally as the suggestion—a knife-blade.

'The operation was a success, they tell me.' She was

aware she should have felt more grateful than she had at the time. 'And I have to say it changed my life, the pain, not just monthly…but I know you are not interested.'

There was no condemnation, just a bleak acceptance in her words that made guilt rush into his head.

'Your stepmother is a bitch, and I am only quoting,' she concluded with a bitter laugh. 'But when this person you so despise—no, loathe—when she spilled her poison you were very happy to believe her.

'You know something, Draco, I think you wanted to see the worst in me, and yes, I know I should have been brave enough to tell you before the wedding, but I was in denial.' She pushed her fingers through her curls and they spilled out like fire against her pale face. 'And, you see, I always knew that you wanted a family more than you wanted me. I was just meant to be… What do they call it? The silent partner, and I loved you so very much that it didn't matter.

'But I am not that person any longer and it does matter. It matters that you believe I am…' As her voice became blurred by tears that she desperately blinked away, she shook her head. 'I would have been happy to be the silent partner but not now. The least I would expect of a partner or even a lover is that they believe in me.

'I apologise for not telling you the truth for that terrible wedding debacle. I should have been braver, but it is hard to know you can't give the man you love the only thing he wants.'

'Don't, Jane!' Draco breathed, holding up his hands as if to physically fend off her words.

'What? Don't tell you that I loved you? That I wanted to give you what you wanted more than anything?'

She saw his twisted tortured expression and said with

a bitter laugh, 'Oh, I know that you didn't love me, even then I knew that and I… I felt inadequate… I felt…' She swiped a hand across her face and sniffed, adopting a tough expression that she was a million miles from feeling. 'Less than a woman.'

Jane was so caught up in her emotions that she barely registered the stricken expression on his face.

'I loved you and I wanted…' She inhaled, her chest lifting. 'But I believe, I know, that I deserve more than you are able, or willing, to give me. But all that is irrelevant. I can't give you babies, Draco, no beautiful babies, no heirs. So let's just say goodnight because this is getting so very, very tiring.'

With perfect timing the baby's bereft cries filled the room.

Jane looked at Draco one more time, drinking in the fabulous features, the man that she loved and always would, and turned away. The heart couldn't always have what it wanted. Sometimes reality got in the way.

It took her a good half an hour to settle Mattie and when she returned to the book-lined living area she knew without calling out that she was alone.

CHAPTER THIRTEEN

'SO IT IS all right for us to travel.'

Marco, who had dropped in every day since they had been discharged, nodded his confirmation. 'If you think that is a good idea?'

'Is that a medical opinion?' Maybe he had read things into Draco's absence or maybe Draco had discussed the situation with him. What had he called it? she wondered bitterly. Awkward?

'No, not at all, it is a friend's opinion. And as a friend I say that you should not be carrying this news alone. You should tell him.'

'Tell who?' she said, feigning ignorance.

He raised a brow and said quietly, 'I was at the wedding.'

'Oh!' She swallowed. 'I didn't know, but I need to be where I don't feel so isolated.' She looked around the luxurious space they had stayed in for the last week.

It would have been easier if it had been an anonymous hotel but everywhere she came across signs of Draco's occupation: the book he'd been reading with its page marked, a scribbled note on a desk in his bold handwriting, the elusive scent of the male fragrance he used, the rows of freshly laundered shirts hanging in a wardrobe, which she had quickly slammed shut.

She couldn't stay here. She couldn't go back to the palazzo. The only option was to go home.

'I really need to think. I need to get my own head around it. I will tell him before I go,' she promised, her hands crossed across her chest. 'God, I can hardly believe it myself. Is it real?'

'It is real and you will do brilliantly. There is no medical reason your pregnancy will not go smoothly. And now I am speaking as a doctor.'

Draco's PR people were deliriously happy about an article written in a major financial journal praising his role in translating knowledge into strategies for driving forward a business model for a green revolution that had been picked up by multiple media outlets across the globe.

They had been confused by his lack of enthusiasm, but they did not recognise the irony. Draco was not deliriously happy. He was not happy at all.

Draco's two days of self-exile had made him realise that he was the architect of his own misery. He'd guarded his heart since childhood, not because it was smart or clever and definitely not wise, but because he was a coward!

People spoke of him as the man who had everything—he was living the dream. But he had been too much of a coward to even admit he had a dream.

A woman who was beautiful and smart had wanted to be with him and she had run away because she thought his only use for her was as a baby incubator. The shame he felt was intense.

It had taken more guts for her to run away than any he had ever shown. Jane had so much love to give and he had thrown it back in her face.

Jane hadn't run away. He was the one who had been running away all his life from feelings he was afraid to own.

Without Jane he had nothing.

Would she listen to him? He had no idea but he would try and he would never stop trying.

Later that morning, after Marco had left, Jane went online to book a flight. She had just completed the booking and was trying to work up the courage to call Draco when she heard a noise.

It made her pause because since her arrival she had barely registered that she was not alone in the building, if you discounted the formal person who appeared every day asking her to state her requirements.

In a brief moment of whimsy she had thought about requesting hair that didn't have a will of its own or the ability to not say the wrong thing at the wrong time...or maybe that was the right thing.

Though in the end she had been gifted her greatest wish.

The truth had still not bedded in her mind. She woke in the morning and then remembered. Despite the signs, if one of Marco's daily visits to check in on Mattie had not coincided with one of her really bad, 'can't pretend it's not happening' nausea events—not pretty—she still wouldn't have suspected.

When Marco had suggested that she might like to do a pregnancy test it had made her laugh—it beat crying. After she had reminded him of her medical history, to her amazement he had still thought it a good idea and produced one from his medical bag.

Jane was still reeling between joy and disbelief, but she had not changed her travel plans. Leaving was the only option open to her. While she felt guilty for not telling Draco the truth of Mattie's parentage, that guilt was outweighed by the hurt she felt that Draco had believed that she had had an abortion.

As she sat down to call him to tell him what he had a right to know, that he was going to be a father, she still had no idea what she would say. This time, though, she planned to be open and upfront. There had already been too many secrets.

Draco had always believed he knew what and who he was.

As he walked into the room that inner certainty had vanished. The truth was his confidence had never come from knowing who he was. It had always been about proving to the world and himself who he wasn't.

His father! His weak, selfish, pathetic father, and he'd become that man because of a toxic love.

The equation was simple: avoid love. See it coming and cross the street. He'd never needed to cross the street and then Jane had appeared.

His confidence had come from the conviction that he couldn't be in love with anyone. Love was selfish and destructive, an indulgence for people who believed in fairy tales past childhood. He had made the argument until he was word perfect, using cold, hard logic and reason.

Now that conviction had been proved a lie. He loved Jane. The foundations he'd built his life on had crumbled and, instead of feeling lost and adrift, he felt liberated.

'Can I come in?'

'You are already in,' Jane pointed out, getting to her feet and walking away from her open laptop. 'And I'm the guest.' Had she overstayed her welcome? Was that why he was here? 'I was just about to ring you, Draco.'

'And now I am here.'

'I have booked our flights home, but first I wanted to apologise.' She swallowed and took a deep breath. 'Apologise for deceiving you. I should not have left you standing at the altar. I just wasn't brave enough to tell you why I had to. I took the easy route and ran.' She huffed out a sigh and squeezed her eyes closed. 'So many lies. I let you think I was Mattie's mother.'

Draco's eyes followed the direction of her glance to the baby.

'You are his mother in every way that counts. Is Mattie fit to travel?'

She gestured to the baby, who was lying on a vivid play mat, a toy stuffed in his mouth as he happily kicked. 'As you see.'

'Has Marco been calling in?'

'Every day. I'm assuming you asked him to?' Distancing himself. As far as she was concerned there was no other way to interpret the situation.

Draco nodded and dragged a hand through his dark hair. 'He won't tell me anything?' he ground out, his voice cracking with frustration. 'Just tells me he can't disclose medical details and if I want to know I should ask for myself.'

'And you came. That was good of you, but, as you see, Mattie is fine.'

'I expect you will tell me to go to hell, but actually I think I am already there! I know I let you down,' he said heavily. 'Believing the lies of that poisonous woman was unforgivable!'

'I was hurt,' she admitted with a catch in her voice.

'And hearing you say that means a lot to me.' Maybe more than you can ever know, she thought. 'But, Draco…there is something I need to tell you. Something that changes everything, but nothing,' she added bleakly.

Draco would never love her.

He took an impetuous step forward and as the light shone on his face Jane was shocked to see how drawn he looked as he caught her hands in his.

'No, let me speak. Ask you if you…' He released her and grabbed his head in both hands. 'Oh, Jane, I have been such a fool!' he cried out in an anguished voice she barely recognised. 'I love you. I have been the world's worst fool, a coward,' he bit out, his voice aching with self-contempt.

Nailed to the spot with shock, she just stared at him. Was this a dream?

'Please, Jane, tell me it is not too late… We have Mattie. We don't need a baby.' He stepped forward and took her hands, lacing his long fingers in hers and bringing them up to his lips. 'All I need is you. All I ever needed was you, but I was afraid to admit my dreams, that you were my secret dream made warm, beautiful, brave flesh.

'This is no excuse, but I saw my father destroyed by a woman, but being without you—*my* woman—would destroy me. I am not a full person without you. Can you ever forgive me? Will you marry me? And this time it will be different because I am different. I am not afraid to tell you that I love you.'

Tears pricked her eyes as she read the anguish on his face, the blaze of hope and fear in his eyes.

She looked up at him, her heart shining in her face. 'I love you, Draco,' she said simply as she stepped into him, laying her heart against his heart and feeling his arms close tight around her.

'Not too tight...'

His arms dropped away and he looked at her anxiously. 'I hurt you?' He looked horrified at the thought.

'I just feel a bit queasy, that's all. Normally I love the smell of your soap but...'

'You are ill.' He went white. 'I will call...'

She shook her head. The rush of emotion too strong now to hold back the tears of joy that spilled out. 'It's fine. You see, I'm not ill. I'm having our baby, our miracle.'

Mattie, ignored for too long, let out a loud gurgle.

'A brother or a sister for you, little one, a playmate.' Draco placed a warm, protective hand on her flat stomach. 'It is safe for you? If not...' He shook his head. 'I will love our child, but I will never ever put you at risk, Jane,' he said sombrely. 'I hope you realise that.'

She slid a loving hand down his face, her vision misting at the sincerity in his voice. 'Marco says there is no danger, though it's possible I might need a caesarean.'

She had started crying and her heart was too full to tell him they were tears of joy.

'Do not cry, do not be afraid—you are not alone,' Draco soothed, cradling her face and kissing her lips with a blend of tenderness and passion that produced more tears.

'I'm not afraid. I'm happy I'll never be alone again,' she sobbed, her voice choked with raw emotion.

'If you don't stop crying I will have to kiss you.'

Jane smiled and let the tears flow, thinking, Bring it on!

* * * * *

UNKNOWN
ROYAL BABY

ANNIE WEST

MILLS & BOON

For Jan Van Engen,
who loves sheikh romances.
It's great to know you're waiting for this one.

CHAPTER ONE

HIS HIGHNESS ISAM IBN RAFAT, Crown Prince of Zahdar, rose from the conference table, walking around it to the interviewee. 'Thank you, Mr Drucker. This has been a most useful meeting.'

Avril stifled surprise. As His Highness's assistant, it was her role to usher guests through the presidential suite before and after meetings.

Drucker realised that too. He couldn't mask his excitement as his host personally escorted him from the room. The visitor didn't even spare her a glance, much less say goodbye to her, though they'd had several conversations prior to today and he'd been surreptitiously checking out her breasts through the meeting.

Repressing a fizz of distaste, she focused on her notes.

It was some time before her boss returned. The hotel was one of London's finest and the suite took up a whole floor.

When the door reopened she looked up, skin prickling in the way it always did when Isam was around.

He'd stripped off his suit jacket. Her gaze snagged on broad shoulders and a body that seemed all lean, hard muscle beneath his perfectly tailored shirt and trousers.

She drew in air, trying to slow her racing pulse. Clearly she wasn't used to being around such masculine perfection! She needed to get out more.

The irony wasn't lost on Avril. She hadn't begrudged her

cloistered life and now Cilla's death had given her more free-dom. Yet these past weeks she'd had to force herself out of the house. Grief lay heavy and she felt bereft. Cilla had given her stability and love for as long as she could remember. She didn't want freedom at the cost of her great-aunt's life. She missed the feisty, frail, wonderful woman.

Her emotions were all over the place.

That was why she was so unsettled. It wasn't just the im-pact of being physically near her boss instead of separated by a continent.

He tugged his tie loose and undid two shirt buttons. 'You don't mind, do you, Avril? It's been a long afternoon and I hate being trussed up in a suit.'

But you wear it so well.

She bit down the words. The fact he was even more attrac-tive in person than in his photos was a shock she still grap-pled with after days working side by side.

It's ridiculous. He pays your salary. You've worked for him for six months.

But her brain had trouble equating this stunningly hand-some, charismatic man with the clever, demanding, yet ap-proachable colleague she'd come to know and like via email, texts and phone calls. The man with whom she'd built a rap-port, even, to her surprise, a level of friendship.

She was his only UK-based PA, working remotely. She was the conduit for his business interests in Britain while he lived in Zahdar or travelled the globe.

Yet sometimes, when he'd anticipated her next words dur-ing a long-distance call, or made her laugh with his wry, in-sightful humour, she'd felt they understood each other in a way that transcended business. Lately she'd felt closer to him than to anyone other than Cilla.

Avril fought an unfamiliar full-body blush. 'Of course I don't mind, Your High— Isam.'

His dark eyebrow had shot high in a look of mock severity. But when she used his name instead of his title he smiled his approval.

Absolutely, you need to get out more, when a man's smile makes your stomach flutter.

Yet his familiar name tasted strange now on her tongue, though she'd been calling him that for months.

Isam in the flesh was an altogether more sensational being than the faceless colleague to whom she'd grown close.

She'd only ever dealt with him, not any of his other staff. Given the frequency of their communications and the growing understanding between them, he'd insisted on using first names. Avril had been surprised, but what did she know about the ways of royalty?

Yet what had seemed practical and easy when he was far away grew more difficult as they worked together in his private hotel suite.

Because now he's not just your employer. He's the sexiest man you've ever met. The first man ever to awaken those dormant feminine longings.

She hoped he had no idea how he made her feel. It was as if her life of sexual abstinence—because she'd had other responsibilities and no time for a boyfriend—finally took its toll.

She'd never had such vivid sexual fantasies as in the last couple of days, since Isam came to London. Last night she'd lain awake for hours imagining how it would be to touch him, kiss him, undress him.

Even now she couldn't stifle the burr of excitement under her skin at being near him. Or the unfamiliar ache in her pelvis.

Hurriedly she pressed her thighs together.

'That was a useful session, don't you think?' Her voice was stilted and she took refuge in her notes, pretending absorption in what she'd written.

Because she feared what he might see in her eyes. It was vital she remain professional, unswayed by his bone-melting smile.

He flopped into a chair beside her. From the corner of her eye she saw him spin to face her, knees close to her, solid thighs encased in charcoal superfine wool. 'Very useful. What did you think of him?'

'Me?'

She shouldn't be surprised. Isam regularly sought her input. But something in his tone made her look up sharply.

Dark grey eyes regarded her intently. Beneath his imposing, straight nose, his sensuously sculpted mouth had flattened. The angle of his jaw seemed sharper. He looked—not disapproving, but not happy.

What had Drucker said to get Isam offside?

'It's not my decision but—'

'That's never stopped you giving input before.'

Startled, Avril hesitated. Isam might be demanding but he was never impatient. She firmed her lips and lifted her chin. 'I wouldn't employ him.'

Something flared in that gunmetal gaze but she had no hope of identifying it. 'Go on.'

She shrugged. 'On paper the deal seems promising. But I'm not sure he has his priorities right and that doesn't say much for his judgement. He pumped money into creating executive suites in his hotel but I think he's overcapitalised. They're underutilised, maybe because of the location. It's the more affordable accommodation that brings in the money there, yet he refuses to take an interest in that. Plus...'

A nod encouraged her to continue. 'He skimmed over the issue of staff underpayment. From what I've been able to discover that's an ongoing issue. If rumours are to be believed, it's a major problem. Apart from the legalities, do you want to take on someone who doesn't value and reward staff? If you acquired the hotel I definitely wouldn't keep him on as executive manager.'

'I caught him staring at you.'

Discomfort lifted her shoulders. 'Some men seem unable to resist leering at a woman.'

Even an altogether ordinary woman in a plain navy suit and white shirt. It was something she hadn't missed when she left her job in an office to work from home remotely as a virtual PA.

'I apologise that he made you uncomfortable, Avril. That's why I cut off the meeting. I won't do business with him. But I needed to meet him and ensure I was making the right decision.' His tone darkened. 'That short session convinced me.'

Isam had ended the meeting because his visitor ogled her? She blinked, digesting the idea. Avril had known there was something wrong—they hadn't got through half the points she'd prepared. She slanted a glance at Isam and discovered him watching her with a look of concern.

'It's all right. I—'

'It's *not* all right, as I made clear to him just now. But thank you for your patience today. I'm sorry it happened.'

He'd called the guy on his behaviour? Avril reminded herself it was only what any decent person would do. She should have done it herself instead of pretending it wasn't happening by focusing on her work.

That Isam hadn't ignored the behaviour, but had done something about it, released a flood of warm emotion.

You're not here to feel emotion. You're here to work.

But she couldn't suppress the warm glow inside.

'I'll tidy my notes and send them to you. And the list of action items from today's meetings.'

She paused, reluctant to continue because, despite the long day, and the session with Drucker, she'd enjoyed herself. Enjoyed being with Isam. She liked the way he worked and that he valued her input.

A secret, feminine part of her thrilled at being with this potently masculine, charismatic man.

Plus she hated the idea of returning to the empty house she'd shared with Cilla. Isam was so *alive*, so real and strong. She craved some of that strength and assurance. Craved the excitement of being with him as an antidote to the bleak loneliness of her home.

'Thanks.'

Isam paused, a couple of frown lines appearing on his forehead. Instead of detracting from his handsome features the hint of extra gravity only enhancing his allure.

Careful, Avril. You sound starstruck.

'I fly back to Zahdar tomorrow but there are some things I still need to sort out.' He shot a look at his watch, a sleek statement piece that probably cost as much, if not more than Cilla's house and all the adjoining ones in their terrace. 'It's late, but can you stay back to work this evening?'

Avril stiffened, hesitating. Not because she begrudged him her time. But because working any longer with Isam in his private suite wasn't a good idea. Not because he'd be anything other than professional. But because her feelings about him were increasingly chaotic.

Face it, woman! They're not chaotic. You know exactly what they are. Excitement. Old-fashioned attraction. Lust.

'The hotel does an excellent dinner and my driver would take you safely home afterwards.' Grey eyes narrowed on her. 'Unless you have another engagement?'

Desolation shot through her, undercutting any half-formed idea of excusing herself to avoid an evening closeted with him.

She had no engagements, except watering her great-aunt's African violets and finishing the job she'd begun earlier, sorting Cilla's clothes to donate to charity.

* * *

Isam watched Avril's mouth crumple for a second before curving into a smile.

Something in his chest clamped painfully tight.

This smile wasn't like the warm ones she bestowed when caught up in their work and enjoying herself. When she forgot he was a crown prince. It was more like the polite expression she'd worn as she'd ushered Drucker into the room.

Abruptly he sat back in his seat. Surely she didn't equate him with Drucker! Isam might be dangerously drawn to his delightful PA but he'd been careful not to reveal it. Despite the fact that over the months they'd worked together they'd developed an easy familiarity, an ability to anticipate each other's reactions, a rare type of intimacy he'd never known with a woman.

The power imbalance between them, the fact he paid her salary, made it impossible for him to act on his attraction. Avril Rodgers was out of bounds. Even if she didn't work for him, he sensed she was a home and hearth sort of woman, not like his usual sexual partners who were happy to indulge in a short-term affair.

Isam had spent the last four days, since his arrival in London, constantly reminding himself that Avril was a work colleague. The difficulty was that too often he caught her looking at him with definite sexual interest that fed his own desire and weakened his scruples.

When her brown eyes shimmered like old gold and she slicked her bottom lip with her pink tongue, regarding him with a mix of eagerness and awe, she tested every good intention.

But not now. Now, he knew something was wrong, and it evoked every protective instinct.

'Avril, are you okay?'

She blinked, banishing that momentarily haunted look,

and sat straighter. Yet her restless hands gave her away. 'Of course. I was just thinking about tonight.'

'It's short notice. I understand that you can't—'

'I can. I'm free tonight. I can stay on.' Her smile this time was more familiar. 'Easier by far if we finish whatever work you have in mind before you leave for Zahdar.'

Isam reminded himself he was a disciplined man. A few more hours in close proximity to temptation wouldn't matter.

Though Avril was like no temptation he could remember. Capable, organised and clever, she was the perfect PA. But there was something else, a warmth, a genuineness, that called to him. Not to mention a sexual allure that frankly stunned him. She wore conservative suits with a minimum of flesh on display, so different from many of the women he met on his travels. But despite her air of wholesomeness...

Better not to think about. Or about how Drucker's lewd appreciation had evoked in Isam something like jealousy.

You want her to look at you, only you.

Who was he kidding? He wanted a whole lot more than Avril's looks. His gaze caught on her capable hands, now neatly clasped in her lap. Too often he'd imagined them on his body.

Isam shot to his feet and strode around the long table, shoving his hands in his trouser pockets in an attempt to hide his burgeoning arousal.

'Excellent. What would you like for dinner?'

Hours later, Avril stretched stiff muscles and rose from her chair. Isam had left the room to take a private call from Zahdar. She'd finish her work. Soon she'd leave.

Would she see Isam again? Probably, but not for a long time. They'd go back to working at a distance.

That was good. She needed that distance.

Yet she wished...

Don't even think about it! You're too sensible to pine for what you can't have. You and he... Inconceivable!

She grabbed her barely touched glass of red wine and stalked across to the window, not bothering to put on the shoes she'd discarded under the desk while they worked.

She'd requested a glass of wine to accompany the superb meal she'd been served, but then hadn't had the stomach for it. It was Cilla, dear Cilla, who'd loved the occasional glass of Shiraz. It must have been sentimentality that made her order the glass.

Avril looked out across the dark street to the leafy park that made this Mayfair location so desirable. It had rained while they worked. The pavements shone, reminding her of the night Cilla died.

Melancholy filled her. She knew Cilla had been in pain. That slipping off peacefully in her sleep had been a blessed release. Cilla had wanted, insisted, Avril not mope. Her great-aunt had even made her create a list of fun things she wanted to do when the time came and Avril had more time for herself.

Her lips twisted. Cilla had been a remarkable lady. She lifted her glass in silent salute and took a long, slow sip, savouring the wine's mellow fruitiness. It warmed her, a comforting glow settling deep inside her.

Tomorrow she'd honour Cilla by reading through that list, though she wasn't in the mood to try new adventures yet.

Unless Isam was on your list. Then you'd be ready for adventure.

'Avril.'

His deep voice came from so close behind her that she jumped, twisting around.

Isam stood there, dark shadows dusting his jaw, making him look even more elementally, bone-meltingly male.

She saw him in the same moment she registered the wave of red wine arc up from the glass that jerked in her hand.

In slow motion she saw it collide with his pristine shirt and horror filled her.

Avril put the glass down to search for a tissue but her bag and jacket were at the other end of the imposing room. The dinner napkins had been cleared away long ago.

'Handkerchief? Tissue?' she rapped out.

A large handkerchief, ironed and snowy white, was pressed into her hand. 'Thanks.'

She held it to his shirt, knowing she was probably ruining both, but unable to watch the spill dribble further. With her other hand she tugged open a shirt button then another and another. 'You need to get this off straight away. Salt will lift the wine stain. Or soak it in cold water.'

Beneath her touch she felt the sudden flex of warm muscle. A waft of air eddied across her forehead and she realised it was Isam's breath, soft as a caress.

Avril froze, eyes widening as she realised what she was doing. Her left hand pressed the damp handkerchief to Isam's chest. His hard, hair-roughened, golden-toned chest.

She gulped. The fingers of her right hand were curled, immobile, around a shirt button halfway to his belt.

Only now did she register the rise and fall of his chest with each breath and the friction of chest hair against her knuckles. A tickle of excitement lifted the hair at her nape and pulled her scalp tight.

'I can take it from here.'

There must be something wrong with her hearing. Isam's voice sounded strained, gravelly rather than smooth. The blood pounding in her ears must be to blame.

Her flesh tingled all over and her nipples pushed hard against her bra, making her shiver.

'Of course.'

Her gaze was glued to her hands against his chest but her synapses weren't firing properly. She should be lifting her hands off him yet they didn't move. Her brain was too scrambled. Or her body refused to heed its orders.

She'd dreamt of touching him, of seeing the powerful body beneath the custom-made clothes. The reality was shockingly arousing. Isam in the flesh short-circuited her ability to move.

Two large hands covered hers. But instead of dragging them off him, those long fingers wrapped around hers. Avril's breath disappeared in a gasp.

Sensations shot through her. His scent, citrus and warm male flesh. The gentle strength of his touch. A sudden twitching movement of his pectorals. The quick thud of his heart against her knuckles. As quick as her own, surely.

'Avril. Look at me.'

Reluctant, because she knew this had to end and the fallout would be embarrassing, she arched her neck, her gaze snagging on the bronzed column of his throat, strong and fascinating. Up to that determined chin, dark with an evening's beard growth. She swallowed hard, taking in the sculpted perfection of his mouth, the long, aristocratic nose, stopping when she reached heavy-lidded eyes.

She jumped and would have tugged her hands away except he held them against his chest.

Because what she saw was unprecedented. Isam's expression was aware. Aroused. Sensual.

All the things she'd believed impossible.

Of its own volition, her body swayed closer, her breasts pressing against his hard torso, stealing her breath from her lungs as his heat engulfed her. Sparks ignited across her skin and her blood shimmered as if effervescent.

Someone's breath hitched. It must be hers, but then she felt the rise of his torso as if he held back the air in his lungs.

Avril couldn't find anything coherent to say. No man had ever looked at her the way Isam did now. As if he wanted to eat her all up. As if he craved her the way she longed for him.

It made her feel different. Powerful.

She swallowed, the movement jerky as though her muscles forgot how to work. Dry-mouthed, she swiped her tongue over her bottom lip.

Heat blazed in Isam's eyes, his nostrils flared, and suddenly he didn't look like the civilised man she knew but some marauder. The glint in his eyes was surely avaricious, and his hands tightened possessively. Avril thrilled at the change in him.

'Isam.'

She had no trouble now, saying his name. It emerged as a whisper, husky with longing. She rose on tiptoe, needing to bridge the gap between them.

Except with shocking finality, he shattered the precious moment. Still gripping her hands, as if knowing her legs were wobbly, Isam stepped back. The room was comfortably air-conditioned, yet it felt as though an arctic blast swept between them. Avril shivered.

His voice was deeper than she'd ever heard it, with an accent edging his previously perfect English. 'This can't happen.'

Yet it *was* happening. Didn't he feel it?

'I employ you. You depend on me for your salary.' He shook his head, his mouth crimping down at the corners. 'It would be wrong.'

Avril understood. There was a power imbalance between them. He didn't want to take advantage of her and she admired him for that.

Yet this need wasn't wrong. It wasn't tainted. It was mutual and ferociously real.

More real than the grey half-life she'd been living lately. She *craved* this as a diver, too long below the surface, craved air.

Even now, as she watched him distance himself, the hammer beat of her heart and the jittery restlessness low in her body were all about *her* needs, not something imposed by him.

'Couldn't we pretend that you're not my boss? That I'm not your PA? Just for this evening?'

At any other time she might have winced at the stark need her words revealed. But this between them was so consuming, it superseded the normal rules. In twenty-six years she'd never experienced anything so visceral.

He scowled and even then she hungrily devoured the sight of him—no longer urbane and in control, but prey to strong emotions, like her. 'No. Absolutely not!'

Suddenly, it was easier than she thought to step away. She wrapped stiff arms around her abruptly chilled body.

What had she been thinking? She'd seen the photos of Isam with a series of stunning women. All glamorous, all beautiful and no doubt at home in his rarefied social milieu. The sort who held down high-flying careers yet found time to look a million dollars at royal events.

'I understand.' Avril struggled not to feel hurt. If she'd thought rationally she'd have known the idea was ludicrous. She didn't fit his world or his expectations. Her stockinged toes curled into the thick, handwoven carpet. 'I'm not sophisticated and sexy and you're—'

'Avril, you've got it wrong.'

She shook her head, pursing her mouth before she blurted out any more foolishness. It was time to leave.

'This *isn't* about you.'

He was trying to soothe her ego but his words had the opposite effect. Her turbulent feelings coalesced into anger, pumping through her bloodstream. She welcomed it because it obliterated, at least for now, embarrassment and disappointment.

'Of course it is. I'm no fool. I know the huge gulf between us. I'm ordinary and you're…you. It was laughable to think—'

'Stop that!' Isam folded his arms, muscles bulging and eyes glinting like molten mercury. He was the image of furious, frustrated masculinity and still he made her knees go weak. But she stood tall and returned his heated stare. 'Do you see me laughing, Avril? I spent today, *all* the days we've worked together, locking my feelings away. Trying to ignore my attraction to you. Pretending to be unaffected and uninterested, when all the time…'

Stunned, she watched a muscle spasm in his cheek as his jaw clenched. The tendons in his throat were taut and she felt tension radiating from him.

He was so angry he *glowered* through slitted eyes.

But instead of dismaying her, his fury had the opposite effect. It told her he felt *something* for her.

She took a half-step towards him. Instantly he pulled back, chin lifting arrogantly. 'That wasn't meant as encouragement, Avril.'

But his hauteur didn't deter her. 'You want me?' The words dropped, soft as petals on dewy grass.

Isam swallowed but said nothing.

'You *want* me!' The realisation eased her racing pulse and soothed the desperate ache just a fraction.

His voice was flinty with authority. 'It would be madness to act on it.'

'Madness, maybe.' She paused to snatch air into oxygen-starved lungs. 'I understand your reservations. Our lives are worlds apart. This can't lead anywhere beyond tonight. You're an honourable man who doesn't want to take advantage.'

Unable to resist any longer, she placed a hand on his arm, feeling the abrupt jerk of muscles in response.

'But what if *I* initiated it? If *I* invited you? It would be a momentary madness and I know it could only last one night. A secret shared by just us.'

She felt a shudder pass from him to her—a quiver of awareness and deep-seated longing. That proof of connection strengthened her determination. And her recklessness.

'Even if it meant we couldn't work together later, it would be worth it. Don't you feel it too?'

Avril knew instinctively this madness as he called it was what she needed. For the first time in weeks the world made sense in a way it hadn't since she'd lost Cilla. Even if the price was to leave this job, she'd take it. With her skills she'd find work. But where else would she find someone who made her feel the way Isam did?

Even the touch of her hand on his arm was enough to banish the shadows that had eclipsed her life, turning her black and white world into vivid colour again.

Lately everything except work had seemed out of kilter. But this was absolutely right.

Avril needed to feel joy and comfort. She needed the touch of someone warm and living. Not just anyone. Only Isam made her feel this way.

CHAPTER TWO

'OF COURSE I FEEL IT.' Isam's words made her sag in relief. 'But I won't take advantage of you. Besides, I can't offer a relationship, not long term. There are expectations on me that I can't ignore. And I certainly don't want to lose the best PA I've ever had.'

Any other time his compliment on her work would have thrilled her. But Avril had more urgent matters on her mind.

She closed the space between them, standing toe to toe, so her breasts brushed his folded arms as she slid her hands over his solid chest and around his neck. His skin was hot and the sensation of his thick hair against her fingertips elicited a frisson of excitement.

'Then I'll take advantage of you,' she murmured, pulling his head down as she rose on her toes.

Her lips brushed his once, twice, and suddenly he was kissing her back. Powerful arms wrapped around her, pulling her close and high. Against her belly she felt the press of masculine virility and fire exploded in her veins.

Yet Isam's kiss was slow, almost gentle, and totally at odds with her rush of urgent arousal.

Avril leaned in, opening for him, giving kiss for kiss. Still he took his time, as if needing to be sure of her.

She'd never kissed like this. Clumsy Christmas party pecks and dates with guys who were either too tentative or way too aggressive had made her suspect she wasn't missing much by not dating.

Isam made her realise she'd had no idea how a kiss could be. But how badly she wanted to learn. She wanted to grab life in both hands and experience everything she'd missed.

Her legs were boneless by the time he lifted his head, surveying her through silvered eyes that shimmered with heat. That look alone would have seduced her. Not that she needed seducing. She clung to his shoulders, fingers digging possessively.

He opened his mouth to speak but she forestalled him.

'I'm absolutely sure I want this. I don't care about your position or mine. I don't care about the future.' Not even her job was as necessary as this. She breathed deep, his spicy, lemony scent making her heady. 'I *need* you, Isam.'

For a second he didn't move, didn't make a sound. His proud features looked so tight they might have been sculpted from metal. Then his chest rose mightily, pressing against hers and he shook his head, murmuring something in Arabic she had no hope of understanding.

Before she had time to guess at his response he moved. One second she was standing, stretched taut against him. The next she was cradled in his embrace, held sideways against his torso, his arms supporting her back and legs.

He turned and carried her from the room with long, decisive steps and her heart soared. They weren't heading for the exit but the bedrooms.

'You lay waste to my caution, Avril. To everything except my hunger for you. I tell myself I shouldn't, I can't, but it's no good. I want you desperately.'

His voice was rough, almost unrecognisable, and she lifted her hand to his throat where he swallowed hard. Tenderness welled up for this strong man humbled by the same urgent desire that swamped her.

He paused in the doorway, looking down at her, that ferocious blaze of arousal tempered by something that made her heart split open in wonder.

'But remember, if you change your mind—'

'I won't.'

She covered his mouth with her palm. She didn't want to talk.

Isam kissed her hand, then opened his mouth and dragged his tongue along the centre of her palm and right to the tip of her middle finger.

Avril shuddered and gasped as heat zinged through her body. She'd never experienced such an erotic caress. Her breasts seemed to swell, her nipples peaking hard while inner muscles squeezed tight.

She quivered, shocked at her response and eager for more. If she felt this way now, how good would it be when they finally came together?

She looked up into his assessing stare. Was Isam thinking the same thing? His eyes looked molten hot and she couldn't keep her thoughts to herself. 'I want you naked. Now.'

She felt a fillip of delight, seeing his eyes widen. But better was her satisfaction as he strode through the suite into a vast, elegantly appointed bedroom.

As soon as she was on her feet she reached for his shirt, scrabbling at the buttons. Yet Isam was quicker than her. By the time she tugged his shirt from his trousers her blouse was unbuttoned and open. He pushed it and her jacket from her body in one smooth movement that reminded her he'd done this many times before.

It would make sense to warn him of her inexperience, but Avril didn't want anything to interrupt this moment, or give him a reason to have any more concerns. Instead she reached for the fastening of his trousers.

What began as a deliberate act became a blur of urgent

movement. Soon they were on the bed, gloriously naked, Avril breathless at the amazing sensations of their bodies together. Dimly she registered Isam reach for the bedside table, retrieving a condom.

As if her body weren't stimulated enough, the sight of him rolling it on took her to a whole new level of excitement. He knelt above her, exploring her spreadeagled body with hands and mouth so thoroughly and perfectly that it was mere minutes before an orgasm rushed her.

Avril arched off the bed, responding instinctively to his mouth at her breast and his hand between her legs. The sensations were overwhelming, utterly sublime. Yet as she finally came down from that amazing high, her eyelashes spiked with frustrated tears. She'd had no time to explore his fascinating body, much less have him inside her as she craved.

'Avril, you are you okay?' His voice was a concerned rumble against her ear as he hauled her close.

He wrapped his arms around her as she sank against him, bones melting in ecstasy. His tone grew imperative. 'Tell me. What's wrong?'

She shook her head, her vision blurry as she opened her eyes to meet his worried gaze. 'I couldn't wait. It was incredible.' *He* was incredible, so passionate yet tender. The way he touched her both reverent and carnal. 'But I wanted the first time to be *with* you. Not your hand but...'

A grin cracked his taut expression as he rolled her onto her back, nudging her thighs wide so he could settle between them.

Her already overburdened senses frantically registered new delights. The weight of him, even though he propped himself on his elbows. The incendiary heat and the fascinating hardness of his erection. The tickle of chest hair against her breasts that made her arch and rub her nipples eagerly against him. That felt incredible.

As she moved his breath hissed and his erection pulsed against her, making her eyes widen.

'Is that what you want?' he growled. The timbre of his voice made every fine hair on her body stand up in anticipation.

'You know it is.'

Avril reached down to touch him but he clamped her wrist, pulling it away. 'Better not.'

There was no time to protest because then Isam moved and her world would never be the same again.

Imagination was no preparation for the wonder of them coming together. She'd known the mechanics but reality dumbfounded her. Strange, yes, with a feeling of fullness she couldn't describe. A momentary flinch of pain, quickly gone, obliterated by delight.

It felt as though she'd waited a lifetime for this. The wild beauty of it. The earthy reality of body joining with body. And something more. Something like relief and glory and compulsion all tangled together.

Isam looked so serious, watching her hawk-eyed as he moved slowly, awakening her body to a new reality. But Avril was eager to learn and share the ecstasy he'd already given her. Soon she was moving with him, hands clutching him tight.

His gaze flickered when she hitched her heel around his muscled thigh. Instinctively she'd wanted to lock them closer together, only to discover the new angle heightened her pleasure. He helped her hook her other leg around him.

Isam paused, teeth bared, nostrils flaring, a man on the edge.

He looked…untamed. And she revelled in the change from urbane businessman to elemental lover.

This was how she needed him.

With gritted teeth he withdrew then bucked his hips, driving her to a new, extraordinary height.

After that there was no more slow. The control he'd so obviously exerted crumpled under a rush of sensual need. They moved together, gasping, hearts racing, and Avril felt a rush of pleasure gathering again in her pelvis, her breasts, her blood. Until her vision started to splinter as ecstasy engulfed her.

She opened her lips to call his name just as he claimed her mouth and their striving bodies hit the summit together.

The world spun out of control as light burst behind her eyelids. There was only Isam, holding her tight as he lost himself in her, introducing her to paradise.

Later, much later, when she could conjure the energy, Avril smiled and pressed her mouth to his damp skin, rejoicing in his tiny shudder of reaction and the murmur of satisfaction that rumbled from his chest into her body.

Life was good. So very, very good.

Get out of bed. Do it now.

Through the curtains no one had bothered to draw last night, the faintest morning light was visible.

Isam had an early flight to Zahdar that he couldn't miss. Before that he wanted to see Avril home.

Avril, who'd tempted him beyond reason, beyond the limits of his control, into reaching out and taking what he wanted. He'd *known* he shouldn't, known that, despite her eagerness, there'd be complications, and *still* his vaunted self-control had proved no match for his hunger. That was a first.

Never had it occurred to him that she'd be an innocent.

A shiver skated through him as he remembered the moment when he'd encountered that fragile, unexpected barrier and her honey-brown eyes had widened in consternation that turned quickly into pleasure.

Isam told himself that if he'd known he'd never have taken her to bed. Bad enough that he'd broken every rule by sleeping with someone dependent on him for her salary. But to take her innocence too…

In front of him Avril stretched in her sleep then burrowed back against him with a little twitch of her *derrière* that brought her flush against his erection. Involuntarily his fingers closed harder around her soft breast and his chest grew weighted as his lungs tightened.

Get out of bed. Do it now.

While he still could. Before she woke. It would be better if he were up and dressed by then because it would be easier to resist her. To talk sensibly about the implications of what they'd done.

Yet he couldn't bring himself to move.

Unfamiliar emotions eddied in his belly. Even when he'd discovered her lack of experience he'd been unable to rein in his desperate hunger. He remembered the final ecstasy of their joining, her clutching tight as he bucked hard and fast. Too hard? Too fast? She'd climaxed. She'd looked adorably sated and smug afterwards but had he hurt her?

Isam wasn't used to such ambiguities around a lover. He wasn't used to questioning his actions.

But you've never had a lover like Avril.

Even before they'd had sex, something about Avril set her apart from other women. Why?

She wriggled again in her sleep, this time arching so her breast thrust into his cupped hand. A spike of heat shot to his already tight groin.

His eyes rolled back and he gritted his molars at how very good that felt.

Everything about her felt good, which was why he'd broken another of his rules and spent the whole night with her.

Usually Isam slept alone, even after sex. He'd learnt years ago that it helped remind lovers that what they shared was mutual pleasure only, not commitment. He wasn't ready for a long-term partner, not yet. For when he did, that partner would become his wife. It was what his country expected of him.

Now he'd spent the whole night with a woman. Not any woman but his PA, who, unbelievably, had been a virgin.

What was wrong with men in Britain that no one had tempted her into bed before?

Even as he thought it, he winced at the idea of Avril sharing herself with some other man.

He bent his head a fraction and nuzzled her hair. Last night it had been a revelation when he'd seen it loose for the first time. Thick and long enough to cover her breasts, it was a sensual curtain that only heightened her seductiveness.

He breathed deep, inhaling her honey scent. Not sugary sweet but like the rich dark honey from the mountains of Zahdar, full-flavoured and lusciously addictive.

Addictive is the word. You need to get up now and—

'You *are* awake.' Her husky, morning voice was a caress, making his erection pulse against her. 'Oh!'

Was that an 'oh' of dismay? Or delight?

Isam lifted his hand from her breast and drew away. Only to have her roll over and fix him with a searching stare.

Desperately he tried not to notice all the delicious curves on display. He swallowed hard and kept his attention on her face. She was flushed, a crease down one cheek from how she'd lain on the pillow, and her hair was rumpled. She looked so delectable he had to curl his hands into fists rather than reach for her. Pain scored his palms.

'You *don't* want to have sex with me again?'

Her mouth turned down in a delicious pout.

When had Avril learned to pout? At work she was all professional decorum. The way her lips thrust out was damned near irresistible.

'I see.' The pout disappeared and her expression grew sombre. 'Of course. I wasn't thinking. It's time I left so you can—'

He grasped her shoulder as she rolled away, turning her back to face him. 'Wait.'

It didn't matter that he'd been telling himself it was time to get up. He didn't like it when she wouldn't meet his eyes.

'It's okay. I understand. I wasn't meant to stay so long.'

The fact her words echoed his own thoughts only made him feel worse. Because, whatever this was, Avril wasn't like any of his previous lovers.

You know what this is. It's a minefield. A potential disaster. Sleeping with your PA! You've never behaved so appallingly.

Yet Isam couldn't bring himself to regret what he'd done.

That, more than anything, should have raised a red flag. But he was too busy reading Avril's dull flush and her unhappy expression.

He kept his voice soft. 'Why do you think that?'

Her mouth turned down. 'Because you're a prince. And I'm...' She paused so long he wondered if she'd continue. 'Me. Ordinary. Last night was a mistake.'

She reached for the sheet as if to cover herself but he was lying half across it and refused to move, because inexplicably her words fired his anger. She'd merely stated the obvious, but he didn't like it. Didn't like her calling herself ordinary. Avril was many things but not that. As for her assuming last night was a mistake...

It didn't matter that he'd thought the same himself. To hear her label it that was insupportable. He didn't stop to question why.

'Do you really think last night was a mistake, Avril?'

Her expression changed. Her jaw set and she met his gaze squarely. 'No. It was wonderful. The most amazing thing I've ever done. But I understand that for you it's problematic, sleeping with staff. Inconvenient. Maybe even embarrassing.'

He knew she was trying to be pragmatic, yet the words felt

like a slap to his face. Even though he'd been torn between berating himself over his behaviour and revelling in the memory.

'You're not an embarrassment, Avril. And you're definitely not an inconvenience. Last night was unfortunate because I overstepped the boundaries—'

'Unfortunate!'

'But I can't regret it. I can't wish it undone.'

He watched her process that, understanding dawning.

During meetings she was the consummate professional, no sign of her emotions. But now he read her like a book. First hurt at believing herself rejected, then regret, then finally annoyance. Now suspicion mixed with something that made her eyes shimmer.

'If you don't regret it, why pull away from me just now? Is it that after last night, you're just not interested any more?'

He felt his forehead twist into a scowl that she should even think him uninterested. He was about to counter with a reference to his painful erection but stopped.

She couldn't know what was going on in his head.

'I know years ago the press painted me as a bit of a Casanova, but I was never as bad as they made out. I'm not so callow.'

Besides, after one taste of Avril how could he conceivably have lost interest?

Only the truth would do.

'I spent the night alternately dreaming about you and awake, fantasising about having you again.' He watched her eyes grow round. 'But I thought you needed your rest so I resisted waking you. Especially in light of your inexperience.'

Isam waited for her to say something about that. To explain why she hadn't warned him, though he suspected she'd feared, rightly, that he'd stop.

Such confidence in your self-control. You were in such a

*lather, chances are you wouldn't have been able to hold back
even if you'd known.*

'You wanted me…after?'

'I did, do.' He saw the spark of excitement in her gaze and
felt compelled to go on. 'You're right, we've created a com-
plicated situation—'

Her voice was breathless. 'You want me.'

There it was again, that satisfied smile he'd found so be-
witching last night. Isam couldn't help but respond to it. His
facial muscles stretched in a grin that he knew was more las-
civious than circumspect.

Because suddenly, despite the caution he should employ,
despite a lifetime learning to put royal responsibilities and
expectations before everything else, he couldn't dwell on the
complications they'd created. He was just a man, bewitched
by an alluring woman. A woman watching him with wonder and excitement.

Blood rushed to his groin, leaving him light-headed.

'I want you,' he admitted again and felt the last shackles
of restraint fall away.

'I'm glad.'

That was all it took. Her sweet smile, her shining eyes and
her welcoming smile. All thought of protocol, duty and the
world beyond this bed became hazy and insubstantial.

Isam stroked her cheek with his knuckle, watching her
voluptuous shiver that made her berry-tipped breasts shake
invitingly. Then slowly, because, despite the thrumming urgency of his need, this was too important to rush, he gathered her to him.

CHAPTER THREE

One year later

'THIS WAY, MS RODGERS.'

The tall man in the sharp suit gestured for her to precede him into the hotel's lift. His smile was perfunctory, not reaching his eyes. He had an air about him that made her wonder if he was a bodyguard, not an administrative assistant.

His stare made her shiver and pull her too-snug jacket close, the hairs at her nape rising. Would he frisk her before she was allowed into the presence of His High-and-Mightiness?

She didn't relish the thought. But she'd see this through. Now she had a chance to confront Isam.

Her emotions were a chaotic jumble and her stomach churned with something close to nausea. Avril had never believed today would come. After a year of complete silence, he wanted to see her.

She'd almost, *almost* refused to attend.

She'd stomped around the house, muttering under her breath about self-centred men and their unconscionable behaviour. The message, not from Isam himself, but from an officious staffer she didn't know, had caught her by surprise. To her horror, she'd found herself blinking back furious tears, bombarded by relief, anger and disbelief.

Not excitement. She'd given up on that ages ago.

How could she be excited to see him again? She'd almost convinced herself that the thrill she'd felt that night with him was her mind exaggerating. He'd been her first lover and, for a while at least, she'd turned him into someone special, more admirable than the flawed, arrogant bastard he'd proved to be.

Her breath caught on a bubble of bitter laughter that felt scarily hysterical. No, he wasn't a bastard. Not as far as the world was concerned. Not long after leaving London, on his father's death, he'd moved from being the legitimate royal heir to being proclaimed King of Zahdar.

But handsome is as handsome does, as Cilla used to say.

He'd treated Avril appallingly. She'd never be able to respect him after what he'd done.

'Are you all right, Ms Rodgers?'

Her gaze snapped up to the man she was sure now was a minder. Did Isam fear she might physically attack him? Unlikely, since she'd be no match for him. More likely royal security was more obvious now he was Sheikh.

'Oh, I'm just dandy. Thank you.'

She watched her companion blink and realised her smile held a feral edge. Drawing a slow breath, she forced herself to be calm or at least to look it.

The lift bell pinged and the doors slid open to reveal the elegant opulence of the presidential suite's foyer.

In the almost thirteen months since *that* night, Avril had never ventured back here. Isam hadn't returned but stayed in Zahdar since commencing his reign.

Because of her?

Unlikely. It was clear the man she'd thought she knew didn't exist. She'd fallen for a mirage. She'd invested Isam with a character that matched his outwardly attractive appearance. Now she had the real measure of the man. Not admirable. Not attractive. Not worth pining over.

Avril smoothed her hand down the russet fabric of her

straight skirt. It wasn't new, she wasn't going to waste her money on a new outfit for this meeting. But it was a favourite, even if the fit wasn't quite as it used to be, and it made her feel good.

'Thank you,' she murmured as the minder led her into the suite then opened the door to the conference room.

She stepped over the threshold and heard the door snick closed behind her. On the other side of the table sat three men in suits. She only had eyes for the tall one in the centre.

Her heart took up a rackety beat, pounding her ribs as she met clear, pale eyes. Something like an electric charge jolted through her. Despite being prepared for this meeting, moisture tickled her hairline and bloomed across her palms, making her tighten her grip on her laptop case.

He stared straight back at her and her peripheral vision dimmed as her focus narrowed to eyes the colour of a grey winter's morning. Eyes that scrutinised but gave nothing away. Eyes that didn't flicker with even the tiniest hint of pleasure or welcome.

Avril *thought* she'd been prepared, thought Isam couldn't hurt her any more, but that unresponsive stare pierced the armour she'd spent so long constructing.

She put her palm to the centre of her chest, trying to hold in sharp stabbing pain.

'Ms Rodgers? Ms Rodgers.' She turned stiff neck muscles to find a man beside her. He was in his forties, with a round face that looked more suited to smiling than the frown he wore now. He wore a bespoke suit and concern in his eyes. 'Please, won't you take a seat?'

Looking from him to the empty seat beside the Sheikh, she realised he'd come around the long table to her. How long had she stood there, aware of nothing but Isam?

'Thank you.'

She sat as he introduced himself and the man still seated

next to Isam. But she didn't retain their names, too frantically
focusing on trying not to show how badly shocked she felt.

'And you know Sheikh Isam,' he added.

Belatedly she realised she hadn't remembered the obliga-
tory curtsey for Zahdar's head of state. Not that the man deserved a curtsey.

Avril inclined her head. 'Yes, we've met.'

Was it imagination or was there a ripple of reaction to that?
No, not a ripple. More a sudden stillness, as if her words put
them all on alert.

Probably imagination. She made an effort to get a grip.
There, that was better. A slow breath out as she clasped the
arms of her leather chair. She was in control of herself now.
The worst moment was over.

They'd seated her on the opposite side of the table. As if for
an interview. Did they think to intimidate her with formality?

Her attention returned to Isam, directly opposite. He leaned
sideways as his companion murmured something. Without
his steely gaze on her she scanned his features, stunned at
the changes in him and even more at how familiar he was.
Her fingers twitched as if remembering the smooth flesh of
his back and rounded buttocks, or clutching at his thick, surprisingly soft hair as they kissed.

His cheekbones were the same, sharply defined with angles a camera, or a besotted woman, would love. His mouth
was pursed rather than relaxed and his nostrils flared as if
something annoyed him.

But what caught her attention were the deep grooves
carved around his mouth. The lines at his eyes hinted now
at pain rather than pleasure. And of course the scars. A web
of them at one side of his brow, extending up into his hairline.

Simmering anger disappeared, replaced by dismay. She'd
known he was injured in the helicopter crash that killed his

father soon after Isam's return to Zahdar. But seeing the evidence brought a sharp, iron taste to her tongue.

It took a moment to realise she'd bitten her lip in distress.

When the accident happened she'd been frantic with worry. The Zahdari press had provided little insight into his condition. Every press release from the palace had seemed designed to obfuscate.

But eventually there'd been good news. Reports of the new Sheikh out of hospital, recuperating privately. Then of him taking up the reins of government. Then a few photo opportunities showing him at a distance, usually consulting with elders or opening some new facility.

Abruptly Isam turned and she felt the force of his stare like an assault. It seemed to drive right into her, probing and analysing. Threatening to shatter the hard-fought-for equilibrium she'd finally achieved.

What did he want from her?

'Thank you for coming today, Ms Rodgers.' It was the man with the round face and glasses who spoke. 'His Majesty is reviewing his interests in the UK, hence today's meeting.'

Did you really expect him to come here to take up where you left off that night? To see how you were? If you were okay?

Pursing her lips, she inclined her head. She'd known this would be a business meeting.

She still had to work out how she could get time alone with Isam. Despite her deep-seated disgust at his behaviour, there were things she needed to say. Things that weren't for the ears of strangers.

'If you don't mind, we'll start with your position.'

Avril started. Her position? Her gaze darted to Isam's but his steady stare was blank. She breathed deep.

She lifted her chin. Two could play at being aloof. 'What do you want to know?'

She kept her focus on Isam but again it was the man beside him who spoke. 'Your role, for a start.'

That wrenched her attention to him. 'I'm His Majesty's PA in the United Kingdom.'

'His Majesty hasn't given you any instructions for some time. Yet you continue to draw a salary.'

It was the thin man on Isam's other side who spoke, the one who looked as if he'd swallowed a lemon. He made it sound like an accusation, as if Avril had done something wrong, stealing from the royal coffers instead of struggling to manage responsibilities beyond her remit because her boss had lost interest in his enterprises here and cut off communication.

Her hackles rose. It certainly wasn't her fault!

'I'm afraid that's something you need to take up with His Majesty, not me.' She turned to skewer Isam with a glare that should have pinned his worthless hide to his chair.

'Since his last visit I've managed as best I can. I was given clear parameters about regular auditing of and reporting from his UK enterprises. There are quite of few of them.' And not all had been happy at the lack of direct contact from Isam, leaving her to handle their expectations when she herself didn't know what to expect. 'You'll find full updates and progress reports in my regular emails.'

As well as her desperate appeals for him to contact her. All of which remained unanswered. Her chest rose on a shuddering breath but she sat straight, shoulders back and chin up.

Still Isam said nothing, yet she saw a flash of something in his expression that told her he wasn't as cool as he appeared. Good! He deserved to squirm, ignoring her calls and emails. Presumably, too, informing his staff not to accept any call she made to the palace.

She'd spent too long and given up too much of her pride

trying to contact him. She wasn't in the mood to put up with any more nonsense.

'As you say, a series of emails, yes.' The first interviewer looked down at his notes. When he lifted his head his smile was easy yet instinct told her he hid something. 'And the email address you sent it to? I'm afraid I didn't have time to make myself a copy of the relevant reports before the meeting.'

Avril frowned, darting a look at Isam, but he was in whispered conversation with the other man. This was beyond odd. Why let his staff question her about her job rather than focusing on the work that badly needed his attention?

She spelled out the email address, watching as it was written down. 'If there's anything in particular you need to see, I can show you now.'

She put her laptop on the table and watched three pairs of eyes swivel to look.

'Your work device?' asked the thin man with the dour expression. At her nod he continued. 'Excellent. If you could call up the most recent report that would be useful.'

Avril did as requested, but, instead of asking questions, the thin man walked around the table and with murmured thanks took the laptop back to his seat.

Startled, she looked at Isam for explanation. Didn't he trust her any more?

He didn't look quite so detached now. Long fingers massaged his temple, making her wonder if he had a headache, and as their eyes met she saw something that might be regret.

As if! She was the one who'd learnt about regret. And that her instincts were severely flawed around this man.

The first interviewer interrupted her thoughts. 'Now, Ms Rodgers, perhaps you'd like to tell me about your work history, your skills?'

'Sorry?'

'I'm interested in why you applied for the position and what you brought to it.'

Indignation rose as a premonition rippled down her spine. They were going to sack her?

Avril didn't mind that. She no longer wanted to work for Isam ibn Rafat. She should have resigned long ago instead of holding out that secret hope that he'd finally contact her and they'd talk. But she'd not allow them to imply it was because of the standard of her work.

She turned to the man she'd once esteemed. More than esteemed. 'Isam.' Protocol be damned. 'Do you want to tell me what this is about?'

In her peripheral vision she saw his minders stare at her use of his personal name. It was probably an offence back in Zahdar. The dour man's jaw actually dropped and the other one darted a wide-eyed look at his sheikh.

Her boss, her one-time lover, took his time responding and every second felt like a new betrayal.

'I know this seems unnecessary, given that you've worked for me for some time. But we're bringing my UK interests in line with my other investments. That means a detailed review of current arrangements.'

It was the first time Avril had heard his voice in over a year and she was shocked by how it affected her. Deep and smooth, with just a hint of huskiness, it trawled through her, snagging on sensitive spots, drawing a flurry of excited response.

Her hands tightened around the chair's armrests and her thighs clamped together in instinctive rejection of that lush softening at the entrance to her body.

How could her body betray her after the way he'd treated her? He'd used then ignored her as if she were nothing.

'Rashid here—' he nodded to the man with glasses '—oversees all palace staff. Before I became Sheikh I preferred to manage my British investments personally rather than through Zahdar's public service. But now, as Sheikh, it makes sense to draw it all together under one umbrella.'

He lifted those broad shoulders in a shrug that should have made his statement reassuring, as if the review were a trifle, but the movement was stiff. Did he still carry injuries from the crash?

Avril jerked her thoughts back. Isam would have the world's best specialists attending him. She needed to concentrate on what this meant for her position.

Avril had told herself that cutting ties with Isam was the only way forward, though it meant finding a new position when she least felt up to it. But to be chucked out on the pretence of not doing her job, just because he was embarrassed by her presence, was beyond the pale.

'So you're rationalising and looking to sack me?'

That, at last, drew a reaction from Isam. He leaned towards her, horizontal lines grooving his forehead. 'I didn't come with any such intention. This is an information-gathering session only.'

He seemed so earnest, so persuasive, she was tempted to believe him.

Until she remembered the man who'd left her over a year ago with a promise to return in two weeks. She'd understood when he didn't. The crash that injured him and killed his father had made international headlines. So she'd waited, hoping, fearing and praying for his recovery.

And then…nothing. Not a call, not an email, not a response to any of her messages. His phone was unanswered and palace staff had been polite yet dismissive when she'd called the switchboard.

'Perhaps it would be easiest if we started with how your previous work fitted you for your current position.'

At Rashid's words she reluctantly turned to him. 'I can supply my résumé if necessary. I worked my way up through a series of positions until I was personal assistant to Berthold Keller.'

That grabbed her audience's attention. Rashid's eyes widened. 'The property magnate?'

'That's him.'

'But you must be no more than in your mid-twenties. That's a very senior position at a young age.'

She'd turned twenty-seven a few months ago. 'I'm pleased to say my previous employer valued competence over seniority.'

She spared Isam a sideways glance, challenging him to comment, but of course he said nothing. At least this session was destroying the last of her silly yearning for a man who'd only existed in her imaginings.

'I'm very good at what I do.'

Cilla had said she had an old head on young shoulders. She was organised and hard-working, with an eye for detail, traits learned from her great-aunt, along with the desire to be financially independent.

'So why did you leave?'

'Working for Mr Keller involved a lot of travel, which was stimulating, but over time I realised I wanted to stay in London.' Because Cilla, her feisty, independent great-aunt, had grown physically fragile. 'It was Mr Keller who recommended me to the Sheikh.'

In response to Rashid's questioning look, Isam nodded. 'He's a friend. I respect his judgement.'

Then he rose, resting his palm on the gleaming wood as if for support. But any thought that his injuries had weakened him physically were banished as he straightened to stand tall and imposing. There was no weakness in this man just as there was no softness.

It had been her mistake ever to imagine such a thing.

Even so, Avril's pulse spurred in anticipation of his invitation to follow her for a private conversation.

'If you'll excuse me…' his gaze swept the three of them '…there's something I must do. I'm confident you'll make good progress without me.'

His gaze met hers for the briefest of seconds. This time it wasn't blankly disinterested. His eyes looked stormy and she could almost imagine a bolt of lightning tearing through the room. She shivered in response to some unseen reverberation.

Then, to her astonishment, Isam left without a backward glance. As if she held no more interest for him.

CHAPTER FOUR

ISAM STRODE THROUGH the suite, his steps growing longer and faster. The straitjacket binding his shoulders and upper arms tightened and the talons ripping through his gut sharpened, threatening to shred his self-control.

Finally he reached the sanctuary of his room.

His head throbbed with a familiar ache that he'd learned to despise. It was the reminder of all he lacked. Of the weakness he hid from all but a trusted few.

But he didn't reach for pain relief. Instead he sank into a tall wingchair, leaning his head back against the upholstery and squeezing his eyes shut.

Instead of darkness he saw grey, shot through with snatches of light. They were fragments, like a shattered window pane, separate and useless.

Like you.

He firmed his jaw. No, not useless. Just not as he was.

A bitter laugh rumbled up from his chest but he didn't let it escape. He couldn't allow self-pity.

Besides, what had he to feel sorry about? He was alive and almost whole. Whereas his father...

Isam breathed through the racking pain of loss that still, sometimes, seemed too great to bear.

Easier by far, and necessary, to concentrate on the problem that was Avril Rodgers.

The disjointed pattern in his mind's eye transformed into

a woman. Thick brown hair swept up behind her head in a businesslike bun. Businesslike, too, her court shoes and skirt suit.

But there'd been nothing businesslike in the way he noticed her. The tight fit of her rust-coloured jacket over her breasts. The purity of skin that he imagined to be as soft as the petal of a creamy rose. The restrained yet unmissably feminine sway of her body as she crossed the room.

Even the smudges of tiredness under her eyes made her controlled professionalism seemed gallant, as if weariness would never interfere with her ability to do her job or stand up for herself.

He swallowed hard, knowing she was different. *Feeling* it in every pore of his body. Despite a natural masculine tendency to notice an attractive woman, he didn't usually react so viscerally.

The radiance of her brown eyes, warmed by glints of gold, made him think of welcoming firelight on a chill desert night. The way her lips pouted when she was annoyed and the flash of hauteur, when she thought her competence questioned, intrigued and invited.

He couldn't prevent a snort of laughter. She'd looked daggers at him. There was no invitation there.

But that hadn't stopped his reaction.

His pulse accelerated as broken images teased him.

The curve where her neck met her shoulder. His nostrils flared on the scent of aroused woman and wild honey and his lips tingled at the brush of velvet-soft skin.

The flare of shock in warm brown eyes, accompanied by a whispered gasp, before she relaxed against him, her eyelids dropping to half-mast in a sultry look of invitation as her body welcomed him.

A ruched, dark pink nipple cresting a breast so perfect the sight of it dried his mouth. The feel of her breast, just the right size for his hand that trembled as he cupped such beauty.

Isam's eyes snapped open as blood surged into his groin. How long since any woman had made him so weak with desire, so quickly?

He'd come to London knowing he had issues to resolve. Things he had to deal with before he could continue to give his full focus to his country. It had been a challenging year. All Zahdar mourned his father and looked to Isam for reassurance, while he still struggled with his loss. This had been one of the most difficult times of his life.

Yet beyond all the urgent demands on his time there had been a niggling urge to set aside his duties and the worries of a nation, and come to London. Of course he'd put his people first and remained at home. He understood they'd feared he might die from his injuries too.

But now you're here, what next?

One look at Avril Rodgers had told him this wouldn't be easy. She'd been left to her own devices for over a year, a situation that needed to be rectified immediately.

But he couldn't concentrate on office arrangements and communication protocols. Not when she bombarded his brain with sensual impressions that sent it into overload.

In the early days after the accident there'd been times when concentration was difficult. When he'd felt his mind fight for focus. When brain fog had been a constant barrier to progress. He'd been told not to worry, that he *would* improve. But to a man used to decisiveness, proud of his mental agility and focus, that had been far worse than the various breaks, bruises and lacerations.

Avril threatened that focus more than he'd imagined possible. Alarmingly so.

There was no way Rashid and his staff could fix that. Isam had to do that for himself. Alone.

* * *

The doorbell rang after dusk and Avril rolled her eyes. Would this day ever end?

She'd gone to Isam's hotel sure that at least she'd have the satisfaction of telling him what she thought of him. But the coward had walked away, leaving her to defend her work and her character to his minions.

Then, as soon as she'd walked in the door hours ago she'd been run off her feet. She hadn't even had time to change out of her office clothes, simply stepping out of her shoes and promising herself a long soak in the bath later, if she could keep her eyes open.

Though, given her indignation at how today's meeting had played out, she suspected sleep wouldn't come easily tonight.

She stifled a yawn as she walked to the front door, then, realising who it must be, she smiled as she opened it. 'Gus, it's lovely—'

Her words died as she registered, not the comfortable round outline of her neighbour, Augusta, but a towering form, all hard, masculine angles. She'd know those shoulders anywhere and the proud angle of that head.

Without even thinking about it she swung the heavy door forward. Instinct was a skittering creature racing up her spine, whispering in her ear that having that man in her home would be disastrous.

The door juddered to a stop. She pushed but it wouldn't budge. Looking down, she saw a large, glossy shoe wedged in the doorway. She hoped his foot was bruised.

'I don't want you in my home.'

From beyond the door a deep voice said, 'You'd rather we had this conversation on the doorstep? For the entertainment of your neighbours?'

Avril opened her mouth to say her neighbours were lovely, unlike him, then snapped it shut.

'Or shall we have this out in my suite? Perhaps over the conference table with Rashid taking notes?'

She yanked the door open so hard it almost bounced off the wall beside her.

'Don't you come here with your threats. You think you're a big man, high-ranking and powerful. But there are more important things in life. Respect, for one.' She jammed her hands on her hips and seared him with her scorn. 'Common decency.'

She was so incensed at his nerve in coming to her house after effectively dismissing her earlier, she could barely catch her breath. *That* was why her breathing was so choppy, her breasts rising so vigorously they tested the buttons of her blouse.

Avril crossed her arms over her chest.

'We need to talk.' Something in his tone quelled her surge of anger. He didn't sound smug, but strained. 'We both know it.'

Finally she nodded. 'We do. Tomorrow. I'll meet you some-where.' Somewhere neutral like a coffee shop. 'What time—?'

'Not tomorrow. Now.' When she didn't respond, merely lifted her eyebrows in a show of disdain, he continued. 'My time in London is limited. Most of it is accounted for. If we want a private discussion it needs to be now.'

'Surely a king can set his own timetable.'

He merely shook his head slowly as if to say she had no idea of his schedule.

And he'd be right. What did she know of royal life? The few days she'd spent with him had been remarkable for their informality.

Informality! Hysterical laughter at the understatement threatened her composure.

Avril had sudden recall of how it had felt when he'd taken her to bliss with his body, then held her close, whispering words of affection. Even now the deep timbre of his voice made something loosen inside her.

She'd wanted to see him for so long. Been desperate to see him. Now here he was and it was like a nightmare. Nothing was as she'd once hoped. Even her determination to despise him was undercut by her body's response to his nearness.

'Avril?' Her gaze lifted to his and was trapped. His eyes gleamed pewter-dark. Did she imagine they looked troubled? 'Let me in.'

Reluctantly she stepped aside and he walked past, so close her skin prickled and she closed her eyes in momentary despair. She loathed this man. He'd treated her badly. Yet her yearning body hadn't yet got the message. But after tonight she'd probably never see him. One way or another she wouldn't work for Isam after this.

'To the left.'

She followed him in to see him standing, surveying the old-fashioned furniture. The packed bookcases and clutter of photos. The thought of him snooping through her life, hers and Cilla's, made her step forward to stand in front of the display.

'Take a seat.' Because she'd feel better if he weren't dominating the room with his height.

But it wasn't just his height. He'd always had an energy about him, a charisma she'd never been able to ignore.

To her relief he sank into a large armchair, looking just as at home as he did at that dauntingly large conference table.

Or naked in bed. His musculature and that fine dusting of hair across his chest utterly fascinating.

Appalled at her thoughts, Avril took a chair opposite him. She didn't offer refreshments. This wasn't a social occasion. Just as well Cilla wasn't here. She'd been a stickler for polite niceties.

'Why are you here?'

'I thought that would be obvious. To talk about us.'

'There *is* no us! You made that clear when you refused to answer my calls and messages.'

A flicker of emotion crossed his face but she couldn't pin it down. He looked down at his hands, triangled in front of him with fingertips touching.

'You tried to contact me.'

It wasn't a question but a statement. Yet there was something about his tone that made her hesitate for a second. But she wasn't in the mood to play games. They both knew how he'd treated her.

'Of course I tried to contact you. Even if I didn't have work issues to discuss, I was worried.' At least at first. 'Your crash made world headlines. But no one seemed to know how badly injured you really were.'

Grey eyes lifted and met hers. 'As you see, I'm fine.'

He didn't look fine, she realised with a shock of clarity that made her insides twist. He looked…gaunt, as if a sculptor had chiselled his features but gone too far, accentuating deep chasms and angles and not leaving enough flesh on the bone. In the conference room she hadn't noticed, too caught up in her own emotions.

'I'm sorry about your father.'

She knew what grief was like. At least her great-aunt had reached a venerable age and her decline had given them both time to prepare. It must be terrible to lose a loved one so suddenly.

'Thank you.' He nodded. 'He was a good man and I miss him.'

For a moment they regarded each other and Avril could have sworn she felt the ebb and flow of understanding between them.

No. No. No! Don't start fantasising now. He's not that man.

It was time to remind them both that she had his measure.

'I emailed you, multiple times. I called but got no answer.

When you didn't contact me, even when you were out of hospital and taking up your duties again, I called both the Zahdari Embassy here and then your palace, leaving messages.'

The memory of those fraught months reinvigorated her indignation and hurt. She hadn't expected long-term commitment as a result of the night they'd shared. She was no blind romantic. But he'd made it clear he wanted to see her again.

He'd acted as if he cared about her.

More fool you.

'And I didn't get in touch.' He rested his forehead on his hand, his elbow on the arm of the chair. 'I'm sorry, Avril. I—' He looked up, frowning. 'What's that?'

The sound began low and soft, like the warning hint of thunder in the distance, making her sit up, dismay filling her. She knew from experience the storm would break all too soon.

She jumped to her feet. 'Excuse me. There's something I need to see to. I won't be long.' She hoped. 'Wait here.'

It was only as she hurried from the room that she realised she was in stockinged feet and wisps of hair hung around her face. It would have been nice to meet him looking cool instead of frazzled. But her appearance was the least of her worries. Her heart hammered desperately.

She stumbled up the stairs, weariness vying with shock. For, after months knocking her head against a brick wall, trying to contact Isam, she'd learnt she was better off without him. Today had just consolidated that, convincing her he didn't need to know about this.

This was her business, not his.

Given the way he'd discarded her without a second thought, without even the courtesy of a call, she'd never trust him with anything so valuable.

The decibels rose as she reached the landing at the top of

the stairs and dived into the first room, closing the door behind her.

A couple of minutes later, arms full, she turned at the sound of the door opening, her heart leaping into her throat.

There was Isam, looking ridiculously splendid in his tailored suit and impeccable silk tie, his shoulders almost brushing the sides of the narrow doorway. He looked as out of place in her little home as she would in a palace.

His eyes rounded as he took her in. Swiftly he surveyed the room, taking in the recent changes she'd made, then returned to the weight in her arms.

'You have a baby?'

Her arms tightened around Maryam as she swayed and jiggled, trying to persuade her to go back to sleep.

'Evidently.'

Now he looked more than surprised. He looked stunned. 'It's yours?'

Avril had thought of this moment for so long. She'd imagined so many different scenarios. But now it came to it, the words stuck in her mouth. Her emotions were still so up and down. Half the time she didn't know if her daughter was a glorious blessing or a test she'd fail, despite her best efforts.

She nodded jerkily and lifted the baby higher in her arms, patting her back.

But Maryam refused to be soothed, her grizzles becoming a full-blown cry that made perspiration bead Avril's nape and her stomach churn. She'd spent ages getting the little one settled to sleep. Was it going to be another bad night like last night?

She turned to pace the room. The warm bundle in her arms was familiar now after almost four months, and she loved her daughter dearly, but she was incredibly aware of her lack of experience as a mother.

She'd never been around young children. Never had

younger siblings or cousins. She'd been brought up by an elderly woman whose friends were, in the main, old. Avril had never babysat before she came home from hospital with this precious, fascinating, demanding bundle.

Gus, next door, was a fountain of useful information and practical help. Occasionally she'd pop around in the evening with a hot meal she'd cooked, offering to keep an eye on Maryam while Avril ate. For Avril's daughter had the unerring ability to wake, crying, just when her mother sat down to eat or take a bath. As for sleeping…

Avril turned to find Isam had moved into the room, making the nursery smaller than ever.

'You should leave. I'll meet you tomorrow. You'll just have to find time for me in your schedule.'

Was he even listening? His whole attention was on the baby. Avril's breathing snared. Was he noticing her mink-brown hair, so dark it looked almost black? Or her grey eyes?

Avril's arms tightened reflexively and Maryam wailed.

'Is she teething?'

Avril frowned. 'You know about babies?'

He lifted one shoulder, his attention still on her daughter. 'A bit.'

Once more Avril swung away, swaying Maryam and trying to soothe her. Without success. And when she turned there was Isam, frowning. Judging her for not being able to calm her child?

'I don't think she is. And it's not hunger,' Avril explained. 'I just fed her and she doesn't need changing.'

Grey eyes lifted to meet hers and fleetingly it felt as though understanding passed between them. 'Sometimes I think they just want company.'

She felt like saying Maryam had her company all the time. Today had been the first time she'd left her daughter, which had only added to the stress of that formal meeting. Gus had assured her that Maryam had been 'as good as gold' in her absence, leaving Avril wishing she could be a bit more content with her own mother.

'You look done in,' he murmured. 'Why don't you sit down and I'll hold her for a bit?'

She couldn't have been more astonished. But Isam's expression was serious and his tone gentle.

Too gentle. It was easier to feel competent and in control without what looked and sounded like sympathy.

His mouth lifted at one corner in a crooked smile that made her insides squeeze. 'It's a long time since I held a baby.'

He *wanted* to hold her squalling daughter? Or was he just being kind?

Of course he's being kind. But why?

'How long has it been?'

His smile stiffened but he stepped closer. 'My sister was eleven years younger than me.'

Was. Of course, she'd read when researching for her job that he'd had a sibling, but hadn't paid much attention. Now she glimpsed something in Isam's face that made her ashamed not to have registered how much losing his sister must have meant to him.

Spurred by emotions she didn't stop to consider, Avril let him lift her daughter from her arms. As soon as she saw his confident hold and the way Maryam, surprised by the newcomer, stared up at him, something eased inside Avril. Her knees loosened and she sank abruptly into the cushioned rocking chair that she'd brought upstairs for feeding time.

Maryam frowned up at him and he bent his head, all his attention on her. It was strange, seeing them so close together.

Her tiny daughter and this big man who sheltered her so easily against his broad chest. The sight of his protective stance and his absorption made Avril feel strange.

When Maryam waved a tiny hand in the air he offered his

finger for her to clutch, and that strange feeling burst into something stronger. A fierce melting, a drawing sensation through Avril's belly, while her heart stuttered before picking up a quickened beat.

She was so lost in her thoughts it took a while to register that her daughter was no longer crying. And that Isam was crooning something she couldn't understand. The baritone rumble of it tunnelled through her body, making taut muscles loosen and easing her jittery tension.

Her brain told her to get up and take care of Maryam herself. But she was exhausted. Would it really hurt to sit quietly just for a few minutes?

How long she sat there, she didn't know. His lullaby worked on her too. She felt her bones melt into the upholstery as she relaxed properly for the first time in what seemed ages. It was only as he moved towards the cot that her drowsy eyelids lifted.

She said nothing as he put the baby down. Maryam's long dark lashes curled across perfect cheeks and her rosebud mouth made her look like an angel. A rush of maternal emotion sideswiped Avril, making her blink and get up to fuss with the blanket until Isam moved away.

Neither spoke until they were downstairs.

'How did you do that?' she asked as they entered the front room.

Avril had lost count of the number of times she'd sung lullabies and walked the floor with her daughter.

He shrugged. 'Maybe I was just different enough to distract her until she dropped off.'

Avril had a feeling it wasn't that simple. Again she wondered about her own competence. Maybe Maryam had picked up on her stress despite her best efforts at seeming calm.

Or maybe you're beating yourself up over nothing.

'What's her name?'

Warily, Avril pursed her lips. But after what he'd just done she owed him this at least. 'Maryam.'

He stiffened, his eyes narrowing. 'That's an Arabic name.'

'Is it?'

You know it is. But you could mention it's used in other languages too.

'You didn't know?'

He paused, waiting for her answer, his gaze searching.

Now the moment had come she wasn't sure she could go through with it. For a year she'd been determined to share this, but today she'd convinced herself that discretion was better. For her daughter and herself.

Yet after seeing him upstairs…

Isam shoved his hands in his trouser pockets, the movement pulling open his jacket to reveal a wet spot on his pristine shirt. Drool from where he'd snuggled her daughter close.

'Avril, you haven't answered me.'

She wrapped her arms around her middle. 'I knew. I looked it up. I like the name but I also wanted something that worked in both English and Arabic.'

He said nothing but his eyes silvered as he stared at her, and she saw his pulse thrum hard.

She drew a sustaining breath. 'She's your daughter.'

He stood utterly still. It was only the flare of his nostrils and that rapid pulse at his temple that proved he was alive, not some graven image.

'My daughter? Our daughter?'

'She was born thirty-nine weeks after you left London.' His head jerked back as if in denial or belated shock. But surely he'd begun to guess upstairs. 'She's ours. Conceived the night before you flew to Zahdar.'

Isam might be good with babies but he wasn't in any hurry to accept fatherhood. He shook his head then turned on his heel and crossed to look out onto the dark street.

Be fair. It took you long enough to get over the shock of being pregnant.

Minutes later he swung back. But instead of excitement or the tenderness she'd seen when he looked at the baby, his expression was set, sending a ripple of disquiet through her.

'We'll need a paternity test. I'll arrange it. Someone will come tomorrow.'

Now it was Avril who rocked back in shock. When she found her voice it was strident but undercut by a telling wobble. 'You don't believe me? You think I'm lying about my *daughter*?'

'It doesn't matter what I think, Avril. I'm a king. Others will need to be convinced. This needs irrefutable proof.'

This. As if her beloved daughter were a *thing* not a person.

She unwound her arms from around her middle. Barely she resisted the urge to walk across and slap him for his unfeeling arrogance. Instead she planted her palms on her hips, feeling the strength of righteous indignation and a rush of adrenaline flow in her bloodstream.

'I don't care that you're a king. I don't want anything from you. Ever.' She moved close enough to make sure he read the fury in her eyes. 'Now get out of my house. I never want to see you again.'

CHAPTER FIVE

IN THE END it was easier the next day to agree to the paternity test than fight it.

Because despite her anger and her hurt that Isam refused to believe her, Avril knew Maryam deserved to have proof of her paternity. Especially since he seemed determined to deny it. Plus it required only a simple cheek swab, no needles.

But what really convinced Avril was the visitor who arrived that morning. A grey-haired woman with one of the kindest smiles she'd ever seen. She said she'd been hired through an agency to provide any assistance Avril required, cooking, cleaning, shopping or helping with the baby.

Avril was in the process of sending her away, hating Isam's presumption that she couldn't manage, when her visitor's wide smile dimmed. She confessed she was finding her recent retirement boring and had leapt at the chance to put her skills to use. She missed being around people, especially babies.

Somehow Avril ended up with a sheaf of recommendations in her hand and a résumé that indicated Bethany had been an early childhood educator before retiring.

A couple of phone calls later, Avril had reassured herself the woman was genuine. By which time Bethany had brought her a mug of tea and a slice of the home-made fruitcake she'd brought. The rich flavour was so like that of Cilla's home baking, it had Avril blinking back tears.

By the end of the day, which included a nap from which

Avril woke feeling more refreshed than she had in ages, Avril and Bethany had bonded. The older woman wasn't bossy or judgemental. She had an easy confidence around Maryam and a caring nature. Her reassurance that Avril was doing well, adapting to a new baby, even eased some of her niggling anxiety.

Isam might not want to take an active role in his daughter's life, but something good had come out of his guilt. Avril would accept Bethany's assistance while she could.

She suspected she and Maryam would thrive with the older woman's assistance, which was important. Especially as Avril needed to start looking for a new job. She had money to tide her over for a while after she left her current position, but the sooner she started looking, the better.

She had so much on her mind she could almost have ignored the fact that Isam didn't contact her that day.

When she'd told him to leave the night before he'd surveyed her for what seemed an age, then turned and walked out into the night, leaving her stricken and trembling with an excess of emotion.

Avril hadn't believed he'd go so easily. But he'd probably been desperate to escape the complications she and Maryam represented. She had no idea how children born outside marriage were treated in his country, but suspected a monarch fathering a child by a foreigner wouldn't be generally approved. Royals were cautious about bloodlines and as a new king he'd be particularly eager to avoid scandal.

Maybe he was planning a dynastic marriage. Probably she and her daughter were an inconvenient embarrassment.

She got through the rest of the day trying and failing not to think about the man with the piercing eyes and tight, angular features that made her wonder how much he'd suffered after that crash.

But the night after Bethany arrived, Avril slept long and deep, and for once Maryam wasn't as restless as usual.

Yet when Avril woke, it was to realise she'd dreamt of Isam. Not the rigid man who'd retreated from his child, then left without a backward glance. But the man she'd fallen more than a little in love with last year. The man who embodied an irresistible combination of tenderness and masculine power. Her skin was damp and there was a twisting ache deep in her pelvis as she shoved the bedclothes back and got up.

Later that day Avril was updating her résumé while Bethany looked after Maryam upstairs, when the doorbell rang.

Isam stood tall and imposing but she noticed the dark shadows in his eyes and tension—or was it pain?—grooved around his mouth.

Avril refused to worry about him. He had a kingdom full of people to do that. Instead she folded her arms and stood her ground. 'What brings you back? We've nothing more to say.'

Someone would send the results of the test, and Avril had decided to accept his guilt gift of temporary mother's help.

His jaw clenched but his tone was disarmingly gentle as he said, 'I'm sorry you feel that way, but we have to talk. For Maryam's sake as much as anything else.'

For a minute longer Avril stood unmoving before reluctantly stepping aside. He was right. For Maryam's sake they had to set some parameters for the future.

She led the way into the front room, feeling the atmosphere change from slightly cluttered comfort to sparking awareness as he followed her in. Once again they sat opposite each other.

'The test result is in.'

'So quickly?' She shook her head. 'Of course, being royal you could pull strings. And so? If you're going to tell me it proved you're Maryam's father, don't bother. I already know. I was a virgin before we got together.'

Something flared in the gunmetal grey of his eyes. It

looked like surprise. Yet her innocence must have been obvious to him that night. She'd been enthusiastic but not adept.

'I'll have a copy of that report please.' She held her hand out. 'I want Maryam to have proof, since you're so keen on denying her.'

'Denying her?'

How could he deny his own child? Why would he even want to? He knew how precious life was and how easily it could be snatched away.

Isam's chest tightened at the thought of anything happening to his tiny daughter. When he'd held her he'd felt a rush of emotion so powerful it had strained his self-control to relinquish her into the cot and walk away.

One look and he'd suspected her identity. Even the shock of that suspicion hadn't diminished his sense of wonder.

The feel of her in his arms, the way she looked, even that clean baby smell, forcefully reminded him of holding Nur all those years ago. The uprush of emotion had almost cracked his composure. But years of training as Crown Prince had come to his aid, enabling him to hide his wonder, excitement and yearning. And the grief that welled at the memory of Nur.

Suddenly, he had family once more. His mother had died when Nur was born. So when his sister, and more recently his father died, there was only him.

He'd been grappling with so much this past year that he hadn't allowed himself to dwell on that, though grief for his father was a constant. But now he was no longer alone.

'Isn't that what you're doing? A paternity test is hardly the action of a man wanting to accept his child. It's what men do to try wriggling out of their responsibilities.'

Avril folded her arms, the action drawing her T-shirt tight across her breasts and making his palms tingle as if wanting to reach out…

'Don't worry, as far as I'm concerned you won't have any responsibilities. I've learnt the sort of man you are. I'll raise my daughter alone.'

He met Avril's accusing stare and realised she was serious.

The sort of man you are.

Bitterness twisted his lips. That was the sixty-four-million-dollar question, wasn't it? What sort of man was he?

Once Isam had never thought that in doubt. He was honest and hard-working. He had a sense of humour and enjoyed time with friends, especially adventuring on desert trips or kayaking, though he didn't have much free time. He'd spent recent years working with his father for the betterment of his country, though mainly behind the scenes while he managed his own business too. His father had had more patience for the restrictions of royal protocol that Isam found so constricting.

But since the accident Isam's character and abilities had been called into question. Not outright. No one would dare. But the arrangements made to govern the country while he was incapacitated had given some a taste for regal power they hadn't wanted to relinquish. Nevertheless, it was disappointing to know there'd been a whispering campaign against him emanating from that direction.

So easy to blame others. But given your...continuing problem, can you be completely sure of yourself?

Isam refused to acknowledge the poisonous voice in his head. It only came on the darkest days, which, thankfully, were growing fewer.

One step at a time.

'A paternity test is also the action of a sensible man in a position of power.' He refused to apologise for that. It was the reality of his life. 'You must realise it was a reasonable precaution. It doesn't mean I'm rejecting our daughter.'

He saw Avril's eyes grow wide at his emphasis on the word

our. She swallowed and he guessed that behind her bravado she was scared.

Who could blame her? The stakes were high and they were all but strangers to each other.

'Maryam is *ours*,' he reiterated. 'Not simply yours, not simply mine.'

'So the real issue was that you didn't believe me. You had to make sure I wasn't lying.' Her expression betrayed disappointment and hurt rather than anger, and Isam felt it like a gut punch, driving hard enough it threatened to wind him. The depth of his reaction surprised him. 'What did I ever do to make you think me a liar, Isam? We worked together for months. We had a good relationship. I thought you knew me.'

'Sex isn't the same as knowing someone. Our affair—'

'I wasn't talking about *sex.*'

She interrupted as no one else did, her tone dismissive.

At home everyone was conscious of his royal status. Trying to have a discussion with Avril Rodgers could be frustrating but he preferred her honest emotion to blind subservience. Or those who paid lip service to respect while manoeuvring against him.

She went on. 'I'm talking about the way we worked together. You respected me then. You liked me too. I didn't imagine that. We shared a camaraderie.' Her mouth firmed. 'And I'd hardly call the other an affair.'

The other?

She sounded scornful, as if she hadn't enjoyed sex with him. Despite the gravity of the current situation, which far outweighed whatever carnal joy they'd had, Isam bristled. No woman had ever found him an unsatisfactory lover.

'What would you call it, then, if not an affair?'

She couldn't have thought he was offering a permanent relationship! Even foreigners understood that a king's bride had to meet a whole slew of requirements.

It would be disastrous for a royal sheikh to marry a woman who wasn't up to the job.

His wife would be more than his companion and lover. She'd be Queen of Zahdar. She'd help him in his work to support their people and keep their country thriving, with the best prospects for the future. She'd be in the public eye every day, a role model to many.

Avril made a dismissive gesture. 'I'd call it a one-night stand. What else?'

Isam heard the words but instantly rejected them. He jerked back in his seat, pulse chaotic and thoughts whirring.

'A one-night stand?'

He felt his eyes bulge. Saw her say something but couldn't make it out over the hammer of his pulse in his ears.

The edge of his vision misted, blurring into grey. But he saw her, every line and curve clearly defined.

She spoke again and this time he caught the words. 'I said, what else would you call it? We were only together for one night.'

A one-night stand!

With his personal assistant.

A woman dependent on him for employment and a reference.

A virgin.

A terrible, crawling sensation began in his belly, slithering all over him, making his flesh shrink against his bones.

What sort of man was he?

It seemed people had been right to question after all.

He shot to his feet, paced the small room, then paced back again, unable to sit still. Emotions thrashed through him, needing an outlet.

He swung around again and there was Avril, blocking his way. When she spoke her voice was softer. 'Isam. What is it? I don't understand.'

Nor did he. If anyone had told him he was a man who'd seduce an innocent then dump her after one night, he'd have been insulted. He'd have claimed it was impossible.

Maryam, their daughter, proved him wrong.

He clutched his head, pain flaring at the effort to dredge up the proof that it wasn't true.

'Isam! You're worrying me. Come and sit before you fall down.'

'I'm not going to fall,' he muttered. 'I'm in peak physical fitness.'

His rehabilitation regime had been taxing. Determined to recuperate quickly, he'd pushed himself even harder. He'd always been fit and now he was stronger physically than ever before.

'You're swaying on your feet. Your face has gone grey.'

She half led, half pushed him into a chair. Despite the adrenaline rush in his blood, he felt as if his bones melted into the welcoming upholstery. He trembled all over.

Shock. More than shock. He sometimes got this heady feeling when he pushed too hard. But not usually this bad.

Soft fingers touched his and he snapped his eyes open, surprised to find he'd shut them.

Avril was crouched before him, curling his fingers around a glass of water. 'Sip it slowly and don't move. I'll be back. I'm calling a doctor.'

'No doctor!'

Her jaw angled pugnaciously. 'You're obviously not well.' When he didn't reply she added, 'I don't want the hassle of a diplomatic incident. Imagine the complications if a head of state collapsed in my home.'

Her pragmatism gave him the jolt of normality he needed. He sipped the water and forced his mind to go blank, as blank as possible in the circumstances. When that didn't work he focused on his breathing. Soon he had himself under control.

'My apologies. I know what's wrong and I don't need a doctor. I didn't mean to scare you.'

He saw he'd done just that. Avril's expression was tense and she was still squatting before him, so near he felt he could lose himself in those golden brown eyes.

She rose but stayed close as if worried he'd stand up. 'You scared the life out of me. Are you unwell?'

'Not unwell.' Technically.

'And? You went as white as a sheet, then grey when I reminded you we'd only had one night together.' She paused, eyes narrowing. 'You looked...stunned.'

Isam knew he should divert the conversation in another direction. He'd become adept at that in the last months.

But something stopped him. Her genuine fear when she thought he was ill? Or the memory, the one that had kept him awake last night, of touching velvet-soft skin and hearing Avril sigh in pleasure?

Suddenly he felt exhausted at the need to keep his secret.

'How could you be stunned? You know it for a fact.'

He didn't answer. But he wondered what she saw in his expression for her eyes widened and her jaw dropped.

'Isam? I don't like that blank look. It's as if you're looking but not seeing.'

He was seeing, all right, but not enough. He drew a shuddering breath and gave her the truth. 'I take your word for the fact we just had one night. I'm afraid I don't remember. I have amnesia.'

CHAPTER SIX

ISAM WATCHED HER stumble back a step, eyes round with shock. 'Amnesia? That's…' Slowly she shook her head. 'Do people really get that? I thought it was only in movies.'

A bitter laugh cracked open Isam's tight lips. 'I wish.' How *much* he wished it only occurred in fiction. 'Unfortunately, I'm living proof it's real.'

'You mean, you don't remember *anything*?'

He hesitated. Very few people knew the full truth about his condition. Given his position as ruler of Zahdar, it was thought best to keep the situation confidential. The last thing his people needed was to lose confidence in him. The potential damage to investment, to the massive development projects he and his father had initiated, even potentially to the peace of his nation, was too great.

But already he and Avril shared a potentially inflammatory secret, their daughter. He had to trust her. Besides, instinct urged that she wouldn't betray him.

But can you trust your instincts? Maybe even the memories you do have are flawed and your image of yourself distorted.

That was what some would have him believe. But Isam couldn't allow himself to think that way. He *had* to believe in himself, and now, in Avril.

'I have lots of memories. It's only what happened in the six months or so before the chopper crash that are foggy.'

Foggy. That's a nice euphemism. Why not admit it's basically a great, yawning gap?

'And I don't remember the crash or its immediate aftermath.'

The doctors said it was because of the blow to his head, but the emotional trauma of losing his father to such catastrophic injuries was partly responsible.

Apparently, despite Isam's own injuries, he'd managed to pull his father and the pilot from the chopper before help arrived, though they were probably dead on impact. He'd heard a whispered comment that the scene was one of the most devastating even the seasoned rescuers had ever seen.

Avril stumbled back and sank into a chintz armchair. It was a relief to focus on her. 'The six months before the crash? Does that mean you don't remember…?'

'I remember some things. But even what I do remember, I can't always trust. I've been told that some of my recollections aren't correct.'

His distant relative Hafiz had acted as regent while he'd been in hospital, and some of Hafiz's comments about Isam's actions prior to the accident disturbed him. Made him question what he knew of himself.

It was frustrating and undermined his ability to move forward as he wished. Increasingly he had suspicions about that, but for now he had more pressing matters to deal with.

Avril. And their daughter.

'What *do* you remember from that time?'

He met her eyes and knew what she was wondering. How much he remembered about *her*.

'Not nearly enough. I remember snippets, scenes rather than complete memories. The visit of another head of state to Zahdar. A friend's wedding.'

He paused, reluctant even now to admit it, but knowing it was unavoidable. 'But not you, Avril. I don't remember you.'

It was a lie. Since seeing her in the boardroom yesterday he'd been getting short flashbacks. Not of any conversation but rather sensual recollections. The honey taste of her on his tongue. The music of her soft cries as she tipped over the edge into bliss. The feel of her body welcoming his.

But were they true memories or wish fulfilment?

Because from the moment she'd walked into the presidential suite yesterday, he'd felt a sensual tug, a deep-seated hunger for this woman who was to all intents and purposes a stranger.

Was it any wonder he'd slept badly?

Isam saw her absorb that, hurt swiftly replacing shock in her expressive eyes.

'You don't remember *anything* about me? You employed me about six months before your accident. We worked together in London the week before.'

Guilt tightened his flesh, making it prickle in discomfort.

How must it be for a woman who'd given her virginity to him, *who'd borne his child*, to discover he had no recollection of her?

Even though he hadn't let her down deliberately, it must feel like a second betrayal, after he'd failed to return to her in London.

It was inconceivable that he could be responsible for the torment he saw in her wide eyes. Yet he knew, with a heavy heart, that it was so.

Isam wished he could make this easier for her. But lying would do no one any good.

'I'm sorry. I don't remember. But when I saw you yesterday you seemed…familiar.'

The fact that he'd been instantly plagued by sensual snapshots had made it impossible to concentrate on the meeting. Snapshots, sensations, yearnings. They had seemed real.

Seemed like genuine memories, but could he be sure? And were they of her as he believed? Or of some previous lover?

Racking his overtaxed brain, he'd been unable to recall any lover who matched those memories.

Avril collapsed back in her chair, deflated. 'That's why you were so brusque?' She frowned, her voice dropping as if she spoke to herself more than him. 'That didn't seem natural. It didn't seem like *you*, to blank me like that. You were never a cruel man.'

He was relieved to hear that. Some of the things Hafiz had said lately made him wonder if his view of himself was flawed.

'But your London investments. You must remember those.'

Isam shrugged. 'Only the long-term ones like the hotel where I'm staying. I inherited that from my English grandmother years ago.'

'When you hired me you were in the process of acquiring some British investments. That's why you wanted an assistant in the UK.'

'So I gather. But I don't recall them.'

For long moments she regarded him silently then shook her head. 'Even so, your staff must have known about them. They must have known about me. It's a long time since your accident but I haven't heard a word from you.'

Her stare was accusing, as if she either didn't believe in his memory loss or thought he'd used it as a convenient excuse to avoid her.

Exhaustion hammered him and he rubbed his temple where the shadow of that familiar ache threatened anew.

'I'm sorry, Avril. I know this seems far-fetched.'

Almost as far-fetched as discovering he had a lover he'd forgotten and a baby. He drew a deep breath.

'It seems you had a personal number for me, not one that was used by my staff. I lost that phone in the crash. The same with my email, I didn't use a palace address. The royal staff weren't involved in my British investments and it seems I channelled that work through you alone.'

Her eyebrows shot up. 'Is that usual? For them not to know anything? I know I only had dealings with you but I'd assumed...'

What could he say? That he didn't know? That he could only guess?

'These UK investments are quite separate from everything else and clearly I'd decided to manage them on my own, with you on the ground here. I wasn't investing public funds. I was using my own private capital, so there is no question of impropriety.'

'I wasn't suggesting that—'

'Of course not.'

But he remained on edge at even a hint of suspicion, Hafiz's innuendos that his priorities weren't always for the public good fresh in his mind.

'That's why your staff were so eager to access my laptop? You really didn't have backup?'

'Of course I have. I just don't seem to have made a note of where. It's not in the cloud storage used for palace records, but then these weren't public service documents. Remember, too, that everyone's focus after the accident was on continuing the usual business of government after so much disruption. There was no reason to look for additional matters off the official books.'

If it weren't so appalling it would be laughable. A king who couldn't even retrieve his own business documents. Because he'd deliberately not wanted to involve the usual channels in these projects.

The few senior palace staff who knew the situation had been utterly discreet, because there'd been enough public anxiety following the crash that killed his father and injured him. For a while there'd been some doubt about how quickly he'd recover. Informing his people that their new king had a faulty memory would hardly inspire confidence.

If word got out about any of this it would be more ammunition for Hafiz, who seemed intent on undermining him.

All Isam knew for sure was that he'd been determined to pursue these investments as separate from any others he owned. He thought he knew why but 'thought' was a far cry from 'knew'.

'So…' Avril drew the word out '…you didn't come to London for *me*. You came to find out about the business.'

He inclined his head. 'I came across a note that made me curious.'

He'd been trying to fill the gaps in his memory, trying to recreate his movements, but his diary had merely said 'London'. Until he'd unearthed a handwritten note with her details, perhaps from when he'd employed her.

'I had my staff investigate and they discovered you'd attended meetings with me.'

They'd also discovered he'd been paying her regularly for some time, which had made even his loyal administrator, Rashid, look askance, until they discovered they were salary payments, all above board, just not organised through the usual channels.

Her tone was sharp. 'You investigated me?'

'Not in detail.' If they had, he'd have known in advance about Maryam. 'I wanted to speak to you myself, rather than rely on others.'

Since being injured he preferred not to take reports at face value. He needed to assure himself that he understood the situations with which he dealt.

A bubble of mirthless humour expanded in his chest. His daughter and his ex-lover were far more than just a 'situation'. They changed everything. For himself and for his nation.

'We need to talk about Maryam.'

In other circumstances he might have waited to bring the conversation around to her. He was conscious that Avril still grappled with the news of his memory loss. He knew the feeling. Every day it was a challenge. And now he'd learned he had a daughter! Not even a year trying to acclimatise to the massive holes in his memory had prepared him for that.

The accident had taken his father from him, robbed him of his memory, and the chance to be there for Maryam's birth. The chance, too, to know her mother better.

But self-pity and time were luxuries he couldn't afford. He needed to protect Avril and Maryam. Their situation left them vulnerable and he couldn't allow that.

They also potentially provided Hafiz with ammunition to undermine Isam's rule. His relative had come to covet the power he'd wielded while Isam was in hospital, but his focus was personal aggrandisement, not the nation's well-being.

Avril didn't look happy. 'I thought you wanted to disown her, but now I understand your caution.'

He told himself not to take it personally. She was still grappling with their extraordinary situation.

One thing at least he could clarify. 'I would never, under any circumstances, disown my child. I know what a precious gift she is. I intend to cherish her and give her the best life I can.'

He'd look after her as he hadn't been able to look after Nur. His failure then was still a raw wound after all these years.

But instead of calming Avril's anxieties, his words made her frown. 'You make it sound like *you'll* be raising her. She has a mother, remember.'

Isam looked at the woman who'd been at the centre of his waking thoughts and even his dreams since their meeting yesterday. It was amazing how much she'd got under his skin. But then that shouldn't surprise him, now he knew he'd broken every self-imposed rule by sleeping with her. Whatever he'd felt for her a year ago had obviously been significant. Compelling.

'Don't worry, Avril. I'm fully conscious that you come as a pair. My amnesia encompasses past events only.'

Even now he could barely believe he'd forgotten this woman. The way his body responded to her, the way she drew his gaze and his thoughts…

Exactly what had been their relationship? How had they come together? He was desperate to know, but that would have to wait.

'I'm just trying to reassure you that I intend to be involved in Maryam's life and do all I can to support her, and you.'

Avril stiffened. 'You think I'm looking for a handout?'

'Anything but.' He'd been told she initially hadn't wanted to accept the assistant he'd arranged. Seeing the shadows of fatigue beneath her fine eyes, he was relieved she'd changed her mind. 'I can see you're proud and independent. It must have been taxing, being alone through your whole pregnancy, and now with a baby.'

Had she been alone? He didn't know her family situation. As for her hooking up with another man since their night together…everything in him rejected the idea. That mightn't be proof but he couldn't believe it of her.

How do you know when you can't remember her properly? Maybe Hafiz is right and the injury to your brain is worse than you want to believe.

Another idea Isam refused to countenance.

'I wish I'd known and been able to support you.'

'I…' She sank back in her seat like a woman overcome by the barrage of shocks she'd received. 'Thank you, Isam.'

He clenched his hands around the arms of his chair, resisting the impulse to rise and gather her close. To offer comfort. But he couldn't. Whatever their relationship had once been, she'd given no indication she'd welcome his embrace, even a purely platonic one.

But your response to her is anything but platonic.

Another complicating factor in an already fiendishly difficult situation.

'We still need to talk about Maryam.'

Instantly her chin shot up defensively. Then she nodded. 'Yes. I'm sorry. I'm still getting used to…' she waved a hand in his direction '…the truth about you. I thought you'd deliberately cut me off.'

'There's no need for apologies.' He paused, not wanting to press the point but knowing it was imperative they move swiftly. 'Obviously we have a lot to discuss and I don't want to overload you today. You've had a lot to process.'

And you don't want to scare her by declaring your intentions out loud.

For there was only one solution he could see to this situation. Marriage.

It didn't matter that his country expected him to choose a bride familiar with Zahdar, its customs and language. A bride with some experience of a royal court and the pressures and expectations that would be placed on a royal sheikha.

It didn't matter that, in the concern about his recovery and the future of the monarchy, a candidate for his bride had already been put forward. Though fortunately it had gone no further than that. Isam had agreed only to consider the suggestion, there'd been no announcement. Despite the increasing pressure from senior advisors that he needed to secure the succession soon.

Avril offered a small smile that made his belly tighten. 'It *has* been a lot. I feel like a cushion that's missing half its stuffing.'

'I understand.' He chose his words carefully. He had to take this one slow step at a time rather than spook her. 'Unfortunately, I can't stay in London. There are urgent reasons for me to return to Zahdar. But we need to discuss how we go forward and I don't want to do that long-distance. We need to talk face to face so there are no misunderstandings. Our daughter's future is too important. Do you agree?'

'I do. I've spent a year wallowing in doubt about you, about us.' She stopped, her eyes widening as if surprised at her use of the word *us*. As if she hadn't written off their relationship.

He was startled too, given her earlier deep mistrust.

'So when are you coming back to London?'

'I'm afraid matters at home are such that I won't be able to leave again for quite some time.'

'You're the King. Surely you can make it happen.' She folded her arms. 'If it's important enough to you.'

If only it were that simple.

He could come and go if he wished but there was too much at stake for him to be out of the country for any length of time. Rashid had been emphatic that he could deal with the London situation, as he called it, alone, urging Isam to stay in Zahdar. But Isam had known he had to find out about Avril in person. It was part of finding out about himself.

Meanwhile Hafiz would take advantage of his absence to undermine him further if he could. Who knew what damage Hafiz was doing even now?

'Believe me, Avril, I'm thinking about the long-term needs of Maryam, of you. *Us.*' He let that sink in and saw her eyes widen. 'That's my primary concern but at the same time it's vital I return to Zahdar. So I have a proposition.'

'Go on.'

'Come back with me.' He raised his hand to stop the protest he saw forming on her lips. 'Please hear me before you object.'

Avril gave a small huff of impatience, her mouth forming a pout that should have looked obstinate and annoying. Yet it was so alluring it sparked a flare of heat low in his belly. A flare of hunger.

It was so instantaneous, so absolute, it took Isam a second to find his voice again.

'Come to Zahdar. The pair of you. And your nanny. You can rest and get your strength back after what must have been a tough year. I'll organise comfortable accommodation for you all. While you're there we can take our time making plans for our daughter.'

He saw doubt writ large on her face. 'Think of it as a well-earned holiday.'

Still she hesitated. 'Surely that's risking complications, us coming to your country? Wouldn't it be better to talk here?'

Complications! She and Maryam were already complications that needed to be handled carefully, not just for his sake but for that of the monarchy and potentially the nation.

'I can promise you private accommodation in Zahdar. If you stay here, I fear it won't be long before the press start bothering you. I can't totally protect you from that if you stay.'

'The press!' She looked horrified. 'No one knows about us.'

He lifted tight shoulders and spread his hands. 'Not yet. But since my accident I'm under immense scrutiny. People were concerned for a long time about whether I was fit to rule, given the severity of my injuries.' He refused to use the word enemies. There was no need to scare her.

'Sooner or later someone will take an interest in what I've been doing in London. They'll make a connection to you, and Maryam. Then you'll be hounded every time you step outside your door. Come with me, Avril. I promise to keep you both safe while we plan for the future.'

CHAPTER SEVEN

PRIVATE ACCOMMODATION, HE'D SAID.

A place to relax and recuperate after a difficult year, he'd said. A place where they could take their time to discuss the future.

Well, two out of three wasn't bad, she supposed.

Avril had seen Isam daily since arriving in Zahdar four days ago. He seemed fascinated by Maryam, wanting to spend time with her and Avril when his schedule permitted, but so far there hadn't been enough time for them to discuss the future in any detail.

Do you really want to?

There would be difficult decisions to make, compromises she wasn't looking forward to, because she couldn't deny Isam the right to know his daughter. Inevitably that would mean time when Maryam would be with her father, not her.

Avril had no illusions. Isam was a king, he wouldn't spend his precious time with his daughter at Avril's tiny London house.

Yet she couldn't imagine being parted from her little girl. The thought made Avril's chest tighten and her hands tremble.

A gusty sigh escaped as she folded her arms, her mind shying from that horrible thought to her surroundings.

The accommodation Isam had organised was private as he'd promised and quiet enough to relax in, if you could forget it was in the heart of Zahdar's royal palace!

It was a small mercy, she supposed, that this luxurious suite of rooms didn't have ceilings gilded with real gold like some of the rooms they'd passed on the way here. Nor were there columns studded with rubies and lapis lazuli like in the entrance colonnade where they'd entered the enormous complex. And that, she'd learned later, hadn't even been the main entrance!

Yet everything here, from the artworks to the vast proportions and sumptuous furnishings, screamed *royal*. Her en-suite bathroom could accommodate a hockey team, the sunken bath clearly designed for more than one person.

An illicit image crept into Avril's mind, of sharing it with Isam. Even after a year she had perfect recall of his lean, powerful body and how it had felt, naked, against hers.

She shivered, not with cold but with a heated awareness that belied the fact she'd given birth only four months ago.

Surely new mothers weren't supposed to be interested in sexy men. Particularly men who'd lost interest in *them* as objects of desire.

Isam was the perfect host. But he never, by so much as a sidelong glance, gave any indication he viewed her as an attractive woman any more. As if the carnal heat saturating his gaze on their one night together had been a mirage.

What do you expect? The man's forgotten that night, erased it from his memory.

If it had been significant enough to him he'd remember. You weren't significant enough.

The carping inner voice had only made a reappearance in Avril's life since Isam left her without a word in London. Before that, with Cilla's help, she'd virtually banished the old self-doubt from her life, the belief she wasn't special enough to make her parents stay. Wasn't special enough to inspire love.

Avril stiffened. She was an adult and knew she wasn't responsible for her parents' actions.

She was capable and strong. Yet she felt undone by the insistent tug of attraction for Isam that still lurked deep inside. Even though to him she was merely an inconvenient problem. She was a complete stranger to the one man to whom she'd ever given her trust. How that hurt.

She grimaced. Scratch the surface and there, after all, was the needy little girl she'd once been. The one who'd cried when Mummy left and didn't come back. Who'd stifled tears when Daddy went away too. But at least by then she'd had Cilla and some stability in her world.

Which is what Maryam will need. Stability and love, lots of it.

She'd deliver that for her daughter. She'd do everything necessary to ensure it. Including negotiating a shared parenting arrangement with a royal sheikh!

Avril stared out at their private courtyard.

Filled with scented flowers, it was glorious, so pleasing to the senses that even she could tell every plant, every path and fountain had been put together by a master. As for the pool with its hand-painted tiles and cushioned sunbeds with embroidered silk canopies and gauzy curtains…

The whole place was beyond anything she could have dreamt. Was it any wonder she felt out of place?

Cilla had raised her to be independent and practical, and Avril had worked for some powerful people, occasionally glimpsing their more rarefied worlds.

But this was on a different scale. This wasn't just wealth. This was royal privilege, complete with liveried staff, a palace bigger than her old neighbourhood, and a labyrinthine web of protocols governing everything right down to modes of address and appropriate clothing. She knew from the compendium of information that had been supplied to help her and Bethany acclimatise.

Acclimatise! Avril had read it from cover to cover and

wished Isam had found them rooms in an anonymous hotel
in the city.

Here everything reminded her of the immense power Isam
wielded. The imbalance between them.

What was she, an ordinary woman from an ordinary background, doing here? Already she felt at a disadvantage and
they hadn't even begun their negotiations.

'Avril?'

Isam's rich baritone slid across her skin as if conjured by
her thoughts. Her flesh prickled, every fine hair on her body
standing alert while her heartbeat quickened.

She whipped around to discover Isam in the doorway. Instead of a dark suit, he wore long white robes and a headscarf
secured with a twist of dark cord. The simple clothes suited
him, emphasising his height and the lean strength of his body.

A dull throb started low in her abdomen and she fought
to ignore it. She no longer had the defence of anger against
him. The news he hadn't deliberately cut her out of his life
changed everything.

Avril feared that at the core of her jumbled emotions was
something too strong, too dangerous to her peace of mind.

'I knocked, several times.'

She nodded, throat catching on a stifled breath of mingled
appreciation and nerves. 'Please, come in.'

Even though she wanted to tell him to leave. She didn't feel
up to the discussion they had to have. She knew, no matter
how reasonable he was, that she'd hate the outcome. The idea
of leaving her precious girl for even a short length of time, a
couple of days, even weeks, churned nausea through her belly.

He glanced around the large room. 'Maryam's sleeping?'

That twist of sensation low in her body changed to something like disappointment.

What sort of woman is jealous of her own daughter?

You should be pleased he's so interested in Maryam. That's as it should be, a father wanting to see his girl.

This isn't about you.

Avril stood straighter. 'Yes, she's sleeping. Bethany is with her, while I—'

Isam crossed the room. It was less than twenty-four hours since she'd seen him, yet she was struck anew by the depth of her response. The softening, low in her body. The spark of heat. The humming need.

As if her body had awoken to one man and one alone. A terrifying thought!

'You…?'

She'd been going to venture out of the palace for an hour, take up the standing offer of a guide to take her into the city. She'd spent too long here, stewing over things she couldn't change, growing more rather than less nervous by the day despite the extra rest she was getting.

'It doesn't matter. Won't you sit down? I want to talk to you about Maryam.'

'She's all right? There's nothing wrong?' Concern sharpened his voice.

'She's fine. As I said, she's sleeping.'

Avril perched on the edge of a damask-covered settee and watched him take a seat opposite.

'Excellent. But if ever you have concerns, at any hour of the day or night, we can summon the palace doctor.'

She frowned, imagining an echo of anxiety in his tone.

She must be mistaken. Maryam had shown no negative effects from the travel. As for Isam anxious… He was one of the most competent, confident men she knew. Surely as Sheikh he had the power to make problems vanish from his life.

Avril wished she could do the same.

Lacing her fingers, she drew a deep breath. She couldn't put this off any longer. 'It's time we talked about Maryam.'

Isam inclined his head. 'Yes, and I want to know more about us.'

'Us?' That hit out of the blue. 'There isn't an us.'

Was it imagination or did the proud angles of his face grow more pronounced, more severe? 'Yet here we are, parents with a child. I want to know more about our relationship. How we came together.'

Avril had assumed that after pregnancy and giving birth, with strangers performing intimate examinations and procedures on her body, nothing could make her blush.

She was wrong. Heat surged up her throat and into her cheeks. She was tempted to blurt *in the usual way*, but stopped herself in time.

He's not asking what the sex was like.

'Does it matter now? The important thing is our daughter.'

He leaned closer, elbows on the arms of his chair and fingers touching. 'As you say, she's paramount. But… I feel at a disadvantage. You have full recall of something intimate and significant between us and I have none.' His mouth tightened and she saw something in his eyes that looked like vulnerability. 'It's a terrible thing to have blank spaces in your memory with no understanding of how you behaved.'

The heat intensified in Avril's cheeks. Not from embarrassment but from shame that she hadn't thought about this from Isam's perspective. The reality of memory loss was something she could barely conceive. He shouldn't have to beg to find out more.

'Of course. I'm sorry.' She cleared her throat. 'We worked together for several months before you came to London. Our working relationship was good. You trusted me and I handled the work well.'

'I didn't interview you in person?'

'You did, but via a video call, after all I was going to be your *virtual* PA, working remotely. You also set me some tasks to do then assessed my performance.' Still he didn't look convinced. 'My previous employer, Berthold Keller, recommended me to you. I'd worked for him for several years but he knew I wanted to work from home.'

Isam nodded. 'Why did you want to work from home?'

Avril paused, fighting a natural instinct for privacy. But there was no harm in sharing this. Besides, guilt at being so thoughtless about his amnesia spurred her on. 'I lived with my great-aunt. She was well in spirit and mind but growing physically frail. I wanted to be on hand to help her.'

'She shares your house? I didn't see her in London.'

Avril looked down at her hands, clenched in her lap. 'Actually, I lived in *her* house. She raised me. But she died after I began working for you.'

'I'm sorry for your loss, Avril. Was it after my time in London?'

She looked up to see dark pewter eyes fixed on her, full of sympathy. She drew a wobbly breath. 'No, just before.'

He jerked back in his seat. 'You were bereaved when we met in person? Did I know?'

'You had no idea.' It wasn't something she'd wanted to speak about. 'It was actually a relief to spend that week with you, concentrating on work rather than everything else.'

The funeral and its aftermath had left her drained. Did that explain her fixation with Isam? Her no-holds-barred need for him? Maybe her yearning had been some sort of reaction to grief.

So what's your excuse now? Cilla's been gone for more than a year and he only has to look at you to make you melt.

Avril lifted her head and discovered his expression was sombre. 'I owe you an apology, Avril.'

She frowned. His amnesia explained why he hadn't been in contact. 'What for?'

'For seducing you when you were my employee. For crossing a boundary that should never have been crossed. For taking advantage of you in your grief.' He shook his head, his gaze leaving hers to fix on a point behind her. 'For taking your innocence. My behaviour was—'

'You've got it wrong!' She leaned forward, aghast at his misunderstanding. 'You didn't seduce me. We… It was utterly mutual.'

'Nevertheless, given our professional relationship—'

'You're not hearing me. We were both…attracted.' What an anaemic word for that full-blooded, desperate craving. Avril didn't have words to describe the urgent compulsion she'd felt that night. 'We'd both been fighting it, and you were adamant we shouldn't act on it, precisely because I worked for you. But I insisted. I wanted, needed you that night as I'd never needed anyone before.'

It was simultaneously terrifying and liberating to admit it. But seeing Isam's anxiety over what he believed his unpardonable actions, she was determined to clear any misunderstanding. The man had suffered enough, losing his father and his memory, without adding to his misery.

It was a relief to know her original assessment of him was right. She'd spent most of the last year despising him for his apparent decision to cut her from his life. This proof of his true character reassured and warmed her.

Not for her own sake, since there'd be no going back to their fleeting relationship. But it was a relief to know Maryam's father was a decent man.

'You didn't pressure me, Isam. On the contrary, you said no, but I wouldn't listen. I understood your scruples. I knew it could be no more than a single night. But I—'

Had to have you.

'I initiated it. I coaxed you into it.'

'You're saying *you* seduced *me*?'

Heat tinged her cheeks and ears. That made her sound like

some femme fatale, alluring and confident. In fact she'd simply been desperate. She shrugged. 'Yes.'

Those grey eyes were narrowed on her. What did he see? A weary mother with bags under her eyes. Hardly a temptress.

She shifted in her seat, uncomfortable, not with what she'd done that night, but knowing he was wondering why he'd slept with someone so ordinary. She'd seen the old media reports, the photos of him at high-profile events with glamorous, sophisticated women.

Avril sat straighter, needing to change the subject. 'That doesn't matter now. It's in the past. We need to discuss Maryam's future.'

His stare told her he knew she was changing the subject deliberately. But to her relief, instead of objecting, he nodded. 'That's why I carved out time from today's schedule. We need to make some decisions. Nothing matters more than our daughter.'

On that they both agreed. Maybe this might be easier than she'd anticipated. Easier yet still distressing.

'She can't inherit the throne, can she? It's males only?'

'As the constitution stands, yes.'

That was a relief. Not that she wanted her daughter to miss out on opportunities, far from it. But if she'd been heir to a throne, Avril might have had a fight on her hands, raising their daughter in the UK.

'Why do you ask? What do you want for Maryam?'

'Don't worry, Isam. I don't have royal aspirations for her. I just want her to have a loving, secure home life. To have a decent education and a chance to pursue her dreams when she's older.'

'Good. I want something very similar for her.'

Similar but not the same? Avril moistened her lips, about to ask where they differed but he was already speaking.

'There are excellent schools and universities in Zahdar.'

She stiffened. 'And in the UK.'

'I know. I attended one for several years. My grandmother was English and a few years being educated in another country was very beneficial.'

The flutter of anxiety in Avril's stomach eased. So he was talking about Maryam, when older, spending some time here. Avril couldn't object to that. Even in the months when she'd thought Isam had cruelly deserted her, she'd been determined her daughter would learn something of her father's culture and heritage. Growing up with two languages and two cultures could only be an asset.

'That sounds reasonable.'

His lips quirked up at the corners in the hint of a smile that brought back memories of that week in London. Memories of his warmth and ready charm, how enthralled she'd been.

But it wasn't all memory. Little shivers of awareness were even now thrumming through her core. Her nipples had peaked at the mere hint of his smile.

Avril crossed her arms then uncrossed them, shifting in her seat. 'But that's years away. In the meantime we need to think about access.' She paused, wishing she didn't have to say it. 'I'm assuming you want to be involved?'

Something flared in those grey eyes. Something that saturated her body with heat then left it shivering with cold. Did she imagine his mouth tightened?

'You assume right. I'm her father. I'll be very much involved.'

He didn't raise his voice but it had a sharp edge that made her think of honed steel.

Avril made herself nod and smile. 'Just checking. I didn't know, given your royal responsibilities—'

'I take those very seriously, Avril. But nothing is more important to me than Maryam's well-being. Than family.'

Emotion coursed through her. If things had been different, if they'd shared more than a one-night stand, his words would have been music to her ears. She'd imagined that one day she'd find love with a steadfast, wonderful man and together they'd create a loving family. In other circumstances, Isam would have made a perfect father and partner.

Meanwhile, her little girl deserved a caring family. Parents who'd always be there for her. Not deserting her and making her feel she didn't deserve their attention.

It was only now she had a daughter that Avril felt the full weight of anger at the way her own parents had treated her. For years she'd felt bereft and insecure, her self-confidence damaged until Cilla did her best to change that. Now she was determined that her daughter wouldn't be abandoned as she'd been.

'I want to be part of Maryam's world. I want to be with her as she grows up, someone she can depend on for love, guidance and support.'

She felt her eyes grow round. That sounded more hands-on than she'd expected. 'And I assume you want the same, don't you, Avril?'

'Of course. But I'm certainly not going to hand her over to be raised elsewhere.'

Isam nodded. 'I agree. We both want her to have the best and we both need to be involved. So there's one obvious solution. We marry and raise her together.'

His mouth curved into a smile that didn't reach his eyes. They looked sombre and she felt a chill run along her backbone, because she knew he was serious.

Yet the idea was preposterous. 'Marry? We can't marry. You're a king and I'm your PA. *Was* your PA.' His minders at that meeting in London had made it clear her services wouldn't be required any longer. 'Royals don't marry women they barely know. Commoners from another country.'

His smile became a twist of the lips. 'You'd be surprised

at how often royals marry virtual strangers, for the good of their country. And there's nothing preventing a king from marrying outside his own nation.'

'But I'm…' Ordinary. Unremarkable. Not glamorous or well connected. 'Not cut out to be a queen.'

'You love your daughter, don't you? We'd be marrying for her. As for the rest, you can learn our customs, learn to be royal. If I hired you as my PA, you must be clever and diligent, trustworthy and dedicated.' He leaned forward, his voice coaxing. 'I don't pretend it will always be easy. But I'll be by your side, *on* your side, yours and Maryam's. You can rely on me. I'll help you through the challenges and it will be worth it to give our daughter a stable, loving home.'

Avril opened her mouth, about to list all the logical, sensible reasons why it was a far-fetched idea.

But his words echoed in her head.

'You can rely on me. A stable, loving home.'

The sort of home her parents hadn't provided, because she hadn't been their priority. Her mother had deserted her to take up with a new lover and the freedom of life on the road. Her father, who'd always travelled for work, had gone for longer and longer periods rather than less while Avril grew up. Until finally he fell in love with a Canadian woman and followed her across the Atlantic to start a new family.

And here was Isam, offering marriage, willing to withstand the inevitable backlash if he married a foreigner with nothing to recommend her as Queen, all for the sake of Maryam.

That he was a man who felt strongly, not just about duty, but about their daughter, was obvious. When he married he expected it to be permanent. It was there in his grave expression and the stillness of his tall frame.

Avril's heart squeezed. That he would do this for their daughter.

But what about you? What about your happiness? Are you willing to throw that away?

But would it be throwing it away? Surely it would be building a future for Maryam. And who was to say Avril wouldn't find happiness here with Isam and her daughter?

It struck her that while she'd inherited her mother's colouring and her father's organisational skills, she was fundamentally different to them. She might not be the world's most adept mother. She still had a lot to learn. But when it came to priorities she put her daughter's needs first.

Avril sighed and sank back in her seat. 'What if you fall in love? Would you want a divorce?'

He was already shaking his head by the time she stopped speaking. 'I've never been romantically inclined. I've known many women and never imagined myself in love. I was raised to expect an arranged marriage.' He paused, pinioning her gaze so it felt as if he saw deep into her soul. 'I'm proposing a *real* marriage, Avril. We'd be partners and lovers. And you have my word that I'll be faithful.'

She blinked in astonishment as unmistakable heat fizzed in her veins, coalescing low in her core. Sexual anticipation. She recognised it now and it made a liar of her attempts to tell herself this was totally about Maryam. For there was part of her that wanted Isam, just as she had from the first.

But suggesting marriage was one thing. Vowing fidelity was another. 'You don't even know if we're compatible—'

'I may not remember the details, Avril. But the fact I broke every rule so I could have you tells its own story.' Those serious eyes glazed hot, intensifying the eager, melting sensation deep inside. As if he now remembered that night and the pinnacles of ecstasy they'd reached together. 'We're sexually compatible. Everything tells me I trusted you and I see no reason for that to change. I hope you trust me too. Plus we have Maryam.' He lifted those wide shoulders in a shrug. 'We have a better basis for marriage than many.'

He made it sound so reasonable. Instead of utterly shocking.

'Once I give my vow, I won't break it. I'm a man of my word.'

She believed him. The gravity of his expression and the tone of his voice, plus all she knew about him, said so.

'I take my promises seriously too.'

If she were to agree to this, she'd commit wholeheartedly.

'Excellent. So you—?'

'It's an…extraordinary idea. I'll need time to think about it.'

His expression told her it wasn't what he wanted to hear. Impatience danced in his glittering eyes. But instead of trying to push her into a decision, he nodded.

'Naturally. But time's of the essence. The palace staff are discreet but the longer you're here, the greater the risk the news will leak. I want to control the release of information, rather than have rumours circulate. I won't allow anyone to turn you and our daughter into fodder for gossip.'

It was a reminder that she'd stepped into a new world under the public spotlight.

Not what she wanted.

He looked at his watch then rose. 'I'll expect your answer by the end of the week.'

CHAPTER EIGHT

SHE WAS DUE to give Isam an answer on the biggest decision of her life.

Was it any wonder Avril couldn't settle?

She'd slept a lot and swum in the clear waters of the courtyard's private pool. She'd begun to feel refreshed in a way she hadn't for ages. Yet she was on edge, and of course Maryam picked up on her agitation, growing more fidgety.

Bethany had practically pushed Avril out the door today, suggesting she go outside while she settled the baby. Avril had thought about exploring the city but decided against it. What she needed was to stretch her legs in solitude, not listening to the patter of a guide.

So she left their secluded part of the palace for the grand gardens within the palace compound. She wanted space. Walking always helped her sort out her thoughts.

A staff member ushered her through magnificent doors onto a broad, marble-lined portico. Avril's breath caught at the beauty of the gardens before her, sloping down past a channel of water and fountains, into rambling parkland.

Someone had spent a lot of time and effort ensuring there was plentiful water for this beautiful green space.

Movement further along the pillared terrace drew her attention. She turned to see a group of people gathered there in the shade, heads turning her way. Hurriedly she plonked on her wide-brimmed hat and strode away.

She didn't want to draw attention to herself. She didn't know what the press was like in Zahdar, but at home the unmarried mother of a king's child would be fodder for screaming headlines and gossip.

Would it be any different if you married him? There'd still be gossip and headlines because you're so unsuited to be Queen. The whole idea is preposterous.

But if they didn't marry, what was the alternative? Sharing Maryam, six months here and six in London? What was to stop the paparazzi making their lives hell in the UK?

Isam would give Maryam the stability and care Avril craved for her. And there'd be no tug-of-love separations as their daughter passed between London and Zahdar.

But it would mean putting yourself in the power of a man you barely know.

Except, she decided as she strode beyond the fountains and into the shrubbery, she felt she *did* know Isam. A man of his word. Strong, yes, but caring.

Even since coming to his palace Avril had seen enough to know he loved Maryam. There was a tenderness, an excitement and pride when he was with their baby, that made Avril's heart squeeze and her insides turn to mush. And not merely because there was something intrinsically attractive about a big, powerful man gently cradling a tiny bub.

She walked for an hour, weighing her options. Yet still she wasn't ready to make a decision. But it was getting hot and Maryam would be awake.

Avril followed the long mirror pools up the rise towards the palace. She'd almost reached it when voices caught her attention. She saw that group again, still clustered in the now scant shade.

She noticed a walking frame and a wheelchair and heads of grey and white hair.

Avril frowned. She'd grown up surrounded by Cilla's elderly friends. She respected and liked them. She also understood the frailties of age. Surely these old ladies shouldn't be out here as the heat intensified?

Caution warred with concern for about a second before she headed towards them.

They were dressed beautifully, as if for a special occasion. Many fanned themselves and several drooped. She couldn't see so much as a cup or glass between them.

She paused, searching her scant knowledge of Arabic. 'Hello. Are you thirsty? Would you like a drink?'

A chorus of greetings came her way, along with smiles and curious looks. One, tall and upright, nodded and spoke at some length.

'I'm sorry. I only know a few words. Do you speak English?'

Murmurs greeted that, but the woman nodded. 'I do. Thank you for your offer. Drinks would be very welcome.' She tilted her head enquiringly. 'Your Arabic may be limited but it's very good. Do you work in the palace?'

The palace employees were perfectly groomed and attired, whereas Avril suspected her cotton dress was crumpled and less than pristine after unsuccessfully trying to settle Maryam. 'No, I'm a visitor.'

Curiosity was bright in the other woman's eyes. 'We're visitors too. We had an appointment to see His Majesty. But there's been some delay.'

And they'd been left out *here*? Something wasn't right. Quite apart from the unsuitability of leaving them in the heat, the palace was full of comfortable rooms.

Avril covered her concern with a smile and inclined her head. 'I'll be back shortly.'

She hurried to the double doors, the temperature dropping deliciously as she stepped inside. The man who'd shown her into the garden was hurrying away. He didn't pause when she called him, as if not hearing.

She hesitated, knowing she couldn't leave the women in the heat any longer. They needed drinks but they needed to be in the cool too. But where?

More footsteps sounded, coming down a long corridor from the opposite direction.

Avril rushed to intercept a man carrying a bulging file. He looked slightly familiar, as if she'd seen him in the distance during her tour of the palace. 'Excuse me.'

'Yes, madam?'

'Can you help me? I need a room, large enough to seat a group of about fifteen guests in comfort. Not on hard seats but in comfortable chairs. Is there something like that in this part of the palace?'

'Well, I'm sure if you put in a request—'

'I'm afraid there's no time for a request. The room is needed *now*.'

Avril read his surprise and feared that if she didn't press her case he might leave, like the servant who'd pretended not to hear. One of the old ladies hadn't looked well and Avril worried. She stood straighter, lifting her chin and sweeping off her sunhat.

'There's been an unfortunate mix-up. The Sheikh has guests who have been left waiting outside in the heat for more than an hour. *Elderly* guests. It's not appropriate. We need a room for them, the more comfortable, the better. We need drinks immediately. A couple of them look particularly fatigued and I'm worried about dehydration.'

The man opened his mouth to speak but Avril pressed on. 'And food too, please. We also need to inform His Majesty so he can see them as soon as possible. Can you do that?'

To her relief, instead of arguing, he gave a small bow. 'You can rely on me. This way.'

He led her down the corridor, opening a door onto a spacious, opulent sitting room. The couches looked comfortable and there were small tables that would be perfect for drinks.

'Will it do?' He nodded to doors on the far side of the room. 'Bathroom facilities through there.'

Avril grinned, relieved. 'Thank you, it's perfect.'

His rather stern features transformed as he smiled. 'Excellent. You bring the guests and I'll see to the rest. When I speak to the Sheikh, who shall I say arranged this?'

She hesitated, feeling she shouldn't broadcast her name to a stranger since she didn't want to stir gossip. But it was too late. 'Ms Rodgers. Thank you so much, Mr—'

But he was already hurrying away, pulling out his phone.

Ten minutes later the women were all comfortably seated. Scant moments after that a parade of staff brought trays of cold drinks, delicate fruit ices and platters of finger food. They circulated among the women, offering refreshment and delicately embroidered napkins.

Soon after, hot drinks arrived including mint tea, cinnamon tea and coffee. Platters of hot food arrived after that, all provided by smiling, attentive maids.

Avril straightened from moving a small table closer to one of the guests, and looked around, satisfied.

'Very nicely done, my dear.' It was the tall woman who'd since introduced herself as Hana Bishara. 'I couldn't have done better myself.'

This was obviously high praise. 'Thank you. Though the kitchen staff have done all the work.'

The food looked and smelled delicious, reminding her she'd skimped on breakfast and she was starving. As soon as Isam arrived, or someone from his office, she'd leave to get her own lunch. Her breasts felt tight too, a reminder that Maryam would need feeding soon.

'You obviously have a talent for organisation, and the authority to make things happen here.'

Again Avril recognised curiosity in Hana's expression.

'Not authority. I just pointed out to the staff that there'd been some mistake, and requested refreshments.'

'If you say so. Ah, here's His Majesty.'

There was a ripple of movement as all the guests rose then bent their heads before the Sheikh, who paused in the doorway, flanked by a number of serious-faced staff.

Over their heads, Isam's eyes met Avril's and heat skimmed her flesh. In that second it felt as though something powerful passed between them. Understanding. Recognition. And something far more powerful.

Or maybe you're imagining it because you want to believe he didn't just propose out of duty. Because you're tempted to accept.

But Avril wasn't into self-deception. His proposal was pragmatic, nothing more.

Yet as he crossed the room towards them, she couldn't prevent the flutter of excitement in her chest. Those grey eyes seemed to flare as they met hers.

Maybe it was time for an eye test.

'Your Majesty.' Her quick curtsey felt ungainly. 'May I present Ms Hana Bishara.'

He greeted the older woman in Arabic then continued in English. 'My sincere apologies for the discomfort your group has suffered. My staff tell me there was a problem with the timetable. But that's no excuse. I'm deeply interested in your delegation's views.'

'Your Majesty is very kind.'

'Not at all. Perhaps you'd like to introduce me to the members of your group.'

As he turned towards her companions, Isam murmured to Avril, 'Thank you for saving the day. We'll speak later.'

His words and his smile warmed her to the core.

Was she really so needy, basking in his approval for something any sensible person would have done? Yet she found herself smiling as she exchanged farewells with the women.

It was late when Isam finally left his office. His already full schedule had been disrupted by the lunchtime fiasco, throwing the rest of his timetable out completely.

It had been a near disaster. If not for Avril…

His jaw clenched so hard pain circled the base of his skull. It wasn't the first inexplicable problem. There'd been a series of difficult, potentially embarrassing situations. The common factor was that in every case the mistake led back to *his* office.

The women's delegation today, there to advocate for better support for the elderly, had been told he'd specifically requested they attend today, whereas his official appointment diary showed them coming tomorrow.

He knocked on the door to Avril's suite, and hearing nothing, knocked again.

A muffled voice called from inside. Opening the door, he heard Avril, in another room. 'I'll be out in a minute. Maryam and I are just finishing up.'

His daughter was still awake? Isam's spirits lightened. She was the perfect antidote to the pressures and problems weighing down on him.

He closed the door and crossed the sitting room, only to halt in an open doorway at the sight before him.

He'd imagined Avril was changing a nappy. Instead he found her seated in a comfortable chair, her long hair curtaining her shoulders, head bent as she smiled down at the baby who'd clearly just finished feeding. Avril's blouse was open, one perfect breast bared.

The air caught in his lungs.

She looked the archetypal mother, tender and life-giving.

And sexy. So sexy Isam felt his blood rush to his groin. Carnal hunger ripped through him, weighting his muscles and tightening his lungs. Hunger and something else that felt like possessiveness.

Given the fact each day brought more teasing memories of them making love, it shouldn't surprise him. He remembered her exquisite softness, her delightful eagerness, her expression as he tipped her over the edge into bliss. She'd looked at him in wonder, as if he weren't a mere man but some hero. As if he'd made the world stop for her alone.

Those memories, though fragmented, made him wish—

'Isam! I thought you were Bethany.'

As she spoke she pulled her blouse closed, a delicate rose pink tinting her cheeks. She looked adorable. Though the word didn't do her justice. It was too passive for such a vibrant woman.

'I said we'd talk. I'm afraid this was the earliest I could get away.'

He walked forward, arms out. 'Let me take her while you do up your buttons.'

Though it was a shame for Avril to cover up.

She nodded and he gently took their baby. *Their baby.* The wonder of it never ceased to amaze him. But his joy was undercut by the way Avril flinched at his inadvertent touch. So different from when they'd made love.

Isam was eager to renew that intimacy. But he couldn't push. It was more important, for now, to convince her to marry him.

He gathered up little Maryam, smiling down into her long-lashed eyes, and turned away, giving Avril privacy. The little one waved a hand in the air and when he touched it, a tiny fist wrapped around his index finger.

Everything in Isam melted. All the barriers he'd built

around himself in the last year. Essential barriers that had allowed him to deal with grief for his father and the loss of his own autonomy.

That was how it felt, as if he'd lost himself, or an essential part, along with his memory.

But feeling his daughter's surprisingly powerful grip, experiencing his own rush of love, made his shattered self seem whole.

As did his longing for Avril. For the first time in a year, he wanted a woman. Not just wanted. Craved. It was a physical hunger yet a superstitious part of him almost believed she could make him complete again. Since meeting her, memories had started trickling into his brain.

'What are you singing?'

He turned to find her close, all buttoned up. 'Just a lullaby. I used to sing it for my sister.'

'You cared for her?'

Of course he'd cared for her. Then he realised what Avril meant. 'My mother died, having her. I was eleven and my father explained that while a nanny would look after her, it was important Nur knew from the beginning that she was loved and part of the family.'

He stopped, hearing his voice turned to gravel. His sister had died years ago yet still, sometimes, the grief hit as if fresh.

Warmth circled his upper arm as Avril touched his sleeve. 'I'm sorry you lost your sister. I can't imagine what that would be like.'

When he nodded but didn't say anything she continued. 'I grew up as an only child. Though I've got half-siblings now.' Her tone was flat.

'You don't get on with them?'

Avril's mouth crimped into a crooked line. 'I've never met

them. When I was in my early teens my father migrated to marry a Canadian. I've never met his wife or their children.'

Fury scythed through him, and outrage on her behalf. 'He didn't invite you to go with him? He left you with your great-aunt?'

She shrugged but her shoulders looked tight. 'He wasn't around much by then anyway. He travelled a lot for work.'

In his arms the baby squirmed and he realised he held her too tight. He eased his grip, rocking her gently. 'You didn't want to go with him?'

What sort of man abandoned his daughter?

Avril lifted Maryam, now yawning, from his arms and put her in the cot. 'By that stage we weren't close.'

Isam bit down a scathing observation about her father. It might relieve his feelings but at what cost to hers? 'And your mother?'

The brief report he'd received had been focused on Avril's professional life, not her family history.

'She died a long time ago.' She cut him off before he could express sympathy. 'It's okay. I was so little I barely remember her. She left to be with someone else and then died in an accident a few years later.'

Isam had come here focused on the difficulties of his day. Talking to Avril put those in perspective.

He wanted to gather her to him and ease her pain, an instinctive response that by its very nature made him pause. That, and her expression, which almost dared him to feel sorry for her.

'No wonder you're such an independent, capable person,' he said as he gestured for her to precede him into the sitting room.

When they were both seated she responded. 'I'm glad you think so.'

'I *know* so. The last few days I've been getting snippets

of memory back.' He saw her sit up, alert. 'When I was in London that week, we had meetings in the conference room of my suite.'

She nodded, her voice eager. 'You remember our time together?'

In truth what he remembered most clearly were the physical sensations and erotic highs of sexual intimacy. Recalling the tight embrace of her body turned him hard with wanting. Memories of caresses and whispered endearments were a siren song that grew in intensity each day.

Better to focus on what they'd done out of bed.

'I remember some of it. A couple of interviews. A man named Drucker, wasn't it?'

Avril sat forward, hands clasped together. 'That's right.'

'You didn't approve of him.' Isam smiled. 'I recall you were quite fluent about his flaws.'

She lifted her shoulders, this time the movement seemed easier. 'You asked for my opinion.'

'Which proves I trusted you.'

Isam was more than capable of making up his own mind, so the fact he'd asked for her input was telling.

'Is that all you remember?'

'Bits and pieces.' He still didn't recall how they'd ended up in bed together, just the delight when they did. Despite Avril's assurances, he was still uncomfortable, wondering if she'd downplayed his actions and he *had* taken advantage. 'But enough for today to make sense.'

'Today? What do you mean?'

'You remedied a potentially disastrous situation with speed and aplomb. I'm grateful for your intervention.'

The colour in her cheeks deepened and her eyes shone. Avril liked being appreciated. Who didn't? But she looked as if he'd handed her a prize, complimenting her on her competence.

Isam thought of what she'd revealed about her family. Having been abandoned by those who should have loved her, did she find validation in achievement?

'Anyone would have done the same.'

He shook his head. 'Not nearly so well. You made the ladies feel valued and appreciated. You anticipated their needs with genuine consideration. They were full of praise for you. I hear you even exchanged pleasantries in my language. When did you have time to learn that?'

'I only know basic phrases. I tried to learn a little for Maryam. I wanted her to grow up knowing something of your culture and language.'

Isam was stunned. 'Even though you thought I'd dumped you?'

Those warm, brown eyes looked away, over his shoulder. 'Especially because of that. I thought if she couldn't rely on her father, it would be up to me to help teach her.'

And she'd called their daughter a name that would work both in England and in Zahdar. For a moment he was silent, awed by her generosity, her determination to make their child's life as rich and meaningful as she could.

'I'll help you learn. You can have a tutor, but I'll help you myself too.'

'While I'm here.'

He stiffened. Was she signalling she wanted to leave? He'd brought her here to marry her. That hadn't changed.

Initially he'd been busy sorting through the difficulties of taking her as his bride so he could counter them. All the ways she wouldn't fit in.

But there were positives. She was kind-hearted but sensible. She was good with people, *his* people. Today she'd held her own with as much assurance as any royal and in trying circumstances, thinking quickly and clearly. No wonder he'd hired her as his PA. She was determined to do her best for their child and he believed, once they were wed, she'd be loyal and supportive.

As for their sex life…he couldn't imagine anyone more compatible.

He *wanted* Avril. She had the values and traits he desired in a partner.

And you've never felt so enthusiastic about the idea of marrying any other woman.

'About that,' he said. 'I'm here for your answer. It's the end of the week and I'd like to announce our engagement sooner rather than later. If you agree.' He paused, watching her tense. Many women would leap at the chance to be his queen, but not Avril. 'After today rumours will be flying about my uncommon guest.'

'It's one thing to make a baby. It's quite another to become a royal—'

'I know it's daunting, but you can do it. Most of being royal is about working hard and putting the needs of other people first. You demonstrated that today and you did it without fuss or panic. You were a natural.'

Yet she looked unconvinced. 'I'm used to being the gofer, the assistant, not the one in charge.'

Isam's laughter escaped. 'Oh, I think you'll do very well. You had no hesitation ordering one of the most senior men in the kingdom to do your bidding.'

Her eyes rounded. 'Sorry? You mean the man who organised the food?'

Isam's smile widened. 'I do. He's head of one of the foremost families in the country and a senior government minister.'

For the first time Avril seemed lost for words.

'He was most impressed with your take-charge attitude in a crisis. In fact he asked if you might be interested in joining our diplomatic team.'

To his delight, she chuckled, reminding him of times he'd

now recalled when they'd shared a joke while working together. 'I'm glad he didn't take offence. After that other man turned away when I called him for help, I wasn't sure if he'd listen.'

'Other man? What did he look like?'

'About my height, slim, with a beard. He was hanging around near the doors when I went outside and when I came back. I was sure he'd heard me call but he hurried away.'

Isam filed the information away for later. For now he had a more important issue to deal with.

'You'll make an excellent queen. And I'll be there at your side.'

Her gaze caught his and a frisson of heat rippled through him. 'But I don't know the country or customs—'

'Nor did my grandmother when she came from England. But she was happy here and much loved by the nation as well as the family.' He paused, considering what arguments might sway Avril. 'Here you'll have purpose and a rewarding life, quite apart from the wealth I can offer. We can build a family, a secure world for our little girl. A place where she and you belong. A loving home. Isn't that what you want for her?'

She licked her lips but didn't answer and Isam, an expert at commercial and diplomatic negotiations, felt his stomach churn with nerves.

'What do you say, Avril?'

His heart hammered as she took her time responding. Tension drew his skin tight. She couldn't refuse him!

Finally, she nodded but she didn't smile. 'Very well. I'll marry you, Isam.'

CHAPTER NINE

RELIEF COURSED THROUGH Isam's veins, making him light-headed for a second.

Her agreement secured Maryam's future.

But this wasn't just about his daughter. He wanted Avril with a visceral need he couldn't explain. Not just as the mother of his child. But not just as a sexual partner either, despite the throb low in his body.

What then? This wasn't a romance.

He shied from the thought. He had no time for sentiment, he had a nation to secure. Besides, all the people he'd ever loved had been taken from him. He wasn't interested in opening his heart up to anyone and risking more grief.

Except for Maryam. How could he not love the tiny mite who was his own flesh and blood?

'Excellent.' He kept his tone measured, disguising a disturbing jostle of emotions. 'Together we can build a solid marriage and a wonderful future for our daughter.'

'I...hope so.'

Hardly an effusive agreement. Isam battled annoyance at her lack of excitement.

He knew Avril wanted the best for their baby, but surely he hadn't been mistaken, believing he read attraction in her unguarded looks.

No, he *couldn't* have been mistaken. She wanted him, and

he'd been her first, her only lover. That gave him an advantage he could use.

But not now. She needed time.

He'd be taking another long, cold shower tonight.

The gravity of her expression quenched any feeling of celebration. She looked more doubtful than convinced, as if unsure she'd done the right thing.

And she doesn't know the half of the problems facing you.

If she knew about Hafiz and his attempts to undermine Isam, would she still have agreed to marry him? Or would she have been frightened off?

Isam thrust away the thought. With the determination born of confidence in his own abilities, he refused to worry over something that wouldn't happen. He'd overcome the plot against him.

Hafiz had acquired a taste for royal power and was doing his underhanded best to make people believe Isam's head injury had permanently affected his judgement and character. Today's problem with the timetable was part of that attempt. But he wouldn't succeed.

'It's been a big day and you're no doubt tired.' While Isam had to fit in several hours of work before he retired for the night. 'We'll talk tomorrow in more detail, but I'll announce our betrothal in the next few days.'

She jumped as if touched by a live wire. 'Days!'

He held her gaze, watching the gold flecks in her soft brown eyes. She was intriguing. Alluring. And his...almost.

'It's better for us to announce our news than for you to become the object of speculation, which will happen now your presence is more widely known.'

She didn't look convinced and it struck him that Avril Rodgers was the antithesis of a gold-digger. She seemed uninterested in his money and his authority, much less the idea of becoming Queen.

He smiled. Perhaps this was cosmic justice for his casual arrogance as a much younger man. He'd been so certain of his desirability, given the number of women who had chased him, eager for attention and to bask in the reflected glow of his wealth and power.

'But once our engagement is announced, we can take our time planning the wedding. You'll have plenty of time to prepare for that.'

The question was whether he could wait that long to claim her.

Two days later, Avril stood in the centre of her sitting room while two seamstresses inspected the fit of her new gown. She couldn't think of it as simply a dress. This made-to-measure, one-of-a-kind garment was made from rich crimson satin that, when she moved, revealed a sheen of deepest amethyst. She looked from Bethany's approving grin from where she sat with Maryam on her lap, to the vast, gilt-edged mirror that had been brought into the room.

The woman reflected there bore only a passing resemblance to Avril Rodgers. Her hair had been professionally styled up in a way that looked stunningly elegant. Her equally professional make-up was discreet except for the crimson of her lips that matched the colour of her dress. The make-up artist had done something that emphasised her eyes, making them look…beautiful.

Avril had never felt beautiful before. She had favourite clothes that made her feel good and gave her extra confidence. But this was a transformation.

The red dress had tight three-quarter sleeves and a V neckline. It was demure yet the neckline sat wider than usual on her shoulders, presumably to mirror her fitted bodice that tapered to her surprisingly narrow waist. She hadn't realised until today that she'd lost the rest of her pregnancy weight.

Below her waist the rich satin skimmed her hips then fell in gleaming folds. The skirt was full and feminine and every time she moved the brush of the fabric felt like a caress.

You're thinking about Isam again. Stop it.

That was difficult, when even the slide of warm water down her body in the shower made her remember his touch.

Avril firmed her lips. Though he'd begun to remember her, he hadn't remembered intimacy between them, only work. He recalled her as his PA, nothing more.

What did that say about his priorities and her importance in his life?

She knew what it said. She'd never been more than a temporary lover, soon forgotten. She'd known that at the time, he'd been upfront about it. And she'd told herself it didn't matter. Yet *now* it mattered.

Avril remembered every word he'd said to her when he'd come for her answer the other day. He'd praised her quick thinking and pragmatism, qualities he'd wanted in a PA, and now apparently in a wife. There'd been nothing about him *wanting* her. Nothing personal.

When will you get it through your head? There's nothing personal between you any more. He's marrying you out of duty. Because of Maryam.

It had to be enough.

The seamstresses moved back and the designer, a sharp-eyed woman with silvery hair, finally nodded. 'It is done. I hope you like it, madam.'

'I do. I never thought I could look so—' Avril shook her head.

For the first time in their acquaintance, the older woman smiled. 'I rarely heed fashion advice from men. But I believe His Majesty chose well, insisting you'd be more comfortable in Western dress for the occasion.'

Isam had insisted? It was a small thing but it warmed Avril.

She'd left everything to the designer, trusting she'd know best what would be suitable.

As if on cue a knock sounded at the door, a footman opened it and Isam swept in, resplendent in white, a heavy ring of old gold, symbol of royal authority, on his hand.

He stopped midstride, his robes swirling about his legs. Dimly Avril was aware of the women curtseying then following Bethany out through another door. She couldn't tear her gaze from the man who today would pledge himself to her. A royal betrothal was almost as binding as marriage.

Her heart pattered faster and her chest swelled on a deep breath. She watched his eyes widen then narrow as he surveyed her from top to toe then slowly, devastatingly slowly, back up.

Avril's flesh tingled. Her nape tightened and so did her nipples, thrusting against her new satin bra. Low inside, heat bloomed and muscles spasmed as if reliving memories of the night they'd been together.

He paced towards her, stopping only when he was so close she could smell the warm citrus scent of his skin and admire the close shave of his angled jaw. 'You look magnificent.'

His voice was husky, catapulting her back in time, making her remember how he'd made love to her, not just with his body, his mouth and hands, but with words of praise and enticement that had made her feel—

'Thank you, Isam. So do you. Every inch the Sheikh.'

She had to wrest back some control of herself. It was daunting enough to face an official photoshoot, knowing the photos would be pored over not only in Zahdar, but across the world. Isam was young to be Sheikh, handsome, talented and with a recent tragedy in his past. The world would be agog to see the woman he'd chosen as his bride.

A dreadful, plummeting sensation hollowed her belly. Was she foolish to think she could do this?

'What is it, Avril?'

She swallowed hard, tasting trepidation. 'I just...' She shook her head. 'How can you believe this will work? I'm not—'

Isam curled his fingers around hers and drew her against him. It was the first time they'd been so close since the night Maryam was conceived. The night he'd introduced her to a world of delight she'd never guessed at. A wonderful, golden world where anything was possible.

'It will work because we'll make it work. And you *are* everything you need to be.' Her gaze lifted to his, those grey eyes mesmerising and bright as liquid mercury. 'You're the mother Maryam needs and loves. You're talented, capable and caring. That's more than enough.'

The intensity of his stare made it hard to remember he wanted her for purely pragmatic reasons. Because when he looked at her like that she could almost believe...

Heat surged in her veins, bringing her skin to tingling life, flushing her throat and face. The way he looked at her, a huskiness in his voice she'd heard only once before, the words branding themselves in her brain... All those undermined her doubts and stripped bare her vulnerabilities. Made her hope.

Something cool touched her finger and she looked down to see him hold a ring to it. He paused, as if waiting for approval or objection, then as she watched, he slid it home.

Her breath seized. The ring was remarkable. A huge crimson stone that she guessed was a ruby glowed with a dazzling inner light. Its setting was of old gold filigree that extended right up to her first knuckle. She blinked, trying to take in the delicately wrought flowers and...were those birds? She'd never seen such a thing.

It was a ring for a queen. A statement piece that spoke of extraordinary wealth and, she suspected, generations of tradition.

Daunting, much?

'I know in your country engagement rings are often chosen by the bride. But in mine they are usually an heirloom from the husband's family. I hope you like it.'

Avril swallowed, shaky at the grandeur and beauty of what she wore. It struck her that her dress was a perfect match for the stone, which was the perfect size for her finger. Had he organised it that way?

Of course he had. Isam was a man who saw details as well as the bigger picture. It was one of the reasons she'd enjoyed working with him.

'It's gorgeous but very grand. I'm not sure—'

'It was my grandmother's. I thought you'd enjoy wearing something from another bride who was an incomer. She was very happy in Zahdar and I hope you will be too.'

Avril looked up into his face, seeking a clue to his thoughts. She read tenderness when he referred to his grandmother but apart from that he wore his inscrutable expression. The one that left her second-guessing his thoughts.

He's probably wondering if you're up to the ordeal waiting for you now. At least it's better than him pretending you're special to him.

Finally she nodded. 'Thank you. That's very thoughtful. I'll wear it with pride.'

And terror at the responsibility. But then it was so big at least she'd know if she lost it.

There was a knock then the door opened and a voice said, 'It's time, Your Majesty.'

Isam's eyes didn't leave hers. His voice dropped to a low hum that resonated across her skin then settled deep in the place where need was a twisting, hungry ache. 'It's time. First the photos. Then to tell the world I want you as my queen.'

He led her to the door before she had time to get even more nervous.

* * *

The photo shoot wasn't as daunting as she'd expected. Just one photographer and his assistant. The only difficulty was smiling on cue.

Isam's words had thrown her into a tailspin. Avril welcomed his reassurance but when he'd spoken of wanting her as his queen in *that* tone of voice, and with so much heat in his eyes it should have made steam rise from her skin...

She'd almost believed he wanted her the way she wanted him, with a dark craving that defied every attempt to squash it.

He'd reawoken all that restless, useless longing inside her.

She knew he meant that he wanted to marry her for Maryam's sake. Because marriage was the simplest of their options. So why look at her and speak to her that way?

He'd admitted he didn't remember being intimate and she couldn't believe he was overwhelmed with desire for a weary, stressed new mum.

Unless it was a ruse to persuade her past her doubts. So she'd go through with today's announcement.

That had to be it. He'd wanted to spur her into compliance rather than have her cower in her room.

Avril lifted her chin, annoyed by such tactics.

'Perfect,' murmured the photographer. 'Just perfect.'

There was movement beyond him. Avril was surprised to see Bethany enter, carrying Maryam, who wore an unfamiliar, delicate gown of cream and gold.

Isam moved from Avril's side to scoop up their daughter. He turned and just like that Avril's heart forgot to beat for a second. Maryam smiled up at her father with wide eyes and he, broad shoulders curved protectively as he cradled her, wore an expression so tender it made emotion well.

Avril blinked and found herself softening.

She had no illusions that their marriage would be easy but

it was the right thing for Maryam. She'd grow up with two loving parents.

'I thought we should include Maryam in some of the photos,' Isam said as he approached. 'Not for public consumption but for us.'

Avril nodded, throat tight at his thoughtfulness. In later years it would be something Maryam might treasure.

The man confounded her. One moment so caring, the next throwing her into utter turmoil.

It's not him that's the problem. It's you. You're an emotional mess. You want a man who can't remember being intimate with you. How can you expect deep feelings from someone who doesn't even know you?

Yet it was easier now to smile for the camera since the photographer didn't need posed shots. In fact, she was barely aware of him as Isam placed their baby in her arms, then settled beside her, offering Maryam his finger. Instantly their little girl grasped it and chortled.

Avril felt a rush of delight, aware of Isam's body warm beside her, his focus on their daughter, and Maryam's joyful response.

Yes. This.

They might have been brought together by circumstance but they could be a successful family unit, united in their love for Maryam.

They could do this.

Isam led her from the room towards the grand public reception spaces on the other side of the palace.

Were her nerves obvious? Isam glanced at her as the corridor widened and the furnishings graduated from luxurious to overtly opulent. Her heart was in her mouth at the idea of being presented to a bunch of VIPs as the country's next queen. Even his steady calm couldn't prevent the butterflies whirling in her stomach. Because of her confused feelings, or the ordeal ahead?

'It's a small reception. You'll be fine,' he murmured, his fingers tightening around hers. 'Pretend it's a business meeting, or a stray group of elderly petitioners come to tell me how to improve their lives.'

'If only.' She turned her head to see his encouraging smile. He was doing what he could to make this easier.

Even lie about wanting her?

Staff opened enormous carved doors and they stepped into a vast room with walls that looked like fields of beautiful flowers. Above soared a ceiling of gold from which hung rows of glittering chandeliers. And below that, a throng of people, all bowing low.

'A *small* reception?' she whispered as she faltered on the threshold.

'A mere two hundred. Tiny by royal standards.' Isam's mouth crooked up at one corner. 'Just be yourself, Avril, that's all you need to do. I'll be with you.'

He led her into the crowd that parted for them. Avril was aware of curious, assessing gazes and then bowed heads as their sheikh approached.

Except to one side where an older man walked swiftly towards a young woman dressed in silver, his expression thunderous. That look and the urgency of his gestures as he spoke to her struck a jarring note, especially as his narrowed gaze was fixed the whole time on Isam.

Beside Avril, Isam stiffened, but he kept his pace unhurried.

Someone stepped up to the podium. She recognised the minister whom she'd co-opted to provide refreshments for Isam's elderly guests.

His speech was short and ended in a burst of enthusiastic applause from the crowd that now encircled them. Then the minister spoke again in English, presumably for Avril's benefit. He announced the Sheikh's betrothal to Ms Avril Rodgers. To her surprise he added that they had a baby daughter and that mother and child were now living in the palace prior to the wedding. Then he concluded by wishing them well.

Another round of applause erupted and people surged towards them. For a second she hovered on the brink of light-headedness, feeling overwhelmed. Until Isam squeezed her hand and murmured that they'd do this together.

Strange how easily that settled her nerves.

She saw a single movement away from them, the scowling man striding for the exit. Then all her attention was claimed by well-wishers. Many had an air of gravitas as if very aware of their importance and many wore obviously expensive clothes, but all seemed genuinely pleased about the engagement.

It surprised her, as had the fact Maryam had been mentioned in the speech. Avril had supposed a foreign bride, who'd borne a child out of marriage, would be frowned on. Perhaps the Zahdaris were too polite to show disapproval.

Then her doubts fled as a familiar figure appeared. The tall, upright form of Hana Bishara, the woman Avril had met several days earlier.

Hana bowed to Isam then to Avril. 'I'm so delighted by the news of your betrothal. I can see our sheikh has chosen his bride well.'

'Thank you so much. It's lovely to see you again, Hana.'

The lady's smile widened. 'You remember my name?'

Avril grinned back at her. 'You were the first person I tried to speak to in Arabic. You were very encouraging and didn't even wince at my pronunciation.'

Hana laughed. 'Your pronunciation was admirable. Perhaps we'll meet again and you can practise with me.'

The friendly offer and the warmth of her manner cut through Avril's anxiety. 'Thank you. I'd like that very much.'

'I'll look forward to it too. But for now I must move on. There are others waiting to meet you.'

There were. To Avril it seemed like far more than two hundred but the short interlude with Hana had given her the boost she needed. Besides, everyone was friendly. She wouldn't be surprised if their smiles hid surprise or doubt, but she was thankful nevertheless.

Until she turned to find a woman in silver bowing before Isam. She'd been with the older man who'd left so abruptly. The woman wasn't precisely beautiful but had presence, an elegance and confidence Avril envied.

Did she imagine a lull in conversation around them as the woman spoke to Isam then turned and wished Avril well in English?

Who was she? Avril thanked her, wishing she'd caught her name, before turning to the next person in line.

After that everything went smoothly. Buoyed by the warmth of her welcome and Hana's encouragement, Avril even began using her basic Arabic to welcome and thank the well-wishers. Which led to more smiles and nods of approval.

Beside her, Isam looked proud and regal but his manner was warm with his guests, even warmer when he caught her eye after it was all over.

'Superbly done, Avril,' he said as he led her back to the palace's private wing. 'Thank you.'

She shrugged. 'You were right. I didn't have to do much.' Even so she felt she'd run a marathon, her body only now beginning to relax. Yet having Isam at her side, a bulwark against nervousness, had made such a difference.

What does that say about your feelings for him? You're supposed to be marrying him for your child's sake, not because of some romantic fantasy you know isn't real.

Avril made herself concentrate on tonight's reception. She didn't delude herself that future events would be so easy. But it pleased her that she'd held her own. In fact she felt that buzz of excitement in her blood that she always got from a job well done. It left her wired and excited rather than tired.

Which had to explain her impulsive decision to invite Isam into her suite rather than say goodnight at the door. She wasn't ready for sleep. She had too many questions.

It had absolutely nothing to do with not wanting him to walk away. Nothing at all.

Avril watched him pace the room with a coiled energy that made her wonder if he felt the same high of excitement and satisfaction she did. Of anticipation…

'Why did you make the announcement about Maryam? Won't it shock everyone that you have a child? I thought you were just going to announce the engagement.'

Isam swung around, a lamp in the corner slanting light and shadows across his harshly beautiful features.

'You'd have me drip-feed the news? To what end? Our child is a cause for celebration.'

His delight stirred feelings she hadn't known she carried.

Because *she* hadn't been important enough for her mother or her father?

Was that the real reason she'd agreed to marry—because Isam clearly intended Maryam would be at the centre of his world? How could Avril resist that?

'Even so, we weren't married when she was born.'

His dark eyebrows drew together. 'In Zahdar we don't have such negative views about illegitimacy as in some places. Maryam will be welcomed here.'

He smiled. 'Besides, her existence proves we're compatible and fertile. One of the Sheikh's key roles is to ensure the succession, for the future safety of the country.'

Avril folded her arms, refusing to be amused. 'You mean they'll like me because I'm good breeding stock?'

That made her feel like a prize-winning sheep!

Isam paced closer. 'It doesn't hurt that we've produced a child. My father's early death was a shock, especially as I was badly injured. It made people wonder about the future and the stability of the monarchy.

'But tonight you showed the grace and strength I need in a queen. People respect and admire that. They'll admire you even more when they get to know you. They'll approve my choice.'

He was doing it again, winning her over with flattery and that searing look, as if he wanted her as more than a convenient bride and mother to his child.

Avril took a step back, chin jutting. She couldn't play those games. 'I understand that. But I'd rather you didn't pretend to things you don't feel.'

She accepted theirs would be a real marriage. There'd be sex and maybe more children. In her secret heart of hearts, Avril looked forward to intimacy with Isam. But she didn't want convenient lies to salve her ego.

'Pretend?'

She looked down at her twisting hands. 'I appreciate all you're doing for Maryam, and to make our relationship appear solid. But I'd prefer you didn't pretend this is your *choice*. We're together because of circumstance, because of our baby, not because you *want* me.'

The silence following her words grew so long that finally she had to look up. Isam wore the strangest expression.

'You're right. Circumstance brought us together. Otherwise I'd probably marry a woman from Zahdar. Someone chosen for me in an arranged marriage. I—'

'Wouldn't that be hard to accept?' She reminded herself

traditions were different here, especially for royals. 'You wouldn't marry for...?'

'Love?' His eyebrows rose. 'I believe my grandparents did but that was an exception. Here royal marriages are settled for dynastic reasons. That's the way for my family.'

He looked so calm, so matter-of-fact. As if the idea of marrying a stranger didn't bother him.

But then, that was essentially what he was doing with her. She wished she could be so sanguine. To her it felt wrong to marry for anything other than love.

Isam closed the gap between them, capturing her hands. 'But that doesn't stop me wanting you, Avril.'

CHAPTER TEN

ISAM LOOKED INTO SEARCHING, golden brown eyes and felt his control snap. His hands tightened on hers.

She thought he didn't want her?

He'd held back, needing to persuade her into marriage and not wanting to rush her physically. But he'd imagined his heated thoughts had betrayed him. After all, they'd been intimate before. He'd assumed she'd read his hunger, despite his attempts to rein it in.

But she was an innocent, remember? And you only had one night together. Maybe she's not adept at reading the signs.

The reminder that he'd been her only lover fuelled that renegade hunger, yet made him feel protective too.

He wrapped his arms around her and tugged her against him. A sigh chased its way up his throat as their bodies made contact.

Just holding her, fully clothed, made him shudder with satisfaction. What was it about this woman? She created a need in him more potent than any he'd ever known.

Her hands pressed to his chest, fingers splayed as she tipped her head back, keeping their gazes locked.

'You really *want* me?'

'Of course I want you. In London I broke every rule to have you.' That he knew for sure. 'Since you came to Zahdar I've been having cold showers every day. I'm trying to give you time to adjust.'

She looked at him with solemn eyes. 'You never said.'

He frowned. Before the reception he'd told her he wanted her as his. But he'd been concentrating on reassuring her, supporting her in preparation for their first appearance together. Maybe he hadn't been completely clear.

'I'm saying it now. I'm desperate for you, Avril. Let me show you how much.'

Isam gathered her up in his arms and, when her lips curved into a fragile smile, marched across the room and into her bedroom, hitting a light switch on the way. He laid her on the bed, almost laughing at her expression of mixed shock and eagerness.

Despite her earlier doubt she didn't protest. Far from it. All the worries and demands of the long day disintegrated as he looked down at her, watching him avidly.

He wanted to take his time cataloguing everything from her velvet skin to the way the rich fabric enhanced her feminine shape. It was a hard-fought battle against the urgency that had tested him since meeting her across that London conference table.

Shucking off his shoes and keffiyeh, he followed her onto the bed, reaching for her foot in one jewelled sandal. Swiftly he released the narrow straps and tossed it away. He explored her instep, her dainty toes, high arch and curved ankle, registering each shiver and twitch in answer to his touch.

She was so responsive that he made himself pause rather than swiftly work his way up her body. He propped her heel on his thigh and worked the muscles of her foot in a deep massage. Her tension dissolved almost instantly. Her soft moan was the most erotic music.

It reminded him of the way she'd gasped out his name as she climaxed. *That* memory was clear and enticing and never failed to arouse.

Isam lowered her foot to the bed and stripped away her other sandal before massaging that foot.

Avril lay before him, fully dressed, eyes narrowed to slumbrous, golden slits, shifting needily, her hands curling into the bedspread.

A shaft of heat tore through him, settling in his already hard groin. He wanted her *now*, without preamble. But it would be even better if he took his time.

Her dress was soft as he pushed it up her legs, but not as soft as her flesh. Unable to resist, he pressed a kiss to her calf, then stroked it with his tongue, feeling her muscle spasm.

'Isam!'

Her voice was husky. It made his skin tight and weighted his groin so he had to take a moment, concentrating on control.

He looked up to find her propped on her elbows, watching him, eyes radiant with ardour.

'Patience, sweetheart.'

He wanted her so badly it hurt. But he wanted to imprint himself on her. To set up a deep-seated need in her that only he could assuage. To make her crave *him*.

Because he couldn't remember everything he needed to about how they'd come together?

Because that gap in his memory made him feel exposed?

He shied from that. Too often in the last year he'd felt that way. He preferred to take charge.

Isam wanted Avril, wanted sex, but he wasn't above using their desire to bind her to him. She'd agreed to marry but he knew she still doubted her decision, and him.

He couldn't allow that. He had to make utterly sure of her. He'd give her time to acclimatise and prepare for the wedding, but having her back out at the last minute wasn't an option. Sex would reinforce the ties that bound them.

How delightful when duty and his own desire dovetailed.

You call this duty? You couldn't pull back from her if you tried.

Isam shoved the crimson skirt higher, pretending not to notice the fine tremor in his hands as he palmed her smooth thighs. Without stopping, he shoved the material over her belly, then stroked his fingers back down her hips, curling them into the pale lace of her panties on the way and dragging them down her legs. A second later they followed her sandals onto the floor and he knelt between her knees, gloating.

Avril was beautiful, more beautiful than he'd remembered. The contrast between her formal dress and her bare lower body only fuelled his excitement. He felt greedy and dizzy with anticipation. Like a teenager, teetering on the edge of control.

That he couldn't allow. He was determined to bring her pleasure before finding his own.

Slowly he slid his hands back up her thighs to her hip bones, not deviating to that V of dark hair, despite the way she twitched and turned, seeking his touch.

'Soon,' he promised. But first, he'd seen something else that fascinated him. The light caught striations low on her belly. His breath hitched as he guessed their meaning. 'Are they stretch marks?'

He'd heard of them but never seen any.

Avril shifted abruptly and Isam looked up to catch her change of expression. Her eagerness had transformed into discomfort, her mouth forming a moue as if of distaste.

He frowned. To him these marks were a badge of honour, proof of her body's miracle in conceiving and carrying their child. Emotion welled at how special this woman was. How extraordinary.

He kissed the narrow lines and felt her stiffen. But he wasn't deterred. He explored each one, taking his time, telling her how proud he was, how thankful and how awed. In

English and Arabic he praised her, telling her, with absolute truth, that he'd never wanted any woman more.

When he'd finished, her thighs were slack beneath him, her hands fisted in his hair and her eyes aglow.

His voice was thick and rough. 'You are so very beautiful, Avril.'

And she was *his*. He felt it deep in his belly, in the very marrow of his bones.

No other woman in his past had affected him like this.

Did she feel the same about him? The possibility that she didn't was unbearable. He wanted to bind her to him, not just with a promise of marriage but with ties of emotion and need.

He pushed her legs wide and settled between them, lowering his head. Her thighs trembled as he parted her folds to unveil that sensitive nub. Her whole body jolted as he captured it in his lips, drawing long and slow.

She gasped, her hands clenching tighter, holding him to her. As if he had any intention of leaving! The scent and taste of honeyed woman and arousal enveloped him and he couldn't get enough.

He needed to take his time, draw this out so that she hovered on the brink of bliss for as long as possible. But his own need weakened his determination. Instead of prolonging her pleasure he drove her further, faster, using his mouth and his hands until her quivering body rose desperately against him and shudders racked her. He felt her climax, tasted it, was part of it as she cried his name again and again, drawing him to her.

When he finally climbed higher to settle beside her Avril burrowed into his arms, her broken breaths hot at his throat, fingers clutching, legs tangled with his.

A tiny, thinking part of his brain triumphed at her response. But mostly Isam was caught in the pure joy of bringing her such pleasure. He wrapped her close, stroking her hair, delighted and possessive in equal measure.

Her eyes, when they opened, gleamed golden rather than brown and he felt something inside him soften and melt.

He wanted her to look at him like that again and again. He'd never tire of it.

Isam's already taut body stiffened with need as she moistened her lips to speak.

Then a wail pierced the night air.

Isam blinked, taking a second to identify the sound when all his thoughts had been on Avril and himself. It had felt as if no one else existed but the pair of them.

The sound came again, louder this time.

Avril slumped against him. 'Maryam.'

For a second he lay there, storing up every wonderful sensation, so much better than his broken memories of them together. Then, with a supreme effort, he rose from the bed and walked stiffly towards the cries.

A nightlight was on, giving the nursery a cosy glow. The baby looked up from the cot with a trembling chin, and tear-washed eyes. Before she could cry again he lifted her, rocking her gently. She didn't want to settle, instead mouthing the fine cotton of his robe.

'Sorry, little one. I can't help with that.'

But he could make sure she was changed and dry before taking her to Avril. When he returned to the bedroom with Maryam, Avril had changed into a cotton robe, sitting back against the pillows and smothering a tremendous yawn. She looked flushed and lovely though her gaze skated from his. Was she shy about what they'd done? Did she regret it?

Then she lifted her gaze from their daughter to him and her smile made something in his chest tumble.

'Thank you, Isam. I should have expected this.'

'What about the nanny?'

'I've told her I'd do the nights myself.' She shrugged. 'Maybe I shouldn't have insisted. It would be nice to get more rest, but she's been working all hours and deserved a break. Besides, I prefer my privacy. We close the door to her quarters at night.'

Isam nodded. He hadn't given any thought to their privacy as he'd set about seducing Avril. He'd been too caught up in his need for her.

That was a first. He couldn't remember any time when he'd been so lacking in caution.

Except when you got your PA pregnant.

What was it about Avril that made him forget everything else?

No time now to ponder. He carried the baby to Avril where she sat propped against the pillows.

Despite the colour in her cheeks and the glitter in her eyes, he registered the shadows of fatigue beneath those eyes. She covered her mouth as another yawn escaped.

It struck him how much had changed for Avril in a short time. She was a new mother in a foreign country where she didn't know the language or customs. She'd been brilliant tonight at the reception, but it must have been an enormous strain.

Isam had been working all hours, managing his royal responsibilities and dealing with crises that he believed were of Hafiz's making. As a result he'd barely focused on how daunting this was for her.

That had to change.

'It might be better if I leave you to finish up then get some rest.'

Her eyes rounded and she stopped in the act of opening her robe for the baby to feed.

'You're leaving?'

He caught her hand and pressed an open-mouthed kiss to

her palm. He tasted honey-sweet woman and the salt tang of sex. A shudder of hunger ripped through him. One taste of her was nowhere near enough.

He swallowed, his voice rough. 'I want to stay. But if I do I'll be tempted to make love to you all night. I suspect you need your sleep now more than you need sex.'

'But you didn't…'

'Don't worry about me.' He hauled in a deep breath. 'Ever since we met again we've been working to *my* schedule, driven by *my* imperatives as King. Let me do this for you, Avril. Feed Maryam then rest. You look like you can barely keep your eyes open. Perhaps we can breakfast together.'

This time when Avril smiled, her pleasure had nothing to do with sexual desire, yet he basked in its warmth. It was the first real smile she'd bestowed on him since his accident. It felt like a rich gift.

Simply at the suggestion they share a meal.

You already knew she was unlike other lovers.

Yet that didn't explain his elation at her unguarded smile.

He kissed her hand again, inhaling the sweet essence of her, then made himself go to the door. He had to leave now or risk forgetting his good intentions. It was going to be a long night.

'Until the morning. Sleep well.'

'The food isn't to your taste?'

Avril started, her gaze locking on Isam's, and reaction rippled through her belly.

'It all looks lovely, thank you.'

She surveyed the food on the table between them, yanking her thoughts from last night. Difficult to do when her brain couldn't get past their renewed intimacy and the pleasure he'd given her.

The table was loaded with every conceivable breakfast

item from fragrant savoury dishes to fruits, pastries, breads, dips, jams and even a large block of honeycomb dripping with sweet bounty.

'Do sheikhs eat like this every morning?'

He chuckled and even that set off reverberations deep inside as if she were attuned to him at a visceral level. 'I'm afraid I eat rather more frugally usually but I wasn't sure what you liked. Please help yourself.'

She nodded and reached for flatbread, cheese and a ripe fig.

It was hard to concentrate on breakfast when her mind kept returning to the magic he'd worked on her needy body. She'd been so sure they'd spend the night together yet he'd insisted on going, leaving her restless now despite the best sleep she'd had in months.

She'd been moved when he'd put her needs above his own. How many men would do that? Maybe there was a chance for her to become more than the bride foisted on him by circumstance.

Her blood sang and her appetite sharpened. She bit into warm bread spread with soft cheese, almost groaning with delight at its nutty deliciousness.

'You like that? Try it with rose-petal jam.'

His tone was husky, eyes glinting as he watched her eat. It was the same expression he'd worn as he watched her climax less than twelve hours earlier. He'd looked at her then as if *she* were the most delectable feast he'd ever tasted. The memory scrambled her brain.

Avril hurried into speech, needing something else to focus on. 'Tell me about the people at last night's reception. Who was the woman in silver?'

The woman had looked at the pair of them with the strangest expression, though her face had been bland when she'd approached and congratulated them on their engagement.

'Silver? Surely there were several.'

'She was with that man who behaved so oddly. You saw him too, he looked upset and he left without a word.'

Avril watched Isam pause in the act of helping himself to baked eggs. His abrupt stillness made her skin prickle.

She'd *known* there was something strange about the man, though the other guests hadn't noticed. They'd been watching her and Isam.

Isam finished filling his plate. 'You really are observant. I remember that from when we worked together.'

Her pulse quickened. 'You remember more about us together?'

'Still not everything, but lots, including your initial interview.' He smiled. 'You were very impressive. And I remember almost all the days we worked together in London.'

Avril struggled not to feel disappointed that it was only their business dealings he recalled, rather than anything personal. Surely if their intimacy had been important to him he'd remember it.

To Isam she'd been only his PA. Now she was his necessary bride. Never someone he wanted for her own sake.

Don't even go there. You need to keep your feet firmly on the ground.

'So who was he, the man who left without congratulating us?'

She watched Isam sip his coffee before replying, his deliberate movements confirming her intuition that this was important. Had he been trying to divert her from her original question?

'His name is Hafiz and he's a distant relative. After my father died and while I was in a critical condition, the Royal Council appointed him as regent. He held that position until it became clear I'd live, and then for a while afterwards until I was well enough to rule.'

Isam spoke matter-of-factly, yet Avril's heart hammered high in her throat. She hadn't known there'd been any question about him surviving.

'You're really all right now?'

'Really. Except for some persistent memory loss that's gradually improving.'

Yet his smile didn't reach his eyes. She could only guess how frustrating amnesia must be.

'You don't like him, do you?'

His eyes widened with surprise. 'As a royal I've spent my life keeping my emotions to myself. But you read me too easily, Avril, better than most people.'

She said nothing, just waited. Finally he said, 'I hadn't wanted to tell you yet. You have enough to deal with. This—' his gesture encompassed their palatial surroundings '—takes a lot of getting used to.'

'I don't need to be coddled. I'd rather understand what's going on.'

His prevarication only heightened her concern. The Isam she knew didn't dither. He was quick to grasp problems and take action. Yet now he seemed reluctant to talk.

Finally he shrugged. 'There have been problems for some time. At first I wondered if they were my fault. That's the way it seemed, or at least the way it was made to seem.'

'I don't understand.'

Isam's expression hardened. 'Nor did I. I was convinced my memory loss was only for the period before and during the accident, not afterwards. Yet important errors kept being made, all stemming from my office, apparently leading back to me. No real damage has been done…yet. But it's been a close-run thing and only because my staff are so dedicated and loyal. There have been whispers among the few who knew about my amnesia, that perhaps I wasn't up to the job of ruling after all. That I was unreliable, my brain too damaged to work effectively.'

A chill of premonition skated down Avril's spine. 'You think Hafiz is behind that.'

Isam nodded. 'Behind the rumours, and, thanks to you, I'm now sure he's behind the problems we've had.'

'Thanks to me? I haven't done anything.'

'But you have. The day you found that group waiting in the courtyard, you described the man who'd loitered nearby. The one who hurried away when you called him. Your description fitted someone who'd already raised suspicion. He's a secretary in the palace with access to my office and he has a close connection with Hafiz. My personal staff have checked his movements over the past several months and his access to restricted information. We believe he engineered every crisis we've faced.'

Avril stared, her stomach churning. 'You mean leaving those people out in the heat was deliberate? That could have been disastrous.'

'Exactly. And because they were told I'd personally requested them to attend that day, some might make a case that it was my fault. That I'm undependable and make erratic, pointless decisions.'

'*Some* meaning Hafiz?'

'It sounds far-fetched but it's no joke. The crises we dealt with were initially to do with leaked confidential information that might affect key commercial negotiations and national security. Now he's stooped to threaten the health of innocent bystanders too.' His voice hardened. 'All because Hafiz has developed a taste for royal power. I think he hoped I wouldn't recover and the council might make him Sheikh.'

'That's appalling! Surely no one would take him seriously.'

Isam's mouth tightened. 'He tries to capitalise on the fact that prior to the accident my work for the country was mainly behind the scenes. He even tried to paint me as a playboy with no interest in governing, based on a few high-profile lovers years ago.' Isam shook his head. 'When I was young I was impatient of royal protocol, leaving most official public duties to my father. But we worked as a team. I've helped run the country for years.'

Avril struggled to take it all in. 'But he can't get rid of you, can he? You're well.'

'I am. The only way I can be removed as Sheikh is if I'm proven incompetent to lead. That *won't* happen.'

She surveyed his grimly set features and relief stirred. The thought of Isam dethroned by a conniving rival chilled her. Not that she knew anything about Zahdari politics, but she knew him. He had immense vision, was dependable and talented, the sort of qualities a leader needed.

The shock of his revelation made her realise her earlier doubts about his motives said more about her than him.

'Don't worry, Avril. Now we've located the mole in the palace we'll be able to prove what he's up to.'

'And Hafiz? What was he doing last night?'

Isam's mouth flattened. 'I can't say for sure but the woman with him was his daughter.' He paused as if searching for words. 'In the months after my accident the Royal Council strongly urged me to marry. Everyone likes the idea of an heir to carry on the succession. Hafiz suggested his daughter as a suitable bride and I agreed to consider the possibility. He was looking at ways to shore up his links to the throne.'

Avril's breath clogged her throat, making her voice thick. 'But then you found out I'd had your baby.'

It was one thing for him to say he'd probably have married a woman from his own country if circumstances had been different.

But it was another to discover that wasn't theoretical, that there *was* another woman!

A sophisticated, elegant woman who looked born to the role of Sheikh's wife. Who'd do it more successfully than Avril ever could.

No wonder the crowd had hushed as the woman in silver offered her good wishes on their engagement.

Avril folded her arms, hugging them close to her body, holding in the sudden wretchedness churning her insides.

'Yes. From that moment there was no question of me marrying anyone else.' After a second he continued. 'I never agreed to marry her, Avril. Only to think about it. As for Hafiz's behaviour last night, I don't know. But only a very few people knew about our engagement in advance. Hafiz wasn't one. My guess is he was furious that his ploy to marry off his daughter to me failed.'

Warm fingers covered hers and squeezed. 'Don't worry. Soon we'll have proof of his machinations. His campaign against me can't succeed. And you can be sure I'll look after you and Maryam. Believe me, Avril, I take my duty very seriously.'

CHAPTER ELEVEN

Duty.

There was that word again. Until she'd met Isam it had never bothered her. She told herself it shouldn't now. She was glad he wouldn't shirk doing the right thing by their child. Besides which, he was clearly besotted by Maryam.

If Avril's parents had loved her more, if they'd been as committed as him to doing their parental duty, they wouldn't have left her behind.

Don't go there. You can't change the past. As for the future, your focus must be Maryam, ensuring she has the parental love and care you didn't.

Cilla had been a wonderful role model and taught her so much, loved her so dearly. But there'd always been a part of Avril ready to believe she wasn't enough, wasn't lovable, and that was why her parents found it so easy to leave.

Now the man she was about to marry reminded her their wedding was all about duty.

She pushed down burgeoning hurt, crushed it into a dark recess behind her ribs and slammed a lid down on it. She couldn't afford to feel hurt, not if they were going to make this work.

'Sorry, what were you saying?'

Isam had spoken but she'd been caught up in her thoughts. But the time for regret and doubt was over. She had committed to this.

'I said we need to spend more time together.' Pale eyes held hers but she couldn't tell what he was thinking. 'Since we returned to Zahdar I've been putting out spot fires of Hafiz's making. But now we have a lead on how he's causing the trouble, I can step back a little, help you adjust.'

Avril tried to ignore her flutter of pleasure. 'What do you have in mind?'

'My staff will organise briefings for you on palace protocol, local history and customs, and so on. Useful things that will help you when you become Sheikha. But you won't just be taking on a royal title, we'll be building a marriage. We need to know each other better, trust each other.'

'You want to get to know me?'

'Is that so bad?'

'Of course not. It makes sense.'

Avril didn't know whether to be pleased at his sensible approach, or disappointed. It sounded as though he intended to schedule slots for her in his busy timetable. Would they do Q and As across his desk?

The difference between that and last night's encounter, when he'd buried his head between her legs and taken her to the stars, made her want to weep. She wished he'd gather her close and make love to her instead of sitting on the other side of the table.

She didn't know where she stood with Isam. Most of the time he acted like a polite acquaintance, but last night... All she knew for sure was that he saw her as key to claiming his daughter.

Avril looked away, reaching for a peach, rather than reveal disappointment that, despite last night's intimacy, he viewed their relationship as something to be planned.

'How do you want to do that?' She bit into the peach, its sweet lushness the complete opposite of their dry conversation.

His expression changed, so quickly she couldn't read his

gleaming eyes before his features settled again into calm lines.

She'd give so much to see him raw and unguarded.

'Sharing breakfast each morning would be a good start, yes?'

She kept her tone non-committal. 'Yes, an excellent start.'

'And perhaps there are some things you'd especially like to see and do. After we marry we'll tour the kingdom and I can show you my country. But for now it will need to be things in or near the capital. What interests you?'

Isam's question stumped her for a moment. She'd spent so long fretting over practicalities, preparing for single motherhood, worrying what would happen if her salary dried up, learning to care for a baby. How long since she'd thought of things she'd *like* to do?

Not since Cilla persuaded you to make that list.

'Avril?'

'There are some things,' she said slowly, remembering Cilla's enthusiasm and her own over the catalogue she'd compiled. She'd done it for Cilla's sake but had found a genuine spark of excitement at the possibility of expanding her horizons one day. Before Isam and an unexpected pregnancy changed everything.

He leaned closer, his clean, citrus smell invading her nostrils and making her tremble. 'Go on.'

'I want to learn to drive. In London there seemed no point but I always wanted...'

'What did you want, Avril?'

His low voice thrummed across her flesh, teasing her so she blurted out, 'Travel. Adventure. To see and explore. I wanted to see the Northern Lights. Learn to navigate by the stars. Go hot-air ballooning. Waterski and scuba-dive.'

She clamped her mouth shut. Adventure and a life of royal duty were hardly compatible. The only thing on her list that she was likely to achieve was to learn another language, not as she'd imagined—to help her on her travels—but simply so she could communicate in her new country.

To her surprise Isam grinned and despite everything she felt a ripple of pleasure deep inside. He looked jubilant, the habitual gravity of his expression morphing into an enthusiasm that made him look younger and stunningly handsome. Her pulse quickened and she leaned closer, drawn by his magnetism.

'You've come to the right place. Not for the Northern Lights, but we can travel to see them some time. For the rest, Zahdar is perfect. Along the coast there are some excellent diving spots and there's a lagoon perfect for waterskiing. Hot-air ballooning is popular inland and as for navigating by the stars, that's a highly prized local skill. Astronomers come from around the world to see our night skies in the desert. We have an excellent observatory. I can show all that to you, Avril. And I can teach you to drive.'

'*You* can?'

He nodded. 'Who better? We'll take a four-wheel drive out of the city.'

'A four-wheel drive? I was thinking of something small.'

'Why not learn to drive something that will take you off road? It's more practical here and all the better when you want an adventure.'

His enthusiasm was contagious, but she couldn't allow herself to be carried away. 'Are sheikhas allowed to have adventures?'

She'd assumed her new future would be hemmed in by strict rules about conservative royal behaviour.

'Why not? My father said…'

Avril watched Isam's expression change, his smile falter. She waited but he didn't continue and she had the feeling that instead of seeing her his gaze was inward-looking. What did he see?

She waited. Was it a memory? Something he'd only now recalled? Surely that was a good thing. Then she saw his forehead scrunch up and taut lines bracket his mouth as if he were in pain. His hand went to the scars near his temple where his pulse throbbed.

'Isam.' She leaned in, her hand on his arm, feeling his tense muscles. 'Are you all right?'

She was used to him being strong and in control. The sight of him frozen in what looked like pain made her heart squeeze.

Finally, to her relief, he seemed to focus again. He stared as if surprised to see her.

She poured water into a crystal goblet and took it around the table to him, crouching beside him and curling the fingers of his other hand around the stem. Surely she only imagined they felt cold.

'Drink this.' She supported his hand, lifting it to his mouth. 'You'll feel better.'

She had no idea if it were true, but she couldn't bear seeing him like that. He sipped then lowered the goblet.

'My apologies.' His voice was a husk of sound and his throat worked as if he tried to coax stiff muscles into action. 'I...'

'Don't apologise. Are you okay?'

He rubbed his temple, frowning. 'I'm fine, nothing to worry about.'

But Avril did worry. Because despite all the warnings she'd given herself, Isam mattered to her.

Not because of Maryam or public expectations that they marry. But because she cared.

Even when they were boss and PA, when he should have been off-limits, she'd felt so much for him. It should be impossible, given how little time they'd spent together, but something about this man called to her. Made her yearn. Made her feel…

'Shall I call for a doctor?'

'No doctor!' He drew a deep breath. 'Thanks, but it's all good.' His mouth hooked up in a crooked smile that tugged at her heart. 'It may not look it but it's true. Sometimes memories come back easily and other times…' He rubbed his temple then reached for his coffee.

'It will be cold now.' She rose to her feet. 'I'll get a new pot.'

'No.' Long fingers shackled her wrist, warm and strong. 'Water's fine. Please, sit down. I don't need caffeine. I've already had enough stimulation.'

His mouth twisted wryly yet Avril saw the sheen of moisture brightening his eyes and knew he was more affected than he pretended. She covered his encompassing hand with hers.

She wanted to quiz him but he was entitled to privacy. They'd been physically intimate but not emotionally. It wasn't as if they…

'I'm sorry I worried you.' He took another long draught of water, his gaze fixed in the distance. 'I've been remembering more and more lately, but mainly less significant things. Now, out of the blue, I remember talking with my father on the day he died.'

Isam turned and fixed her with that turbulent grey gaze, heavy with emotion.

Her chest squeezed. Was he remembering the accident? 'Oh, Isam.'

'It's okay.' He moved his hand, threading his fingers through hers. 'It's a *good* memory, from before the crash.'

Yet her heart went out to him. Though she'd been prepared for it, Cilla's death had left her distraught. How much harder to lose a loved parent suddenly?

'I'm glad. Good memories are to be treasured.'

'He was particularly happy that day. I'd agreed to stand in for him so he could have a week off. He'd planned a couple of nights in the desert with a few old friends. I ribbed him about getting too old for camping and he said that a little adventure now and then was good for the soul. That it was important to take a break occasionally from the stress of governing.'

'He sounds like a wise man.'

Isam's eyes met hers. 'He was. The best man I knew.' He paused and she wondered if he was reliving that precious memory. 'He was pleased for another reason too, something else I've just remembered. I'm glad I could tell him that day.' Isam's voice roughened. 'That he knew before he died.'

Avril heard his raw emotion. 'You don't have to tell—'

'I want to.' Eyes that before had been pewter-dark now shone silver. 'Besides, it's related to your old job, my investments in Europe. Given everything else, I haven't had time to go through all the reports in detail.'

Her curiosity rose. 'Your business is doing very well.'

'Yes. So well that I told my father that day that I was in a position to invest some of the profits. There was an initiative I wanted to start in Zahdar. When I'd initially raised it my father liked the idea but said other matters took priority, like funding medical facilities, infrastructure and schools. He wouldn't divert public money into it when there were too many other areas of need.'

Understanding dawned. 'So you decided to invest your private funds to raise money for it?'

He inclined his head. 'It will be a long-term project but it's important to me. I'd floated the idea with members of the Royal Council. Most liked it but Hafiz was against it, said it showed my priorities were wrong.' He frowned.

Avril broke the growing silence. 'I'd back your priorities over his any day.'

A smile tugged at the corners of Isam's mouth and the look he gave her made something inside sing.

'Thank you, Avril. When I was recuperating he'd mention things I'd apparently said or done that seemed to make no sense. For a while I wondered if my faculties *had* been affected by the accident. Before I realised he was trying to gaslight me.'

'He sounds like a poisonous man. I wouldn't trust him.'

'On that we're agreed. No doubt when I announce my initiative he'll try to undermine it.'

'But what *is* it?'

'It was inspired by my sister, Nur. You know she died young?'

Avril nodded, watching his expression cloud. Clearly his grief was still profound, both for his father and his sister. She thought of losing Cilla and what a relief it had been to talk about her aunt with friends rather than bottle up her loss.

'Was it a long illness?'

Isam's expression sharpened and she feared she'd said the wrong thing. Would he see this as prurient curiosity? For a long time he didn't speak. But eventually the words came.

'I was at home the night Nur became ill. She'd complained of a headache so I got her pain relief and sat with her while she rested. But when she opened her eyes a little later she winced at the light and she had a temperature, so I called the doctor.' He paused, swallowing, and Avril felt his pain. 'By the time he arrived she was complaining of a stiff neck and her temperature had spiked. It was meningitis, swift and fatal.'

Avril heard the desperation in his voice, saw him turn rigid, felt his hand tense around hers.

Not just with grief, she realised, but with guilt. Her heart ached for him. He had such drive, he was used to solving problems and making things better for people. How it must have hit him to be helpless to save his sister. No wonder he was distressed.

'I'm sure the medical staff did all they could.'

Isam inclined his head but his features remained strained.

'*You* did all you could, Isam. You were there for her, *with* her. You got help as soon as you realised there was a problem.'

'If I'd realised earlier—'

'How could you, when it just seemed like a headache? I'm sure the doctors told you that.'

He nodded but said nothing and she wondered if there was anything she could say to ease the burden. 'What was she like? Do you want to tell me about her?'

She saw his shoulders ease down. 'From the time she could walk she was always on the move. Most of the time she ran rather than walked. She was happy and curious, always busy, often laughing, and she had a kind heart.'

Isam's mouth formed a crooked smile that tugged at Avril's heart. 'She sounds lovely.'

'She was.' He paused and rolled his shoulders back. 'Nur was enthusiastic and energetic but sometimes found school difficult. She passed all her subjects but teachers expected much more and some of her peers were eager to see her fail.'

Avril must have voiced her dismay because he squeezed her hand. 'Sometimes being royal isn't easy. My father could have had her taught privately but he thought it important that she learn to mix with others and hold her own.'

Avril's respect for his family grew. 'That sounds tough.' Like most people, she'd thought of royalty mainly in terms of wealth and privilege, not its difficulties.

'Nur was athletic and sport became an outlet for her. She found her niche in team sports. She was a born leader, encouraging other players, building bonds between them. It was marvellous to see and all the girls gained confidence and abilities from what they learned together.'

'She was lucky to have such a proud big brother.'

Isam looked startled, then shrugged as if it was nothing. But Avril knew many children didn't have such loving support, and how much difference it could make, having someone who cared.

'You have to understand we don't have a strong history of female sport here. Sport isn't included in our school curriculum for either sex. That's what I want to change, to give them all the chance to participate no matter where they live or what their gender. Health experts and educators talk about the benefits of physical activity, and from watching Nur and her friends I saw so many positives. Not just fitness but self-confidence, teamwork, discipline and, for some, a chance to excel.'

He spoke so eloquently, it was easy to read the strength of his feelings as well as the work he'd put into exploring this. She felt caught up in his enthusiasm.

'I want to establish facilities across the country so all our young people have the chance to engage in sport, in school and outside it. I want to tie it into programmes on healthy living and give every child and adolescent chances simply to enjoy themselves. Life can be short and for some it's very difficult. This is another way to bring people together, building bonds and individual benefits.

'Sorry, I'm on my soapbox. It's something I want to do in Nur's memory. My father was fully behind it, if I could raise the funds.'

Avril sank back, moved by his passion. For his beloved sister and his people. How many political leaders used their own money to achieve something for the public good?

'I think it's a terrific idea, giving chances to people who don't already have them.'

She imagined there were plenty of remote locations in Zahdar. She wondered if Hafiz's objection were solely because of the cost or because the project would specifically include females.

'I'm not particularly sporty but I used to play volleyball.' Before her hectic job with a previous employer cut into her free time. 'I joined to keep fit and I definitely felt healthier for it, but I loved the camaraderie most of all.'

She hadn't realised until now how much she'd missed it. She'd had less time for friends after that.

Abruptly she became aware she and Isam still held hands. She looked at their intertwined fingers. There was nothing sexual in their touch yet it felt...powerful.

This man evoked such strong feelings, far more than a sexual yearning. He'd moved her with his talk of his sister and father. It was clear Isam had loved them, that their loss still hurt.

He felt deeply. How that appealed to her. Imagine being loved so steadfastly.

Now he was truly letting her into his life, sharing his hopes and emotions. Excitement rose. He'd opened up in a way that made her wonder if their future might be brighter than she'd thought. Perhaps, in time, there was a chance...

'What are you thinking, Avril? Tell me.'

It wasn't a command, but that coaxing, velvet voice was irresistible. She looked up and felt a beat of something pass between them. Heat rushed through her. She felt it climb her throat and pool deep too.

She could blurt out her neediness. How much she wanted from him. She could fret over his feelings. Or she could follow his example and simply commit to what now felt right.

Because she loved him.

Amazing that she hadn't recognised it before.

'You're a good man, Isam. I know an unknown, foreign wife isn't an ideal sheikha. I know Hafiz and others will try to use that against you, but I'll do my best not to let you down.'

CHAPTER TWELVE

FOR THE REST of the day Isam battled a headache. He got them less frequently now but occasionally, when the flood of memory returned, pain came with it.

Pain because he was still healing? Or because the memories were bittersweet?

But he couldn't wish them away. The memory of that last morning, his father's ebullience at the prospect of his short vacation and at Isam's news that his initiative for Nur could begin soon... That was priceless.

Isam rubbed the back of his neck and rolled his shoulders as he sat back from the desk. He knew the real reason for his pain—guilt lingering beneath his grief.

Because he'd lost his family and hadn't been able to save them. Everyone, the doctors and his father, assured him he couldn't have done any more for Nur, yet the burden of guilt would always lie heavy.

Now his father was gone too.

Isam had been told he'd done everything conceivable to save his father and the pilot. There'd even been amazement that, despite the severity of his injuries, he'd managed to drag them free before the chopper exploded. Yet that didn't ease his guilt.

How could he alone have survived? Why him?

He felt as though he'd let them down.

An image of earnest brown eyes swam before him, dragging his thoughts from the past.

'I'll do my best not to let you down.'

He shook his head. As if Avril would ever let him down!

Technically he hadn't known her long. Their working relationship had lasted less than a year and they'd only been reunited a short time. But he knew, as surely as he knew the view from this window, that he could rely on her.

Employing her had been a masterstroke. She'd handled every task assigned her and far more with competence and integrity. She'd so impressed that he'd wondered, during that week they'd worked side by side in London, why she'd settled for an assistant's job, working remotely rather than aspiring to a more high-flying corporate job. He could imagine her managing her own enterprise.

He hadn't realised then that she'd curtailed her career to care for her aunt. That made him respect her more.

Now she was to be his wife.

His pulse quickened, excitement stirring. And not because of her sterling work qualities.

He wanted her with a blood-deep hunger that defied all past experience. Wanted her body and her rare smiles. Wanted the excitement that had shone in her eyes when she spoke of having adventures. Adventures that he, with his privilege, took for granted.

And he wanted her tenderness. He saw the way she looked at their baby and felt almost jealous.

The few times they'd been intimate were emblazoned on his brain and his body, leaving him needy.

With Avril everything seemed magnified. Every sensation, every feeling.

Was it because, since the crash, he was starting out afresh? That previous relationships seemed faded and insignificant? Or was it, as he suspected, more to do with Avril herself?

Something about the intense spark between them? A spark he had no name for.

Then there was the fact she was the mother of his child. Emotion blindsided him whenever he dwelt on the miracle of Maryam's birth and the debt he owed her mother.

He'd changed Avril's life and was asking her to take on even more. He knew she was up to the challenge. It wouldn't always be easy, especially in the beginning. She'd have to face down the doubters.

Isam resolved to do everything he could to ease her way, to influence those who could make her life easy or difficult. He'd strive to arm her with the skills and knowledge she needed. That had to be his priority.

He glanced at the computer and the stack of paperwork on his desk, awaiting his attention.

Never had he ended the day without completing his work. Yet he shut down the computer.

He needed to be with Avril. His surge of memory this morning had interrupted their time together so they hadn't finished their discussion before his secretary came to chivvy him to his first meeting.

His blood coursed heavily in his arteries.

Are you sure it's a discussion you want?

'Isam!'

Avril put down the book on Zahdari customs and culture, staring at the tall figure who'd let himself into the sitting room.

Her heart stuttered then accelerated so fast she felt lightheaded as she rose from the sofa.

His jaw was shadowed and his thick hair slightly rumpled as if he'd run his hands through it. Even his scars looked rakish, accentuating rather than detracting from his charisma. His dark suit emphasised his straight shoulders and long legs.

His tie had disappeared and his white shirt was open at the throat.

An invitation to touch, whispered a subversive voice.

'Who did you expect when you invited me in?'

'I thought you were a maid. From what your secretary said, I assumed you'd be working well into the evening.'

Avril watched him flex his fingers as if trying to ease tension.

Could it be the same tension she felt? It had drawn her to her feet, heart hammering as adrenaline pumped in her blood and heat pooled low.

Don't be stupid. He's here to discuss something pragmatic.

Maybe the full schedule of appointments she'd acquired today to meet dressmakers and various experts who would supposedly turn her into someone fit to be royal.

'I should be working.' His voice sounded strained. 'But I needed to see you.'

'Is something wrong?' When he shook his head she continued. 'You wanted to talk about another public appearance?'

'No. We do need to talk.' His voice was harsh and she watched him swallow, tracking the jerky movement of his throat and feeling something like triumph. 'But later.'

Avril waited but he seemed in no hurry to explain, merely stood there, watching her.

Isam moved from the door and the gleam in his deep-set eyes made her nape prickle.

Another step and another, slow, almost languid, yet there was a decisiveness in the set of his jaw and something in the flare of his nostrils that rooted her to the spot, excitement igniting. Her breathing shallowed and she felt the laboured lift of each quick breath as he closed the space between them.

Her heart had bled for him this morning as she'd witnessed his grief and joy at remembering his father on that last day.

This man had the ability to wring her heart but it was too late to retreat. For she'd already surrendered hers.

She'd feared that would make her weak but now, watching his absolute focus as he closed in on her, like a man drawn by a power he couldn't resist, she felt strong. Excited. Thrilled.

As if, for the first time, she was truly *seen*. Not as an employee or a complication. Not as someone he was duty-bound to acknowledge. Nor as the bride he felt obliged to claim.

As a person in her own right. A woman he couldn't relegate to a neat pigeonhole. A woman who got under his skin the way he'd burrowed under hers.

'Why are you here, Isam?'

She had a fair idea but she had to be sure. Her experience with men was limited.

Because no other man ever tempted you. No one else made you feel this way.

'I couldn't stay away.' He stopped before her and she angled her chin to hold his gaze. 'I've been trying to hold myself back and give you space and a chance to rest. Each day it's more difficult. And after last night…' He shook his head. 'I want you, Avril. I can't concentrate, can't work. I need to be with you.'

It was there in the tension honing his striking features. In the glitter of his eyes and the set of his shoulders. Avril felt it too, the ponderous beat of her heart and the melting between her legs.

'You want to have sex with me.'

Tiny vertical lines appeared in the centre of his forehead. 'Not just that but yes. Definitely, yes.'

If anything had been needed to banish last night's fear that he'd brought her to climax simply to make her more amenable, it was the sight of Isam now.

Avril's mouth curled into a smile that felt sultry with invitation. 'Yes.'

He blinked, pupils flaring dark in that sizzling stare, and for a moment there was utter stillness. Then his mouth curved in one of those devastating smiles that had always gone straight to her heart.

'Avril.'

Her name sounded like relief and joy. Acknowledgement and invocation. No one had ever turned her name into something so glorious.

His name formed on her lips but before she could speak he wrapped his arms about her, drawing her up against him and claiming her mouth.

His strong body and his embrace held her securely as her knees weakened. The taste of him, the urgency, undid her. The perfection of their kiss snapped the last ties of her self-control that had already been loosened by the realisation she loved him. How could she hold back?

She slid her arms up between them to lock her hands behind his neck, holding him to her as he dipped her back. There was a feeling of weightlessness, as if the world spun away, but she had no fear of falling from Isam's arms.

This was where she belonged.

Avril kissed him back with an enthusiasm born of old fears and new hope. She was ardent and clumsy. Far from minding, his low growl hummed with approval. And was that possessiveness? Her heart leapt.

'The nanny?' he murmured against her lips.

'Gone for the night.'

Isam lifted one hand to cup her jaw, the weight of those long fingers branding sensitive skin. Fire trailed from her throat to her breasts, her nipples budding. Even the scratch of skin against bra felt arousing.

'The baby?'

Avril turned her head, catching his thumb between her

teeth and biting down. His gaze heated and she felt the fire in her breasts arrow straight to her pelvis.

'Asleep,' she mumbled against his thumb. He tasted better than anything she knew. 'I just put her down.'

His chest expanded hugely, pushing against her swollen breasts as he drew a deep breath. 'I need you, Avril.'

She speared her fingers up to clasp his skull. Even the sensation of thick hair against her hands was an erotic assault, making her quiver with need. Her breathing was almost a pant as desperation rose.

'I need you too.'

There, she'd said it. Instead of weakening her, the admission felt like triumph. Because whatever she'd feared, there was no mistaking Isam's hunger for her. It didn't take the impressive arousal hard against her belly for her to realise he was on the edge of control.

Isam straightened, one arm around her waist and another around her buttocks, lifting her clean off the floor. The proof of his strength only turned her on more.

Their mouths met again, not so neatly this time, clashing a little in their desperation. But Avril wouldn't change a thing. She preferred raw and real to any practised seduction.

Their first night together had been wonderful. But this was on a new level. Despite his strength she felt tremors running through his big frame as if he struggled against a force too powerful to withstand.

'Need a bed.'

His muffled words fell into her mouth, another aphrodisiac, and she feared she couldn't take much more.

'Why not here?'

Avril felt his body jolt. His mouth lifted just enough that he could hold her gaze. She stared straight back then deliberately arched, pressing her aching breasts against his chest.

He whispered something that might have been a prayer

or a plea and then he was moving, striding across the room until her back met the wall. He held her there, pressing her with the weight of his tall frame.

His arm around her waist slid free so he could cup her breast. Her eyes shuttered as she pushed into his palm, at the same time registering the thrust of his thigh between hers. Instantly her legs parted, allowing him to wedge himself against her so she was caught between him and the wall.

Sensations bombarded, inciting a voluptuous shudder.

'Isam. I need—'

'Yes. Me too.'

Avril opened her eyes and drew her hands around to his face. Tenderly she traced the web of scars that ran into his hairline, her heart overflowing at the idea he might have died.

She stroked lower, hearing the scrape of her fingers on his scratchy jaw over the pounding of her heart. She spread her fingers to cup his jaw as she met his eyes and emotion filled her. 'Can we? Here?'

There'd never been a sexier sound than Isam saying, 'We can and will,' in a baritone growl that reverberated through her chest and right down into her feminine core.

Relief soared as together they tackled his belt and zip. Seconds later her hand closed around firm male flesh and her internal muscles clenched needily.

Callused hands skimmed up her legs, pushing her dress to her hips. A second later knuckles brushed her splayed thighs and fingers hooked around her underwear. One tug brought the sound of tearing fabric and her eyes rounded. Avril wondered if it was possible to climax just from anticipation.

Did Isam read her thoughts? Obviously he read her body because that tiny knowing smile reeked of male smugness.

In answer she slid her hand the length of his erection.

She would have laughed as his smile disappeared and he

swallowed abruptly. But there was no joking now, only a compulsion to mate. As if she'd die if she couldn't have him.

'Avril.' The single word held all the longing that filled her.

'Yes, now.'

He touched her again and she tilted her pelvis, hungry for the contact of slick flesh against clever fingers.

Isam eased her hand away from him then lifted her leg, hooking it around his hip. Eager, she raised the other with his help and locked her ankles, encircling him. She was wide open to him, and unbearably excited.

Gently he lifted her higher against the wall and when she slid down a little there he was, waiting for her, probing soft flesh.

Even that felt almost too excruciatingly arousing. She needed him, all of him.

Hands on his shoulders, she bore down just as he thrust up. A lightning flash of silver heat. A precarious moment of stunned disbelief as their bodies met in perfect harmony. The nagging hollowness filled with proud virility. Hardness melded with softness, need with need.

They hung together, suspended on the edge of perfection. Then, as if their twin bodies responded with exact synchronicity, they moved together. Friction deepened perfection. Sensation heightened to awe. Until it became too much and pure joy consumed them.

Avril lost herself in the grey eyes of the man who'd stolen her heart.

It felt as if she glimpsed paradise.

'We do have things to discuss, Avril.'

They were fully dressed again though she knew she must look rumpled. She *felt* rumpled, her dress creased, her body quivering with sensual after-shocks and her brain dazed with delight.

How she wished they'd moved straight to the bedroom after that exciting coupling. The last thing she wanted was to talk about the world beyond these rooms and all the daunting responsibilities she faced.

Sated as she was, Avril hadn't been ready to end their sexual encounter. She wanted to lie naked in his arms with the freedom to explore his superb body. Perhaps tempt him into another erotic venture. He'd opened the doors to a world of sensual fulfilment and she had so much catching up to do.

In contrast Isam, sitting beside her on the sofa, looked as vibrantly handsome and centred as when he'd walked in. As if he'd strolled into her sitting room for a business discussion.

She resented that. He'd swept her away on a tide of passion and she wanted to linger there. In that blissed-out place she could pretend, for a little while, that she was precious to him, that what they shared *meant* something.

She suppressed a sigh. It *did* mean something. That he was still attracted to her physically.

Avril's mouth tightened. Since they were going to marry that was a good thing. Even if he wasn't emotionally engaged, they'd have a satisfying sex life.

She ignored the voice screaming silently that it wasn't enough. It *had* to be enough, for her sake and Maryam's. Avril would care for her daughter as her parents hadn't cared for her. Even if it meant—

'Did you hear what I said, Avril?'

'Sorry. I wasn't really concentrating.'

She looked across and met his surprised stare.

Obviously he was used to holding his audience's attention. One of the prerogatives of being royal.

But as she remembered him this morning, grieving and vulnerable, her indignation disintegrated.

Avril wondered if his determination to accept and raise Maryam had roots in his feelings for Nur. He'd lost the people closest to him. Now he was determined not to lose the tiny girl who was his only family.

Her heart turned over, as she thought of the lengths he was going to for Maryam's sake, courting scandal and bringing in an unsuitable wife.

It wasn't Isam's fault he didn't love Avril. He was doing his best. And from what he'd told her about the situation with Hafiz and his own recovery, doing it under incredibly difficult circumstances.

Her voice softened. 'What is it, Isam? What did you want to talk about? Is it my next public appearance?' She repressed a shiver of trepidation.

'That's important, but for now we need to agree on something more urgent.' He covered her hand with his. 'More personal. I want us to live together, now. I see no point waiting to marry.'

'Live together?'

The smile forming on his face faded. 'Why not? After last night and tonight, I know you're as eager for intimacy as I am.' Before she could respond he went on. 'I see the shadows under your eyes, Avril. If we spend the nights together I can help share the burden of looking after Maryam.'

'You want to help look after the baby, hands on?' She recalled that he'd helped care for his sister but despite his assistance last night he surprised her. 'Surely you're already carrying enough of a burden with your official responsibilities?'

His fingers firmed around hers and the hint of a frown carved his forehead. 'I want a real relationship with my daughter, not just to see her for half an hour between meetings. My family is as important to me as my country.'

His family. He meant Maryam, not her. Avril forced down a sigh, refusing to wallow in self-pity. She was grateful he felt such a strong bond with their daughter.

'I'm not arguing, Isam. I'm just surprised. I was thinking of potential scandal. I imagined people wouldn't approve if we were—'

'Sharing a bed?' His chuckle ignited a flare of feminine arousal that made her shift on the seat. 'I'm sure people assume that's exactly what we're already doing. They'd be surprised to know I haven't been regularly bedding the beautiful mother of our child.' His level stare told her he was serious. 'As to scandal, we've already done that. An affair and a baby born outside marriage.'

It was as she'd suspected. 'Will that play into Hafiz's hands?'

Isam raised his eyebrows and she glimpsed hauteur in his proud, uncompromising features. An arrogance that startled her, reminding her he was the hereditary Sheikh, born to power. A man used to succeeding and winning what he wanted, no matter what the odds.

'Don't worry, Avril, I have his measure. He won't succeed. You and I have had an…unconventional relationship so far but that doesn't matter. People are pleased about our baby and delighted at our upcoming marriage.'

Because they wanted their sheikh to provide an heir. Not because they approved his choice of bride.

He was sparing her feelings but she suspected there must be a lot of negativity about her, despite her proven fertility. Her lips twisted, because that was her real value in this equation. Her ability to provide an heir to the throne.

Warm fingers curled under her chin, raising it so their eyes met. She saw warmth there and something that made the tightness within her unfurl. 'There's nothing for you to worry about, Avril. I promise.' He paused and for a moment she almost thought he looked nervous. But Isam didn't do nervous. He was the most confident, capable man she'd met. 'You still haven't answered me.'

'What was the question?'

He leaned in. 'Us. Living together. Now.'

Avril licked suddenly dry lips and saw his eyes track the movement. Heat bloomed across her flesh as his eyelids grew heavy in a look of sultry expectation that opened up an emptiness in her pelvis. Her breath was a shuddery sigh. He only had to look at her that way and she turned to mush.

She feared the power he had over her, the strength of her own yearning. The desperate desire to blurt out a *yes*.

But why hold back? She wanted intimacy, wanted to build a family with him and Maryam. Wanted Isam.

'Yes.'

Her mouth was still forming the word when he leaned across and scooped her up onto his lap. 'Excellent.' Then he smiled and the devil was in his eyes. He rose, holding her effortlessly against his chest. 'Come and tell me what side of the bed you'd like to sleep on.'

But as he carried her to the bedroom she knew it wasn't sleep on his mind. Anticipation fired her blood.

CHAPTER THIRTEEN

AVRIL HURRIED TO put on her make-up. She'd been distracted, playing with Maryam.

At six months, her little girl was such fun, babbling happily and blowing bubbles. She could roll over now, reaching for her toys, and sit up with only a little assistance.

Isam, an adoring father, insisted she was gifted. Avril was just happy Maryam was thriving. Seeing her with her father confirmed Avril was doing the right thing.

So why did the fact the wedding was mere weeks away create a chill deep inside?

Avril ignored the sensation, telling herself it was nerves before another royal event. They still made her edgy. She knew Isam took a risk, marrying her, an outsider who had little to recommend her as Queen. As a result she worked hard to learn everything necessary to take her place at his side.

The last two months had been a roller coaster. Intimacy with Isam was even better than before, and there were times when she felt the connection strong between them. She often accompanied him to official events and it was getting less fraught each time.

She muddled through with his help and that of Hana Bishara. It transpired that Hana was a retired language teacher and she'd become Avril's tutor and friend. Through her Avril now knew a number of women, regularly meeting them for coffee afternoons. Gradually the sense of isolation began to ease and she knew that in time, if she worked at it, she could make a niche for herself here.

Avril put down her mascara and pressed a hand to her churning stomach, turning from the mirror.

Did she *want* to make a niche here?

In theory, yes. For Maryam. And for herself, since she would marry the man she loved. The man whose ardent passion turned their nights together into bliss.

Yet disquiet stirred. Despite her best efforts it was getting worse, not better.

On the threshold of the bedroom she paused and made herself focus on the beauty before her.

Isam had moved them into a different suite, one that had been his grandparents'. It was grand, as everything in the palace was, but something more too.

The walls of the bedroom were hand-painted to create a romantic bower. The wall behind the bed was a trellis of lush roses, so realistic it felt as if she could reach out and pluck one. The other walls depicted a beautiful spring garden and the rolling green hills of England.

His grandfather had presented it to his wife as a wedding gift, afraid his new bride might pine for her homeland. Isam thought Avril would like it too.

She did, enormously. But she couldn't prevent a poignant ache, wondering how it would feel to be so loved by a husband that he'd create such a romantic place for her.

Avril frowned, guilt stirring.

Isam was doing everything he could to make her feel at home. Teaching her to drive, his patience and encouragement making it easier than she'd thought.

There'd been private outings, just the pair of them, to places he thought she'd enjoy. An idyllic private beach where they'd swum and made love. A superb lunch high in a modern glass tower with a bird's eye view of the city, where he'd pointed out new developments and traditional parts of the city he loved so much.

One evening he'd taken her outside the capital for a supper picnic. Away from the city lights they'd gazed at the brilliant stars and he'd begun teaching her their names. They'd go hot-air ballooning after the wedding too.

Isam was thoughtful and kind, and his passion excited her. But there was something missing.

Unlike his grandfather who'd had these beautiful rooms decorated for his bride, Isam didn't love her.

Avril told herself it didn't matter. This was the best solution to their situation.

You want more than a solution. You want love.

The one thing she'd always craved.

She shook her head, discarding her robe and putting on the clothes laid out for her. The beautiful green dress and shoes had been custom made. Yet she barely registered their luxury. She was too busy telling herself, as she did daily, that she was doing the right thing.

She'd promised to marry and she would, for Maryam. And because she couldn't bear the thought of leaving Isam.

'Ms Rodgers, it's very kind of you to single me out again. There are so many who'd like to talk with you.'

Avril met the elegant brunette's eyes, reading pleasure there as well as tension. She felt sorry for Hessa, Hafiz's daughter, guessing how difficult public appearances must be. Word had got out that Hessa had been suggested as a royal bride but rejected by Isam. How many in the crowd also knew her father had plotted against his sheikh?

Even at this celebration to open Zahdar's new national library, Avril had seen the nudges and whispers.

She moved closer. 'Not at all. It's nice talking with someone of a similar age.'

'His Majesty doesn't mind?' Hessa looked past Avril as if expecting Isam to stride through the throng and separate them.

'Of course not.' On the contrary, he'd thanked her for talking to Hessa at a previous event, when others had treated her like a pariah. Avril suspected he felt sorry for her, tainted by Hafiz's behaviour.

'But my father—'

'You're not your father.' As far as Avril could see, the man had left his daughter to face public curiosity alone. He hadn't attended any public or royal events since the engagement announcement.

'You're very understanding. I'm so glad the trouble he stirred this week hasn't affected you after all. It would have been a shame.'

'This week?' Avril hadn't heard anything about him lately. Isam had told her things were under control with Hafiz.

'Yes, that incident in the marketplace and...' She shook her head, eyes shadowed. 'I apologise for his behaviour. It saddens me that he used you in that way.'

Avril was about to find out more but thought better of it. This wasn't the time or place. Besides, a tickle of awareness down her spine told her they weren't alone.

It was the sensation she got whenever Isam came close. Her body recognised and responded to his nearness even when she hadn't seen him.

Excitement stirred as it always did. She *wanted* his company. But there was something else too. A despairing ache that swamped everything else.

Despair because their months living together had confirmed what she'd feared. The love she'd recognised so recently was as potent as ever. It showed no sign of diminishing. Her emotions grew deeper as time passed. She was in his thrall, totally responsive and eager for him.

But to Isam she represented duty.

She doubted that would ever change. He was considerate and tender, passionate too, so passionate her toes curled thinking about it. And his love for Maryam…

Her heart clenched. He was capable of love, just not for her.

'Your Majesty.'

Hessa sank into a curtsey. As ever, Avril admired her grace. She was elegant, arresting, and knew so much about the country and its politics.

She'd make a much better sheikha than you.

A deep voice spoke. 'Hessa, it's good to see you.'

Isam reached out to take his wife's hand and felt the tiniest flinch. He watched her shoulders rise, a sure sign of tension.

Concern speared him. For the past few weeks, despite his best efforts, something had gone wrong between them. But what? Whenever he tried to broach the matter she changed the subject, telling him everything was fine.

Fine. Such a bland word. He didn't want to settle for fine.

Initially she'd seemed to enjoy being with him as much as he wanted to be with her. He'd thought they bonded over Maryam. They'd even shared the once familiar camaraderie that had characterised their working relationship. As if they understood each other, almost without words.

She'd never physically withdrawn from him before. On the contrary, her passion for him seemed endless. Even, of late, almost desperate. Now her composure seemed brittle.

He sensed her fragility.

Hessa spoke, drawing his attention. 'Thank you, Your Majesty. May I congratulate you on the new library? It's a stunning building and a wonderful resource, particularly for researchers.'

'I'm glad you think so.' He and his father had sponsored the project together and he was proud of it. He explained to

Avril, 'Hessa is a historian and this building will house prized ancient texts and records as well as being a library for the general public.'

Avril immediately began asking the other woman about her work and the documents she consulted in her research.

Pride filled him. That Avril should make such an effort to put Hessa at ease when so many avoided her now. That showed a generosity of spirit that he admired. But it wasn't just Hessa. Avril happily engaged with everyone from VIPs to market vendors, treating them all with courtesy and interest.

Yet concern overshadowed his pride. Something was wrong and he didn't know what. It worried him, seeing her so on edge. Was Avril overwhelmed by her royal responsibilities? Or by the unfamiliarity of her new country?

Gently he squeezed her hand, signalling his support. But she didn't respond.

Anxiety stirred in his belly. Whatever problems they'd faced, she'd never been indifferent to him.

'It's time for the official opening.' His voice roughened. 'If you'd like to come and help me cut the ribbon, Avril.'

'Of course. This will be a first for me.'

Her lips curved into a wide smile. But it didn't reach her eyes. Her gaze was curiously blank and fear feathered his nape.

He needed to get to the bottom of this. Today.

Two hours later he followed Avril into their sitting room. Despite his worries, his gaze lingered appreciatively as she crossed the room, hips swaying because of her high heels. Her dress, fitted around the upper body and skimming her hips and thighs, was modest, except he couldn't help visualising her body beneath the gleaming silk.

His blood heated. Months living together had done nothing to assuage his need for her.

He struggled to focus on something other than his primal

hunger for her. Calling on years of practice, Isam turned to assessing today's event. Avril had been a huge success and not just with the attendees.

Zahdar's fashion designers loved her, vying for the chance to dress her. It helped that she was gorgeous. But she also went out of her way to support local makers. That green silk had been manufactured by a new enterprise reinvigorating the old art of silk production. Even the pattern of the fabric was an advertisement for Zahdari design. The delicate white lilies grew in the mountains and were a symbol of his people.

'Isam. You're staring.' She brushed her hands down her skirt, inadvertently drawing attention to the swell of her hips and the line of her thighs. 'Is there something wrong with the dress?'

He shook his head and followed her further into the room, arousal stirring. But this wasn't the time for sex. He turned to pour them cool drinks.

'On the contrary. I was thinking it perfectly balances support for local industry with chic style. I applaud you on your choice.'

She was stunning, beautiful and utterly sexy.

He opened his mouth to tell her then paused. So often she brushed aside his compliments on her appearance as if not believing him. On the other hand she was anxious about measuring up to her new role and liked feeling competent. That gave her confidence.

He held out a glass to her, trying to stifle disappointment when she took it without even a brush of fingers against his.

'Today was a resounding success, and you played a big part in that,' he said when they were both seated. Again Avril distanced herself, choosing a chair instead of the sofa they'd shared so often.

Another pang of disquiet arrowed through him.

'Thanks for your efforts with the head librarian and the

mayor.' He smiled, remembering the way both men had responded to her attentive questions. 'I'd feared that, given their past differences, we'd have some awkward moments, bringing them together. But it worked out well with your help.'

Instead of looking pleased, Avril nodded and frowned down at her drink. Each day she seemed to withdraw further from him. Despite their physical intimacy, something had changed. Something that made her eyes sad when she didn't think he was looking.

He couldn't bear it. 'Avril—'

'Isam, I—'

'You first,' he said.

His expression was unreadable and Avril was worried. Despite his encouraging words she knew Isam had something weighty on his mind.

Was it the trouble she'd caused? Hessa hadn't given details but it was clear there'd been problems Hafiz had used as ammunition in his campaign against Isam.

'Why didn't you tell me?' She leaned forward. 'I had to find out from Hessa of all people that I'd done wrong.'

Isam frowned as if he didn't know what she was talking about. How much had he withheld? 'I don't know—'

'Don't, Isam. I know Hafiz used something I did recently, some *things* I did, trying to discredit me and, through me, you.' She looked at the glass grasped tightly in her hands and put it down before she spilled anything. 'You treat me like a child, not trusting me with the truth.'

'Hardly like a child!'

Heat blazed in his eyes, a combination of sexual awareness and indignation, as if he wasn't used to being called on his behaviour. Of course he wasn't. He'd been raised royal, trained to expect deference and obedience.

It was a side of him she didn't see often. But those occasional glimpses of innate arrogance, however tempered, were an important reminder of who he was. Sheikh first and foremost. Not her soulmate, however much she wished it.

'You withhold important information. How can I learn if I don't know when I've done things wrong? How can I feel confident I'm doing the right thing in public?'

The royal aspect of this new world was daunting. Yet she'd happily face that if she felt she and Isam were truly partners. Increasingly, however, she realised that was a pipe dream.

'There was nothing important—'

'You're still denying it. Why can't you be straight with me?'

Isam shook his head. 'I *am* straight with you. Despite what you heard from Hessa, you didn't do anything wrong. It was just Hafiz trying to twist things.'

Isam sighed, scraping his hand across his scalp. In his dark suit, tie undone and hanging loose around his open collar, he reminded her of the vital, fascinating businessman she'd met in London.

Her heart squeezed as she wished, not for the first time, that he were just that, an ordinary man. For there was a chance an ordinary man might fall in love. But royals in Zahdar were immunised against that, taught from the cradle to expect loveless marriages.

Isam had so much love to give. She'd seen how deep his feelings ran for his sister and father, and she saw every day how much he loved Maryam.

But romantic love? He'd inferred romantic love wasn't for him. and Avril feared he was right. Even after everything they'd been through he was busy protecting her. He didn't see her as an equal, just a responsibility.

The enormity of what she faced overwhelmed her. She'd thought she had enough love for the pair of them. That she could make do with what he offered her.

Was she fooling herself?

'The main thing to know is that Hafiz wasn't successful.' Isam paused, as if making sure she digested that. 'He saw a video of you dancing at the community centre last week and spoke out about it in an interview.'

Avril frowned. She'd been at the centre with Hana and some of her friends, attending a women's afternoon. It hadn't been an official royal function and she'd enjoyed relaxing with the welcoming group.

'I wasn't very good at it but they were all eager for me to try.' There'd been laughter and encouragement and her participation had broken the ice. 'I did stumble a lot, not a good look in someone about to be Queen.'

Hessa would know the dance and probably perform it flawlessly.

'It wasn't about your competence.' Isam's mouth compressed. 'It was because the dance is one traditionally performed by young women before marriage. By virgins.'

Avril's eyes widened. She wasn't married yet and everybody knew she wasn't a virgin. 'But I was *invited* to dance with them.'

He nodded. 'Exactly. You did nothing wrong. Hafiz was trying to turn it into an insult. To say that the dance is only for sexually inexperienced women rather than simply for those about to marry. His statement reflected badly on him rather than you. As soon as he spoke out, pretending to be affronted, he was howled down.'

She digested that, forcing down distaste. 'And the incident in the market?'

Isam's pinched mouth and set jaw signalled discomfort. Or was that anger? 'He heard about your visit to the sweet shop and tried to turn it into something it wasn't.'

She thought over her visit to the vast covered market and the couple of minutes she'd spent in a delightful stall. The owner had invited her behind the counter so she could see how some of the delicacies were made and she'd left, smiling, with a box of tasty treats.

'I don't understand. I didn't do anything except taste some food. Shouldn't I have accepted the sweets?'

'As I said, you didn't do anything. It was just about you standing close to the stallholder.'

'But it was a tiny space.' Her eyes rounded. 'And we were in full view the whole time, apart from the counter between us and the rest of the market.' Her words tailed off as she read his expression. 'You're not serious! He thought the man hit on me?'

Isam looked uncomfortable. 'No, the opposite.'

Avril opened her mouth then closed it, words failing her. Eventually she managed, 'He accused me of what? Trying to seduce the guy?'

She shot to her feet and stalked across the room, arms wrapped around her middle.

'I told you it was nonsense. It's not about anything you've done or could do better.'

'No,' she croaked from a tight throat. 'It's about what I am. A scarlet woman, is that it? Because I had your baby.'

She turned to see Isam on his feet, concern pleating his forehead. He strode across to her, reaching for her hands but she whipped them behind her. She didn't want him to soothe her. She wanted, *needed* to know.

Isam froze as if she'd slapped him and instantly she regretted her action. But at the same time, she'd grown too used to being lulled by his reassurances.

'Tell me. *Please*, Isam.'

He shoved his hands in his trouser pockets, the action somehow making his straight shoulders seem even more powerful.

'You're right. Hafiz has tried to run that story. Since his

attempts to disrupt my work haven't succeeded, he tried to blacken your character. But,' he continued when she would have protested, 'he hasn't succeeded. In fact his outlandish claims have rebounded. He's made himself a laughing stock and will soon lose what little support he thought he had. Everyone can see that you're not the sort of woman he claims. In fact, you're becoming very popular and admired.'

That might be true, yet Avril felt sick, nausea churning her stomach and her skin prickling hot then cold.

'Why didn't you *tell* me?'

'Because of exactly what's happening now. I wanted to avoid upsetting you. It was so patently untrue. No one believed his insinuations. Besides, Hafiz is about to abandon his political aspirations. You don't need to worry about him any more, Avril. I've seen to that.'

Avril frowned. That was good news but it didn't change the fact Isam had hidden the truth from her. 'I deserved to know!'

His steady gaze held hers. 'I apologise if you feel I've let you down. I didn't want to worry you. I put you in this position and I'm responsible.'

Her voice climbed an octave. 'Stop saying you're responsible for me. I'm responsible for myself!'

If he said it was his *duty* to protect her she might just scream. It was unreasonable but she'd come to hate that word.

Because she wanted to be so much more to him than a duty, someone he needed to protect.

Hurt as she was, it also pained her that the loathsome Hafiz used *her* to get at Isam.

'I know you're trying to do the right thing, Isam, but you're not helping. You're making this harder for me. I'm trying desperately to fit in but you won't trust me with the truth about things that concern me. You don't treat me as a real partner.'

His horrified look spoke volumes. 'You must know I trust you, Avril.'

Slowly she exhaled a shuddery breath. 'I do.'

Of course he trusted her. He was spending so much time helping her learn to act like a royal. That was his focus, securing his daughter by moulding Avril into a suitable queen.

Then she stunned herself as well as him by blurting out, 'But that's not enough.'

When they'd entered the room she'd felt a burst of exaltation, imagining he found her attractive in her new dress. But he'd just been thinking how her appearance would please his subjects, because she supported local industry.

He praised her often, but always about her ability to learn or her performance in public. All he cared about was her future public role. Her ability to undertake royal duties.

Isam said something but she didn't hear over the tumult in her blood.

Avril felt a ripping sensation inside, white-hot pain streaking through her then turning into a heavy anguished throb. As if some vital part of her had torn in two.

She stared into his stubbornly set features and confused eyes, and knew they could never go back to the way things had been.

This might have started with dismay at him keeping things from her. But now, suddenly, all the doubts and fears she'd battled for months coalesced, filling her with regret and resolution. And a terrible, terrible sadness.

Because finally she faced what she'd avoided ever since he'd proposed marriage.

'I can't do this any more, Isam. Coming here, living with you like this, was the biggest mistake of my life.' She sucked in air on a half-sob half-sigh, misery overflowing. 'I've tried so hard to convince myself, tried to believe we'd be happy and everything would work out for the best. But I can't marry you and be your queen. I just *can't*.'

Avril had spent so long pushing down her feelings, pretending it would be all right, that duty and a great sex life would be enough. And their shared love for Maryam.

Her eyes glazed so that when Isam towered over her, his hands grasping her arms, she couldn't read his expression clearly. She blinked but her vision didn't clear.

'Tell me, Avril. Tell me everything.'

To her amazement, instead of anger, she thought she heard the deep resonance of concern in his voice.

That's what you want to hear. When will you stop fooling yourself?

His hold was supportive. That only made the pain well higher and faster, filling her till she didn't know what to do with it.

'Please, sweetheart. Talk to me.'

Something cracked inside her chest. When he used that endearment he almost undid her. It took her back to those intimate hours in his arms when they reached heaven together. When for a short time she'd believed the illusion that they were two halves of a single whole.

But it was an illusion. There was no romance, no love. There never would be. He used the endearment occasionally because he knew she liked it. That was all.

She told herself she was weak and selfish. She should put her daughter's needs above her own. But it did no good. Avril had reached the end. She couldn't go on.

'Please, Isam. I can't...' She swallowed, emotion thickening her throat. 'I can't do this now. I need to be alone.'

It was all she could do to stand there, blinking back the hot tears prickling her eyes, refusing to let them fall.

He said something she couldn't make out over her thundering pulse. When she didn't reply he finally let her go and stepped back.

It was a measure of her distress that his withdrawal made her want to cry out. Because despite her words, she wanted to be in his arms, wanted him to reassure her it would all be okay, though that was impossible.

She swung away from him, arms clutching tight around her middle, trying to hold herself together.

When he silently left the room, desolation engulfed her.

CHAPTER FOURTEEN

ISAM KNEW PAIN. Or thought he did.

He'd been to hell and back after the chopper accident.

He still missed his father every day. And though his memory had substantially returned, he was always aware of the gap around that fatal day and those last precious hours with his father.

For years he'd lived with guilt and grief over Nur's death.

But the despair he felt, having Avril tell him she'd tried but couldn't bring herself to marry him… That coming here and living with him was the biggest mistake of her life…

He felt undone.

Because *he* was the cause of her unhappiness.

He stared at the city view beyond his study window but saw instead Avril's face, pinched with pain.

How could it have come to this? He'd thought until recently that things were going so well. As they'd spent time together their relationship had blossomed. He could have sworn an intimacy was developing between them, ties that weren't re-lated to their child or simple sexual attraction. The latter had always been phenomenal between them, yet that was only part of what he wanted with her.

In his youth he'd taken for granted the benefits of wealth, privilege and a physique that appealed to women. He'd never met a woman horrified at the prospect of being with him.

He felt wrong in so many ways. Because Avril hadn't been

annoyed or impatient. She'd been upset. More than that, distraught.

And in her pain she'd turned away from him!

He'd wanted to hold her to his heart and assure her they'd find a way through this.

All his life he'd believed he could deal with whatever he had to face. He knew deep inside that if everything else in his world was stripped away, he'd be content if he had Avril and Maryam. Once he'd have been amazed by that. He'd never expected to feel so deeply for a lover, had assumed that respect, liking and sexual compatibility would be enough to cement a marriage.

Now he saw he'd had no idea. His feelings for Avril, like those for his little daughter, ran as deep as the marrow in his bones, as strong as the fierce desert wind and as constant as the North Star.

But Avril didn't feel that way about him. He repelled her.

A dreadful plummeting sensation carved through his chest and belly, leaving him gutted.

He'd taken her for granted, assumed that because he wanted her, and it was logical for them to be together, he could make her happy.

He'd thought the worst he had to deal with was acclimatising her to her new role in his country.

It hadn't occurred to him that *he* wasn't enough for her.

A shudder began somewhere deep inside, growing in force until he had to plant his hand on the wall to keep his balance as the floor seemed to shift beneath him. Through his study window he saw the lights of the city dip and blur as if shaken by an earthquake.

But it wasn't the world that shook, it was Isam.

Reeling, he turned from the window and collapsed into the leather chair behind his desk.

He could insist. He could hold her to her promise.

If he wanted, he could force her to stay, blocking any exit from the country.

There had to be an argument he could make to persuade her to stay.

But then he remembered her torment. The anguish in her drowned eyes. The catch in her throat that spoke of despair and heartache.

Was he so arrogant he'd discount all that to get his own way?

Avril was many things. A tender mother. A passionate lover. An honest, dedicated worker. Someone who cared about others. Her joy in things like a picnic under the stars or learning a new language was a constant reminder that it was the simple things in life that made it worth living. Not the pomp and power. But the smiles and warmth.

Could he risk forcing her to stay and losing that for ever?

He braced his elbows on the desk, his head sinking into his hands.

He could have her by his side if he was ruthless enough. But at what cost?

It was hours later when Avril began to worry.

She'd fed Maryam and got her back to sleep. She'd paced and fretted and tried to talk herself into accepting the world Isam offered her. She'd tried to imagine herself flying back to London, returning to the little house she'd shared with Cilla. Tried to imagine her and Maryam there.

Tried to imagine life without Isam.

Her current situation was unworkable but she couldn't imagine a future without him. Where did that leave her?

The antique clock in the sitting room struck two and she realised how many hours had passed since Isam had left.

It was stupid to worry that he hadn't returned.

Why would he? He wouldn't choose to spend the night

in her bed. He had a palace full of sumptuous bedrooms to choose from. She was the last person he'd want to see.

But he was always here to settle Maryam for the night after her last feed.

And he had so much riding on their marriage, Avril knew he wouldn't take her rejection at face value. He'd want to discuss it, try to persuade her to stay.

And…ridiculous as it was, she missed him. He was the one she needed to escape yet at the same time she craved the comfort of his arms about her, the sense she had when he held her that everything would work out well.

She ran her hands up and down her arms, trying to rub in some warmth.

Wait till the morning. Talk to him then, sensibly and calmly.

That was the logical thing to do. Except she remembered how he'd looked as she unravelled before him, almost incoherent, saying she couldn't stay and needed to be alone.

He'd been utterly shocked, her rejection coming out of the blue. She'd told herself she couldn't read his expression because of the tears blurring her eyes, but her conscience said otherwise. It told her he wasn't just surprised but grievously hurt.

She couldn't wait until tomorrow. She couldn't leave him hanging simply because she craved solitude. Isam deserved better.

Avril found him in his study. Seeing the light under the door, she didn't knock but gently turned the handle and let herself in. Isam sat behind his desk, shoulders hunched as he looked down at a paper in his hand.

She paused just inside the door, drinking him in, wondering if this would be the last time she'd see him. That made her gasp, palm pressing to her aching chest.

'Avril.'

From under dark, straight eyebrows, cloudy grey eyes met

hers. Her heart gave that familiar bump before quickening. But this time there was something else too, a stark pain of loss that echoed through every part of her body.

Even though she hadn't left yet.

For the first time she could recall, Isam didn't get up and come to her or invite her to sit. He simply stayed where he was, staring. Once she might have imagined his look was avid, as if eating up the sight of her. But that wasn't possible after what she'd said.

She told herself she was doing the right thing, ending this now rather than later. Yet it didn't feel right.

Legs shaking, she crossed to the desk, hyperconscious of the elegant green silk dress swishing around her legs. She didn't feel chic, she felt drab and heartsore as she sank into the chair in front of his desk.

Close up, he looked older, lines she hadn't noticed carving around his mouth and eyes. The scarring at his temple looked more livid and his mouth flatlined.

Was he angry or just disappointed?

He had to be both. After all he'd gone through with his amnesia and Hafiz, he didn't need this complication.

'I'm sorry, Isam. I should have told you much earlier. I should never have agreed to marry you.' She hitched a shallow breath. 'Hafiz will use this against you, won't he?'

She faltered to a stop, imagining the fallout of cancelling a royal wedding.

Isam had worked so hard to shore up his position after the trauma of the accident. If they separated there'd be a huge scandal. She'd played into Hafiz's hands.

'Don't worry about him.'

'But I do—'

'I told you. Hafiz is a spent force. Once we identified his spy in the palace we were able to catch him red-handed trying to sabotage not only me but senior members of the government. He's just confessed everything in a formal interview. The transcript of that tape will be shared with members of the Royal Council tomorrow. That's when I was going to tell you, as soon as it was over.' He paused then seemed to force himself to go on. 'The council will need to discuss it but Hafiz's bid for power is finished. Too many influential people will know about his underhand ways.'

Avril slumped back in her seat, relief filling her. If by her actions Hafiz had been able to wheedle his way onto the throne she'd never have forgiven herself.

But there was no relief from the pain she saw ahead, the pain even now racking her body. She bowed her head, staring at her tightly clasped hands, wishing there were some easy way out of this.

'Are you really so unhappy, Avril?'

Her vision blurred and she blinked, refusing to let the tears come. She nodded.

'Is there nothing I can say to persuade you to give us another chance?'

The breath caught in her throat as she heard tenderness and pain in that warm baritone voice.

He was a good man, a wonderful man, trying to do his best for his daughter, his country and even her. It wasn't his fault he didn't love her.

Avril moistened her lips and swallowed hard, tempted to tell him there was one thing that would change her mind. But she'd never hear those words from him. He'd make a loyal and dutiful husband, but that was all. She'd never be the light of his life.

She cleared her throat. 'I'm sorry,' she whispered.

At least, she realised, this wouldn't be goodbye for ever. He wanted an integral role in Maryam's life. The obvious answer was for Avril to move with her somewhere close. It would be tough living in Zahdar without Isam, but her fantasy of returning to London was just that. Their daughter deserved both her parents and Avril had too much experience of parental neglect to deprive her.

That was the answer. A home in Zahdar's capital, or a smaller town along the coast a little where Avril wouldn't have to look up and see the palace every day.

That was an option at least for the first few years, so father and daughter could bond. After that maybe she'd return to London, with Maryam visiting her father for holidays.

Surely, Avril thought desperately, they'd find some workable arrangement.

The sound of Isam's chair being shoved back from the desk made her stiffen. He wasn't going to try to tempt her into changing her mind, was he? She knew what she needed to do but seriously doubted her ability to withstand Isam's kisses, even now.

Her head snapped up.

But instead of circling the desk towards her, Isam stalked to the window, staring out into the night, a crumpled paper falling from his hand. He shoved his hands in his trouser pockets, the action drawing the fabric tight across his firm buttocks, making her drag in an unsteady breath. She was still vulnerable to his potent attractiveness. She guessed that would never change.

Avril saw him in profile, proud, almost austere with his rigid posture and tight jaw.

'Very well.' His voice was gravel, scouring her flesh and her aching heart. 'I won't try to change your mind.'

His chin lifted and she saw his throat move convulsively. In this light he looked powerful, almost arrogant, yet that movement betrayed vulnerability. Pain bloomed. Not for herself but for Isam.

'I've been thinking,' she began, but he cut her off.

'You don't have to worry. I'll arrange everything. The an-

nouncement, the travel. But it may be better to wait a day
or two before you and Maryam return to London. That will
give my team time to sort out the security logistics, not just
for your travel but longer term.'

Avril frowned. 'Longer term?'

Isam nodded, the movement brisk. But he kept his gaze
fixed on the view beyond the window, as if he preferred not
to see her.

'If you and Maryam are going to live in London I want
to make sure you're safe. Let us do a security audit. In fact,
it would be better if you let me buy you another house, one
that's more private. Meanwhile you can stay in my London
hotel suite.'

Avril swayed, momentarily unsteady, and had to reach for
the desk to keep her balance.

He was agreeing to let her take their daughter away? To
raise her in England?

'But if I take her to the UK you won't see her often.'

She saw him flinch, shoulders rising high under that dark
jacket before he pushed them back down.

'I'll visit her when I can.'

The silence following his words made Avril feel empty inside. She knew what Isam's schedule was like. He tried hard
to carve out time for them every day. But to visit London?
Such visits would be rare.

'You wanted to be a hands-on father,' she whispered, feeling her insides turn over in a sickening tumble of distress.

This time he didn't flinch, just stared at the distant city
streetlights. Was he thinking of the millions of people out
there who looked up to him as their leader? 'We can't always
have everything we want. I'll have to try to make it up to her
when she's older.'

Avril put her hand to her mouth, stifling a cry of horror.
That was one of the saddest things she'd ever heard. She

knew how Isam loved their daughter. He positively revelled in being a father. For him family came first.

Was that why he was letting them go? Did he think Maryam would fare better if Avril was happy?

Isam was sacrificing his own bond with their daughter and it made Avril ashamed. She'd tried to make Maryam's need to be with both parents a priority, but when it came to the crunch she hadn't been able to go through with a loveless marriage.

Avril found herself circling the table, drawn to the pain radiating from the big man at the window. Hating that she was the cause. Wishing there were a better way for all of them.

Something crackled under her foot and she looked down to see the paper he'd been reading. Except he hadn't been reading. There was no text on it. Instead it was a large photo. She scooped it up.

Her heart beat louder and something snagged high in her throat. It was one of the photos taken on the day their engagement was announced but she'd never seen it before. It certainly hadn't been released to the public. It showed her and Isam sitting together with Maryam. Avril was smiling down at their daughter but Isam wasn't. Nor was he looking at the camera. His head was turned to Avril, his expression unguarded.

She told herself the camera lied, that it was the angle or the light making it look like something it wasn't.

Yet something leapt inside her. Something bright and hopeful. His expression as he looked at her was familiar. Not because she'd seen it before but because it was how she felt about him.

She trembled and the photo fell from her unsteady hands.

'It's late. Go to bed, Avril. We'll talk when the sun's up.'

Still he didn't turn. Because he'd washed his hands of her? Was he already planning his future without her? She didn't believe it.

Avril moved closer until she stood just behind him, near

enough to inhale the comforting scent of citrus and warm man. 'You're not going to try to persuade me to stay?'

Suddenly he was facing her, his grim face just above hers. This close the pain in his eyes made her want to cry.

'You said there's no point and you wouldn't lie about that. You're not that cruel.' Yet as he looked down at her his eyes widened. What did he see in her face? 'Avril?'

Her heart pounded and she felt something like the mix of fearful exhilaration she'd experienced the first time she drove a four-wheel drive on a mountain road.

'But maybe I was mistaken,' she murmured. 'I was so sure…'

Warmth enveloped her shaking hands. She looked down to see Isam holding them tight.

'What were you sure about, sweetheart?'

Her heart dipped and soared. 'That you only wanted me for Maryam's sake. And to avoid scandal.'

Those long fingers tightened around hers. The blood beat through her body again and again as silence grew.

'That's what I thought, in the beginning.'

Avril's gaze flew to his. Her mouth dried at what she saw there.

'You must remember, I was raised expecting to contract a marriage of convenience. My family never married for love.' As if anticipating her interruption he shook his head. 'My grandparents were the sole exception to that and I know my grandmother missed my grandfather every day after his early death. If anything, that warned me off the idea of romance.'

He breathed deep, his chest rising. 'But that's not how I feel now. Now I understand exactly how my grandmother felt. These last months have been—'

'Wonderful,' Avril murmured, hardly daring to hope. 'More wonderful than I could have imagined.'

Isam's hands firmed around hers. 'But then that changed.'

She nodded. 'I told myself I could marry you and be happy for Maryam's sake. But every time we drew closer, something would happen to remind me our relationship is all about duty.'

'Avril, I—'

She interrupted, needing to explain, knowing he deserved the absolute truth, not just a snippet of it. 'Sometimes I hoped you might begin to love me just a fraction of the way you love Maryam.' Her voice wobbled. 'Because I love you. I think I always have. But all your praise was for when I did a good job, learning quickly or behaving the right way at an official function. It felt like your approval was never just for *me*.'

She hurried on when he would have interrupted. 'I *understand*, Isam. I know nothing is more important to you than Zahdar. That's always been your absolute priority. But you never saw me as a real *partner*. You were too busy protecting me. It didn't feel like trust or partnership, much less love.'

'And you deserve love.' His piercing eyes held hers and she felt the weight pressing down on her chest lift as he smiled. '*That's* what's been holding us apart. That's why you couldn't go through with our marriage.'

He was smiling now, his expression tender, and Avril was shaking so much he had to wrap his arms around her to support her, drawing her close.

Or maybe there was another reason for his action, because he needed her as much as she did him.

She looked up into his proud, dear face and warmth flooded her. The warmth of love and belonging.

'You were wrong about me not caring, Avril—'

'I know. I realised when you started planning to send me and Maryam back to London, and without a word of complaint. Even knowing the enormous scandal you'd face. You put my happiness above your own interests and desires.' Avril clutched his shoulders.

Isam met her stare with a look she'd never seen before.

'I'd sacrifice all I have, if it meant having you, Avril. You say nothing is more important to me than Zahdar, but if—'

She pressed a hand to his lips. 'Don't say it, Isam. I would never ask that.'

The thought of him giving up the role he'd spent his life preparing for didn't bear thinking about. He wasn't just devoted to his country, he was excellent as its leader and his people loved him.

Isam pressed a kiss to her fingers then drew her hand away, planting it over his chest so she felt his powerful heartbeat.

'I love you, Avril.' His words made the world still and all her senses heighten. 'In a different way but just as strongly as I love our daughter. I want you to be happy more than anything. Because I love you with all my heart.'

She stared in awe, everything inside her jangling in delight. 'That's why you agreed to let me leave?'

'What else could I do? You tried your best to fit in here, I knew that. And if you weren't going to be happy here I had no alternative.'

'It wasn't the place that was the problem, Isam.'

'It was me.' He drew a deep breath, his chest rising beneath her palm. 'If only I'd known. I was attracted to you right from the first. That night in London I knew you were out of bounds but I just couldn't resist. None of the arguments in my head could deter me.'

'You remember that?'

His mouth curved into a crooked, endearing smile that she felt deep in her core. 'I remember it all now, every glorious detail. In fact, it was seeing you again across the conference table that ignited my memories. That's why I had to leave you with my staff. I was getting flashbacks, of very intimate moments.' His chuckle delighted her and she found herself smiling back. 'I tortured myself for ages, believing I'd seduced you.'

'And now you remember how it really was. That I was responsible.'

'It was mutual. We were both responsible.' Isam shook his head as he hugged her to him. 'I took a long time, realising exactly how I felt about you. It was only tonight, at the prospect of losing you, that I found a name for it. I've broken with family tradition and fallen in love, Avril.'

She laughed breathlessly. 'Your grandparents would be proud of you.'

'I think you're right.' He paused. 'I confess I've spent a lifetime learning to shoulder responsibility and protect others. In theory those are fine traits but you've taught me they need to be tempered.'

His arm tightened around her waist and he drew himself up. 'If I promise to share more with you, rather than assuming I need to take charge, will you reconsider and stay?'

'Don't, Isam! Of course I'll stay. I love you. Don't make this sound like it was all your fault. It's mine too. I accused you of not sharing but I didn't either. I hoarded my feelings to myself, too scared to talk about them, because I've spent too long thinking myself unlovable. If I'd spoken out—'

'Shh.' Isam's lips grazed hers and nothing had ever felt so good. For she tasted understanding, love, and her own hopes for the future there. 'Let's agree that we both made mistakes and we'll trust each other with the truth from now on.'

Avril wrapped her arms around his neck and smiled with all the joy in her heart. 'That sounds absolutely perfect, my love.'

EPILOGUE

'YAY!' SHAKIL BOUNCED in his seat, clapping.

Beside him, Isam smiled indulgently. Over his son's head he caught Avril's gaze. Laughter lurked in those golden-brown depths.

'I know it's not approved royal behaviour,' Isam murmured as their son jumped to his feet in the grandstand, still applauding. 'But he's young and excited for Maryam.'

He was determined the children's education in royal behaviour would be tempered with the fun of simply being children. He wanted them to have balance in their lives as he now did. Thanks to his beloved wife.

Shakil loved football and couldn't wait to go to school next year and join the local schools' football competition. To him, having his older sister's team win their grade competition was the next best thing.

Beside Shakil, his twin, Sara, applauded just as enthusiastically. But Isam knew that when they returned to the palace, instead of picking up a football or basketball, she'd curl up with a picture book or draw today's events with her prized new coloured pencils.

He and Avril were blessed with children who were all fascinating individuals. He wondered what the future would bring them and knew that, whatever it held, there'd be an abundance of love.

'What are you thinking, Isam?' Avril had risen to her feet and paused beside him.

Isam rose, catching her hand in his and drawing her closer. Inevitably there'd be cameras trained on them but by now Zahdaris were accustomed to seeing signs of affection between their sheikh and sheikha. The friends and VIPs sitting around them didn't even turn to look.

'I'm thinking how very lucky I am to share this with you, sweetheart.' His gesture encompassed the children beside them and their older daughter down on the football field, lined up with all the others who had participated in the schools' competition. His words were pitched for Avril's ears alone. 'You make me whole.'

She stood there, in her dress of amber silk, wearing the heirloom ring he'd given her and matching ruby earrings. But it wasn't what she wore that made her gorgeous, it was her inner beauty and the light of love in her eyes.

Suddenly he became aware of the silence around them as the crowd waited for the VIPs to reach the microphone and begin the presentations.

His wife blinked, eyes bright. 'You do pick your moments, Your Majesty. But just so you know, I feel exactly the same.' She leaned in and whispered in his ear. 'Let's continue this discussion when we're home and the children are asleep.'

Isam squeezed her hand then released it, feeling the zing of anticipation low in his body.

He sat down and watched as Avril made her way to the podium where she and one of Zahdar's most internationally successful athletes would begin the presentations.

Applause swirled around the stands. For the children on the field and for the two women on the podium who were both crowd favourites.

Sara came and sat on his knee to get a better view. Shakil

climbed onto his other leg and Isam cuddled them both close. Then he lifted his gaze to his beloved wife, his smile full of pride and love.

* * * * *

If you just couldn't put down
Unknown Royal Baby,
then you're certain to love these
other emotional stories by Annie West!

The Housekeeper and the Brooding Billionaire
Nine Months to Save Their Marriage
His Last-Minute Desert Queen
A Pregnancy Bombshell to Bind Them
Signed, Sealed, Married

Available now!

COMING SOON!

We really hope you enjoyed reading this book.
If you're looking for more romance
be sure to head to the shops when
new books are available on

Thursday 21st November

To see which titles are coming soon, please visit

millsandboon.co.uk/nextmonth

MILLS & BOON

MILLS & BOON ®

Coming next month

RESISTING THE BOSSY BILLIONAIRE
Michelle Smart

She stepped through the door. 'I am your employee. I have a contract that affords me rights.'

The door almost closed in his face. Almost as put-out at her failure to hold it open for him as he was by this bolshy attitude which, even by Victoria's standards, went beyond minor insubordination, Marcello decided it was time to remind her who the actual boss was and of her obligations to him.

'You cannot say you were not warned of what the job entailed when you agree to take it,' he said when he caught up with her in the living room. She was already at the door that would take her through to the reception room. 'It is why you are given such a handsome salary and generous perks.'

Instead of going through the door, she came to a stop and turned back round, folding her arms across her breasts. 'Quite honestly, Marcello, the way I'm feeling right now, I'd give the whole lot up for one lie-in. One lousy lie-in. That's all I wanted but you couldn't even afford me that, could you? I tell you what, stuff your handsome salary and generous perks – I quit.'

Continue reading
RESISTING THE BOSSY BILLIONAIRE
Michelle Smart

Available next month
millsandboon.co.uk

LET'S TALK

Romance

For exclusive extracts, competitions and special offers, find us online:

- **f** MillsandBoon
- **X** @MillsandBoon
- **◎** @MillsandBoonUK
- **♪** @MillsandBoonUK

Get in touch on 01413 063 232